O. Douglas

Taken by the Hand

e-artnow 2021

O. Douglas

Taken by the Hand

Scottish Novel

e-artnow, 2021
Contact: info@e-artnow.org

ISBN 978-80-273-4035-4

Contents

DEDICATION

CHAPTER I

"Finish, good lady: the bright day is done . . ."

Antony and Cleopatra.

Two ladies stood on the doorstep of 14 Park Place, Glasgow. They had not been asked into the house-had not, indeed, expected to be; they were there merely to enquire. First they had parleyed with a maid, then a nurse passing through the hall had been brought to speak to them, and now, satisfied that they had heard all they could hear, they were withdrawing. They were both a little more than middle-aged, stout, comfortable-looking women, obviously well-to-do, with Persian-lamb coats, expensive handbags, and hats of the type known as "matrons" set high on their heads.

In silence they came down the handsome flight of steps from No. 14 and only began to talk when they had got well away from the house.

"Dear, dear," said Mrs. Murray, the older and the stouter of the two. "Poor Mrs. Dobie! Who would have thought it? Such a healthy woman and so full of life. I don't think I ever met anyone more 'on the spot' as they say. It was a treat to see her get things into shape at a bazaar or anything like that. Just the way she turned herself-so purpose-like. Of course, as a minister's daughter you may say she was brought up to that sort of thing, but still . . ."

"I'm awfully sorry," said the younger woman, with a note of genuine feeling in her voice. After a pause she went on: "She was Janie Boyd. I was at school with her, and a wild girl she was, minister's daughter or no minister's daughter! The pranks she used to play! And her father such a saint! I'm sure St. Luke's thought the world of him."

"Not only St. Luke's but the whole of Glasgow. He was a good man. . . . Wasn't Mr. Dobie an elder in St. Luke's, Mrs. Lithgow?"

"He was. D'you not remember him? A tall man with a beard. His first wife was a Duthie. She had a lot of money. I expect it all went to her only child-Samuel, Sir Samuel now. . . . Mr. Dobie would be sixty when he married again, and Janie Boyd wouldn't be very young either, thirty-five, mebbe. I never knew why she married him, he was so like a waxwork, and a beard and all, and fussy wasn't the word. Peggy would tell me that waxworks aren't fussy, but, well, you know what I mean. But, anyway, Janie seemed quite happy with him. It was wonderful how she managed to keep him contented, and yet get her own way in everything that mattered. But since he died-it must be ten years ago! Fancy! —and she had all the money at her disposal-she's come out wonderfully. I'd hardly have given her credit for so much organising power. How many things is she president of, I wonder? And it's always a pleasure to see her on a platform. She not only speaks well but she looks well. I always wondered where she got her hats; they're so becoming. She'll be greatly missed. I'm sorry for Be'trice, poor thing."

"Yes," said Mrs. Murray mournfully, "it's Be'trice who's to be pitied. . . . She's a friend of your Peggy's, isn't she?"

"Oh, well, they played together as children, and the two families have always been intimate, but I wouldn't call them great friends. To tell you the truth, Mrs. Murray, Peggy can't be bothered much with Be'trice; she says she's too *deprecating*. Did you ever? I'm sure if she is it's a good fault, for most of the girls I know are impudent hussies. I said that to Peggy, but she just laughed. . . . I like Be'trice because she's so civil, it's a relief to find a girl pretty-mannered in these days, but perhaps she is a little inclined to be listless and-and unenterprising. She never seems to want to do anything but stay at home beside her mother."

"Mebbe," said Mrs. Murray, panting a little with the walk, "mebbe the girl's shy."

Mrs. Lithgow turned to give a beaming bow to a passing acquaintance, then said: "Have you noticed, Mrs. Murray, that a very energetic mother has often a tired kind of daughter? Just as a very sort of diplomatic mother will have a disconcertingly honest girl?"

The older woman laughed. "I daresay you're right. Well, anyway, you've got a very satisfactory daughter in Peggy. So clever in the house and yet so good at games, and a fine, upstanding creature! I'm sure you and her father must be proud of her."

"Oh, we are. I don't deny it. She's a good girl, Peggy. And what d'you think? She's just got engaged! It's not out, but I'm telling you because you've always been so kind about Peggy. Harry Lendrum. Yes, Aitkin & Lendrum. The eldest son. Yes, isn't it nice? 'A neighbour's bairn' as Granny says; they've grown up together. And I'll have her beside me-that's the best of it. I hope I wouldn't have made a fuss, but I'd have been very vexed to let her away to India or Kenya or any of those places-though she'd go like a shot. Nothing dauntons our Peggy. . . . You're tired, Mrs. Murray: I hope you haven't walked too far?"

"No, no. I'm just a —wee thing-wheezy. I walk too little. Indeed, Mr. Murray sometimes tells me I'll soon lose the use of my legs! That's the worst of a car. I'm awfully pleased to hear about Peggy. I wonder what she'd like for a present?"

"Oh, anything will be acceptable. They've got to furnish from the foundation, so to speak."

"That's fine. If it's a widower with a house furnished already, or a bride going abroad, you feel so cramped in your choice, don't you? We'll have to think of something specially nice for Peggy. . . . It won't be for a time yet?"

"In the beginning of the year, we thought, but there's nothing fixed. Well, here we are at your own door, and I do hope you haven't felt the walk too far."

"It's done me good, Mrs. Lithgow. Now you'll just come in and have a cup of tea with me. You're a good wee bit from home yet."

"Thank you, Mrs. Murray. I'll be glad of my tea, for I've got a great blow this afternoon. Poor Janie Dobie. I can't get over it at all."

They went in together, through the hall, up the handsome staircase, to the large and richly furnished drawing-room, where a tea-table stood invitingly near the fire.

Tea was brought up at once, and Mrs. Murray, busying herself at the tea-tray, sighed. "Dear, dear, it seems no time since poor Mrs. Dobie was sitting in that chair you're in. . . . She always admired that fire-screen, and I said 'I'll leave it to you in my will, Mrs. Dobie,' just for a joke you know. How little I thought. . . . How d'you like your tea, Mrs. Lithgow?"

"Both, please, and a good kitchen cup. I'm old-fashioned, I suppose, but I must say I get tired of the people who say, 'Two spoonfuls of milk and hot water,' or 'Neither sugar nor cream, and very weak. . . .' Yes, it's the way we must all go, Mrs. Murray. D'you know, I sometimes find myself wondering why the world was made so full of interesting things and beautiful places, and why we're allowed to get so fond of each other when we've got such a short time in it. And Janie Dobie was enjoying life so *heartily*. She always did everything with such gusto. I can't picture her ill and weak. . . . I'll call again to-morrow and ask to see poor Be'trice. It must be so lonely for her with only strange nurses, though, of course, there's always Fairlie. She was nurse, you know, and stayed on as sewing-maid, housekeeper, a bit of everything, and she's devoted to Be'trice. . . . I don't know of any relations on the Boyd side: Janie was an only child; and I don't know of any on the Dobie side either, except the step-son Samuel, *Sir* Samuel. Did you ever meet his wife, Mrs. Murray?"

"Never," said Mrs. Murray firmly. "Does she come here much?"

Mrs. Lithgow pursed her lips. "She used to come years ago, and she was glad enough to send her children-she has a son and daughter-when she and her husband wanted a holiday on the Continent, but now she's too busy ascending the social ladder-you see her name and her photograph often in the papers, in connection with charity balls and things-to trouble about the humble connections in Glasgow. I'm told she says Glasgow's so common."

"Poor thing," said Mrs. Murray, quite sincerely. "And will Be'trice have to make her home with her?"

"Well, I don't know what else she could do. It isn't as if she was a girl with a lot of spirit and enterprise. At her age-she's nearly twenty-five —with plenty of money she could give herself a splendid time, travel and see the world, or take up some special work, there's no end to what she might do. It's what the girl of to-day's always asking, freedom to live her own life, but I doubt if poor Be'trice'll see it in that light. It's the way she's been brought up. If she'd been sent to a good school where she'd have got to know all sorts of girls, and got accustomed to the rough and tumble of life, instead of going about with a governess, for all the world like a cloistered nun. I'm sure Janie Dobie meant it for the best, but she didn't show her usual good sense in bringing up her girl. She taught Be'trice to depend on her for everything-and now what's to happen?"

* * * * *

Mrs. Dobie lay in her large, comfortable bedroom, surrounded with gifts from her many friends-flowers, books, baskets of fruit. It was the same room she had shared for fifteen years with her husband, and every day of the fifteen years she had wished in her heart that she could get rid of every article of furniture it contained. The first Mrs. Dobie had had a sombre taste in bedrooms, and everything was dark and heavy, and so good that there was no hope of its getting shabby in reasonable time.

His first wife had been a favourite topic with Joseph Dobie. Her portrait hung above the dining-room mantelpiece (a tall woman in a Liberty gown of olive green) and his eyes often sought it at meal-times while he recalled some instance of her philanthropic zeal. Indeed, so much was said of "Isabella's" excellencies that her successor, half-irritated, half-amused, sometimes felt that it would have evened things a little had she had a first husband whose portrait she could have hung above the drawing-room mantelpiece and whose virtues she could have extolled. But, untroubled by jealousy, Janie Dobie bore no grudge to the dead women either for her excellencies or her taste in furniture; all the same when Joseph Dobie died she wasted no time in reforming her bedroom.

Ten happy years had followed. She enjoyed the importance that her position as Joseph Dobie's widow gave her. In a small way she blossomed into a personage. Other women recognised in her the makings of a leader. When she spoke she was listened to. When some one was wanted to plead a cause, or preside at a function, Mrs. Dobie's was often the name suggested. As one of her friends said: "Mrs. Dobie has both common sense and mother-wit, she's easy to look at, and there's a sort of cosy you-and-me-ness about the way she addresses people that puts any meeting in a good humour, and then-she's a good woman."

When first she realised she was ill Mrs. Dobie had been inclined to be resentful. She, the healthiest of women, who hardly knew what it meant to have a headache or a common cold, who had always pitied half-contemptuously her feebler sisters as they coughed and ached their way through a Glasgow winter! Why, she *enjoyed* the cold weather, she often said, and always began the winter with eagerness. Summer was all very well and it was delightful at Greenbraes, their house on the west-coast, but how exhilarating to get back to Glasgow in the end of September, back to all her friends and interests, back to a telephone that was always ringing —*Mrs. Dobie: Mrs. Dobie*; she seemed in request everywhere. Her engagement book was full, she dove-tailed engagements, she had rarely one hour all day to herself, and when people in wonder asked her how it was done, she would laugh, and say with perfect truth, "I *like* it!"

It was in June that she first began to feel that all was not well with her; she became conscious of a feeling of malaise, something quite intangible yet oddly compelling, and she told her friends that she was "run down," and smiled wryly as she said it-that she should own to such a thing! And all her friends agreed that what she needed was a real rest. Mrs. Dobie worked far too hard, they said, put far too much of herself into everything she did; no wonder she was tired out. "What about a voyage?" they asked. She ought to get right away from every one and recuperate in new scenes.

Mrs. Dobie listened to them and appeared to be weighing the advantages of this scheme and that, but all the time she was saying to herself, "I won't go anywhere; I'm too tired to start; all I need is to get into my own comfortable bed at Greenbraes and lie there till I'm rested." But to her great disappointment she found that she was just as tired in bed.

In the middle of September she came back to the house in Park Place to be X-rayed, and when the result was known she asked only one, question. It was answered truthfully, and she began to set her house in order.

One day she was lying thinking over matters. Having always had a tidy mind and methodical ways she had not now to wrestle with a mass of things left in confusion, but there was some money of her own which she wanted to go where it would be most needed. Beatrice would have more than she could easily spend, the old servants were provided for, but Mrs. Dobie knew of several people to whom a hundred or two would make all the difference in life. She thought of them as she lay there propped up with pillows, and, reaching out to the table beside her for a pencil and block, wrote down some names and addresses.

There was that poor man George Clark with the delicate wife. He had come back from the War to find his little business ruined, and she had interested herself in him, and got him started again. He was working day and night to keep a footing: he deserved encouragement. And the boy with hip-joint disease whom she visited in his eyrie in a gloomy tenement near the river: the doctors said if he were kept in the country he might be cured. And Alice Wilson who had given her youth to an invalid mother, and for long years had kept herself with sewing, she was now in deadly fear that she would break down before she could claim the Old Age Pension-how good to set her free from anxiety. There were others, too . . . she would think of them later, and what was left would go to the Aged and Infirm Ministers' Fund and the Indigent Gentlewomen.

It was with something of her old briskness that, having decided this, Mrs. Dobie laid down the pad and pencil. She had forgotten for the moment why she was doing it, and the realisation flooded over her like the shock of a cold wave. Surely it was impossible: she was only sixty. And such a young sixty! The obituary columns were full of people, eighty, ninety, even a hundred. Some one had said not so long ago that ninety now was what seventy used to be, and she had agreed and thought comfortably that she had a long way to go.

And had she not? Doctors were often mistaken; another might take quite a different view of the case, but even as she doubted something told her there had been no mistake. She had the sentence of death in her own body, that healthy body in which she had taken such pride, that had never let her down. . . . She looked round the room with a smile that was a little bitter. Carnations by the dozen, roses, violets, great curly chrysanthemums; so much money spent in these hard times. Well, she told herself, at least invalids were a blessing to the florist, to the chemist, to the doctor, if they were a weariness to themselves!

But how much she had to be thankful for. She was in her own house-that in itself was much; she had good nurses, a doctor she both liked and trusted, and if the days seemed long and the nights troubled and confused, the pain so far was not excessive and her mind was clear. There was really only one thing that worried her greatly, leaving Beatrice: and, lying there, heavy thoughts came to her about her girl. Always a timid, shrinking child, it had been her mother's instinct to shelter her. But had she done right? Would it not have been better had she hardened her heart and sent the child to school, trusting that the society of other girls of her age would make her a normal, self-confident schoolgirl? One thing she could not regret, that Beatrice and she had been so much together, had meant so much to each other. As a baby she had never given Beatrice over to the rule of a nurse. Fairlie, good soul, had understood and had welcomed her mistress to the nursery at any time. Later, the governess, Miss Taylor (christened "poor Miss Taylor" after the adored instructress in Miss Austen's *Emma*), had been content, when necessary, to be the shadowy third in the trio. What happy times they had had all learning together! The long motor tours through foreign countries, the winters in Rome and Florence, when pictures and churches were studied in leisurely manner and enjoyed, not gulped down like a nauseous dose.

Beatrice had loved every minute of those years. It was later, when they had settled down in Glasgow, Mrs. Dobie told herself, that the real mistake had been made. She herself had become so interested in public work that she had not realised what was happiness to her daughter. She should have seen to it that Beatrice was more with other young people, playing games with them, acting, dancing, interesting herself in Guides. But it was so difficult, for the child was bookishly inclined, shy, retiring; it was positive misery to her to be sent out with a laughing band of young people. Having lived her life in a middle-aged atmosphere she hardly seemed to speak the same language as her contemporaries, and certainly did not understand their jokes. She went to dances to please her mother, charmingly dressed and most willing to be pleasant, but she always returned from them with the same plea-couldn't she stop going to dances? And she seemed so happy at home that the mother had weakly acquiesced, rather proud, perhaps, that she was so all-sufficient to her daughter, when other mothers complained that they hardly ever saw their girls.

But now-when Beatrice no longer had a mother, to whom could she turn? They had so few relations. Samuel, Beatrice's step-brother in London, was the nearest. Mrs. Dobie had written to him when she realised that her illness was serious, and he had replied very kindly, saying that his house was always open to Beatrice, and he was sure that Betha his wife would do everything she could for her. But Janie Dobie's heart was not at rest, and as she lay there the tears she would have scorned to shed for herself flowed for her daughter.

The days passed, and the disease which for a time had seemed quiescent now began to develop rapidly. Mrs. Dobie found it difficult to avoid showing her suffering and she tried to arrange, with the help of the nurses, that Beatrice should be as little as possible in the sickroom. But Beatrice was not to be kept out.

"Your Mamma," said the night-nurse, who was middle-aged and Victorian, "thinks it isn't good for you to sit so much with her. She's happier when she knows you're out taking the air."

"The air can wait," said Beatrice. "As if I wouldn't a hundred times rather be in her room than anywhere else!"

Beatrice was in the habit of reading the newspapers to her mother-the *Glasgow Herald* and the *Bulletin* in the morning, *The Times* when it came in later, but one evening when she was about to begin as usual the patient said:

"I think we won't bother with *The Times* to-night; I want to talk to you, darling."

There was a pause while she rallied her failing strength-then, "Beatrice," she said, "we must think what you are to do. . . . I'm not getting better. No," as the girl protested, "one knows oneself, and my mind would be easier if we decided on a plan. . . . Would you care to stay on in Glasgow? This house and the furniture go to Samuel; Greenbraes is yours-but you never cared much for Greenbraes; besides, it's too lonely in winter. We have so few relatives; no one who could come and live with you. . . . What do you think of going to London with Samuel? I know . . . I know . . . we've got out of touch with Betha —I blame myself for that. I was too taken up with the work I was trying to do; I neglected your interests. Forgive me, darling."

"Forgive!" said Beatrice, staring at her mother with misery in her eyes. How small and grey her face had grown even in the last few days. Other people's mothers, she thought resentfully, went on living to any old age. And her mother had been like a girl, almost; a big happy girl, with her rosy face unlined, her brown hair with hardly a grey thread, her erect carriage. It had been so delightful to have a mother who did the work and the talking, leaving her to dream. Beatrice quite realised that she was an anomaly in this age of competent young women. She liked to look on at life, and the very thought of driving a car, or gliding, or indeed doing anything on her own, terrified her. But what was to happen to her if she lost her bulwark? If this mother so big and strong and dear was going to leave her she was lost indeed-But this was not a time to think of her own plight; she must try to calm her mother's fears.

Janie Dobie had drifted away for a minute in a half doze, and when she opened her eyes Beatrice was smiling at her.

"You're not to worry about me, Motherkin. What you've got to do is to set your mind on getting well. Here comes Nurse to get you ready for the night. While she's removing the flowers-how many offerings to-day, Nurse? Oh, film stars haven't a look in with you, my dear-let me smooth your forehead and perhaps it will make you more inclined to sleep. When I used to get hot and nervous and off my sleep, you would come up after dinner to the night nursery and stroke my hair, and sing *Rothesay Bay* until I forgot all my troubles. Do you remember?"

The girl lay on the bed with her left arm under her mother's head while with her right hand she softly stroked her brow, and the nurse walked backwards and forwards, carrying out the flowers to a table on the landing.

When she had tidied the room and put on a "standing" fire, she came to the bed with a basin of water and a sponge to freshen her patient before she began another night. Beatrice slipped carefully from the bed and bent and kissed her mother. "Good-night, precious. If you're not sleeping let me come and have a cup of tea with you. May I, Nurse? I often wake about two and lie for an hour or so."

"You're too young to lie awake," her mother told her. "Shut your door to-night and never give a thought to me till morning. We have very comfortable nights, haven't we, Nurse? Run away now, dear, and listen to the wireless. Have you an interesting book? Good-night, good-night."

The nurse looked after the girl.

"It's lonely for Miss Dobie," she said. "I was one of six myself."

"Have you sisters? Three. How rich you are. If only my girl had a sister!"

"Yes," said the nurse, "it would make a difference. Not," she added, "that my sisters have ever done anything for me. We had all to go out and fend for ourselves, earn a living the best way we could. But we like well enough to meet at a time; blood does count for something. Is that comfortable? There's quite a touch of frost in the air to-night: I hope it doesn't bring the fog."

She turned off the lights and went in to the dressing-room to arrange things as she wanted them for the night. The servants had brought her up sandwiches and cake, and she had a kettle and teapot and little pan, so could make tea or heat soup when she pleased. She was sorry for the handsome, kindly woman who lay dying next door; sorry, too, for the girl who would soon be left alone, but she had a comfortable chair, a good fire, an exciting book, and some of her favourite chocolates, so life at the moment, she told herself, wasn't too bad.

* * * * *

Mrs. Dobie lay still, watching the firelight, till a sound made her raise her head.

Fog on the river!

How often she had lain in bed and heard through the misty night the hoarse hooting of some ship. It had always given her a vaguely excited feeling . . . ships bound for far-away ports going down the Clyde; stars hanging like lamps in tropical skies; life; adventure; wonderful things she was missing.

Again from the river came the distant sound.

The sick woman heard it, but the drug she had been given was taking effect, and she only thought drowsily that everything was going on-ships sailing, men working, boys and girls re-joicing in their youth. . . . What was it she had to think of? *Beatrice* —she must plan for Beatrice. But she was so tired, too tired to plan, too tired to pray, almost too tired to care. . . . "Surely" she thought, as she turned her head on the pillow, "surely some one will take her by the hand. . . ." Then she slept.

CHAPTER II

All through the five-and-twenty years of her daughter's life Janie Dobie had striven to make plain paths for her feet, and Beatrice found that her mother, in dying, had not failed her. Plans had been carefully made so that everything would be as easy as possible.

It was to be a private funeral, with no flowers. "For," as Mrs. Dobie had told her lawyer, "it's no use bothering busy people to come to a funeral; ask the few that it would hurt not to be asked. As for flowers it would simply mean that numbers of people who couldn't afford it would order wreaths; I hate a mass of decaying vegetation anyway. I know I have my friends' good wishes on my journey and that's all I want."

On the evening of the funeral day Beatrice was ashamed to find herself conscious of a distinct feeling of relief. These dreadful days were past, days of drawn blinds and hushed voices, dress-maker's boxes and masses of crinkling paper; herself standing before a mirror which reflected an unfamiliar black-clad figure with a blanched scared face; the arrival of her step-brother Samuel, the difficult conversation, the length of the meals; the terror of the nights when sleep kept far off and she lay and listened for she knew not what, thinking all the time of the voice that all her life had fallen so comfortably on her ears: "*Are you all right, darling? Mother's here.*"

Surely, thought Beatrice, the worst was over. Samuel was going away in the morning, the blinds would be pulled up, life would begin again. There was even a vague feeling of anticipation, for now that she was on her own she would be able to do exactly what she pleased. Clothes, for instance. Her mother had always chosen things for her, or, at least, had advised, and sometimes Beatrice had not had the things she liked best. And her hair. Mrs. Dobie had thought it a pity to cut the wavy golden fleece. She had said, "It's too soft, my dear; not thick enough to shingle, you'd look like a canary!" Beatrice had not believed it, and now she could make sure.

But even as she made up her mind to change things, desolation flooded over her at the thought of what she had lost. How could she find her way in a cold world, deprived of the personality that was like the sun in its warmth and cheer?

They sat together, Sir Samuel Dobie and his step-sister, at dinner. It was a good dinner, for the cook had been many years in the house, and knew exactly what her mistress would have ordered, the waiting was perfect, and Sir Samuel was feeling mellow. He looked at Beatrice in her black lace dress, with her shining hair smoothly combed into a loose knot, with approval. He told himself that she looked lady-like. Of course it was an absurd thing to look in these days-he had a highly-coloured wife and daughter at home, so he knew-but still, it was rather nice. Poor little thing! She must be feeling lonely. He had told Betha when the telegram came summoning him to Glasgow that he would have to ask his step-sister to come to them at Portland Place. Betha had replied, "*Must* you?" in no very cordial tone, and had rushed off to her next pressing engagement. But Betha must understand that in this matter he was master in his own house. After all, blood counted for something, and this was his father's daughter; he was her trustee and nearest relative, and it wasn't as if the girl was not well dowered; with her looks and the money she would soon be somebody else's responsibility. . . . He thought kindly, sitting there, of his step-mother. A sensible woman. They had always got on well together. She had been no trouble to him in life, nor, as it happened, in death, for it suited him quite well to be in Glasgow at this time. Not, of course, that he would have grudged coming up on purpose, but still. . . . He was truly sorry that she should have died in the prime of life-why she was only five years older than he was! —but there was no blinking the fact that the money that would now come to him would be very welcome. True, he was a wealthy man, but these were anxious days, and he had an expensive household, a terribly expensive household. Really Betha seemed to have lost all sense of the value of money. It was ridiculous, because it wasn't as if she had been brought up in luxury. Quite the reverse. He had rather stooped, he always felt, in his marriage, but Betha had had taking ways as a young girl, and he was only human after all. She had made a good wife too, up to her lights, but she had always insisted on over-indulging the children, and now the boy and girl absolutely ruled the house; the place was turned upside down at their pleasure. . . . He turned his head and studied the face of the lady in the velvet gown above the mantelpiece. What would his mother have thought of her granddaughter?

He sighed, then realised that he was eating an excellent bit of fish.

"Very good salmon," he said.

Beatrice, deep in her own thoughts, started slightly.

"Yes," she said, "we always get good fish."

"The best of everything in Glasgow, eh?" said Sir Samuel jocularly. "Well, there are worse places. After London, of course, it's provincial, but quite a good place to live in. The people are easy to know, and pleasant to deal with. Your poor mother seems to have been quite a personage. Yes, you would have been gratified at the tributes paid to her by old friends whom I spoke to at the funeral."

"Yes," said Beatrice, trying not to mind the condescending tone, "mother did a lot of public work. She liked it."

"And was well fitted for it," said Sir Samuel, handsomely. "Ah, yes, women are coming more and more into public life. It seems ungallant to object, but one wonders, one wonders."

Beatrice looked rather hopelessly at the slice of roast beef on the plate laid before her, as she said, "Don't you think women are as capable as men of doing most things?"

Sir Samuel was helping himself to mustard, and paused with the large Georgian silver pot in his hand, pursing his lips at his step-sister.

"I think not," he said finally. "Many of them have a superficial cleverness, but they don't last the course, if you understand the expression."

"But," Beatrice protested, not because she cared, but merely to keep the ball of conversation rolling, "surely there are many women who are much more than superficially clever. The Duchess of Atholl, for instance, Maude Royden, and, and, oh, dozens more."

Sir Samuel smiled kindly. "Those are merely the exceptions that prove the rule. What, I ask you, have women done in the House of Commons?"

Beatrice was about to reply, but realising in time that it was a rhetorical question she laid down her knife and fork, drank a little water, and prepared to study her step-brother while he addressed her.

He was a tall man, with a large smooth face, a high, slightly receding forehead and a fluent-looking mouth with slightly protruding teeth. He was good-looking and very well dressed, and his appearance always predisposed an audience in his favour. As her mother had reminded Beatrice he was her nearest relative, almost, in fact, her only one. She sat, hardly listening, wondering what he was like, this large man, in his own house, what his wife thought of him, if his children believed in him. . . . She hardly knew Lady Dobie. There was nothing to bring the lady to Glasgow, and when Beatrice and her mother had passed through London it was generally holiday-time and the house in Portland Place was in the hands of caretakers. When the children were quite small they had been sent for several summers to Greenbraes, the house at the coast, and she, Beatrice, had adored the funny, sophisticated little Londoners, and had played with them by the hour. But that, she reminded herself, was years ago. They would be very different now. Why, Elaine was twenty and Stewart was at Oxford.

The dinner, which had seemed to Beatrice endless, was drawing to a conclusion. Sir Samuel, who had passed the sweet, was having a second helping of savoury, explaining as he did so, "I've no use for sweets; leave them to the ladies. Sweets to the sweet, as the immortal William said. . . . I hope you're fond of poetry, Beatrice? I used to read reams. Poetry's good for the young. Browning, now. I used to write papers on Browning. But the cares of the world, you know. Ah, yes, yes. '*Grow old along with me, the best is yet to be.*' I hope so, I'm sure, but really one has little time to think of anything but the things of the moment. . . . All week I rush between the office and the House; on Sundays I like a round at golf and a rest, but Betha and Elaine have generally other views. But tell me about yourself. Did you help your mother in her various activities? Or have you branched out on a line of your own?"

Beatrice shook her head. "I'm afraid," she said, "that I'm not really much good at anything. I don't seem to have been given any special talent, so I do the listening."

"Delightful," said Sir Samuel. "And so necessary! So many people want to talk and so few to listen. Your popularity must be great."

"I haven't noticed it," said Beatrice. "No, I don't think I'm a success in any way. It didn't matter when I had mother. I helped her, and basked in her popularity, but now — —"

Sir Samuel made a grave face. "Ah, yes, this is indeed a sad blow to you. . . . Have you thought at all what you would like to do? I don't suppose you would care to stay on here? No, I thought not. I mean to sell this house, in fact I've had an offer for it. Yes, it's remarkable in these days when large houses are going for an old song, but of course it's a very good position, and your mother kept it in such a beautiful state of repair. As you know, Greenbraes is yours. Would you care to live there for a bit? No-no, there's no hurry in making a decision. You must look on my house as home in the meantime. You will come to us when you finish up here. It will only be a case of packing your own belongings, and disposing of your mother's personal effects. . . ." He looked round the room. "If there is anything that you have a special liking for just let me know and it'll be arranged. I've forgotten what's in the house. If you're not too tired d'you mind if we go over it to-night? I shall have to leave after breakfast-and get my business done and catch the midday train to London. No, no," as Beatrice sprang up, prepared at once to do as was suggested, "let's have our coffee in comfort; the house won't run away. . . . Yes, it really is exceedingly fortunate to find a purchaser just to my hand, so to speak. And did I tell you he's willing to take the furniture if we can come to an arrangement? I gathered it was wanted for a club or something of that sort. It's none of my business so long as the money's forthcoming."

He laughed, and Beatrice smiled as seemed required, but she was almost dazed at the sudden way things were happening.

When they had drunk their coffee Sir Samuel rose, saying, "Well, Beatrice, shall we go through the house now? If a thing's got to be done get it done at once. That's a good rule in life-whether it means getting out a tooth or an appendix, or anything else unpleasant."

Sir Samuel laughed aloud at his little joke; and Beatrice politely echoed the laugh, while she said to herself: "Mother's funeral day and I'm *laughing!*"

She rang the bell and told the maid who answered it that Fairlie was wanted, and presently Fairlie appeared.

She was a short, stout woman with a comely face and the manner of a privileged old servant.

Beatrice said, "You remember Fairlie, don't you, Samuel? She knows what's in the house much better than I do."

"Oh, yes." Sir Samuel beamed in his best "constituency" manner and shook hands heartily, remarking: "I remember you in my father's time."

"So you will," said Fairlie, encouragingly. "I came here when Miss Be'trice was one month old, and Mrs. Dobie was the best friend I ever had or am like to have. What we've lost! And not only us but dozens of folk she kept on their feet; it's as if we'd all lost a shelter and a support."

Beatrice turned quickly away, and Sir Samuel said, "Quite so. Mrs. Dobie was a splendid person in every way. . . . Ahem . . . I was telling Miss Beatrice that I thought perhaps we should go through the house together while we have time. To-morrow I must get back to London. . . . It seems you can tell us about things. You'll have an inventory?"

"No' me," said Fairlie. "We never had any use for such a thing; we never let the house. But I've looked after the napery and silver and everything for years, and I can tell you what's in the house almost to a towel."

"Ah, yes, but everything will have to be gone carefully over by a valuator. What about the silver? Is it any good? I've forgotten. We might look at that."

"Ay," Fairlie agreed. "It's quite handy in the chest in the pantry. You just sit down and I'll get some one to give me a hand with it."

Beatrice and her step-brother sat down as directed, and Beatrice, looking across at the face of the first Mrs. Dobie over the fireplace, said, "You will take that picture, won't you?"

Sir Samuel walked over and studied the portrait.

"It's large," he said, "and dull. I can't think where I'd hang it in Portland Place. Elaine wouldn't let it into the drawing-room, and it would be hopelessly out of place in the dining-room. It's well painted though-that velvet. . . . If you'd care to have it, Beatrice . . . ?"

The girl hesitated, but before she could speak Sir Samuel hit on a plan.

"I'll tell you what," he said. "Let's send it down to Greenbraes. It would look very well in the dining-room there. That sort of large coast villa is the proper setting for that sort of portrait. Besides, I remember my mother was very fond of Greenbraes, so it's quite fitting that her portrait should find a home there — I suppose you'll let the place? There's no point in having it stand empty."

"It isn't empty exactly," Beatrice said. "A couple live in it as caretakers, and in the spring and autumn mother used to send people down who needed a rest. She called it her private holiday-home."

Sir Samuel was looking at the other pictures. "Ah, yes," he said, "that was very nice of your mother. She had a large heart and — I may add — a large income. My father left his widow exceedingly well provided for, and she had full control of everything."

"I expect," said Beatrice, flushing pink, "I expect he knew he could trust mother to use the money as he would have wished. He was generous too."

"Quite, quite," Sir Samuel's tone was conciliatory. "They both belonged to a generous age. People could afford to give in my father's day. Those were solid secure times. Now everything is uncertain. It's no joke, I can tell you, Beatrice, to have large responsibilities in these days-Ah! here comes the family plate."

Fairlie, assisted by a housemaid, carried in the chest, which she unlocked solemnly, and proceeded to exhibit its contents with pride.

Sir Samuel picked out a spoon. "About 1875," he said, "when my father married."

"There's three dozen of each of these," said Fairlie, "soup-spoons, dessert-spoons, forks, big and little, and further down there's awful bonnie thin plain ones-Georgian, I think, my mistress called them. She liked them best, though of course they hav'na the look of the heavy ones. . . . And then there's three tea-and-coffee services. Oh! and ongtray-dishes and a silver soup-tureen, and trays and salvers galore. I aye wanted the mistress to keep them in the bank, the world's that lawless turned."

"Yes-well, I might keep the Georgian stuff, but the rest had better be sold. Thank you, Fairlie; lock it up again. I'll see that an inventory's made at once. . . . Now, Beatrice, shall we go to the drawing-room? Excuse my going first," and he ran like a boy up the stairs.

Beatrice followed slowly, wondering what her mother would have said to her stepson's interest in his new possessions. She would have been amused, Beatrice thought. She wondered if her mother could see them now. Did she notice, perhaps, that the new black lace dress that Beatrice wore did not fit? It was part of the "mourning order" she had given to the shop where she and her mother had been in the habit of getting most of their clothes. The head dressmaker had come herself-tightly encased in black satin, and sniffing mournfully, for she had sincerely liked the cheerful, considerate customer who had been so easy to dress-and advised Beatrice as to what she would need.

"Just a nice morning frock, and mebbe a coat and skirt, and something for the evening is all you need to begin with. Black is not worn as it used to be. I remember when it was a year's deep black for a parent, but now it's black and white or grey from the very start, and every vestige off before the year's out. But I'm sure, Miss Be'trice, you'll want to wear real mourning for your Mamma, for she was a dear soul." She slipped a frock over the girl's head. "Yes, I used to feel that the sun had come out when she dropped in. She always asked after my mother, and wanted to know how my neuritis was keeping before she began about her own affairs. Ucha, that's not bad, Miss Be'trice. You're stock size and that's a great help at a time like this. . . . Look in the glass. D'you like it yourself? You can wear black with your hair and skin, and you should be thankful, for some people look awful! Though it's wonderful, too, what you can do with a touch of white, and there's this about black, I always say it subdues ladies who are too what you might call rash in their colours. You'd be surprised at the trouble I have, to keep high-coloured, full figures away from puce, and even bright red. Some of them seem to have no control over themselves with regard to colour-just like some people with drink-so it's a mercy in a way, though of course it's a pity for the reason, when they're compelled to wear black. Yes, I don't think you could do better than that. Will you try this lace dress? I thought it would be nice and soft for you and younger than satin or crepe de chine. You suit the cape at the back. Isn't it awful graceful?"

But it was the cape at the back that was the trouble, and Beatrice almost imagined she could feel the twitch her mother's hand would have given it to make it hang properly.

Sir Samuel looked round the drawing-room with an appraising eye, and Beatrice watched him. This was the most familiar place in life to her. Here she had played as a child while her mother wrote letters, for she had never been kept strictly to the nursery. She had often done her lessons here too, and painted pictures, and made up stories and games. Here, later on, she had helped her mother to entertain, making anxious conversation with middle-aged gentlemen and their comfortable, complacent ladies. And what happy evenings they had had when they were alone, reading aloud, listening to the wireless, talking, laughing, never tiring for a moment of each other's company.

"I remember this room when I was a child," said Sir Samuel, "in my mother's lifetime. It had a sort of terra-cotta silk panels then and was considered very magnificent. I'm afraid there's nothing of any particular value in it." He peered at the china in a cabinet. "There may be some good things here; we'll know when they're valued. I remember my father was keen about china. Some of these rugs might go to Portland Place; I wish I could find room for that bureau and those chairs, for there's no market for antiques at present. . . . Anything here you'd like to have as a keepsake?"

Beatrice had an impulse to gather the room in her arms and cry, "You can't take it from me; it's mine because of its memories." But what was a room when the spirit that had made it home was gone? So she replied, "I think not, thank you."

"It seems you're no sentimentalist," said her step-brother. "Perhaps it's as well. There's no place for sentiment in the modern world. What a hard world it is I hope you'll never know. I've been blessed-or cursed-with a feeling heart, and when I've got to tell men who've been all their lives in the business, who thought they were safe for life, and were educating their children well, and buying their little suburban villas, that we can't afford to keep them on and must replace them by younger, cheaper men —I assure you, Beatrice, it makes me utterly wretched."

"But *must* you dismiss them?" Beatrice asked. "Couldn't you keep them on-perhaps at a lower salary-till you see if things improve? It's too dreadful to think of those men and their wives and families left stranded-for how could they save when they had to buy their houses and keep their children at good schools? Clerks, too, who won't easily get another job. And those are the people you can't help, for they won't speak. Sometimes-often, I'm afraid, it's a case of the whole firm coming down, but if the heads of the business have still money to go on with, I do think it's up to them to help on their men."

Sir Samuel gave a short laugh as he said, "Ah, my dear girl, it's easily seen that you know nothing about business questions; business isn't a charitable institution. We can't afford, as I said, to be sentimental. To keep going at all means the strictest attention to details; no leakage allowed anywhere. The same thing in my own house. I go over the books carefully myself. Of course economy in a house like ours is very difficult, for we entertain largely. Have to. My position, you know, and Betha has a wide circle of friends, Elaine, too, has her own. I can't insist on economy as I would like, for servants have to be carefully considered. One daren't disaffect them for they are more difficult to find than hid treasure. Fortunately we have a most efficient cook-housekeeper who runs things very well, for Betha hasn't really time, and Elaine is taken up with her own affairs. But you will see for yourself when you come. Betha will write. . . . I see you have the wireless here-what time is it? We might listen to the news . . . a great invention, isn't it?"

CHAPTER III

"Nothing but peace and gentle visitation."

Love's Labour's Lost.

Sir Samuel departed the next morning immediately after breakfast, to finish his business, and get the train back to London, and Beatrice saw him go with a relief that she felt slightly ashamed of, for, as she told herself, he had really tried to be kind.

As she turned from saying good-bye to him Fairlie stopped her with:

"Excuse me, Miss Be'trice, but could you spare a minute to say what's to be done with all the things? Oh, I know" —as the girl turned away —"it's awfully hard for you, but it's better to do it now when your heart's as sore as it can be, than put it off and have it hanging over you. Come, ma dearie. I've laid out everything and all you need to do is just to nod your head, for I think I know where the mistress would have liked the things to go. I mean, of course, the ordinary things. The furs and lace you'll be keeping. . . . But she had such a lot of good, well-made, sensible clothes and shoes-and they'll be a fair godsend to some decent bodies. Mistress Gregor, for one; she's worn the same coat for that many winters I've lost count."

As Fairlie talked she guided Beatrice upstairs and into her mother's bedroom, fresh and sweet as it had always been, with a west wind blowing in through the open windows, and the crystal and silver shining just as she had liked it. The sight of the garments, many of them so familiar, forced the hot tears to the girl's eyes, but Fairlie talked on as if she noticed nothing.

"I wouldn't send anything to a Jumble Sale if I were you, Miss Be'trice. It's different to give them where you know they'll be valued. My, this costume would be a treat to that poor delicate woman-what's her name? Miss Ralston-that the mistress set up in a wee shop. You see, it's decent clothes that's the difficulty. They can manage along no' that bad, but there's little over for clothes and boots."

"Oh, I know, Fairlie, and I'm more than willing that the things should go where they'll be useful, but ——"

"That's all right then," said Fairlie, in her comfortable, reassuring way. "I'll see about getting them all parcelled up. And the-the personal things? Will you take them with you?"

"Is there any hurry? I won't be leaving for some weeks probably."

Fairlie stopped folding clothes and asked, "Did Sir Samuel not say to you that he wanted everything out of the house as soon as possible? I understood that all your own things were to be stored or sent down to Greenbraes at once, because the house had been sold and they wanted immediate entry. . . . The things in this room, dearie, are all yours, mind that; they're your mother's things."

Beatrice looked round. "I'd hate," she said, "not to keep the dressing-table and anything that goes with it, and those painted bottles, and the Morland prints, and the worked stool that stood before the dressing-table . . . . they can be sent to Greenbraes in the meantime."

"Of course they can. I'll take them there myself and see that they're put in a proper place. . . . You wouldn't like to live down there, Miss Be'trice? It's a bonny place."

"Yes. You always liked Greenbraes, Fairlie. I don't know, I may settle there some time, but I was thinking that I'd like you to go there for the winter. Mr. and Mrs. Shields would be glad of your company, and I would feel that there was something to bring me back to Scotland. At present I'm like a knotless thread."

"Toots, you're nothing of the kind. You'll be having a grand time in London with Lady Dobie. And I'd like fine to go to Greenbraes, for I get on well with the Shields, and I'd have the things *she* liked round me. No, no, we'll no greet, ma dearie. . . . Here's Agnes. What is it, Agnes?"

"Mrs. Lithgow wonders if you could see her, 'M? She's waiting in the library."

Beatrice shrank back, crying, "Oh, I couldn't, Fairlie; I couldn't —No, that's silly. I've got to see people some time. Please tell Mrs. Lithgow, Agnes, that I'll be down in a minute."

"There's a brave lassie," encouraged Fairlie. "Just you give your face a sponge with cold water and you'll be fine. Away down afore you've time to think about it."

Mrs. Lithgow's eyes filled with tears as Beatrice came in in her black frock, and she kissed her, and murmured sympathy, and sat down still holding the girl's hand. Beatrice felt very uncomfortable. She did not know whether to let her hand lie in the visitor's warm suede-covered grasp, or gently withdraw it finger by finger, and the problem so absorbed her that she hardly heard the first part of the conversation. When she did become aware of what Mrs. Lithgow was saying —"And now, dear Be'trice, I want you to come home with me. Yes, just now. I don't know what your arrangements are for the future, but I can't bear to think of you alone here. So long as you stay in Glasgow our house is your home. I daren't go back without you. Both Mr. Lithgow and Peggy gave me my orders, 'Bring Be'trice back with you' " —Beatrice gasped with horror. To go, at this time, to stay with strangers-though she had known the Lithgows all her life she had never been intimate with them-to leave Fairlie and her mother's room and the loved familiar things! It was unthinkable. And yet here was Mrs. Lithgow, dressed in black to show nice feeling, positively exuding kindness and sympathy; how could she throw it back in her face?

"The room's ready, the fire burning and all, and Peggy's away out to get flowers," said Mrs. Lithgow, and every word seemed to draw the net closer round the girl.

"Oh, but-you are too kind," she murmured.

"Kind? Nonsense. I was at school with your mother, and we put our hair up the same day. I'm very sure Janie Boyd wouldn't have let my Peggy be alone if I had been the one to be taken. Now, you ring for Fairlie and get a case packed and I'll call for you in about an hour. I'm just going down town to do some shopping. . . . Now, my dear, you mustn't mind me being so, so *precipitate*. Sometimes we're the better of having our minds made up for us. . . . Don't you worry about things here, Fairlie will manage. Your mother always said she could trust Fairlie with anything. You'll be better out of the way —I'll be back about twelve. Ta-ta."

As the door shut behind Mrs. Lithgow Beatrice stood and apostrophised herself as a weak fool. Why had she not said firmly that it was impossible for her to leave Park Place in the meantime, that there was much to arrange and that she must be on the spot to direct-instead of allowing herself to be dictated to like a child. There must be some way out of it. What if she went to bed and left a message with Fairlie that she wasn't well? She could imagine how Mrs. Lithgow's kind face would lengthen! All her preparations wasted, the fire, Peggy's flowers. . . . It wasn't fair, perhaps, to thwart people's efforts, but oh, why were people so set on being kind?

Reluctantly she went upstairs to tell Fairlie. "I shan't stay more than two nights," she promised herself.

"You'll just see," said Fairlie soothingly; "you'll mebbe like it fine. . . . You've nothing much to pack-just the coat and skirt and the lace dress (I took off the cape last night after you went to your bed and I think it hangs better now), but Mrs. Lithgow won't have company when you're there; it wouldn't be seemly. And I'll try to do everything here just as you would like, and of course I can always ring you up if there's anything I don't know about. Sir Samuel didn't say when they'd expect you in London?"

"No. He said Lady Dobie would write. Now that everything's changing and breaking up, perhaps the sooner I go to London the better. After all, Fairlie, they *are* my relations in a way, and I ought to feel nearer to them than I do, say, to the Lithgows."

"Of course," Fairlie readily agreed, "blood's thicker than water."

"I'm Elaine's step-aunt. It's a ridiculous relationship."

"Oh, ay, but you're aged more like sisters, only four or five years between you. I mind Miss Elaine at Greenbraes long syne. An impident wee thing she was, ordering us all about! She was as dark as you was fair; she was but a bairn then and you were a long-legged lassie."

"It sounded an alarming household," Beatrice went on, "from Sir Samuel's description. They seem all so occupied that I doubt if they'll ever take in that I'm coming!"

"No fear of them; they'll be only too glad to have you. . . . Is Mistress Lithgow calling for you, did you say? See you're ready in good time, dearie. Mistress Lithgow's a lady that's always rather before her time than after it, and it wouldn't be nice to keep her waiting. I'll take the suitcase to the front hall to be ready."

Beatrice smiled faintly. "I'll not be late, I promise you. It's a blessing I've still got you to keep me right."

True to her word she was in the hall when Mrs. Lithgow's Sunbeam drew up at the door, and earned for herself a word of praise from that lady.

"That's right, always be punctual. I've simply no use for the haphazard ways of the girl of to-day. Some of Peggy's friends are just awful: don't reply till the last minute and then refuse, or else accept and never turn up. But I can tell you if they treat me like that once they don't get the chance again. Peggy just laughs and says, 'What does it matter?' But it's not good manners and it *does* matter."

Beatrice smiled non-committally and made some remark about the beauty of the day, a subject her companion eagerly followed up, for she was anxious that there should be no pauses.

"Yes, isn't it? I think Glasgow on an autumn morning's just lovely, and there's such a nice cheery feeling of everything beginning again, people settling down after the summer, ordering winter clothes." She stopped, feeling she was being tactless, and started again brightly and at random. "Did you ever see anything lovelier than that flower-shop there? So tasteful the way the autumn leaves and the flowers are arranged! It's a very good shop that. I always go there for my wreaths . . . I've been reading a very nice book just now. I wonder if you've read it. It's called-what *is* it called? I'll forget my own name next, anyway it's awfully nice. I'll let you have it when I've finished reading it. Oh, there's Mrs. Murray! She doesn't see us." Mrs. Lithgow leant forward and waved frantically but without success. "She's been tempted out by the good morning to take a walk; she's heavy on her feet, poor body. And here we are at home, and here's Peggy."

Mrs. Lithgow's daughter had been watching for the car from the dining-room window and came running down the front door-steps to welcome the guest. She was a happy-looking girl, with a mop of dark hair and breezy manners, and after she had kissed Beatrice affectionately she began to chaff her mother about some mistake that lady had made.

"You who are so particular, Mother! Always down on me for my slap-dash ways. But I don't put wrong letters into right envelopes. Mrs. Morris has just been to ask if you're going to help her with her beano for mothers —I don't know what it is-next Wednesday, for the reply she got from you this morning began 'Dear Lucy,' and as Mrs. Morris' name is Janet she gathered it wasn't for her."

Mrs. Lithgow sat down on the settle in the hall, and clucked with her tongue at her own stupidity.

"Now, isn't that awful! I was writing to Lucy Beatson at the same time. I never did such a thing in my life before. *Anno domini*, I suppose! But you needn't look so triumphant, Peggy-need she, Be'trice? —it's easy done."

"Ah, but it's fine once in a while to get a handle against Mother! Come along, Bee, and I'll show you your room. It's nice of you to come to us!"

They mounted two flights of stairs, Peggy explaining: "Mother wanted you to have the spare room on her floor, but I thought you might like to be up beside me-the view's nicer." She went to the window. "If it's clear you can see right away to the hills. And we can share a bathroom. It's a shabby affair compared to the one downstairs, but it'll do. And I've put in lots of books, and a comfortable chair, and you stay up here just as much as you like. Now, don't mind refusing if Mother wants to take you out and you'd rather stay in. You're to do just what suits you best. They've brought up your case; shall I ring or would you rather unpack your own things? All right. Is there anything else I can get for you?"

"No, oh no. What a lovely, comfortable room! And the flowers! You've taken a lot of trouble, Peggy."

"Bless you, no. I liked it." She bent down to sniff at a bowl of violets, hesitated for a moment and then said, "I'll leave you now. Lunch is at 1.15 *prompt*."

Beatrice went over to the window when the door closed, and stood looking out at the neat little back gardens of the crescent, the roofs of innumerable houses, and, far away, a line of blue hills all glorified by the noonday sun. It was odd to find herself an inmate of Mrs. Lithgow's household, but then, she told herself, everything from now on would be odd and unfamiliar. Sometimes-not very often-she had gone to stay for a night or two at some one's house, for a dance, perhaps, or some festivity, but how gladly had she hastened back to Park Place and her mother. That had always been the real fun of a visit, to recount to her mother everything that had taken place. And now there was no mother and very soon there would be no Park Place.

But no, she wasn't going to pity herself. . . . Glancing at the clock she remembered Peggy's warning and began laying out what Fairlie had packed, and her hands were washed and her hair smooth when the gong sounded. A sister of Mrs. Lithgow's, a Miss Turnbull, who lived quite near in a very select boarding-house, was also at lunch, and the conversation never flagged, chiefly owing to Peggy's efforts. Beatrice was grateful to her for behaving naturally, more especially as Miss Turnbull felt it right to adopt for the occasion a subdued manner and a lowered tone, and kept casting sympathetic glances at the black-frocked girl opposite to her.

"Peggy has such high spirits," she said, apologetically, across the table.

"And why not?" demanded that young woman. "If I hadn't high spirits now when would I have them? I'm only rejoicing in my youth as the Bible tells us to do."

"Before the evil days come," added her mother, helping herself to red-currant jelly with her mutton.

"Oh," said Peggy, "I expect the evil days'll come all right, but I should think you're better able to bear them if you've done some rejoicing before. Life's good and bad for everybody, but more good than bad for most. I'm sure, Mother, you haven't much to complain of."

"Indeed I haven't," said Mrs. Lithgow. "So far I've had what you might call a flowery path. And even in these hard times Father's business isn't too bad. Not what it was, of course, but so far he's been able to keep on his men, and that's a great relief to his mind. When I think of some people I know with big houses they can't sell and practically no income, I can tell you I'm a thankful woman. And you, Ella," she turned to her sister, "you're about as well off as it's possible to be-not a worry in the world."

"Oh, I wouldn't say that," Miss Turnbull protested. "These are difficult days for every one, and my dividends aren't what they were, and the taxes take a big slice. But, of course, I've nothing to keep up, and I know exactly what my living costs me. Oh, I've many blessings; a nice circle of friends, books — —"

"And bridge," supplied her niece. "Bridge is your great stand-by, Aunt Ella. I forget if you play, Bee."

"I don't," said Beatrice. "Somehow-we seemed always to be doing something else, and only two of us. . . ."

"Of course," said Mrs. Lithgow quickly. "I don't know that I'd ever play myself if it weren't for Father; he likes a game of an evening. But I'd as soon have my work or a book. . . . Ella, I read that book you recommended, but I must say I thought it very queer. The mother going on like that! Such notions writers have now, hardly one of them can write a decent, straight-forward story."

"Well," Peggy explained, "they're not writing for you or your friends. They'd scorn to. . . . If they think of you at all it's only to wish you were out of the world."

"Well, I never!" said Mrs. Lithgow, looking round helplessly. "Peggy, what a way to talk! What have I ever done to writers? The only one I ever met was that brother of Mrs. Warwick's, and I never thought he was right in the head, but I'm sure I've done nothing to deserve — —"

"The fact that you exist is enough," said Peggy inexorably. "You're middle-class and middle-aged, two of the things the bright young writers hate most. . . . and you're decent and clean-minded and you can't expect them to pardon *that*."

Poor Mrs. Lithgow could only shake her head, and her sister, with something of a conde-scending air, as of one more used to the ways of the world, began to comfort her. "It's true in a way what Peggy says, Nettie; some of these younger writers are quite unbearable. You'd think no one over thirty and respectable had a right to live! But most of the people they're hitting at are blissfully unaware of their efforts, don't know the writers exist, in fact, so no harm is done. I must say it rather amuses me to read those books just to see how far they'll go." She addressed Beatrice. "I find reading a great comfort. I hope you are fond of books?"

Beatrice said she was, and Mrs. Lithgow broke in, "I should say so. She's been brought up among books. I think her mother read about every important book that came out; and highbrow weeklies and quarterlies; there was always a table piled with them. I used to feel such an ignoramus when I looked at them. *I* never get further than a novel."

Immediately after lunch Miss Turnbull hurried away to keep an engagement, Peggy went off on some business of her own, and Mrs. Lithgow ordered the car and took Beatrice for a long drive, during which she spoke without intermission, except when for a few minutes she was overcome by sleep. Beatrice was rather miserably aware that had her kind hostess not been so keen on doing her duty by her guest, she would have spent the afternoon asleep in her comfortable chair by the fire.

Mr. Lithgow was at home for dinner, a small man with a cheerful, ugly face. His way of showing sympathy with his guest was to press on her the choicest viands at his disposal and a large selection of beverages.

"You wouldn't like a little white wine? No? Well, what about some green ginger-Crabbie's green ginger, a grand warming thing in cold weather? No? Well, some cider then? Well, lemonade?"

Beatrice, touched as well as amused, could not refuse the lemonade, whereupon Mr. Lithgow told her the story of a country girl at a dance who said that the worst of lemonade was that it was "sae bowffy." He chuckled with delight, and advised Beatrice to tell that story to her London relatives and see what they made of it.

After dinner Peggy's fiancé, Harry Lendrum, came in, and he and Peggy indulged in a war of words which seemed to afford them much satisfaction. They were as good-looking and cheerful a young couple as anyone could wish to see. Mrs. Lithgow's pride in them was obvious, though she pretended that Beatrice must be shocked at their behaviour.

"Children," she commanded, "stop arguing and behave yourselves. We'd better have a quiet game, something we can all join in. Be'trice doesn't play bridge."

Beatrice was conscious of nothing but a burning ache at her heart. Peggy, with her mother and father and her big Harry-how rich she was! No wonder she could laugh and be glad, with life so full of interest, so crammed with things to do, so crowded with people who were fond and proud of her. Lucky Peggy, she thought. And kind Peggy, she added, as, noticing the wistful look on her friend's face, the girl held her hand for a moment in a warm grasp.

Mrs. Lithgow absolutely refused to let Beatrice go back to Park Place.

"Nothing of the kind," she said. "Here you'll stay till you go to London, and the longer that is the better we'll be pleased. Fairlie can come here every day and report. You need more things? Well, we'll send for them. I'll take you along this very day to Park Place and you'll tell Fairlie what you want; that's easy enough surely."

And Beatrice, comforted in spite of herself by the warm kindliness of the Lithgow household, was thankful enough to remain.

On the fourth morning of her visit she got a letter from Lady Dobie saying they would be glad to see her in Portland Place on the 15th of October-the Monday of the following week.

She told Mrs. Lithgow as they sat in the morning-room after breakfast. It was Mrs. Lithgow's time for reading the paper: she went through the *Herald* and *Bulletin* from cover to cover, exclaimed at the different brides, mourned over any premature deaths, shook her head over political muddles, and turned hastily away from reported crimes.

This morning, just as she was finishing the papers, Mrs. Murray was announced. She came in explaining that she was out very early as Mr. Murray had gone with the ten train to London, and she had been to the Central to see him off.

"I'm interrupting you," she said, "but I won't stay a minute."

"Who are you interrupting?" asked Mrs. Lithgow. "I'm doing nothing, nor is Be'trice. Peggy's the only busy one-just listen to her."

Peggy used the morning-room for many purposes, sewing, telephoning, writing notes for her mother. To-day she was carrying bowls of bulbs from one place to another, and as she worked she whistled loud and clear like a boy. Her mother, remembering a saying of her country up-bringing, told her that "whistling maids and crowing hens were not canny about any man's town," and turning to her friend said, "Did you ever hear that proverb, Mrs. Murray?"

Mrs. Murray shook her head rather hopelessly. "I daresay I have," she said, "but I hardly dare commit myself to a statement now. My memory's something awful. It's a humiliating thing to have to confess, but I have to write down everything I mean to do in a wee book, and then, as likely as not I lose the book! And my purse! And my spectacles! It's become a joke in our house, 'What's Mother lost now?' but I can tell you it's no joke to me. I take many a cry to myself. I often wish I had a daughter like Peggy to run and search and keep me right."

"You needn't wish that," said Peggy, pausing with a bowl of bulbs in each hand. "You'll get daughters-in-law all in good time; when Tom and Richard have stopped butterflying from flower to flower."

Mrs. Murray sighed and said, "Daughters-in-law are no better than they're called. I really came in this morning to see if Be'trice wouldn't come and pay me a visit. It would be a real kindness on her part."

"Oh, but you mustn't steal her from us," cried Mrs. Lithgow. "Why, she's only just come, and I said this would be her home so long as she stayed in Glasgow, didn't I, Be'trice?"

"You did indeed, and I'm more than grateful for your kindness, and for Mrs. Murray's, but I've just had a letter from my step-sister saying they'll be ready for me on the 15th. That is Monday, isn't it?"

"I'm sorry to hear it," said Mrs. Lithgow. "Still, of course, they are your nearest. D'you know Lady Dobie well?"

"Hardly at all," said Beatrice. "D'you care to see her letter?"

Mrs. Lithgow took it eagerly. She had a passion for reading letters, anybody's letters, even if she knew nothing of the writers, but in this Lady Dobie she took a profound interest.

"Yes," she said, handing it back a minute later, "*quite* a nice letter. I'm sure I hope you will be happy with them. And now," briskly, "what about getting things ready? You would need to have everything as nice as possible."

"Why, Mother," Peggy protested, "are you implying that Beatrice hasn't?"

"No, no, I'm sure she has everything perfect. But London, you know. And Portland Place. Not to speak of Lady Dobie. You've seen her photo in the papers, haven't you, Mrs. Murray?"

"I may have," said Mrs. Murray guardedly, "but you see so many queer sights in the papers."

"And you'll need to be a lot smarter in London than in Glasgow," Mrs. Lithgow continued. "Will you order some things at once, or would you rather wait till you get to London, Be'trice?"

"What do you think?" said Beatrice, while Peggy broke in, "What a mercy that it's Beatrice and not me! Bee is all right, she's been a lot abroad and picked up an English accent. They'll never suspect, Bee, that you hail from Clyde-side. But I'd give away the show at the start."

"What show?" said her mother. "Are you pretending to be ashamed of Glasgow, Peggy?"

"Only pretending," said Beatrice.

"I should *hope* so," said Mrs. Lithgow.

CHAPTER IV

"I will even take my leave
Of you, and pace softly towards my kinsmen."

The Winter's Tale.

Beatrice was not allowed to leave Glasgow like a knotless thread. Not only did Mrs. Lithgow and Peggy accompany her to the Central Station, but Mr. Lithgow delayed going to his office for an hour, and bought every variety of magazine as well as several daily papers to help to while away the journey for her. Fairlie was waiting on the platform with a carefully prepared luncheon-box, in case, as she said, Miss Beatrice didn't fancy a big hot meal on the train; and Mrs. Murray, panting a good deal with her early start and the effort of walking the length of the platform, and holding tightly a bunch of violets and a large box of Manson's chocolates, arrived just before the train started.

"How can I thank you all?" Beatrice said, quite overcome by the kindness shown her.

"Uch, thanks!" said Mrs. Lithgow, "we've done *nothing*. Let us hear from you, my dear; you know how I love letters, and I'll be interested in everything you tell me. And remember, when you come back to Glasgow there's always a welcome with us."

"And with us," panted Mrs. Murray, "don't forget that."

"But I've first claim," said Mrs. Lithgow, "for I was at school with your mother." Fairlie poured a long, half-whispered story into her nursling's ear, cried a little, wiped her eyes and said, "But there, we must just hope that everything'll turn out for the best."

Mr. Lithgow stood with his watch in his hand. "Off in half a minute," he announced. "Good-bye, Be'trice. Don't marry an Englishman if you can help it. What? Oh, not at all, not at all. The kindness was yours in putting up with us; that's the way to look at it, eh?"

"Good-bye, Bee," Peggy cried. "See and stand up for yourself."

"Good-bye! Good-bye!" Beatrice leant out for a last wave and stood for a few minutes in the corridor before going back to her compartment. There was only one other occupant, a woman who was established in a corner, with a neat pile of papers on her knee, and a business-like leather case at her side. She glanced up for a moment as the girl entered, gave a quick half smile, and went back to her papers.

Beatrice's own side of the carriage presented a distinctly festive appearance, piled as it was with fruits, flowers and chocolate boxes, not to speak of novels and magazines. Where, she wondered, would she find such kindness as in Glasgow? Never would she forget what the Lithgows had done for her. She had thought she would be better left in the Park Place house for a little, among the familiar things and with the servants who had lived with and worked for her mother, but now she saw that Mrs. Lithgow had been wise to insist on her leaving at once. It had done her good, living with the Lithgows; the homely, happy atmosphere, Peggy's noisy fun, Mrs. Lithgow's motherly understanding, and Mr. Lithgow's pressing offers of food and drink, they had all warmed and heartened her, chilled and saddened as she was. She had had to make a great effort, so that it wouldn't be too difficult for them to entertain her, and she had ended by enjoying herself-almost. There was always now-would always be, she supposed —a queer lonely feeling behind everything, a feeling that accompanied her by day, and at night when she shut her bedroom door became so overpowering that she often had to throw herself into a chair and cry and cry. But when she broke down she took herself severely to task, reminding herself that she was now alone no longer a child but a woman grown, and she must see to it that she got over her silly fear of the largeness of the world, her dislike of strangers, her inclination to shut herself up and hide.

Having put everything tidily on the rack Beatrice opened the morning papers. She was not acutely interested in any of the news, and kept glancing in her companion's direction. She was interested, obviously, absorbing every word. Forty-five, Beatrice judged her to be, trim, pleasant to look at, with a clever mouth. There was something about the quiet face that was rather fascinating.

Once she glanced up and, finding the girl's eyes fixed on her, dropped hers quickly.

"She's afraid," said Beatrice to herself, "that if she makes a remark it'll make an opening for conversation, but she needn't be," and she sat conscientiously reading every word of the leaders, hoping she looked as intelligent over it as her companion in the other corner.

She had taken off her tight little black hat, the better to cope with the affairs of the world as reported in the press, and the woman opposite, having finished her paper, looked at her, thinking what a pleasure it was to see a pretty girl whose face was left alone. She congratulated herself on having something refreshing to look at through the day's journey. Was she in black for effect, she found herself wondering, or because she had lost some one? The latter, probably; there was a pathetic droop at the corner of the mouth, and shadows round the eyes. Perhaps she was going to London to take up some job. But a second glance at the girl's clothes, her fur coat, her dressing-case, decided her against that theory. Well, it was no business of hers. Later on she might make some advances. Meantime, she had work to do and she took a bundle of MSS. from her case and forgot everything except the matter in hand.

After lunch Beatrice stood in the corridor for half an hour, watching the landscape fly past, and when she returned to her compartment found her companion busily knitting.

As the girl settled herself in her corner the older woman said:

"Do you find the journey long?"

"Oh, no. I like it. I wish it were longer."

"That doesn't sound as if you were in any hurry to reach your destination."

"No," said Beatrice.

"Personally," her companion went on, "there's nothing I enjoy more than a day in the train; it's such a rest."

This was a new light on travelling. Beatrice had been in the habit of hearing people make rather a fuss about it. Kind Mrs. Lithgow had urged her that morning to eat more breakfast, "because, you know, you've a journey before you," and she had been sent early to bed the night before for the same reason.

"I daresay it is," she said slowly, "if you're busy for ordinary."

"Well, I am," said the knitting lady, "very busy indeed. I edit a woman's magazine, you have it there-yes, that one."

She smiled at the eager interest in her companion's face, as she took up the paper. "Why," she said, regarding it almost with awe, "we've always taken this. My mother liked it; she said there was something in it to interest every type of women. And you really-Oh, aren't you lucky?"

"I don't know about luck, but I certainly don't pity myself; it's work I love, though it's worrying enough at times. . . . But everybody with a job just now should be down on their knees thanking heaven fasting. I'm almost ashamed of the good fortune when I see the misery on the faces of men-and women too-who delight to work, and have nothing now to work at. It must be so difficult to keep your self-respect when it seems there is no longer a place for you anywhere. Some are clever and adaptable and can turn to anything and there's more hope for them, but so many could only do one job really well-and they've lost it. . . . London's a hard place to live in if you haven't learned to harden your heart."

"Have you been long in London? You're Scots, aren't you?"

The knitting lady laughed. "That isn't very tactful of you. How do you know that I'm not trying to bury every trace of my Scots descent? As a matter of fact I was born in Glasgow and educated there, but I've been in London for the last twenty years. You don't speak like the Glasgow born-that's a fact, not flattery."

"Don't I?" said Beatrice. "I've lived all my life in Glasgow, except for two years when we were abroad, but I haven't much ear so perhaps that's why I didn't pick up the accent. I didn't mean that you spoke with any particular accent, simply that your voice was deeper and slower than most English voices. . . . I expect I'll be very homesick for the Glasgow accent before long!"

"You're leaving Glasgow then?"

"Yes. You see —I've no one left. There was only my mother and myself, and mother died." Beatrice finished with a gulp, rather surprised at herself for suddenly confiding in a stranger.

Her companion did not make the mistake of attempting to sympathise. She merely nodded and bent her head over her work.

Presently she said: "It's hard for you. But you're young."

"Does that make any difference?" the girl asked.

The older woman smiled. "I think so. In spite of yourself new interests will claim you. Life is before you. . . . Have you any near relations?"

"A step-brother and his wife and family; I'm going there now; I hardly know them."

"But that's rather interesting; it'll be fun for you finding out all about them."

"Fun!" said Beatrice. "Well, I suppose it might be to some people, but the thought of it simply makes me stiff with fright. It sounds too silly and babyish, for I'm twenty-five, but I've hardly done anything on my own till now. Mother had me educated at home, and took me herself to the Continent as I got older, so I've never had to rough it among other girls. The consequence is I don't know enough about them to feel at home with them. Perhaps if I'd taken up Guides, as mother wanted me to. . . . You see mother herself was so splendid that I wanted no one else. I leant on her. She didn't care how many responsibilities she took on and she failed no one. The people she kept going! Backed them up with her courage! I simply can't think why God took my mother out of a world where she was so much needed. And only sixty!"

"Did you help your mother in her work?"

"Not much," Beatrice confessed. "I'm not much good at public work, and I'm shy of poor people. I never think they believe much in my interest. I don't blame them for I don't believe in it much myself."

"Then what are your interests?"

The girl gave a little shame-faced laugh as she said:

"I don't believe I've got any-specially. I was so much a part of mother that her interests were enough for me. She always told me about everything and I liked to listen. . . . Now, of course, it must be different."

The older woman was touched by the forlorn note in the girl's voice, but she said bracingly:

"If you don't interest yourself in people, no one will be interested in you, and you'll have a very dull time."

"Oh," said Beatrice, looking consideringly at her companion, "I wonder if that was why I was a failure when I went to dances?"

"Who said you were a failure?"

"Does one need to be told? The ill-concealed relief of my partners when they had done their duty and danced with me was enough. I never enjoyed going out because I always came home feeling I had been no success. Mother thought it was because I was shy and that may have had something to do with it, but there was more than that. D'you suppose it was because I wasn't interested enough?"

"Well, you weren't playing the game, were you? What have we got to be interested in except each other and the way life deals with us? If you think of it-that's what all the books are about more or less."

"But a pretence of interest wouldn't be very convincing?"

"But why shouldn't it be real? Train yourself to be interested. Realise that it's more a lack in yourself than a want of appreciation in other people that makes you less popular than you might be. Realise that in standing aloof, keeping yourself to yourself, you miss a lot. And-forgive this flood of advice, but you did ask for it-now that you are alone it's very important for yourself to get all you can out of living. Though you are alone that's no reason why you should be lonely. You must make a niche for yourself."

"Where?" Beatrice asked. "In Portland Place among my step-relatives?"

"You don't know much about them, you said?"

"My step-brother I know best. He's a member of Parliament, a knight, a successful business man. He tried to be kind when he came to-to the funeral. His wife I hardly know at all. She seems a very busy person, important enough to have photographs of herself in papers and magazines. The children used to come and stay with us down the Clyde, dear little people they were, but much more sophisticated than I was —a big girl with pigtails. I shudder to think what they are like now. The girl is twenty, and something of a beauty; the boy is at Oxford. So you see, it's rather an alarming house to enter."

But Beatrice found her companion determinedly cheerful.

"Oh," she said, "it seems to me you'll have a very good time, meeting all sorts of people and going about with your step-sister and her daughter. I know exactly how you are feeling at the moment. It doesn't seem so very long since I came up to London, a very shy, backward girl. But with me it was needs must; I had my living to make and couldn't afford to give way. At first I endured tortures, and do even now, when I have to meet some one whose opinion of me and my work is of importance, but I've learned to look calm and assured and that is half the battle. Go through the world giving and expecting courtesy and ignoring rudeness and malice. Not that you're likely to meet with malice. You look as if it should be roses all the way with you. You're a silly child to get it into your head that you are unattractive. Why, my first thought when you came into the compartment to-day was-No, having given you such a dose of good advice (I believe I must have been meant for a school marm) I won't spoil the effect with sweetmeats."

Beatrice blushed, and laughed shyly, as she said, "I think you're more of a mother-confessor than a school marm. At least I never had the slightest impulse to confide in anybody, and think how I've talked to you to-day, a stranger."

"But wasn't it partly because I was a stranger? Now, what about tea? Let's go in together. D'you ever knit jumpers? It's fascinating work, and this is rather a good pattern. . . ."

It was getting dark when they got back to their compartment after tea and all Beatrice's fears returned as she realised that in another hour they would be in London. How she envied her companion, calmly putting away her work and papers! No wonder she looked quiet and happy. She knew what she was going to. Meeting her glance Beatrice said desperately, "I wish I were going to a job!"

"Why, what would you do with a job?"

"I'd be independent," said Beatrice, thinking of her step-sister, who would probably want to decree what she should do.

"Oh," said her companion, imagining she had been mistaken in the signs of affluence about Beatrice, and deciding in her own mind that Sir Samuel had made the money, and was kindly supporting his young step-sister. "No one who has a comfortable home should try for a job. Jobs are for people who can't live without them."

Beatrice was about to explain that it was the job, not the salary that she wanted, but the older woman at that moment handed her a card. "I'm always at home," she said, "on Sunday afternoons. If you should ever have an hour or two to spare I'd like very much to see you and to hear how things go with you. Don't forget."

"I'm not likely to forget," said Beatrice. "I know almost no one in London and it would be a great treat to see you again."

She looked at the name on the card as she put it away safely in her bag; *Miss Jane Naesmyth*, and thought that it suited her companion well.

"I'll look forward to seeing you," said Miss Naesmyth. "Here we are! Will you be met?"

Beatrice had never thought of anything else. She or her mother had always gone to the station with the car and brought home any expected guest. But she told herself London was different. Probably the car would be engaged, and Betha and Elaine too, and they would expect her to take a taxi. It would be easier for her, really, than looking about for people she didn't know by sight.

"Oh," she said lightly, "I don't suppose so. It's so easy with lots of porters and taxis." But she could not help peering round her as she followed the porter from the luggage-van, and presently she spied in the crowd the large, satisfied face of her step-brother. He was looking very impressive in a tall hat, and coat with a fur collar, and greeted Beatrice with urbanity, complimenting her on having got out her luggage with such celerity and pointing out his waiting car.

As they got in Beatrice saw her fellow passenger pass with a porter to a taxi, and over her shoulder she gave Beatrice such an encouraging smile that the girl drove away warmed and heartened.

CHAPTER V

"See, your guests approach,
Address yourself to entertain them sprightly."

The Winter's Tale.

Although far from feeling at ease in her step-brother's company, Beatrice would have liked to prolong the drive from Euston to Portland Place, and put off the moment when she must meet the rest of the family, whom she pictured as grouped in the hall prepared to receive her. But when the front door closed on them only the butler was there. Her ladyship, he said, and Miss Dobie had not yet come in.

"After your journey," said Sir Samuel, "I expect you would like to go straight to your room. Betha and Elaine must have been detained. I know they expected to be in when you arrived. I told them the time-Ah, here is Higgins, she will take you to your room and be sure you ask for anything you want. . . . See you at dinner —8.30."

Beatrice went up two flights of long stairs and was shown into the room that was to be hers. The maid turned on the electric fire, showed her the nearest bathroom, and suggested that she would lay out what Miss Dobie meant to wear that evening, and unpack the boxes while she was at dinner.

"You may want to rest now, Miss," she said, "and it would make such a litter in the room."

But Beatrice assured her that she was not in the least tired.

"I think I'd like to unpack myself, if you don't mind, and then I'll know where everything is. Not that there's a very great deal to unpack," she added.

"Being in mourning," said Higgins, "you don't want an accumulation."

Beatrice agreed. She liked the look of Higgins, her middle-aged figure and round face and spectacles. There was something rather countrified and innocent about her.

"Perhaps I could get you a cup of tea, Miss?"

"No, thank you. I had tea in the train. It's a very short, comfortable journey from Scotland."

"So I've heard, Miss, but I've never had the chance to try it. . . . Can't I put those away for you? It's a pity to have you stooping and I'm used to it, being her ladyship's maid."

She was a most efficient maid, Beatrice realised, as she speedily and neatly unpacked and disposed of the boxes, and tidied the room.

"There now, Miss, you're quite settled in as you might say. Everything put away under your own eye. . . . Now shall I turn on a nice hot bath? The bathroom's practically your own so you need have no fear of being disturbed; a lady hates to be hurried with the bath."

"Oh, thank you," said Beatrice, wondering to herself how Fairlie would have behaved under the same circumstances. "Only," she reflected, with a somewhat wry smile, "it couldn't have happened in our house, for never would a guest have been left to a maid."

Still, she admitted to herself, it was much pleasanter and easier for her to be in her own room with the kindly, helpful Higgins than sitting, as she might have had to do, downstairs, making difficult conversation with strange relations until it was time to dress for dinner. Now, at her leisure, she could have a bath and dress, and become accustomed to her surroundings.

She looked round the room which was furnished in a way that she had hitherto only seen in advertisements. Everything was the last word in modernity, and, the girl thought, hideous. The carpet was puce, and had a most irritating pattern that looked as if packs of cards had been thrown on it by some untidy person. There was one picture above the bed and after Beatrice had studied it for a long time and made nothing of it, she decided that it might be better turned upside down.

"Not a very restful picture for a bedroom," she said to herself. "I'd rather have 'Sleep sweetly in this quiet room' embroidered with lavender!"

She couldn't think at first what was wrong with the room, then she realised that it lacked the personal touch; it might have been a room in a furniture warehouse. There were no books, no flowers, nothing to make it look welcoming.

Well, she had her own belongings to put out, some of her favourite books, a few photographs, and her own pretty toilet things. They certainly made the room more human, but how awful her rose-pink satin dressing-gown (so much admired by Mrs. Lithgow) looked on the puce coverlet.

About twenty-five minutes past eight, when she was trying to make up her mind to go downstairs and find the drawing-room, there came a tap at the door, and before she could say "Come in" Lady Dobie entered.

"So here you are," she said, kissing the girl. "I was *desolated* not to be in when you arrived, but Elaine and I simply *had* to put in an appearance at two parties. I hope Higgins looked after you properly? Had you a nice journey? How long is it since we met? You haven't seen Elaine since you grew up, have you? Nor Stewart? A giant, simply a giant, six feet two! And oh, my dear, your poor mother! But we won't speak of sad things; after all the world must go on. . . . Are you ready? Then, let's go down-you must be famishing. I hope they gave you tea?"

To this rush of questions Beatrice merely returned a vague murmur, aware that no answer was required, for her step-sister flew from subject to subject like a busy sparrow. She was a small woman grown heavy, with golden hair and a bold taste in clothes. All the way downstairs she chattered, giving little staccato cries at intervals. "Is that my darling? Yes, it's Missus! Missus is coming-my precious Pekie," she explained over her shoulder to Beatrice.

Sir Samuel was waiting for them in the hall and Beatrice was startled to hear him greeted by his wife: "Down first, Big Boy? I've been making my peace with Beatrice about being out when she arrived and she's forgiven me. Of course no one in London would ever *dream* of staying at home to welcome a guest, but I expect they still do that sort of thing in Glasgow."

She glanced roguishly over her shoulder at her step-sister, repeating: "They do, don't they?"

"Yes," said Beatrice, "I'm afraid we're as old-fashioned as that."

Lady Dobie laughed again; it was a trick she had, a way of filling up gaps in conversation. If a silence fell she laughed and said "*Well?*" Thus had she earned for herself a reputation for high spirits.

They took their seats at a round table and Sir Samuel said:

"Is it quite impossible for Elaine to be in time? We put back dinner for her, for she couldn't be ready by eight, but if there's to be no improvement we'll have it at seven-thirty. That's when I like my dinner." He turned to Beatrice, explaining that he very often dined at the House, but he had arranged to be at home this evening in honour of her arrival.

"That was very kind," said Beatrice, with conviction, and her step-sister added, "Yes, isn't he a sweet thing?"

Lady Dobie was responsible for most of the conversation.

"And had you a pleasant journey, Beatrice? But I think I asked you that before, and, anyway, what does it matter when it's over? I hate railway travelling myself. Flying is what I love. So bird-like! No more Channel streams for me. Of course the air's quite as sick-making, more so, if anything, but not quite so humiliating, somehow. . . . Ah, here's Elaine! Come and kiss your step-aunt, dear thing, and tell her you're sorry not to have been on the platform at Euston! In Glasgow they still meet their guests at the station."

Beatrice saw a very tall, very slim girl, with a small tired face under a mop of dense black hair, and a vivid mouth. She seemed to advance reluctantly, and Beatrice, rising to meet her, wondered at the absorbed frown she wore, when, suddenly, a most charming smile broke over her face, and she bent and kissed her new relative.

"Well, Elaine," said her father, as she took her place.

"Well, Papa," said Elaine.

"You're a quarter of an hour late. Did you know that?"

36

"I gathered it from the fact that you had reached the fish. But as you didn't wait for me, does it matter?"

"Of course it matters. I like things done decently and in order, and to have to go into dinner raggedly, with one missing-well, I don't like it."

"I'm sorry, Papa."

"Well, don't let it happen again. I have so few evenings with my family."

"I know. Busy public man. Don't get pathetic, Papa."

"And don't you be pert, my girl."

Lady Dobie laughed and cried: "Stop sparring, you two, or you'll give Beatrice a bad impression of our happy home." She turned to the new-comer, adding, "It's worse when Stewart's home from Oxford; Samuel's down on him all the time. It comes of being well brought up. Nothing makes one feel so superior all through life. Take warning, you girls, and never marry a man who has been well brought up-it's too wearing." She kissed her hand to her husband, saying, "That's too bad, Big Boy, isn't it?"

Sir Samuel went on eating as if he hadn't heard her. Beatrice stole a glance at Elaine's unsmiling face, but it was inscrutable.

The meal proceeded; the servants walked softly round the table; Beatrice and her brother conversed a little about the Park Place house; Lady Dobie threw remarks about like shuttle-cocks.

Afterwards, in the drawing-room, which Beatrice thought interesting but unpleasing, they passed what seemed a very long evening.

Elaine settled herself beside a lamp with a workbox beside her and a gramophone playing at her ear; and worked feverishly at something, hardly raising her head. Lady Dobie fiddled with the wireless, turning knobs till she had almost five stations at once, then wearied of it, and went into the adjoining room to do some telephoning. Her voice could be heard laughing and ejaculating, and Beatrice reflected that there can be few sillier sounds than a person giggling into a telephone. Sir Samuel was peacefully asleep, with the evening paper on his knee.

Some books lay on a table, and Beatrice went to look at them. They were new novels from *The Times Book Club* by authors unknown to her. Picking out the most likely-looking she took it to a chair near a light, remembering a remark of Mrs. Lithgow's —"You can always bury Beatrice in a book."

What would they be doing now, the Lithgows? Peggy, she remembered, was going out with her Harry. The couple at home would be peacefully reading, talking a little, listening to the news, perhaps-such an evening as she and her mother had delighted to spend. How quickly the hours had gone! To-night time seemed to stand still, but that was the result of being in new surroundings. But anyway the worst was over, the first plunge taken.

She found that she liked her step-brother better in his own home than in Glasgow, and found him rather pathetic. Lady Dobie, though odd, doubtless meant to be kind. Elaine interested her; she seemed so withdrawn. What a curiously sad little face it was-but what a charming smile! How did she come to be the daughter of Samuel and Betha Dobie? Elaine, the lily-maid. The name on most girls would have been ridiculous, but it suited her. What was she making so diligently, surrounded with odds and ends of old finery, tinsel and sham emeralds, ermine and rose velvet?

Elaine, looking up for a second, caught her guest's eyes fixed on her, and turned off the gramophone.

"I'm sorry," she said. "I should have asked if you minded this noise. I rather like it myself. . . . I'm making things for some *tableaux* —that's the picture," she pitched it across to Beatrice who caught and studied it.

"You see," said Elaine, "the striped muslin and the scarf? That's the one I've to be, but I'm helping with the others as well. People are so lazy."

"You like to make things?" Beatrice asked.

"If I didn't I wouldn't do it."

"I wonder," said Beatrice diffidently, "if I could help. I'm not much good, I'm afraid, but —
—"

"Oh, don't trouble, Higgins does all the long seams. I like to do the fiddling bits that take
time." She glanced round the room, at her sleeping father, at the open door through which
issued sounds of her mother on the telephone, and remarked:

"This is pretty deadly for you. As a family we make wretched home-keepers. My father
always sleeps if he's in for an evening-bored with our society. My mother doesn't know what
to do with herself and flies to the telephone for distraction. I don't know how other families
manage, but we don't seem able to stand each other undiluted."

Beatrice laughed. "Then it's a good thing you live in the midst of distractions. I don't suppose
you are ever much alone?"

"Not if mother can help it. Father issued orders-he doesn't often do it, but when he does it's
as well to obey-that we were to be in to-night, and alone, in order to welcome you. I pointed
out that it was a poor sort of welcome, that we were at our worst *en familie*, that one or two
well-chosen acquaintances would make things easier for you as well as for us, but father knew
best-and this is the result."

"I see nothing wrong with it," said Beatrice. "Your father's having a rest; you are getting
some work done; your mother's amusing herself; I am sitting in a comfortable chair with a
book that is-quite fairly interesting."

"What is it? Oh, that. It's like a plum-pudding, so full of rich ingredients you get a surfeit
after a little. I've one upstairs you might like. At least —d'you care for history?"

Lady Dobie's voice came shrilly from the boudoir: "Elaine, is it Tuesday we dine with the
Bartletts? You made the arrangement; I haven't it in my book."

"Yes, Tuesday."

"Is Wednesday free? Can we dine with Lady Talbert?"

"*I* can't. I'm dining with Susan and going on to something."

Another talk on the telephone and then Lady Dobie emerged.

"Do forgive me, Beatrice; this is boring for you, but arrangements have got to be made. I've
asked the Vivians here on Thursday. Is that all right, Elaine? . . . Think of some people to
meet them."

"The Prestons," Elaine suggested.

"We don't owe them."

"Don't we? What a nuisance. They're about the only amusing people we know. What about
the Cozens?"

"I might try them," said Lady Dobie, "but they're always about three deep."

Elaine pondered, and said: "Joyce and Philip might come. They're always glad of a meal-
and they work for it. Joyce can talk to anyone, so can Phil when he likes; and they're both
decorative."

"Yes," Lady Dobie agreed, "I may have to fall back on them, but I think I'll try the Laceys
first. Oh, I know they're dull, and Lord Lacey's a perfect nuisance with his diet, but they're
the kind of people the Vivians like. And I might try the Stamfords, though they always seem
to be engaged when I ask them."

"It'll be deadly," said Elaine gloomily.

"Oh, I know, but they'll all be dull together and not notice it."

Lady Dobie returned to the telephone, inviting Beatrice to accompany her.

"This is my den," she said, introducing the girl to the most littered room she had ever seen.
"It's a little crowded at present. You see Elaine turned practically everything out of the drawing-
room when it was done up, and these are the things I simply couldn't part with. We're not
allowed to be sentimentalists in these days, but I confess I cling to my old things. When I can
find time I mean to get everything arranged. . . ." She waved her hand vaguely. "These pictures
hung up and photographs and ornaments disposed of. . . . Just look at my bureau! Piled!"

"Have you a secretary?" Beatrice asked.

"Not a full-time one; three days a week. Such a competent creature. I can leave everything to her. She knows my style so well that I can trust her to answer all but my most intimate letters. And, really now I hardly ever write an intimate letter; there's no time for them. The telephone is so much more convenient. And intimate friends are out of fashion, too; we call each other pet names and dear and darling each other, but it doesn't amount to much. I sometimes wish — —"

But what Lady Dobie wished Beatrice was not to know for she had again taken up the receiver.

Beatrice amused herself looking at the contents of the room, and wondering how any house-maid ever coped with the dusting of it. There were prints stacked against the wall, cabinets of china, tables crowded with silver, piles of photographs, many of them in heavy silver frames. It was amusing to find Elaine as a self-conscious schoolgirl photographed with her brother.

By eleven o'clock, Lady Dobie, exhausted but satisfied, announced that she would go to bed.

"A night in," she said, "is such a luxury, and I feel I've made good use of it. Such luck getting on to so many people; everybody seemed to be having a night in! I've got next week practically filled up, and the next again. I expect you want to go to bed too, Beatrice, after your journey. Don't get up to breakfast. I seldom do, and be sure and ask for anything you want. Yes, well, good-night."

When Beatrice found herself back in the room which already seemed to her a haven of refuge, she started to undress briskly, determined to get out of the habit of breaking down and crying when she got away from people. In bed perhaps, but to the world she must keep a brave face.

A tap came to the door, a genteel tap. "Higgins!" thought Beatrice, and when she said, "Come in," Higgins appeared, her spectacles shining benevolently, in one hand a tray with a tea-pot and a cup, and under the other arm a small white kitten.

"I wondered, Miss, if you'd care to have anything to drink-China tea, or Horlick, or Ovaltine? Some ladies sleep better after a hot drink."

Beatrice, not liking to repulse a kind thought, decided on the tea, which was there, and exclaimed in delight at the sight of the kitten.

"Yes, Miss; I thought it'd cheer you. There's something so homely about a kitten, especially in a strange house. Kittens are the same all the world over."

"He's purring," said Beatrice. "Hear! He's quite happy with me. What's his name?"

"Well, Miss," Higgins cleared her throat and blushed a little, as if not certain that she was being quite delicate, "we're not quite certain downstairs of his sex (if you'll excuse me mentioning it), so we've christened him 'Impudence,' which is suitable to either as you might say. He's the kitchen kitten, quite a common little thing; but he's got a sweet face; it's unlucky him being white, for the coal-cellar's his favourite playground. . . . But he's clean to-night, is Impudence, for before I brought him up I did him all over with cloth ball."

CHAPTER VI

"Let us now go out into London."

H. V. Morton.

Worn out by nights of broken sleep and many emotions Beatrice slept like a tired child, and when she woke, could not for a moment imagine where she was. Her bed had got turned round, the window was in the wrong place-then she remembered. With a rush it all came over her, and she buried her face in the pillow.

Perhaps Higgins noticed the tear stains when she came in with the morning tea, for she announced with much emphasis that it looked to her like being a good day. "October's been very fine," she said, "and even in November I've seen some lovely days; and then December brings Christmas and that's heartening. It's wonderful the helps we get in this world-and we need 'em all, I'm sure. It's eight o'clock, Miss. Breakfast's at 8.30 for the Master, but the ladies don't come down. You will have a tray up here, won't you, Miss?"

"Oh, no, thank you," said Beatrice. "I'll have my bath now, if I may, and go down to breakfast. I've had such a good night. I think your tea was a sedative. How is Impudence this morning?"

Higgins paused, with the towel she was holding in her hand, and shook her head. "Well, if you'll excuse the expression, he's a regular child of Satan. He's got at cook's knitting and pulled it all down and dirtied it something horrid, and he went straight from the coal-cellar and walked on the clean breakfast cloth! Payne-the butler, Miss-he was in a way! Oh, he's not popular downstairs this morning, is pussy. And he looks up into your face so innocent-like. . . . I'll get your bath ready, Miss."

"Cold, please, Higgins. I always have a cold bath in the morning."

"Oh, but, Miss, *should* you? Not dead cold. Why, it's enough to make your 'eart fail. I suppose it's just as one's accustomed, but the very thought makes me shudder-with a touch of frost in the air too!"

Whether it was the cold bath or the good night's rest, certainly Beatrice looked a picture of freshness when she greeted her brother in the dining-room. That gentleman also wore a cheerful morning face and seemed well satisfied to begin another day. He was getting through a good breakfast, with *The Times* propped up before him.

"It is almost my only opportunity of seeing the papers," he explained. "I'm hard at it all day-first in the office, and when Parliament's sitting, at the House. Not that I'm complaining. My word, how I pity the retired men, lounging all day in their clubs. I enjoy every minute of my life, as much now at fifty-five as I did when I was a youngster beginning. Just now, I grant you, it's anxious work, but I'd rather be anxious than live in a stagnant peace. Time enough for that when I'm not fit for anything else. . . . I must get them to bring you to dine with me at the House. It would amuse you to see how things are done, and look at the men whose names and faces are familiar to you in the papers!"

Sir Samuel finished his toast, drank up his tea, then threw down his napkin and prepared to rise, but the chances of an audience were too tempting, and he sat down again.

"Ah, yes, Beatrice," he said impressively, "I can't be sufficiently thankful that I struck out for myself. My father didn't like it, you know. No. He wanted me to settle down in Glasgow and carry on his own business; didn't care for risks. But I must say when he saw I'd made up my mind the old man was generous enough-gave me my portion, like the Prodigal Son, and wrote to all the people he knew in London to keep an eye on me! Most of them were canny Scots, pillars of the Presbyterian Church in London, supporters of vernacular circles and Burns' Clubs-you know the kind, and they received me with great kindness and made me free of their houses. . . . Of course I began very quietly, but gradually I got on. And I was ambitious. Even as a youth I saw Parliament before me, and I made my first attempt at public speaking at the

Church Debating Society in Clapham, where I had rooms. Then I took rooms in Kensington and joined a church there, and got to know more people, began tennis and golf, spent where spending paid, but lived carefully, you understand, for everything I could spare went to the enlarging of the business. And I was lucky, I acknowledge that, Things just seemed to fit in-with a well-directed push from me here and there!" He laughed gleefully and then sobered, as if he felt his theme too big for levity and continued:

"Well, I got to be noticed and talked about as a man who'd get on; my opinions were known to be sound and moderate and I was asked to stand for Parliament. I had plenty of confidence so I accepted. I didn't get in, but I put up a jolly good fight and learned a lot. So when the next Election came, I got a constituency with a good sporting chance. I worked like a nigger and made every one work with me-result, a thumping majority. And I've sat for it ever since. I've always had a knack of managing people without letting them know they were being managed, and down at Lettington they eat out of my hand. I'm popular with all parties. They like my Scots decency and trust me, and yet I'm not too much a Scot, if you know what I mean. I'm not always flinging myself about over the rights of Scotland. I don't blench when people talk about England when they mean Britain. I'm very well satisfied with what I've got out of England, and then, I suppose, having an English wife makes a difference-Well, well, I must go, I'm chattering. . . . I hope, my dear, that you'll be happy here. Elaine must take you about a bit. . . . Both she and Betha are always up to the ears in engagements. Indeed, I seldom see them; they go their way and I go mine. Times have changed since my father's day when a married couple were like the Siamese twins. But perhaps we go too far the other way. The swing of the pendulum, you know, the swing of the pendulum."

He stood up, threw out his chest, brushed a crumb from his waistcoat; passed his hand over his carefully brushed hair and with a "Good morning, Beatrice," left the room.

The girl went to the window to see him step into the car and was impressed by the important-looking leather case with "Sir Samuel Dobie" blazoned on it, that Payne handed in after him. Then she returned to the table to begin her delayed breakfast, for it had hardly seemed the proper thing to be calmly helping herself to eggs and bacon when Samuel was reciting for her benefit the tale of his life.

There was plenty to choose from; three hot dishes, a large ham, and both tea and coffee. Beatrice, who always liked her breakfast, sat down contentedly to enjoy it. It was rather nice, she told herself, to have a hostess who remained upstairs in the morning. But why did Elaine not come down to keep her father company? It seemed odd, but perhaps Samuel preferred it so. Probably he would not have appreciated the bright young daughter of Victorian novels, who was always at the breakfast table, fresh as the morning, to make Papa's coffee as he liked it, and cheer him on his way with a daughterly embrace. The old ideal still reigned, more or less, in Glasgow. She remembered how Peggy Lithgow had, with much chaffing, accompanied her father along the terrace, advised him to be good, and had then returned, springing up the steps, as her mother told her, like a wild goat on the mountains.

Well, it was wonderful to be here, in Portland Place, in the middle of everything. To out-ward appearance it was not unlike Glasgow or any other large city: the same dignified houses, maids doing front doors, message boys whistling, motor-van drivers exchanging badinage with servants, girls on their way to work, walking past with very neat legs and feet. An Indian with a dirty white turban and a bulging cheap suitcase was going down area steps to try to tempt people with his wares. . . .

Nine-thirty! Evidently no one else was coming for breakfast, and the maids would want to clear away. Her own room would be in process of getting tidied. Should she go to the drawing-room? As she went through the hall she saw through a half-open door the glow of a fire, and went into the door. Here was a refuge, a comfortable room, with bookcases and a large writing table; probably Samuel's own room, where she might sit and disturb no one. There were papers here too, picture papers as well as the more solid dailies, so she sat down by the fire and enjoyed them for half-an-hour. Then she remembered that Mrs. Lithgow would be eagerly looking for a letter and went over to the writing table, where she found an imposing blotter, an array of pens, and a well-filled case of note-paper.

"Dear Mrs. Lithgow." No, "dearest," the other looked cold and formal. Then Beatrice stopped. What had she to tell her? She would have to make a story about the journey and about her arrival and what the house was like and her relations. . . . And above everything she must try and thank, however inadequately, the Lithgow family for their great kindness to her. She did her best, but was far from pleased with the result; it was a wooden letter. Perhaps if she waited till the afternoon she might have more to say; the post didn't go till after six, so she took up a book.

About eleven o'clock Betha appeared dressed for out-of-doors.

"Here you are!" she cried, sitting down and stretching out her feet to the fire. "You early bird! I feel I should scold you for not lying still and having a nice rest, but I believe in letting every one go their own way. Yes, it is a nice day, so far as a day can be nice at this time of year in England. I am a sun worshipper, I admit it. Yes. But now that we are alone together, I want you to tell me all about your dear mother's illness. I do hope she didn't suffer, and that it wasn't too terribly trying for you."

There was a pause, then Beatrice said: "She didn't allow it to be terrible. She managed to make it almost a happy time, at least one to remember with-pride."

"How marvellous! But she was such a fine type. I do wish I had known her better, but really, as I often say to Elaine, the world is too much with us. One hasn't time for the quiet friendships and intimate talks one would so enjoy. Instead, one rushes here and there. Just take to-day. I have three appointments before one o'clock. I'm lunching with a most amusing woman, an American. In the afternoon I've a committee meeting about a Charity Ball, a tea, and a cocktail party—I wonder what Elaine is doing. I do hope she'll be able to go out with you. . . . Oh, here she is! Good morning, darling."

Elaine, looking very modish in a small hat that appeared to be glued to her head, wandered in in an absent-minded way.

"Oh, Beatrice, good morning. Good morning, Mother. I don't suppose anyone saw an engagement book." She pushed the things about on the writing-table. "I'm always losing it, but some one generally finds it and puts it here."

"Is this it?" Beatrice produced a small blue book that she had noticed lurking beneath a picture paper.

"Oh, bless you, darling. Now I shall see what I am doing to-day. It's my life's comfort this book. You see it's got a space for every hour of the day, and it begins at 8.30 which gives me such a delicious feeling of possessing all the time there is!"

"I hoped you'd be able to take Beatrice out," said her mother.

Elaine considered the page before her. "I could cut the lunch," she said; "and make my hair do another day, and-yes, we could have the morning together, Beatrice, if you would care to. After lunch I'm afraid I'm hopelessly entangled."

"But, please," said Beatrice, "I'd hate you to alter plans for me. I'll be perfectly happy, I assure you, reading a book here, or going out by myself."

"You can have the car all afternoon," Betha told her. "I shan't be using it and Elaine has her own."

"But I don't need a car, thank you. It isn't as if I were going anywhere in particular. I enjoy shop windows and I'd like a walk in the Park-but what I can't bear is to be a nuisance."

"You could never be that," Betha assured her. "Well, I must fly. You won't forget, Elaine, we're dining with the Staceys to-night. Good-bye, darlings."

Beatrice put on her fur coat and a small black hat and went out with Elaine. She told her she wanted some new clothes, and asked for advice on where to go.

"Now I wonder," said Elaine. "It's not much good taking you to my woman, or to mother's; they'd make you look all wrong. I know. Bunsens-you're their style exactly. D'you mind paying a good deal?"

"Not too much," said Beatrice cautiously. "One wears things such a short time that it doesn't seem to me worth it, but I would like something really nice."

It was easy and pleasant, Beatrice found, to go with a clever young woman who knew exactly what was wanted, and see sylph-like creatures parade in lovely frocks in a restful room, while an older woman with white hair and a sympathetic voice cooed in the background.

It was after one o'clock when they came out, and Elaine, whose breakfast consisted generally of a cup of coffee, announced that she was starving.

"Luncheon's my meal," she said, "and I know where we'll get a good one. Come along to the Black Cat," and while they ate what, to Beatrice, were new and delicious dishes, Elaine pointed out well-known actors and actresses, and constantly leapt up to greet some acquaintance.

"You don't smoke?" said Elaine, over their coffee. "Why?"

"Because I don't like it," said Beatrice; then she flushed and finished, "and because my mother didn't care to see women smoke."

"I see. I rather think you're right; it wouldn't suit your style, and you can't be too careful to be all of a piece. . . . Now, shall I drop you at Portland Place? Or is there anywhere else I can take you? I must be getting on."

"No, no. I'll find my way back. I'll have a look at the shop windows and there are one or two things I'd like to get. Thank you so much for your help . . . ."

Beatrice walked along Oxford Street, enjoying the life and bustle, shopped a little, had tea, and went back to Portland Place in time to finish her letter to Mrs. Lithgow.

> "Elaine and I have been shopping and I've spent a great deal of money on clothes! Two evening dresses —a black velvet one, a beauty, and an embroidered net one, also a day dress and coat. After the buying was finished we lunched at a place called the Black Cat, a very smart place, to judge from the numbers of actors and actresses that seemed to frequent it, and most expensive. Later, walking in Oxford Street, I met so many poor men selling things, I felt guilty about spending so much, and so had to give each one a shilling! London looks very prosperous, there are crowds everywhere, but, I notice, not many buyers in the shops. The evening dress you got from Petrie and Pollock is the very last word in fashion. I am sure Glasgow gets the very best models. Elaine has a car of her own and drives very cleverly through the traffic. She is a pretty girl, and clever. She works beautifully, and seems to read pretty well everything that comes out. Her friends seem to be mostly writers and artists and actors. Betha doesn't appear to be much older than her daughter, and has the air of enjoying life to the full. It is a very large house. I don't know if you would care much for the way it is furnished. The drawing-room has very little furniture and only one picture! But the library is a comfortable room with a coal fire. I miss you all and think about you much. How can I thank you for your great kindness to me? I shall never forget it. You were all so good to me, and patient with me, you and Peggy and Mr. Lithgow. I felt quite home-sick when I left you yesterday morning.
>
> "Your loving and grateful
>
> "Beatrice."

When the letter was finished, she looked at the evening papers and then went up to her room, where Higgins, assisted by the kitten, was laying out her things for the evening.

"You're not going out to-night, are you, Miss? No? I daresay you'll be quite glad to have dinner by yourself and get to bed reasonable like. I can feel for you, Miss, if you won't think it a liberty on my part to say so. I lost my father only a year ago. Of course it was different, I had been away since I was fifteen, still it was always home so long as my father was there, but now-well, I have my sisters, but they're both married and have their own interests. Sometimes when I get low, I feel like a knotless thread."

"A knotless thread," thought Beatrice, "that's what I am." Aloud she said: "You need never feel that, Higgins. You are so useful. You've made a niche for yourself."

Higgins was deftly laying out the lace dress on the bed, the black satin slippers, the underwear, and she gave a small sigh as she said:

"I don't know about an 'iche, Miss, but I do try to be of some use in the world. You see, I belong to the chapel close by here, and they give me work to do. I can generally have my evenings after eight o'clock, so I can attend the meetings, which is a great privilege. And I've got some of the other maids in the houses round to go with me and they're interested too, and help a bit. . . . You'd be surprised, Miss, what a difference it makes to have something outside the daily round. Every Wednesday there's a work party to make things for a missionary sale, and we're all as keen as can be to raise a lot. It sort of widens out your life thinking on big things like Foreign Missions and such like. Of course you understand, Miss, it's only a few that go with me. I don't blame them. Girls get a better time than they did when I was a young thing. . . . Come along now, Impudence, that's not for you to sharpen your claws on."

At eight-thirty Beatrice went down to the dining-room and to a solitary dinner, waited on by Payne and the footman. She had never noticed the presence of servants at the table before, but eating in solemn silence made her nervous and self-conscious. She was glad to escape to the drawing-room, where she sat in lonely state beside an electric fire, and tried to interest herself in a book. At ten o'clock she turned off the lights in the drawing-room and went slowly upstairs to bed.

CHAPTER VII

"There is in London all that life can afford."

Dr. Johnson.

Beatrice had been accustomed at home to a quiet life, but one full of interests. Her mother had seen to it that she had lots of small jobs to occupy her time; she had given her cases to investigate, sick people to visit, begged her company at various functions, asked her advice on one point and another, and made her feel always that she had her part in everything that went on. In Portland Place it was very different, bound to be, as Beatrice frequently told herself. Her step-sister and Elaine had innumerable engagements and interests that she knew nothing of; it was absurd to expect them to drag a young woman about with them everywhere because she happened to be a relation, and at present staying in their house.

True, she had had dreams of finding in Elaine what she had never had —a girl friend, and of enjoying London life in her company, but when she met Elaine these dreams vanished. It was not that Elaine was unfriendly, far from it; she was always sweetness itself to the new-comer, kissing her and calling her "darlingest," but Beatrice did not flatter herself that those endearments meant anything at all. Even when Elaine was at her sweetest and most caressing she felt her as far away as the inconstant moon. Beatrice sometimes wondered if Betha did not feel the same about her daughter. The various members of the family rarely met each other except when they were entertaining, and about a week after her arrival Beatrice had the privilege of being present at a dinner-party.

Helped by the sympathetic Higgins Beatrice got herself into the new black velvet dress and decided that, expensive as it was, it was well worth the money. She had never looked so well in her life, and she wished, childishly, that her mother could see her. The woman had been right to advise her to have the black velvet, though her mother would have said that black velvet was more appropriate to dowagers than young girls. But this was cunningly contrived, it made her look so slim and supple, and so dazzlingly fair. So she peacocked in front of the mirror, very well pleased with her own appearance. There was no need to hurry, for in order to get Higgins' help she had had to dress very early, and she had time to get accustomed to herself. She would try her very best to-night to be a help at the party and not a dead-weight. Miss Jane Naesmyth, the lady in the train, had told her she must be interested if she wanted to be interesting, and she determined she would be. But she prayed that she might not be given a clever young man as a dinner partner; she feared the species. Shy but excited, hoping humbly that she would not make a fool of herself, she set off downstairs.

The guests had nearly all arrived when she slipped into the drawing-room. Betha was talking volubly to every one. Samuel stood sipping a cocktail, and Elaine, in a green velvet dress and red slippers, sat with her hands on the arms of a Charles II chair listening passively to the conversation of a handsome affected-looking youth.

To her relief, Beatrice found that she was to go down with a middle-aged man who seemed disposed to be conversational, and she thankfully seconded his efforts. Before they had finished their soup she knew that he was a member of Parliament, his majority at the last election, his opinion of the National Government, his views on India, and on several other subjects. Beatrice was somewhat at a loss to understand why he had been invited ("Probably for me!" she thought), for the other members of the party were utterly different. She found them terrifying but exciting, and their conversation, at least the snatches that came to her, was entirely unintelligible.

When the friendly, talkative M.P. turned away to confide in the lady on his other side, Beatrice glanced at the young man beside her, who, happening at the same moment to glance her way, said:

"Oh, ah-no, I won't talk about the weather. I don't think I've met you before."

"No," said Beatrice, "I've only just come up from Scotland. I'm staying here. I'm Sir Samuel Dobie's step-sister."

This seemed to amuse the young man.

"Sir Samuel's step-sister!" he repeated. "What a priceless thing to be! Then you're Elaine's step-aunt. Of course one knew vaguely that Sir Samuel was a Scot, but I never thought of Elaine as having any connection with across the Border. . . . I expect you're only in Scotland in the autumn."

"On the contrary," said Beatrice, "I've lived in Glasgow all my life."

The information seemed to solemnise the explosive youth. He said: "You haven't really? By Jove! But isn't it rather uncivilised? I mean to say, you know, Burns suppers and haggis, and red men from the Clyde preaching Communism?"

Beatrice shook her head. "I've never been to a Burns supper nor met a Communist."

"But the weather, isn't that unspeakable?"

Beatrice forgot her shyness in annoyance. This was the affected-looking young man whom she had noticed in the drawing-room talking to Elaine. What business had the effeminate creature to try to be funny at the expense of Glasgow? She turned to him and quoted in the soft broad speech her mother had loved: "*It's no aye rainin' in the misty Ochils*. . . . People get such silly notions about places they haven't seen. Take Ireland. I've never been to Ireland, but I picture it as a place bright emerald green, where men with long upper lips and wide mouths go about saying incredibly witty things to 'colleens' with ravishing complexions. I don't suppose it's really a bit like that, nor is Glasgow the wild, dirty wet place that strangers picture it. If you lived in Glasgow five years I don't believe you'd want to leave it."

"I don't suppose I would, for I'd probably be dead! But you seem to have torn yourself away."

"Only because my home there was broken up," said Beatrice.

"Well, you were wise to come to London; it's the only place to live, and I've tried a few in my young life."

He leant across the table to reply to some sally from a vivacious lady opposite, and Beatrice was left to enjoy her dinner.

Certainly, she reflected, Betha's way of running a house seemed a good one. She relied on her servants and they did not fail her; the cooking was perfect, the service quick and deft. And food tasted better eaten in company. . . .

"Do you read, Miss Dobie?" asked her Parliamentary neighbour.

"Yes," said Beatrice, amused at the question, "quite a lot."

"I envy you. There is nothing I enjoy more than an evening by the fire with a book, but I seldom or never get such a treat. Few people realise what a hard task-mistress politics is. It isn't only when the House is sitting, it's the engagements that pursue one. You'd be amused at my mail, Miss Dobie, the variety of the subjects I'm asked to speak on-anything from the problems of the Far East to Infant Visiting. I seem to have the faculty of suiting myself to my company-at least I'm told so. I mean to say, I can be grave and weighty over important matters, but I've a light touch at women's meetings, and at whist drives and so on I'm positively an acquisition. One thing that helps me greatly is that *I never forget a face*."

"A royal memory," said Beatrice.

"Quite. Quite. Of course I've cultivated it, for nothing pleases people so much as to be remembered. You know by yourself, how squashed you feel to get a stony stare when you expect delighted recognition, more especially if you've worked hard for a man and his cause."

"Yes," said Beatrice, "but wouldn't it be better always to wear a tentative smile? Surely a stony stare is completely out of place."

"I see what you mean, but constituents, my dear young lady, would not be content with a vague smile, they want chapter and verse so to speak, some reference to the work they have done, perhaps some particular meeting recalled."

"It all sounds very difficult," said Beatrice.

"So it is, very difficult, but there are great compensations in the life-the interest of the debates, the companionship of the country's best brains. Look at me, if I weren't in the House I'd be mouldering in the country, thinking of nothing but crops and breeding pheasants."

"With your qualifications," Beatrice said, "I hardly think that would be allowed."

The politician laughed in a pleased way and said he certainly thought he was of more use in his present position.

Beatrice was sorry to leave her contented companion and face the women in the drawing-room.

It was quite a pretty scene, she thought. Most of the women present were fairly young and decorative, and the room, somewhat dreary and formal for a home evening, made a charming setting for a party. Elaine was surrounded by three young girls, Betha was talking to an impressive woman in black, and Beatrice tried to enter into conversation with a long, slim creature in red, who lay inertly in a chair, but her effort met with so little response that she at once desisted. Having expected nothing, Beatrice was neither surprised nor disappointed to find that no one seemed to regard her with the slightest interest, or showed any desire to become better acquainted with her.

When the men came up the confiding politician came at once to her side, explaining that it could only be for a few minutes, as he was due elsewhere.

"You don't play bridge?" Beatrice asked.

"Not seriously. It's a good relaxation for a busy man, and a refuge for idle women, but I haven't time to become proficient. Ah! I see an opportunity to say good night to my hostess —I must take it. Most interested to have met you, Miss Dobie. Get your brother to bring you to the House. . . ." With a last bright smile he departed.

"Dear me!" thought Beatrice, "I might be a constituent!" and wondered what it felt like to be so pleased with oneself.

That evening Beatrice regretted never having learned to play bridge, it seemed so stupid to sit with no one to talk to, with nothing to occupy her hands.

When, at last, the guests departed, she found she was not the only one who had found the evening long. Sir Samuel, standing before the fire, smoking a last cigarette, said: "Well, thank goodness, that's over! Who were those people, Betha? That screaming woman in red gave me a headache. I envied Leathen slipping away. . . . You and he seemed to have lots to say to each other, Beatrice."

"Leathen-was that his name? I wondered if he were some one I should have heard of. I hardly needed to say a word, he had so much to tell me. A very cheerful person."

"Yes. He talks too much, but he isn't a bad sort-old Leathen. At least his talk is intelligible, and interesting in a way, but those young men of yours, Elaine, are hopeless. They may be clever, they may even be geniuses, but preserve me from having to try to keep up a conversation with them."

"Papa! Why so severe?" Elaine yawned as she stooped to pick up her bag. "Let's go to bed! How I hate entertaining-falsely so called."

Her mother, who was looking particularly well in pale grey chiffon and pearls, said, "I can't understand you, Elaine. I *love* entertaining; I'm in my element surrounded by people; I enjoy feeding them. Didn't you think it was a very good dinner to-night?" Not waiting for an answer she went on: "I feel it's a sort of duty to entertain now; so many people can't because they're economising and cutting down their establishments; but as long as we can keep going ——"

"It may not be long," her husband said gloomily. "This last week ——"

"Don't croak, Big Boy."

"I *wish* you wouldn't call me that, Betha. . . . I'm tired any way. Nothing tires me so much as vapid conversation."

"Poor darling," said Elaine lightly-then, "Mother, doesn't Beatrice look charming in black velvet? I do think that was a good buy."

"Very," said Betha, studying her own reflection in the mirror. "Is it too late to telephone to-No, it's only a little after eleven. Odd how long an evening in one's own house seems!"

* * * * *

The days passed, one very like another to Beatrice. She breakfasted with Samuel, glad to listen if he were in a talkative mood, content with her own thoughts if he seemed moody, then read the papers in the library-she was becoming exceedingly well informed about the world's news-or wrote letters till Betha and Elaine came down. She generally only got a glimpse of them, for more often than not they had luncheon engagements, and things to occupy them all afternoon.

Sometimes they had luncheon or afternoon parties at home. At those Beatrice appeared, though she never felt herself anything but an outsider. Sometimes Elaine, holding her by the hand, introduced her prettily to the guests, sometimes she ignored her, and Betha had to murmur her name, but it made no difference, Beatrice felt, who sponsored her, she seemed to make no impression.

For the first few weeks she wandered about trying to kill time. About twelve o'clock she went out, walking slowly down Portland Place, turning off at the Langham Hotel and making for Wigmore Street and *The Times Book Club*. There she usually spent about half an hour, browsing among the books and listening to what other people asked for. It was odd how many seemed to be choosing books for other people. One young man she was sure was a footman in mufti, and he wanted "three good novels and none of them sloppy." A lady in mourning with a long upper lip and spectacles asked for "A pleasant book suitable for reading aloud," and went on to expostulate, somewhat unfairly, with the girl clerk about the type of book that had recently been coming into her house.

From *The Times* she walked slowly past Debenham's, stopping to hand a copper or two to the old man with the long white beard, who stood on the edge of the pavement selling groundsel for birds. It was odd to see anything so fresh in the hands of one so ancient. Then she generally went through Marshall & Snelgrove's, enjoying the gleam of crystal, the shimmer of satins, the glimmer of gold and the piles of cushions of more than Oriental splendour, and out into the bustle of Oxford Street. . . . It was always interesting to go into Selfridge's and lose oneself and one's identity in the crowd that surged through the bargain basement; interesting but nightmareish.

As a rule she had lunch in one of the big shops, because she thought it was rather unfair to make the servants have a meal for her alone; it was bad enough always to be in to dinner. There was a small table by a window in a delightful luncheon room that she had begun to think of as her own. There she went almost daily and was welcomed by a smiling waitress, who didn't seem to mind how long she sat over her meal.

If the weather was good it was quite enjoyable. After lunch she would walk down Regent Street, down Haymarket to Trafalgar Square, and spend an hour in the National Gallery. Or Bond Street was always interesting, and a walk in the Park was a pleasure.

One afternoon Elaine took her to a matinée of a not very edifying play by a young dramatist of her acquaintance whom she called Bobby.

"What d'you think of it?" she asked Beatrice.

"It's interesting," Beatrice said, "but I don't think I quite understand why things happened as they did."

"No more does anyone else, least of all Bobby! This is his first play —I'm afraid it'll come off pretty soon. He published some poems, which he reads to anyone who will listen. Mother was caught one day; her face was a study, for Bobby is always unintelligible and often obscene. Happily he's got a father somewhere, with money, for I don't believe he earns a penny."

On the whole, Beatrice found London boring, and had the grace to be ashamed of it, for she felt that it was not London but herself that was lacking. She reminded herself of what others had found in London, what magic, what mystery, what undying romance. Dr. Johnson in his sledge-hammer way had said that if a man were tired of London he was tired of life. Mr. H. V.

Morton could stroll out and be thrilled, puzzled, charmed, and amused by the tide of common humanity flowing through the streets. He could go behind a hoarding where workmen were digging the foundations of some great new building, and gazing down into the pit read the record of London clear "as layers of cream in a cake." Victorian, Georgian, Stuart, Plantagenet, Norman, Anglo-Saxon and Roman. He could pick up a fragment that looked like a flat cake of sealing-wax and find a morsel of deep red pottery with something written, "F. C. Germanus F." —the trade-mark of Flavius Germanus, a potter who lived in the time of the Cæsars!

She remembered reading that in the drawing-room of Park Place and how she had thrilled over it, and over the descriptions of the docks at sunrise, of the coffee-stalls, of the Sunday Market, where you could sell "an elephant, a werwolf, or your second best aunt" without attracting the slightest curiosity; and, best of all, London Bridge with its old magic that has given London "merchants and adventurers, sailors, poets, and millions of poor, discontented men who must needs take their burning hearts to Balham and shut their ears!"

Beatrice had thought then how wonderful it would be to have time and freedom to roam about London and see for herself these magical places, but now she realised that though the magic was all true and all there, it wasn't for every one. It needed some one to reveal it. For instance, she might look all day long over London Bridge and only see dirty water and grimy barges where the writer saw romance and high adventure. If she wandered through the Bagdad market, timorous and distrustful, she would not meet things on the way or see the man who had bought "a dog, a birdcage and a pair of pink braces, and treated himself to a pair of handle-bars." She had time to see, to enjoy, to admire, but she needed a companion to help her. And there seemed no probability of such a thing coming her way.

CHAPTER VIII

"Langour is not in your heart,
Weakness is not in your word,
Weariness not on your brow!"

Matthew Arnold.

When Beatrice woke up one morning and realised that it was her third Sunday in London she determined that it would be different. The other two Sundays had been miserable days. Sir Samuel had gone off early and rather apologetically to golf. "You see," he explained, "it's really the only day I have for exercise. All the same, I sometimes wonder what my old father would have said to me, for he believed in keeping the Sabbath with all strictness. But times are changed. One has a duty to oneself. Tell Betha I'll be home for lunch-she has some people coming, I believe. I expect you'll want to go to church; there are lots all round."

But Beatrice did not go to church, and spent a very dull and unprofitable day, sitting mostly in her own room, too listless to write letters or even to read; brooding over the past and seeing little prospect in the future.

The second Sunday had been worse if anything. But this would not be a heathen Sunday. For one thing she would go to church, her own Scots church, and hear the metrical psalms sung, and listen to a real sermon; and in the afternoon she would make an expedition to Hampstead and call on her friend of the Scots express, Miss Jane Naesmyth.

To Beatrice this seemed a great adventure and one needing much screwing up of courage. Suppose, as was very probable, that Miss Naesmyth had forgotten all about the girl who had travelled with her from Glasgow and to whom she had given advice, and she, Beatrice, had to explain who she was before a roomful of people!

Well, even supposing these things happened, she was going, and she jumped out of bed, gathered up her towels and sponge with a purposeful air, and actually sang in her cold bath to show how bold and firm she was. She noticed, too, how pretty the big green bowl of bath salts looked with her rose-pink wrap thrown beside it. Back in her room she decided that, seeing it was Sunday and a good day, she might wear one of her new London frocks, and went down to breakfast when the gong sounded, looking so well that her step-brother said:

"London seems to suit you, Beatrice. A very healthy place, I always say. Why, just look at the children in the park-pictures of health. And then, you see, you lead a very regular life, early to bed and early to rise; nothing like it. . . . And where are you going this fine day?"

"I thought I'd go to St. Andrew's," Beatrice said helping herself to kidneys and bacon. "I always like the service there."

"Yes, yes. It's a great church for Scots people; they go in crowds. And he's a fine man, Dr. Stronach. I hope he'll be able to go on for a long time, for I know no one who could fill his place. . . . I thought of joining St. Andrew's when I first came to London, but it was a long way, and it seemed better to join an English Presbyterian Church that was near. I was a great worker in the Sunday school and so on. Now-well, for one thing I'm fairly silted up with work, but oh, I don't know. I daresay if I had the interest I'd make the time. . . . I'm sure I began with the best intentions-of course I'm a member still, and so is Betha. Elaine and Stewart were confirmed at school, and so I suppose you'd call them Church of England, but how much it means to them I don't know. I don't know."

He stopped, helped himself to what he wanted, and returned to the table.

"The young people of to-day, Beatrice, are beyond me. I don't understand their way of look-ing at life; I don't know what they want to be at; their values are not my values. Betha pretends to understand our two, but I sometimes think she's as much at sea as I am. Elaine's a beauty and has everything money can give her and yet she never looks to me happy. I don't believe either she or Stewart ever give a thought to anything beyond their own interests."

After a pause, he said rather wistfully:

"You'd think, wouldn't you, when Stewart's down from Oxford he'd be glad to have a round of golf with me now and again."

"Surely," said Beatrice.

Sir Samuel, eating pensively his Sunday sausage, shook his head.

"He has always the best of excuses, but there it is. I'm only useful for producing the money. . . . D'you know, Beatrice, I sometimes think he wouldn't be the worse of having a taste of doing without."

"It's what many people are having and taking it very well too. But, Samuel, you can't be surprised if Stewart's perhaps a bit above himself. I expect he's always had a big allowance, and been tempted to be luxurious and rather to lord it, perhaps, as a rich man's son. There's nothing the average person has such an admiration for as the power to make money."

"That's true, of course" (Sir Samuel straightened his shoulders unconsciously). "And there's no doubt about it, I've always had the golden touch. My father had it before me. They used to say in Glasgow that anything old Dobie touched turned to gold. A good thing for you and me, Beatrice."

"I suppose so," said Beatrice.

Her step-brother laughed good-naturedly. "Well, we'd be pretty sorry for ourselves if we lost it now, wouldn't we? You mustn't think, Beatrice, that I'm complaining at all of the children. I'm as proud as Punch of them. Elaine is greatly admired, and Stewart's a very handsome fellow, though he hasn't his sister's brains. He excels in games. . . . And you can't expect old heads on young shoulders; time will teach them."

When Beatrice went upstairs to get ready to go to church, she met Elaine in her dressing-gown coming out of her mother's room.

"Hullo, Beatrice! Had breakfast? Come in and see mother. She's suddenly found that she has nothing to wear!"

"Yes, do come in," urged Betha's voice, and Beatrice entering, found her step-sister sitting in an ornate bed, looking, in her rosy draperies, like a full-bloom peony; the large room had a built-in wardrobe with sliding doors, right along one side, in which were massed the clothes of Lady Dobie.

Never, outside of a shop, had Beatrice seen such an array of garments, and Elaine repeated, "Nothing to wear!"

"I know it sounds absurd," said the owner of the display, twisting round to pour herself out some chocolate from a silver pot on a tray that stood by the bed. "This is all I have for breakfast," she said, pathetically, "and I wouldn't have this if I did as I was told. Gracious, Beatrice, you and Elaine don't know how well off you are with figures like fishing-rods! And I've such a healthy appetite. There's nothing I'd like better than to eat kidneys and bacon and paste rolls with butter and honey. The very thought makes my mouth water, but instead I've to deny myself all the time."

"But why do you do it?" asked her daughter. "Why not eat everything and grow old fatly?"

"Young people are so callous," said Lady Dobie, sipping her chocolate, and looking disconsolately at the garments Higgins had spread out for inspection.

"I don't want to put on that green thing again-It's not becoming. I saw myself suddenly in a mirror one day when I had it on and I looked *awful*."

Higgins went to the wardrobe and brought out a black dress, looking to Elaine for guidance.

"That's charming," said Elaine. "That with the Persian-lamb coat-the one with no trimming of other fur, and the black hat with the green-blue feather arrangement, and you'll look your best, mother. No, don't make a face. I'm right. Don't you agree, Beatrice?"

"Black *is* smart," said Lady Dobie, "and that coat is certainly very slimming." She went on to explain: "I'm lunching with old Lady Wharton. I helped her with her Play-Centre Scheme, and I suppose this is my reward. She is old and poor and untidy, and yet in her presence I feel like a child at a school-treat, and not a very well-behaved child either. It's absurd, but there it is!"

"Lady Wharton," said Elaine, "is one of the last of her order. She's a sort of Canute trying to keep back the waves by sheer force of will: don't have a complex about her, Mother; are you off, Beatrice? Church? Oh, good child! I'm going to have a lazy morning till I go out to lunch."

Beatrice hurried out into the winter sunshine. The crisp air felt particularly good after the atmosphere of clothes and scent and cosmetics she had just left. There was time to walk part of the way and she strode along, enjoying the emptiness of the streets and the ring of the footsteps on the pavement, stopping now and again to peep into shop windows, wondering why shops were so much more seductive when they were shut.

She knew St. Andrew's Church well. It was the one she and her mother had always attended when they were in London. To-day, as usual, crowds were flocking, and Beatrice felt vaguely surprised. So there were still lots of people in London who went to Church. She was taken forward to a seat near the front, and glancing round her found the pews full of decorous worshippers, many middle-aged and elderly, but with a fair sprinkling of girls and young men. The woman next to her offered a hymn book and Beatrice thanked her with so friendly a smile that she felt constrained to whisper "Do you come to the Work Party? I'm introduced to such a lot of people there that I find difficulty in recognising them again."

Beatrice assured her that they had not met before and the conversation was stopped by the service beginning.

It was good to sing again the Psalms of David, to feel that she was in her own atmosphere, surrounded by people who were all of the same way of thinking. She waited eagerly for the sermon, for the preacher's voice had a special significance for her. He was one of the most successful broadcasting preachers and she and her mother had often enjoyed together his service on the wireless.

The congregation settled down to listen to their minister as he tried to give them some idea of directing their course on the troubled sea of life. He had everything needed for the task, the wisdom and experience that a long life well spent gives, tenderness for the old travellers, and an understanding pity and admiration for poor brave youth. But it was his voice that brought back so much to Beatrice, that quiet, assured voice that gave listeners confidence, the voice of one having authority. Beatrice listened eagerly, and stood up to sing Bunyan's words *Who would true valour see*, feeling as if, there and then, she would like to set off "to be a pilgrim." And the feeling lasted all through a lonely lunch at Portland Place, for even Sir Samuel was out that Sunday, and braced her up to pay the visit she had planned to Hampstead. "I'll go," she said to herself, "about half-past three, so that she needn't ask me to tea unless she likes. If I feel that she's had enough of me I'll rise to go about four o'clock and she'll think I'm going on elsewhere."

The fine morning had darkened to a grey, dingy afternoon so there could be no walking. A maid whistled for a taxi, Payne being out, and Beatrice set off, as scared, she told herself in bitter scorn, as if she had been going to Buckingham Palace. She found the drive very interesting, and never having been in Hampstead before, amused herself wondering which houses contained artists of note, authors, actors, but in a disturbingly short time her taxi stopped before a door in a wall, and she got out, while the taxi-driver obligingly rang the bell.

After receiving his fee-taxi-drivers always touched their hats to Beatrice when she paid them-he lingered to see what would become of his fare, but the door in the wall opened by some mechanism and she at once disappeared from him. Inside Beatrice found herself in a covered entrance leading by a short flight of steps to a front door at which stood a tidy, middle-aged woman (rather like her own Fairlie) who said Miss Naesmyth was at home, and took her across a little black-and-white tiled hall to a book-lined room, with a big rounded window looking out on the garden.

Jane Naesmyth was writing letters by the fire, and rose quickly when she saw her visitor hesitate at the door. Sunday was the one day she could count on being at home, and she gave many people, more especially people who were strangers in London, a warm invitation to visit her on that day. For a moment she couldn't place this girl, but she went to meet her, and put her into a comfortable chair not too near the fire.

Beatrice said: "I expect you've forgotten, but you said very kindly that day we travelled up from Glasgow together that I might call on you some Sunday. I'm the girl who was going to stay with relations."

"I remember very well," Jane said, in her slow, rather deep voice, and she did, for the girl had interested her at the time and the thought of her had crossed her mind more than once. "I'm so glad you've come, for I've wondered sometimes how things were going with you. It's tantalising, don't you think, to hear a little bit of some one's life and then be switched off-like losing a magazine when you're reading a serial story. You were going to almost unknown relations. I hope they proved friendly folk."

"Oh, yes," said Beatrice eagerly. "Yes, indeed; they're very nice to me; I have everything I want."

"That's good."

"Yes. They're a very busy family. My step-brother one would expect to be, he has both his own business and his work in the House, but my step-sister and her daughter are just as busy! I didn't know it was possible to have so many engagements. I used to think my mother had a lot, but she was generally in to meals and we had a lovely quiet evening to ourselves, but Betha and Elaine just fly from one thing to another; come in and change and rush out again, unless they are having a party themselves which quite often happens."

"And you, of course, won't be going out much just now."

"No. But even if I weren't in mourning, I don't think I'd be wanted. The people who come to Portland Place, they're either very smart or else they're literary or something; young men and girls who write poems and plays or paint pictures or design clothes. I can't talk to those people; we don't even speak the same language."

Jane smiled. "I know what you mean. They speak a sort of jargon of their own, and they're only interested in the doings of their own little set; every one's alluded to by a nickname, and they're all terribly *intimate*. No wonder you feel an outsider! Couldn't you treat it like a game? Try to learn the rules and compete. It might be rather amusing."

"I couldn't," said Beatrice. "I'm not clever enough."

"I shouldn't think it needed much cleverness."

"It needs something I haven't got. I'm slow. I'm dull. Perhaps I'm provincial. No, I'm not saying it to be assured of the contrary, it's only too obvious. Elaine's friends try to talk to me, I do my best to respond, but the relief with which they turn from me isn't very-well, it isn't very *gratifying!*"

"Is 'Elaine' very charming?" Jane asked, after a pause.

"Very. I love to look at her. But she's very remote. No one ever knows what she's thinking or feeling about anything. She treats life as if it was rather a boring joke. She's fascinating but terribly world-weary. Her mother is just the opposite, absolutely full to the brim of energy, determined to get all she can out of life."

"That may account for the daughter's apathy," said Jane.

"I sometimes think so. Betha is so restlessly energetic that perhaps Elaine may have developed that still indifference in self-defence. Anyway, it's very kind of them to be bothered with me. I'm still as far away as ever from having a plan in my life. If only there was something I had to do, some place I *had* to stay, I believe I'd be quite contented; it's the choosing. . . ."

"Have you enough to live on?" asked Jane bluntly.

Beatrice flushed. She never liked to talk about her money, feeling, for some reason, rather ashamed of it.

"Yes," she said.

"Then," said Jane, "you should be a grateful woman. You will be able to do voluntary work."

"Yes, I'd like to —I've been wondering if I should go back to Scotland, to our house on the West Coast. My old nurse is there. . . . Just now, homesick in London, it's a very appealing thought, but once settled there I might feel differently about it."

"Don't do anything in a hurry," Jane advised, "you've all the time in the world before you. How old are you? Twenty-five. Ah, my dear. . . . Would you like to see my little house before we have tea? Why, of course you must stay. D'you suppose I'd let you come out here on a wet November Sunday and depart without tea? It's such luck having you to myself; the rain seems to have frightened away all other visitors. . . . This is an Adam house and it was the most extraordinary luck that I got it. It belonged to an old lady, Mrs. Menzies, who had known my mother as a child, and who, for that reason, took an interest in me when I came to London. I used often to come out here to tea on a Sunday afternoon. Mrs. Menzies always sat there in the window in a wheeled chair, with a cage of love-birds beside her, *The Times*, and a magnifying glass. She was ninety-four when she died and kept all her faculties to the end. We had always the same things for tea —a plate with four pieces of thin bread and butter, a very small seed cake, and a plate of 'fancy' biscuits. And how good everything tasted! I could have eaten everything on the table, a hungry young girl, and I had to take tiny little bites to make things last. I was really very much afraid of the old lady. She always looked at me as if I amused her, which was disconcerting, but she fascinated me, so did her house, and I kept coming. And when she died I found that she had made it possible for me to live in the house as long as I wanted it. It is left to some charity she was interested in, but so long as the rent I pay (quite a small one) goes to them they must let me remain. . . . Don't you love the circular window? My bedroom upstairs has the same. When I'm very busy and fussed in the office it's always such a delight to think of the little house with its flowers and books waiting for me, and Katie, my housekeeper, and Timothy the cat."

"I'd like to see him," said Beatrice. "There's a kitten at Portland Place," and she began to tell Jane about Impudence as they mounted the stairs to see the rest of the house.

Everything she saw delighted the girl, Jane's own room, the two guest rooms, the bathroom that had been made out of another small bedroom, the staircase with its shallow steps and graceful rail, the dining-room, that she imagined was like the one in which Cowper and his Mary sat in candle-lit comfort and watched the antics of the tame hare.

She said this to her hostess and Jane nodded understandingly and said, "It has an atmosphere, the little house. You see, it has never been disturbed. Everything has been here for about a hundred and fifty years and it has passed from one placid occupant to another. Perhaps that was why my old lady let me live in it. She recognised that I was something of an anachronism in a bored hurrying age and, as far as was in her power, insured me peace."

They sat long over tea, looking at books and discussing them, very happy together, and when, at last, Beatrice tore herself away, Jane Naesmyth said: "I don't know when I've enjoyed a Sunday afternoon so much. Come again soon," with such a note of sincerity in the voice that Beatrice went back to Portland Place greatly uplifted.

CHAPTER IX

"She thinks herself very weel aff
To be woo'd and married at 'a!"

Joanna Baillie.

Beatrice did not as a rule get many letters. To get letters one must write them, and there were few people with whom she was on writing terms. So the sight of two envelopes on her morning tea-tray was an excitement, and she took them up eagerly. They were from Mrs. Lithgow and Fairlie, and she opened Fairlie's first.

Fairlie reported that everything went well at Greenbraes-very mild weather; primroses out in the garden; a sale of work in the church-hall, a new baby at the gardener's lodge, and then the letter which had been formal and precise suddenly became colloquial and very natural.

"Do you mind, Miss Bee, how you always wanted to know my age and I aye said, 'Just as old's my little finger and older than my teeth!'? I'm sure I needn't have been so blate to tell my age, I was young enough in those days, but now I'm fifty, and what do you think? I got my first offer the other night. It's queer I never had one before, for I'm as good looking as the lave, but I wasn't much in the way of seeing men, mebbe that was it, anyway this is my first.

"You will be wondering who the sensible man is, and you know him fine. He's the 'smith in the village-John Gordon. You used to like to go when you were a bairn and stand at the door and watch him shoe the horses, a fine big man with a leather apron. He's fifty-five and his wife died a year ago, a real decent woman. It seems last summer he had enjoyed the few words we used to have in passing, and he had me in his mind when it came to replacing the first Mrs. Gordon. As he says it's both cheaper and better to have a wife than a housekeeper, so up he came last night in his Sabbath suit and a silk hanky. Since I came here he's been up several times, so I suspected something, but nothing so sudden. But, as he says, what's the use of waiting? His sister who has been doing for him-she lives next door-is grumbling about the extra work, and he hasn't been comfortable. It's a good house, three rooms and kitchen and hot and cold, and a back door opening to the burnside-real handy if we kept ducks. The furniture my dear mistress left me will look a treat in it, and we could sell some of the old things. I don't think I could do better. He's a sober man, an elder in the kirk, and has always plenty of work. I told him I would need to think it over, but I doubt he didn't go away very anxious! All the same he can't say I jumped at him. There are others he could have got. They say Miss Allan, the dressmaker was never done asking him in to supper. Well, it just shows you that you can't get away from your fate. I little thought that that was why your dear Mama was taken and the Glasgow house sold up, and me sent down to Greenbraes. The workings of Providence are indeed past finding out. I think I'll be married in pale grey with a touch of pink, or do you think beige would be better? I'd be glad of your advice. Are you looking after yourself, in that dangerous London? I'm often very anxious about you, for I never hardly open a paper but I see somebody's been murdered there.

"Yours obediently,

"M. Fairlie.

"P.S. —His first wife died of bronchitis and a weak heart."

Beatrice laid down the letter, and sipped her tea which she had allowed to get cold. This was startling news! She was glad for Fairlie's sake that she seemed about to acquire a decent husband and a good home, and amused at the practical way she regarded the affair. Had she any affection for the 'smith? More, perhaps, than she would have admitted. Beatrice remembered the "smiddy" vividly. She had adored as a child to watch the 'smith blow his bellows and see the flames leap up, lighting every dusty corner of the dark place. It all came back to her-the patient horses, the smell of the sizzling iron on the hone, the music the hammer made on the anvil —*ding* ding-ding-ding-ding. . . .

The 'smith had a brown beard, and she had always supposed him to be the original of the poem about —

> "The smith, a mighty man is he,
> With large and sinewy hands. . . ."

To think of Fairlie, in pale grey with a touch of pink, wedding the 'smith! Though she smiled she was conscious of a cold desolate feeling at her heart. She had always thought of Fairlie as belonging to her, some one to whom she could turn if the need arose. But now Fairlie would belong to the 'smith, she would have her own interests, her own responsibilities, no longer would she be at Beatrice's beck and call. It was much better so of course, but still . . . Beatrice pushed away the tray and opened the other letter.

How well she could imagine Mrs. Lithgow writing it! Sitting down squarely at her bureau where everything was so meticulously neat-ink bottles spotless, fresh blotting paper, good pens-and Beatrice's latest letter spread out before her for reference. The letter ran:

"My Dear Beatrice,

"Many thanks for your last. Glad to hear that you are keeping well so far, also your step-brother and his family.

"To think we are well on in November already! I'm sure I don't know where the time goes. You will be feeling quite at home now in London, and Lady Dobie and her daughter seem to be doing their duty by you.

"The shops must be very pretty, as you say. They're all dressed for Christmas here already. I say Christmas starts now about Hallowe'en and goes on till January! But you can't wonder that the shops make the most of it, for they've had a poor time lately. I really don't know what things are coming to. I can see father is fairly worried sometimes, but what can we do? I try to save where I can, but it's only a drop in the bucket. You may be thankful that you're safely under a Trust with no responsibility! But we are all well and that's the main thing. I will say this about Glasgow, it's a place that keeps wonderfully cheery; we take most things with a laugh. I told you I was helping to get up a dance for the Cripple Children? Well, it came off last Tuesday and was a great success in every way. They all said they had never been to a nicer dance. Everything was good, the band, the floor, and the supper. (*I* saw to the last!) Peggy looked very well in a bright rose taffeta. And how that girl enjoyed herself! I begged her to stop dancing, for I thought she would be fair worn out —(she had been on her feet the whole day) but she just said she'd only be young once, and off she went! Father and I left about one o'clock, but it was four when she came back. What a girl! And yet she will sit and sew for hours at her trousseau as douce as you like. She's a grand sewer and a grand cook, so perhaps she has more sense than we give her credit for!

"I told you that she and Harry had got a house —a new one, right away out in the country beyond the tram lines. A dear wee house it is, just the six rooms and kitchen, quite enough to start with, and beautifully fitted up with every modern contrivance. Two bathrooms. It's all decorated so we can be putting things in and, as Mr. Lithgow said to me the other night —'For all the world, Nettie,' he said,

56

'it's like watching a pair of birds building, first the one carries something to the nest and then the other!' And it is just like that. People may write and talk as they like about a new age and modern trends of thought and all that, but when it comes to what really matters we're back again at the beginning of things. It's making father and me quite young again, bad times and all! Last night the two of us went off and dined at the Grosvenor, and went to see *The Barretts of Wimpole Street.* . . . We missed seeing it when it was here before and we've heard so much about it. It's very nice, of course, but I got tired of that girl lying on the sofa, saying, 'Yes, I think so.' And why nobody clapt the father into an asylum I don't know.

"You will be sorry to hear that Mrs. Murray isn't too well at present. High blood pressure. She gets giddy fits that make her very depressed. How thankful we should be who enjoy good health! She was a little brighter yesterday when I called. Her husband has given her a new fur coat. They're in that line of business, so he probably got a bargain of it. It's a beauty-mink-but she has no more use for it than a cart for a third wheel, for she has a perfectly good one already, and she hardly ever goes out. I was making her laugh over Peggy's house. She is getting a new dress for the wedding and I'm sure I hope she will be there, but I don't like the colour of her lips; however, she's as interested as possible in hearing news. You might write to her, if you have a minute.

"I can see that it's going to be an awful skirmish getting ready for the wedding in February, Christmas coming and all, but it's all very interesting. I often think of you, Beatrice, my dear. You will have many a thought of your dear mother, but don't dwell too much on your sorrow, try to get all you can out of life, for it's grand to be young and it only happens once. Be sure and write soon for we all enjoy your letters. . . ."

It was a wet morning and Beatrice spent it in letter writing. Fairlie had to be written to first, and sent the warmest of good wishes. Beatrice told her how well she remembered the 'smith and his pretty cottage by the burnside, and said how pleased her mother would have been to think of her settled near Greenbraes. She advised beige for the wedding-garment, pointing out that it would make a suitable Sunday dress for the next summer, and that it was more becoming to Fairlie's colouring than the colder and more trying grey. "You remember," she wrote, "how nice you looked in a beige dress that mother gave you one summer, and how well it lasted? The next time you are in Glasgow I want you to go to Hay & Fleming and ask to see Miss Caird, and she will advise you what to get, and make it for you. I shall write to her about it. I expect the house will be fully furnished with what was in it, and what you have of your own, but if you want napery or blankets or anything let me know. Tell Mr. Gordon that I think he is the luckiest of men."

"I wonder," thought Beatrice, "if she'd like a personal present like a brooch or a watch, or if a silver tea-service would be more valued! I'll open this and ask her."

She next wrote to Mrs. Murray, not mentioning her blood pressure, but giving any cheerful details of her life in London that might interest the invalid, then she read again Mrs. Lithgow's epistle and decided to reply to it at once, with the sort of letter that would be appreciated.

First she made suitable comments on all Mrs. Lithgow had said. She knew that was expected, for she had witnessed the indignation of the lady on receiving a reply which ignored the items of news that she had given. "I don't believe she *reads* my letters," was her cry.

After telling Fairlie's news she made as interesting a story as she could out of her own small doings.

"Saturday was a fine day, and Betha took me down with her to Eton. She has a godson at school there whom she sometimes visits, as his mother is in India. I was very much interested to see the place. The boys look so funny in their battered tall hats and tail coats as if they had all been to a wedding and not behaved too well. The boy we went to see (Arnold Dalston by name) is a little chap, small for his age, which, he told me, was fourteen. He showed us his room with pride and offered to fry us a sausage for tea, but Betha didn't accept the kind offer. We went to a very nice place where they know how to cater for boyish appetites, and how that small boy did eat! We had taken fruit and chocolates for him in the car, and Betha tipped him handsomely, so I think he must have felt that it was a successful visit. We saw a good many of the old buildings, but I'd like to go again and hear a service in the Chapel; the boy's voices must be ravishing.

"Yesterday I was at St. Andrew's for the morning service. I go there practically every Sunday because I like the feeling of being with other Scots. Old Lord Grierston handed me the collection plate. I remember he once stayed with us when he was doing something for some scheme mother was interested in, and I almost forgot to put in my collection I was so interested in his handsome old face.

"We had a big luncheon party here yesterday, and the cook tried several new dishes which were very successful; I must get you the recipes-Higgins tells me that cook is quite flattered to be asked.

"In the afternoon I went to tea with Miss Naesmyth in Hampstead, the lady I met in the train coming up from Glasgow. She gave me her card then and I went to call on her one Sunday (I think I told you) and she asked me to tea yesterday. It is amazingly kind of her, for she has hosts of friends. I know you don't care for old houses and positively dislike antiques, but I think you'd like Miss Naesmyth's house. She has almost as great a sense of comfort as you have yourself, and that's not saying little.

"Yesterday there was quite a party, and I found myself next to Giles Lambart, the novelist. I don't think you liked his book that had such a tremendous success. I'd certainly never have guessed from his appearance that he had anything to do with literature. He is fat, and fresh-coloured, and, somehow, seemed to have more of the stable than the study about him. He has certainly nothing of the 'pale cast of thought.' I was feverishly trying to think of something I could say about his books, but I never so much as got a word in. He talked all the time about *teeth*! It seems he had some back teeth taken out recently and has now to wear a plate, and he described to me every detail of the process. He said he had no longer any pleasure in eating, so life would never be the same to him again, his mouth felt as if it were full of small stones from the brook, that 'store teeth' (as he called them) were the worst infliction that could have been devised for poor mankind. All I needed to do was to murmur broken words of condolence, and while I spoke he kept his eyes fixed on my mouth, and groaned hungrily, 'All those teeth of yours belong to your mouth. Oh, my goodness!' It was quite pathetic to watch him at tea. When offered raspberry jam he said, 'My favourite jam; but I can't eat it now: the seeds get behind my darned plate.' "

Beatrice finished her letter, smiling to think of Mrs. Lithgow's anger at the novelist's lack of decorum, and indeed that good lady was quite as disgusted as Beatrice expected her to be.

She and her husband, along with most of their middle-aged acquaintances had had to resort to what she called starkly "false teeth" —no facetious allusions to "store teeth" for her-but it never occurred to them to mention the fact outside the privacy of their own bedroom, or at least of their own homes. She had thought poorly of Mr. Giles Lambart ever since she had been induced to read one of his novels; it was no surprise to her to find that he was indelicate in his conversation.

"Just imagine your father," she said to Peggy, "choosing his teeth as a topic of conversation with a young girl."

"Oh, why not?" said Peggy; "aren't we taught that to be natural is the best of manners? Teeth were uppermost with Mr. Giles Lambart, so he babbled of them. Be thankful it was only teeth. If it had been less mentionable parts of his anatomy he'd probably have been equally frank."

Mrs. Lithgow quite agreed. "There's nothing these writers wouldn't say. . . . But isn't this great news about Fairlie? Her bit of money has soon got her a man. But that's not a nice thing of me to say, for Fairlie's a very personable woman and a treasure to any man. Many a time Janie Dobie told me what a comfort and help she was in the house. She left her independent for life, so she didn't need to marry for a home, but she's quite wise to take a decent man when she got the offer of one. I've a good mind to write a wee note to Fairlie and send her a present. I'm hoping that one of these days we'll hear that Beatrice is going to settle down with some nice fellow, if there's such a thing in the Dobie set. I'm often uneasy about her, I don't know why. Men like that Lambart talking to her about his teeth. . ."

CHAPTER X

"O cheerful colours! See where Oxford comes!"

Henry VI.

Beatrice's days continued on their rather meaningless way, though, after she began to visit Jane Naesmyth, the girl did try to fill them more adequately. She studied the newspapers and went to lectures that seemed to promise interest and information; she attended a verse-speaking class in the Polytechnic which she found quite enthralling, and she visited picture-shows given by young artists.

Driven back on herself she was learning to escape from herself by thinking more than ever she had done about her fellow-creatures. She began to realise the struggle to live that is the lot of so many, and tried to help when she could. There was not much that she could do, but she did buy some pictures (which had to be stored until she found a place for them), and, through a friend of Jane Naesmyth, got in touch with a children's play-centre, which introduced her to many poor mothers.

She made friends, too, with people she was in the habit of passing almost daily on the streets, like the old woman who sat by the Langham Hotel reading aloud from a Braille Bible and stopping at intervals to ejaculate "Buy a box of matches," and who turned out to be a most cheerful happy creature, in spite of the many things that might have made her otherwise.

There was an Aberdeen terrier that she kept a watchful eye on and would have dearly liked to buy from his owner, a street-artist with a plausible tongue. The dog seemed well fed and well cared for and had a bit of carpet to keep him from the wet street, still it was a humiliating position for a Scots dog and he seemed to feel it, hanging his head dejectedly.

And there was Franky. In one of the side streets near Portland Place Beatrice had found a small "antique" shop with some good and uncommon things. She had gone in one day to ask about an eighteenth-century glass goblet she had seen in the window, and had made the acquaintance of the proprietor's only child who had just left school and was now, most proudly and importantly, helping his father. He was a delicate-looking boy, small for his age, and slightly deformed, but with a singularly sweet face and smile.

Beatrice had bought the goblet, and while waiting for her change had happened to give a short cough, whereupon a rasping voice had said, "You've got a cold, you old devil!" Considerably startled Beatrice turned round and found a parrot sitting on a perch, regarding her with deep distaste.

The boy, returning, told her the parrot had been given him by a sailor and that his name was "Charlie Thomson," and that he was a very clever bird.

"He doesn't like ladies," he added.

"Poor Charlie Thomson," said the bird, "he has to go to church all day. . . . Scratch my head, Franky."

"I'm Franky," the boy explained, complying with his pet's request.

After that Beatrice often went into the shop in passing, and looked at, and sometimes bought, pieces of furniture that would be useful if ever she set up in a house of her own. Trade, she knew, was very quiet in their line, and they were very willing to store anything she bought until she needed it. She found that the boy was not only keen on old furniture and china, silver and prints, but also loved reading, and was, rather oddly, a devotee of sport. She found him full of enthusiasm for the South African "Springboks," whom he had seen play. "Aren't they fine big fellows," he said, and Beatrice, looking at the frail child, agreed rather sadly. His father, a thin, anxious-faced man with a cough, told her that "Franky" had always been delicate, and had to be wheeled in a chair till he was seven, but since then he had got on wonderfully, was a clever scholar at school, and had even been able to play games.

"He's neat-handed," he added, "and very knowledgeable and it's a nice quiet job for him, but the wife and I never dare look forward. He's such a little fellow and it's such a big hard world; it would be a thought to leave him-but there, what's the use of dreading a day we may never see."

When, in the beginning of December, Stewart came down from Oxford, it made a difference in the life at Portland Place, but not, Beatrice thought, for the better. Admitting his good looks, his taste in shirts and socks, she disliked his manners, the way he condescended to his father, the very casual attention he gave his mother, and the fact that he almost completely ignored her own presence. Betha was inordinately proud of her son, of his looks, of his success in games, even, it seemed, of his rudeness.

"You see," she told Beatrice, the day he was expected home, "he's had nothing but admiration all his life. He was such a handsome little boy that his nurses could deny him nothing; his governesses spoilt him, his father and I —well, what could you expect? our only boy-and when he went to school he was so good at games that he quickly became a personality. The same at college. So you can't wonder that sometimes he's a little autocratic, don't you know. His father resents it and says: 'Where would the fellow have been without my backing?' So absurd! As I tell him there's no good expecting anything from the young people of to-day; they must be allowed to go their own way, and we ought to be thankful if there's nothing *criminal* in their pursuits! So many seem to get mixed up with the police, and Samuel and I would hate that. Oh, yes, we've every cause to be proud of Stewart. He's in such a good set in Oxford, all sons of well-known people, which is so nice, for we can ask them to dine and dance and so forth, which we couldn't do if . . . I wonder if they've remembered the muffins he likes. Ring, will you, Beatrice?"

Stewart Dobie's manner was more than autocratic: it was rude. He took no trouble with people who seemed to him of no importance. What they thought did not concern him. He only desired the approbation of what he considered the elect. He remembered that there had been some mention in letters from his mother about a dim sort of female who was staying at Portland Place, a relative from Glasgow, of all places, but he did not mean to let her presence annoy him in any way. She was quite good looking, he admitted that, but when he found that she knew nothing about anything that interested him, he dismissed her as unworthy of notice.

The young man, it seemed to Beatrice, had almost as many engagements as the other members of the family, and when in the house was constantly drawling on the telephone, but he was generally out, driving very fast in a bright red car.

After Stewart's coming Beatrice felt even lonelier than before. Here was a family circle, and she was outside it. They gave her house-room, but she mattered nothing to any of them. Even to Samuel, though he was always kind, she feared she was more of a problem than a pleasure. If there had been a place that she could have fitted into, but "I'm only an excrescence," she told herself ruefully. It was no use, she could never feel at home among Betha's friends, or Elaine's either. She remembered, and grew hot remembering, a party Elaine had taken her to. That horrible Bobby with his nasty stories and his mad games! "I thought I had a sense of humour," Beatrice told herself, "but I can't have, or, at least, it's too old-fashioned to appreciate the new fun. It wasn't that I was shocked, but I was disgusted-and terribly ashamed. The sooner I get me to a nunnery the better." But though she laughed at herself, she couldn't help feeling that hers was rather a weary lot at the moment. She was so alone amid all the bustle of coming and going; door-bell and telephone-bell constantly ringing, but never for her. "I shouldn't feel so lonely," she told herself, "in the Sahara."

A few days after Stewart arrived the whole family dined at home one evening without guests —a most unusual occurrence.

"How is this?" asked Elaine, trailing in when they had all begun. "Has every one's engagement fallen through like mine, or are we merely unpopular this evening?"

"Frightfully clever, aren't you?" said Stewart. ". . . as a matter of fact I'm sick of bands and restaurant food; home cooking's a pleasant change, and the society of my brilliant sister an unexpected pleasure."

Elaine made a face at her brother, while Sir Samuel, looking blandly round the table, said: "It's pleasant to be by ourselves for a change. No need for conversation; we can enjoy our food in peace."

"Now that's a point," said his wife. "Does one enjoy food more in private than in public? Does companionship and the effort of making conversation not give a stimulus to the appetite?"

"Depends on the companionship," said Stewart. "Some people won't let you eat for talking; their whole idea of conversation is to ask questions. If they'd tell one an anecdote it might be soothing."

"Like an orchestra playing at a discreet distance," said Elaine.

"I hope it's a good dinner," said Betha.

She looked round the table. "Now that we're all together for once it seems quite the moment to decide about Christmas."

"Christmas!" said her husband. "I thought we decided long ago to spend it here, at home."

"*You* did, darling," Elaine reminded him gently; "we forebore to argue;" while Betha went on:

"You know, Samuel, that was in the autumn when everything looked so bad that we expected to be ruined any old minute. But nothing has happened so far, and people are getting tired of the economy stunt. Why shouldn't we go away as usual? What about Madeira? Quite a lot of our friends are going there, the d'Arcys and Phil and Topsy, and Sylvia Neatham. Or South Africa, if you prefer it. You know, Big Boy, you badly need a holiday after your hard work in the House."

Sir Samuel, Beatrice noticed, began to wear the baffled look usual with him, when his wife and daughter joined forces against him, but he said:

"No, I don't want to go. We should show an example. I've talked so much about economy in my constituency and if they hear I've gone off on pleasure bent, it'd create a bad impression."

"Never mind, Papa," said Elaine, "memories are short and they'll have forgotten all about it before another election. And we do all terribly need a little brightness. Just think of bathing in glorious sunshine when London is creeping about in a black fog! It's only for a very few weeks. We can get cabins in the *Pandora* sailing on the 15th."

"I've got to be back at the beginning of January," Stewart reminded her.

"Well, there are always boats coming and going; you could leave when you liked. If we're having a good time we might stay on for a bit."

Sir Samuel gave an ostentatiously loud sigh, remarking, "I have no authority in my own house, it seems. Well, anyway, it will be a nice change for you, Beatrice. You haven't been to Madeira, have you?"

There was a moment of pregnant silence, then Beatrice spoke:

"No," she said, "I've never done any sailing except on the Clyde, and crossing the Channel of course. But —I don't think I'll go this time, if you don't mind. I've half-promised to spend Christmas with friends, so please don't feel for a moment that you have me on your conscience."

"Oh, but that's too bad," Samuel grumbled. "Isn't it, Betha? Isn't it, Elaine? I thought if we went you'd go, naturally."

"Of course," said Betha, breaking a piece of toast.

"But after all," Elaine said in her tired voice, "we're almost strangers to Beatrice. There's a tradition that you should spend Christmas with old friends."

"What nonsense!" said her father. "Relations are never strangers. The tie of blood stands for a lot-with me, anyway."

"With us all," said Elaine, turning to Beatrice with her charming smile. "And we've so few relatives that's it's been particularly nice having you, Beatrice, dear."

Beatrice smiled in response, feeling she should murmur, as in the same circumstances Mrs. Lithgow would have done, "Not at all," and the subject dropped.

After dinner, in the drawing-room Stewart, after fiddling about for a time, turning the wireless off and on, found that he could not stand a home evening, and went out to seek distraction; the others played bridge and Beatrice slipped off early to her bed.

Once up in her room she was in no hurry to undress, but sat and watched the kitten who was fond of playing in her room, pretending that her moccasin? was an enemy which he must approach with the most absurd heraldic attitudes. But all the time her thoughts were full of the conversation at dinner, and of the pause that had followed her step-brother's perfectly genuine invitation. It was quite natural, she kept telling herself, that they wanted to go as a family, but still — — Determined not to think about it she jumped up to look for the book that she had been very much enjoying, a new volume of Queen Victoria's Letters. There was no sign of it, and she realised that she must have left it downstairs, in the back drawing-room, she thought, when she was looking for something for Betha. She would slip down now and get it.

Lady Dobie must have been at her favourite pastime of telephoning and had left a light burning, so Beatrice had no difficulty in finding her book. She was turning to go back when her step-brother's voice through the half-open door arrested her steps, and she stopped involuntarily.

"It is not fair," he was saying. "We're her nearest, almost her only, relatives, and it's up to us to do our best for her."

"Well, haven't we?" came Betha's light tones. "We've had her here for two months, occupying our one guest-room, and I call that doing pretty well. I'm sure no relative of mine would be allowed to stay here for two months."

Sir Samuel made the exclamation that is spelt "Pshaw!" and added: "How much have you and Elaine done for her? The poor child seems to me to have been alone most of the time. Did either of you ever give up an engagement for her?"

"Oh, my goodness, yes. I took her to Eton and to Kew, and Elaine saw about her clothes and took her to the play and parties. Really, Samuel, I don't know what you're talking about. Beatrice has had every chance, met heaps of people; it isn't our fault if she's dull and provincial and makes no impression on people."

"Provincial!" snorted Sir Samuel. "What rubbish! She's a most lady-like girl."

"That's just it, Papa," said Elaine. "Beatrice would be perfect in her own environment, but this is quite the wrong background for her. She is, as you say, 'lady-like.' "

"Well," said Sir Samuel, "I'm sorry to think my house isn't the proper environment for a nice, well-brought-up girl. It's all very well, Elaine, but — —"

With a start Beatrice realised what she was doing and fled.

On reaching her room she found that she was shaking all over, and put a hand on the bedpost to steady herself. Listeners never hear good of themselves. But how horrible to hear oneself discussed, labelled. . . . Oh, why had she stood as if mesmerised and listened? "Dull and provincial" —and what had Elaine said in her smooth voice —"Lady-like! . . ."

Mechanically Beatrice began to undress; she longed to get the lights out and hide her hurt and humiliation in the dark.

And yet, she asked herself, trying to brace up her shattered pride, had she heard anything she did not already know quite well? She had been aware from the first that there was no place for her in this household. Samuel-poor old Samuel-had been consistently kind and would, she believed, be glad to have her stay on indefinitely, but Betha and Elaine were bound to feel her an encumbrance. She found that she really cared nothing for what Betha said, but Elaine's tone had hurt her deeply. Elaine whom she could not help admiring! Elaine whom, given the slightest encouragement, she could have loved-that Elaine should have been so cruel!

Beatrice tried to be philosophic. They wouldn't have hurt her intentionally; she should not have listened. And, anyway, there were worse misfortunes than having your relations tire of you, and she must set about getting a house of her own. But in the meantime what was she to do? She had spoken of friends with whom she would spend Christmas, but that was simply to save her face; she knew no one who was in the least likely to ask her. She might go back to Glasgow, but there was no place for her there-any more than there was in London. She knew, of course, that they would make her welcome for her mother's sake, but there would have to be explanations. Mrs. Lithgow could be very searching, and then she could imagine the verdict:

"Poor Be'trice, she went to London to live with her relations, but she doesn't seem to have got on very well with her step-sister-in-law. Oh, yes, I daresay there would be faults on both sides."

As Beatrice sat on her bed and kicked off her slippers she remembered disconsolately the advertisements in the daily papers she was sometimes driven by boredom to read, offering happy homes to any with money to pay for them. Some such place might be her destination.

She looked round the bedroom, at the puce hangings, at the futurist picture (she was still in the dark as to its meaning), at the ugly furniture, and sighed. She had spent many lonely hours in it, relieved only by visits from Higgins and the heraldic kitten, but it was a refuge. Outside was a large, cold world. Her eyes were smarting, heavy with unshed tears, but cry she would not. She brushed her hair vigorously, washed her teeth with a flourish, and squared her shoulders in her pink night-gown. Dull and provincial she might be, but —— —

Letters. Higgins must have brought them up and laid them on the dressing-table, and she, after her guilty flight from the boudoir, had been too perturbed to notice them. Now she opened them eagerly. One was from Franky's father to say that the boy was ill in bed and would be very glad to see Miss Dobie if she happened to be passing; the other was from Jane Naesmyth, an invitation to lunch with her the following Sunday.

So, slightly comforted by the fact that she was not entirely unwanted, Beatrice went to bed.

CHAPTER XI

"On London stones I sometimes sigh
For wider green and bluer sky — —"

Austen Dobson.

Jane Naesmyth looked forward all the week to Sunday, and when it came delighted in every minute of it. Spring and summer were the perfect times, then she had the pleasure of living in the garden, but December had its own charms, fireside talks, and the satisfying companionship of books.

On this particular Sunday she and her friend and secretary, Cicely Sellars, were waiting for Beatrice Dobie to come to lunch.

"I'm hungry," said Cicely. "Who are we waiting for?"

Jane was hurriedly scribbling a note at the bureau. "Oh, yes," she said, addressing the envelope. "I want you to be very kind to this girl."

"Well —I'm not in the habit of assaulting any friends of yours that I meet."

"Don't be absurd," said Jane, "you know quite well what I mean." She stamped her letter and continued, "I think I told you about meeting this girl-her name's Beatrice Dobie. It was in the train coming up from Scotland; we were alone in the compartment and she told me her mother had just died and that she was on her way to London to live with her step-brother and his family whom she knew hardly at all. She looked so desolate, poor child, and was so obviously shrinking from the thought of going to strangers that I gave her my address and asked her to come and see me if she ever felt like it. I hardly expected to see her again, but she turned up here one Sunday afternoon and seemed so grateful for my small hospitality that I begged her to come back again. It seemed to me that the fact that she was so glad to come to a stranger didn't say much for her happiness in her step-brother's house. . . . No, she didn't say she was unhappy, indeed she rather insisted that every one was very kind, but I gathered that she was left a great deal alone, naturally-her relations being much engaged in the social round. The step-brother is Sir Samuel Dobie, a member of Parliament, and there is a Lady Dobie and a daughter. . . ."

"Elaine Dobie," Cicely supplied. "I met her in connection with a Charity Ball she was helping to run, a weary young thing, very affected, but rather a charmer with it all. So your friend is-what? a step-aunt, I suppose, to the lily-maid. A poor relation?"

"That I can't quite make out. She says she'd like a job to be independent, but when I asked if she had enough to live on she said she had."

"And not ill," said Cicely, "or cripple or slightly insane? Then what's wrong with her? With health and an income of her own-even a small one-she needn't feel lonely. Doors open readily to such as she. It's poor souls like me who have to knock and knock."

Cicely lolled in her chair and laughed up at her friend who said:

"You don't look an object for pity, my dear. How you keep that complexion of rose and brown I can't imagine. You look as if you had come in from a summer garden, with some of the sunshine still in your hair, instead of from the dampest and dreariest of December days."

"I don't pinch up with the cold," said Cicely, "that's something to be thankful for. . . . What d'you want me to do about this girl?"

"Oh, nothing really, except just to be nice to her. As you say, it's perfectly absurd that she shouldn't attempt to make a path for herself, but evidently all her life other people have decided what she should do-she and her mother, especially, seem to have been bound up in each other-and now that her props have suddenly been removed — —"

"She's like a hop without a pole?"

"Ye-es. Perhaps a little like that."

"Well, it's an amazing thing to find in this age of self-reliant, not to say impudent, females. A refreshing change, don't you think? Ah! the bell! Now for it!"

Beatrice had hoped that she might be alone with Miss Naesmyth, and shrank into herself when she saw Cicely Sellars. But Jane gave her such a warm welcome, and the other guest smiled in such a friendly way, that in a few minutes she felt quite at her ease. It was so pleasant in this orderly room, with the chairs drawn round the blazing fire. A bright rose cyclamen on the bureau made a note of colour, and several dishes of brightly painted French pottery filled with bulbs gave a promise of spring. But there was no profusion of anything, except, perhaps, of books and papers. And talk was so easy in this quiet room, no need to search feverishly for topics, it didn't seem to matter if one spoke at all, and filled with a sense of well-being, Beatrice listened idly to Cicely Sellars, who was talking of something she had seen coming out in the tube that morning, telling it with every bit of herself; her eyes and smile, and the rich rose in her cheeks all adding to the interest, and they rose and went into lunch in a gust of laughter over the *dénouement*.

Three of them at the little gate-table made a cosy party, and before the meal was over Beatrice felt as if this Cicely were already an old friend. There was about her something so gay and yet so kindly, that she fascinated the shy girl, and Cicely, who always liked to make a conquest, was pleased, and tried to draw her out.

As they sat over their coffee, which Jane made herself, Cicely said:

"Jane, what about the Christmas holidays?"

"I don't know. I can't decide. I'm in straits betwixt two. I've a desire to depart for Scotland and see my friends and sniff the snell East sea; but the thought of a quiet time in my own little house is very tempting."

"Oh, but Jane," Cicely protested, "just think what London is like at Christmas-time. Three Sundays in succession. Could you stand it?"

"Why not? I'd never go out. It would be a beautiful rest — —"

"But so dull."

"Not to me. I'd revel in it."

Cicely began to declaim —

> "Her life was ever turning
> In mazes of heat and sound
> But for peace her soul was yearning . . ."

"It's nothing but laziness, Jane. You can't face the thought of the journey and the crowded trains and all you'd have to arrange. May I have some more coffee?"

"You don't deserve it, you scoffer. . . . Are you going away for Christmas, Miss Dobie?"

Beatrice flushed and hesitated. "My step-brother and his family are going to Madeira, but — —"

"Perhaps," said Jane, "you don't like the thought of the voyage?"

"Oh, no, not much, and . . . I rather thought I might go to a hydropathic somewhere."

"Do you like Hydros?" Cicely asked.

"I've never been in one," Beatrice confessed. "What do they do in Hydros?"

"Oh," said Cicely, "it's very bright. There are crowds and crowds of people, mostly in parties, and they dance, and play badminton and bridge; there is never a moment unfilled. It's absolutely the last word of enjoyment to many people, but I hardly think it would be your ideal holiday."

Beatrice repressed a shudder as she said hastily, "No, oh no, indeed. It was stupid of me, I ought to have known better, for friends of ours in Glasgow used to visit Hydros and report marvellous gaieties, but, somehow, I had it in my mind that they were quiet, rather invalidish sort of places that one could retire to. . . . I want a really quiet place, quite in the country, and as plain as possible."

"That," said Cicely, "sounds rather like my home — 'Twixt Bears," and added in answer to Beatrice's look of astonishment, "Yes, I assure you, that's really the name of our cottage in the village of Oxlip. No one knows the origin of the name, though there is an old inn near called *The Two Bears* which may have something to do with it." She hesitated, looked at Jane Naesmyth, then leaning across to Beatrice she said with an engaging smile —"We are very quiet and very, very plain at 'Twixt Bears. What about spending Christmas with us?"

"That would be lovely," said Beatrice lightly, "but I'm afraid — —"

"No, don't please dismiss my invitation as a jest. I really mean it. . . . Perhaps it's forward of me to push in like this; you must have many friends who want you, but you said you wanted to be quiet-as one can well understand-and ours is a small household in a small village, a real four-ducks-in-a-pond village, and we've one spare room."

"But-why should you ask a stranger? I'd be taking some one else's place."

"Oh, no, you wouldn't. We won't have anyone, probably, if you don't come, for, naturally, we wouldn't ask anybody, but it seemed to me you would fit in. . . . I ought perhaps to warn you that after Portland Place you may find it roughish. There's only one bathroom; it's a good one, we put it in ourselves at great expense, but there isn't always hot water. The kitchen grate is of an uncertain temper. Whether the water heats or doesn't heat depends, our one retainer says, on the way the wind blows, but I'm inclined to think it depends on whether or not she got out of bed in time to clean it out properly, but no matter. . . . Have you ever had a Christmas in the depths of the country? No? Then you never felt the true spirit of the season."

"But," said Beatrice, looking rather dazed, "wouldn't your people simply hate having a stranger thrust on them?"

"Oh, dear no, my mother would love to have you-she's like that-and there are only my two brothers, one a schoolmaster and one a schoolboy. Oh, and my grandmother. We're rather proud of Granny-she's inclined to be *thrawn*, but she looks as if she were made of ivory and ebony and might go off at any moment on a broom-stick. You won't mind if she's rather rude to you, will you? She's rude to us all."

Beatrice hesitated, sorely tempted to accept, but unwilling to appear too eager.

"Of course," Cicely went on, "as I said, you would have a far better time at a big hotel or Hydro so far as stir and bustle and gaiety go, but, if a homely Christmas appeals it's to be found at 'Twixt Bears, Oxlip. Think it over." She took out a notebook and scribbling an address, tore out the page and offered it to Beatrice. "Write to me there when you've made up your mind. There's no hurry, for something may turn up that you'd like better, but if you do come I'll be honestly pleased."

Presently Beatrice took her leave, and the two friends remained, sitting by the fire.

"I ought to go," said Cicely; "I've three reviews to write and a page of Home Topics before I go to Ann Barclay's for my evening meal."

"Wait for a cup of tea," said Jane; "it will save you making it."

"That's true, but I'd probably have done without it! You gave us such a good lunch, I could go on easily till dinner-time. So that's your young friend."

"My dear, it was too good of you to ask her to go to you for Christmas. I never thought of such a thing. You astonished me."

Cicely laughed. "I astonished myself! It was a sudden impulse. Did you see her face when you asked her where she was going to spend Christmas? Such a hurt look came into her eyes. . . . I'm pretty certain that those relations of hers made it clear to her that she wasn't wanted in *their* party. Don't you suppose that if they had assumed that she would go with them, or if they had asked her with any warmth, that she wouldn't have gone? She would have been only too glad to have had arrangements made for her and hold on to the people she had got accustomed to. I expect the lily-maid was at the bottom of it. . . . She won't want to trail about with her a step-aunt, quite pretty and well dressed, but hopelessly unsophisticated, who blushes at the wrong moment, and — —"

Jane interrupted her friend's eloquence by laughing sceptically, and Cicely finished with, "Oh, of course, I may be quite wrong, but — —"

"Well, anyway, it was more than good of you to give the invitation. You've sent the poor child away walking on air. I must say it seemed dreadful that she should contemplate going alone to a Hydro or hotel-the first Christmas that she hadn't been safe and sheltered with her mother. But won't your mother feel that it rather spoils your time at home to have a stranger in the house?"

"Not a bit. I've only got to tell her the facts of the case and everything we have will be put at Beatrice Dobie's disposal. I hope she decides to come. I like her. I like her very much, though she irritates one rather. She lacks backbone. She's not decided enough about anything to be really interesting. But it may be the result of her upbringing. What nice manners she has, gentle and dignified. . . . How good this tea is! I'm glad I didn't miss it. I wonder if it's the particular brand you use, or whether it is that Katie makes it with the teapot warmed and the kettle bubbling. . . . Katie is a treasure. I think after all, you're right, Jane, to stay at home this Christmas. You've only cousins in Scotland, and though they'll miss you, they won't be desolated as your own would have been by your absence. . . . Oh dear! I've such a lot to do before the 22nd."

"My dear, you try too much. You've enough and more than enough with me in the office and you do so many extra things, reviewing and so forth."

"Home Topics!" said Cicely. "Oh, I know. But I rather want some extra money just now. Mother is having an expensive time, with Watty at school, and less and less coming in from her dividends. Christopher helps all he can, but his salary isn't large. My word, Jane, I ought to be thankful for my job. Not only for the money, though that is considerable, but because it's such fun working with you."

CHAPTER XII

"My father dead, my fortune lives for me."

The Taming of the Shrew.

Beatrice walked most of the way home, pretending to herself that she was considering Cicely Sellars' invitation, but well aware in her heart that there could be no doubt about her acceptance. To go to a village in the country-and English country was still a sealed book to her-to live with a family that must be pleasant and kind if Cicely truly represented them, in a cottage called 'Twixt Bears, where there was trouble with the hot water, and everything was simple, and as plain as bread! To the lonely girl it seemed like a foretaste of paradise. As she let herself into the Portland Place house and slowly went upstairs to her room she heard from the drawing-room sounds of revelry. Nothing had been said to her about a party; probably they had expected her to be out to tea. She debated whether she ought to tidy herself and go down, but decided that it would be better not; she might only be in the way, so she continued on her way upstairs and on reaching her room, turned on the electric fire, drew the curtains and told herself that she was not at all to be pitied.

Presently she heard a mewing at the door and when she opened it Impudence jumped into her arms, patting her with soft paddy paws and giving little purrs of pleasure.

Later, Higgins came in exclaiming —"Why, Miss, I thought you'd be downstairs! Haven't you had any tea?"

"No," said Beatrice, "I came in rather late and was too lazy to make myself tidy for a party so I didn't go down. I didn't feel tea mattered for once; one always eats too much on a Sunday anyway. . . . This isn't your Sunday out?"

"Well, as a matter of fact it is, Miss, but Wilhelmina's got such a gumboil, poor girl, she's had to go to bed, so I stayed in. Lucky I did, for a friend from the country came to tea with me, a sort of cousin she is, in town for the week-end with a married sister to see the shops all dressed for Christmas. She's living out at Clapham and I would have been sorry if she'd come all this way and found no one. . . . Well, well, to think that Christmas will soon be here again. You'll enjoy getting right away, Miss, always supposing of course that you're a good sailor."

"Oh, but I'm not going to Madeira," said Beatrice. "I'm not very fond of the sea and Christmas in a hotel doesn't much appeal to me. I'm going to friends in the country to have a real Christmas."

Higgins was folding the bed cover and turning down the blankets and she stopped to beam approval.

"Now, isn't that nice! Ideal, I call it. I always loved Christmas at home-the bells and the children singing. It don't seem the same in the town, somehow. Shall it be the lace dress to-night, Miss?"

"Oh, I suppose so. . . . I must get some country clothes. Tweeds and strong shoes."

"Gumboots, Miss. They're the only thing to keep out the damp of those country roads. Awful they are, Miss, you've no idea."

"Will you get home for Christmas, Higgins?"

"I think so, Miss, but it won't be a very cheerful Christmas, for my brother's been out of work for months, and his wife she's lying with a bad leg, and two of the children are ill. Things happen unfortunately at times, don't they? But we haven't got the ordering of them, and I do hope you will have a good time, Miss, for you've had your own sorrows, and it's been dull for you here, with her ladyship and Miss Elaine so much engaged."

"Oh, well, I wouldn't want to go out much just now, and in any case I'm afraid I always like to shirk gaieties."

Higgins shook her head. "When would you be gay, Miss, if not when you're young? And you with your looks so above-board, if I may put it so. As I said to Mrs. Goodfellow the other night when there was a dinner-party, I said, 'Miss Beatrice is my idea of what a lady should look like.' "

Beatrice, feeling that the conversation had better end, held up the kitten.

"D'you see what I've got here, Higgins? He's a most affectionate pussy."

"Too affectionate for a gentleman, I fear, Miss. He's a lady cat to my way of thinking. Hear him purr! He's apologising for being a female. . . . Come away, Impudence, and don't be so free with your company. No one ever spurns him, Miss, and it makes him overbold."

"He's a darling," said Beatrice, "I'd like to take him away with me;" and as Higgins left the room carrying the kitten, she added to herself, "The only thing I do want to take away with me from this house."

She felt bitterly dissatisfied with her visit to her relations. To have lived more than two months with people and to go away with no regret-nothing indeed but relief on both sides. There was something wrong, she felt. Perhaps if she herself had been different, she might have managed to endear herself to Betha, and to find the real Elaine who lay behind all the affectations and foolishness, the Elaine who had never had a chance to grow. . . . On the other hand, it was too humiliating to be treated as a thing of no importance, to be housed and fed, but otherwise unnoticed, going in and out as unconsidered as a shadow. Indeed she was beginning to feel like a shadow. Somehow or other she must manage to become more tangible. She must make herself useful in this world where so many needed help. And she had found some one who would put her in the way of finding out what she was good for. Cicely Sellars was brimful of ideas which she aired without reluctance; there would be time at 'Twixt Bears to discuss most things.

The Dobie family were leaving for Marseilles on the 15th, and Beatrice left Portland Place the day before for the Langham Hotel, where she proposed to stay until she went to Oxlip on the 23rd.

At breakfast, the last morning, Sir Samuel grumbled over the arrangement.

"You're going to friends, you say. Do I know them?"

"I shouldn't think so," Beatrice said. "Sellars is the name. They are Scots, Edinburgh, I think, but they live in Oxlip, a village about twelve miles from Oxford. The girl, Cicely, works in London. I'm going down with her on the 23rd."

"And till then you're going to the Langham? I remember your mother always liked to stay there. A great howff for Scots folk. Well, I don't like the arrangement at all. It would have been much better for you to come with us to Madeira, cheered you up a bit after your quiet time. People don't mourn long, and a good thing too. We're all going the same road and it's no use being gloomier than we can help-Anyway, I hope you will have a nice time with your friends." He hesitated, for his wife had been speaking to him, then went on determinedly. "And when we all come back you and I must have a talk about your future. You must always look upon this house as your home, remember that! You will always be welcome here. . . . But I think you ought to travel a bit and see the world. You've money enough, and if we found the right companions for you you would have great fun. I only wish I'd the time. But I'm a poor slave chained to a routine; all the same, I'd hate to have nothing to do but play golf. Work is the best fun, Beatrice, believe me."

"I do believe you," said Beatrice, "and it's what I want. I don't think I'm any good at enjoying myself. I'd be happier feeling myself of use."

Sir Samuel laughed. "Nonsense, my dear. What could you do? I don't see you in an office, besides-you surely don't want to take the bread out of another girl's mouth."

"No, I don't mean a paid job. But don't trouble about me, please, Samuel. I want to say thank you for all your kindness to me. You've been very good and I've enjoyed our breakfasts together."

"My dear girl —" Sir Samuel laid down his napkin and rose to his feet as if about to make a speech. "Don't talk about goodness, *please*. It's been delightful having a companion in the morning. As you know, Betha and Elaine have no use for breakfast as a meal, even Stewart is very uncertain, but you are our father's daughter as far as punctuality goes. . . . Yes, well, we'll be meeting soon again. Meantime, put that away till Christmas morning. Good-bye, my dear, and a happy Christmas when it comes."

Beatrice found Betha and Elaine in the final flurry of packing when she went to say good-bye. Higgins was kneeling beside a cabin trunk in Lady Dobie's room, putting in what her mistress decided she would need.

"Doesn't it make one shiver to look at these things on a day like this?" said Elaine. "I *wish* you had been coming with us to the sunshine, Beatrice dear."

"Isn't it too bad," broke in Lady Dobie. "No, Higgins, not that bath wrap. But of course we quite understand your preferring to be quiet with friends this Christmas. Another time I shall insist on us having a jolly together. We have your address? Be sure and let us know what you are doing. Higgins, you haven't forgotten-No, I see it is there. . . . Well, good-bye, dear Beatrice, it has been so nice having you."

"Come again soon," said Elaine, kissing Beatrice on both cheeks. "I'm glad we're going away, for the house would seem so empty without you. Good-bye, darling. I'll write."

Beatrice had already said good-bye to Higgins and the heraldic kitten, and left handsome tips for all the servants, and now Payne whistled her a taxi, her boxes were taken out and another chapter of her life was finished.

She found it distinctly pleasant to be conducted to a comfortable bedroom with a blazing fire, an unobtrusive carpet, pretty chintzes and a delightful window looking right up Portland Place, and to go down to tea in the cheerful lounge with people all round her that she could watch and wonder about. It was much less lonely than her life at her step-brother's; there were others here solitary like herself.

For the first time for months Beatrice felt as if she really were alive, and a part of the life going on around her. She had feared that it would be painful to be in surroundings so familiar to her mother and herself, but she found that the thought of her mother having been there with her made the place seem home in a way that the Portland Place house never had been.

As she nibbled her hot toast Beatrice could not help overhearing the conversation going on at the next table between two women, a mother and daughter evidently, and as evidently from Scotland.

"I knew it was nonsense, Mary," the mother was saying, "to send us to Cornwall. I'd have been far better at Skelmorlie. Warm? It was perishing."

"Oh, but we were very comfortable, Mother; pleasant company and lots to do indoors."

"I daresay. Perhaps you enjoyed it, but I wearied terribly. I can hardly believe I'll be back in Edinburgh in my own bed to-morrow night. It seems too good to be true. I'm in a perfect fever in case anything happens to keep us here. I just wish we had arranged to go straight on to-night, for one is never sure if one'll be able to get up in the morning-especially after an illness such as mine."

"No, no, Mother," the daughter spoke soothingly. "After our journey to-day you'd be sure to get a good night's rest, and we'll start fresh in the morning. . . . Father will be meeting us at the station, I expect, and Joan says the maids have been working so hard getting everything clean for us. You'll be glad to get into your own big chair by the drawing-room fire, won't you?"

"Oh, won't I! I'm afraid I've been a trying patient, Mary; I'm not one who enjoys ill-health. But once home I'd soon shed all my invalid ways. Up in the morning to breakfast, do my own housekeeping. . . . I doubt Joan will have let the maids get into slack ways, though she's done her best, poor child. I know that."

The daughter smiled as she said, "Well, we'll soon know. Have you finished? Then come and have a rest before dinner?" And as the two departed, arm in arm, the girl at the next table turned away as if the sight hurt her.

Beatrice found much to occupy her time in that week before Christmas. She had got a list from Fairlie of all her mother's pensioners and she greatly enjoyed ordering a hamper for each, carefully choosing the contents herself. And there were presents to buy for her Glasgow friends. Mrs. Lithgow needed careful thought, she would thank no one for a useless present. Peggy was quite easy, and Mrs. Murray, she thought, being much in bed, would probably appreciate a glorified bed-jacket. The family at 'Twixt Bears had to be planned for. She must have something to give each member on Christmas morning, the question was-what? A trinket of some sort would probably be best for Cicely, but her mother, her grandmother, her brothers? She decided that books would be the safest choice.

So Beatrice went shopping all day long, enjoying being one of the eager crowd that thronged the streets. There might not be much money to spend that Christmas but there was no lessening of the spirit of good-will.

On her last afternoon she took care to see all her friends-the blind woman with her Braille Bible, the Aberdeen terrier, with his master, the street-artist, the old man with the groundsel.

It was beginning to get dark when she reached the little shop where Franky lived with his parents. The father came forward, anxious-eyed as usual, giving his nervous cough, and Beatrice made a few purchases —a string of amber she had noticed in the window and liked, and a pendant in the shape of a galleon, silver and enamel, very delicately wrought. Having paid for them, she got to the real reason for her visit.

"And Franky," she said, "I do hope he is better and able to be up now?"

"He was up, sitting by the fire, but the doctor has put him back to bed. You see, it's the old trouble in the leg begun again. An abscess-tubercular." The man rubbed his cheek nervously, while Beatrice looked sorrowfully at him, then he said: "I think Franky would like to see you. You did him good last time. Of course-you wouldn't say anything to him about it being serious. He's very cheerful, you know; pretends to like his bed. . . . Just a minute and I'll fetch his mother."

The mother came, a gentle little woman with the same blue eyes as her boy and the attractive smile.

"Yes," she said, "it's a great disappointment. He's hardly ailed anything for the last few years, got on with his lessons, and actually was able to play games. His father and I had begun to hope he had thrown off his delicacy. . . . And so he may yet. The doctor says it may not be much, and Franky himself has such a spirit. That's half the battle. The interest he takes in football, knows all the names of the different players! Will you come in and see him, Miss? Yes, through this door, you know the way."

Franky was lying in his own little room looking out on to the yard of a garage.

"It's a bit noisy," his mother said, "but Franky likes the stir, don't you, sonny?"

The room was tidy, with a bright fire, some chrysanthemums in a vase, and the parrot in its cage. The boy was sitting up in bed busily making something. He looked well, for his colour was bright, and he greeted Beatrice happily, talking away to her about the aeroplane he was trying to make, and about a book he was reading.

"And there's this about having to lie in bed in winter," Beatrice told him, "you know you're not missing much outside."

"I'm missing the matches," said Franky. "Daddy used to take me."

A thought struck his visitor. "Franky," she said, "I've been wondering and wondering what I could give you for Christmas, now I know. I'll give you a portable wireless. And then you'll be able to hear the descriptions of the matches if you don't actually see the players."

"*Mother!*" The boy's face was very pink. "D'you hear? I'll be able to listen in to all the big matches."

"So you will, dearie. But aren't you going to thank the lady? . . . I'm sure, Miss, I don't know what to say. It hardly seems right to accept such a valuable gift, but how can we refuse what will give the boy such pleasure-and his father and me too. We've often wished we could hear the concerts and all the things, but times have been so bad with us there was never any hope of getting a wireless."

"There's a good place quite near," said Beatrice, "and if the thing doesn't work as it should, send it to them. You know the place, don't you, Franky? Just round the corner."

72

"Armstrong's," said the boy promptly.

"Yes, that's the name. I'll go now and see about it. . . . I'm going into the country for Christmas, but I won't be gone long, and when I come back I'll hear how you and the wireless are getting on. Good-bye, and a merry Christmas. Would you dress a little tree if I sent it in, as the Germans do? It would stand beside your bed and look festive. Very well, I'll see about it."

Beatrice was conscious of a load at her heart as she hurried round to order the wireless and leave instructions that they were to send to see if it worked all right. She had always had a great liking for small boys, and Franky had attracted her from the first. To know that he was marked out for suffering hurt her badly. There might be nothing before him but years of ill-health. He might never be able to help his parents in their struggle for a living, and would have to feel himself a burden.

As she chose a tree and got ornaments and trifling toys to decorate it at Hamley's, Beatrice tried to comfort herself by reflecting that at present the boy was quite happy. He had a good home and parents who simply lived for him; he had a buoyant spirit and many interests, and, after all, no one knew what the future held. . . . She was rather surprised at herself for being so concerned. Her mother had felt other people's troubles as her own, often to her daughter's bewilderment. Now, Beatrice asked herself, when there was no one else to worry was she to take on the job?

CHAPTER XIII

"You must understand, my dear, that when poets talk of cottages and hermitages and such like things, they mean a house with six sashes in front, two comfortable parlours . . . bedrooms . . . in short such a house as this is."

A Letter from William Cowper.

Cicely Sellars had said that she would call for Beatrice at the Langham at two o'clock on the 23rd, but she was fully half an hour late, and Beatrice had time to get seriously perturbed, as she sat in the entrance hall and watched the swing doors admit people of every age and size, but never the form she waited for. Indeed she began to tell herself that 'Twixt Bears had always seemed too like a fairy tale to be true; something had happened to keep Cicely from going and she would have to stay on in London and have a hotel Christmas after all. She was almost despairing, when Cicely came bounding up the steps, buttoned into a leather coat, rosy and laughing, breathlessly apologising for being late, but protesting that she was surprised to find herself there at all.

"Such a morning as we've put in; Jane almost lost her temper, so you can realise what provocations she had. . . . But all is well and off we go. . . . I say, I ought to have prepared you for the sight of Ulysses. You'll be rather affronted to see him among the lordly vehicles that throng this doorway, but he's a famous old roadster for all that."

Ulysses was a shabby little car, not very clean, and rather battered, and what Beatrice did feel ashamed of was the size and opulence of her two cases strapped on behind. She found it amusing to sit so near the ground, as it seemed to her, and watch Cicely thread her way deftly through the maze of traffic. Once out in the suburbs they went at a good pace, and as Cicely seemed to prefer to drive in silence, Beatrice could sit and watch fields and woods and villages flit past them in the gathering dusk, and try to picture her destination and the people she both longed and dreaded to meet.

Suddenly Cicely began to talk, to tell of the home they were going to.

"I hope you will like my mother," she said. "You mustn't think because she doesn't say much, or make a fuss, that she isn't glad to see you. It's her way to be quiet about everything. My father died thirteen years ago-in 1919; quite suddenly. The doctors said it was the effects of the war; he was out all the time. Watty was a tiny baby; and he's thirteen now. He was an after-thought. The two next me died while my father was in France, Jimmie and Jill. They would have been eighteen and twenty now. It was typhoid fever. We were living in the country and the drains of the house were all wrong. It was awful for mother, all alone with us, having to send such news to my father in the trenches. I think she and my father were absolutely happy for the first years of their married life, but 1914 shattered everything for them. There was no peace after that, nothing but tragedy. Mother was left with three of us and very little money when my father died, and things were complicated by my grandmother who, when mother decided to go to Oxlip, insisted on accompanying her. It was a case of Naomi refusing to be parted from Ruth! And we don't hear that Ruth grumbled, whereas my dear old Granny does nothing else! My father was her only child and she loved him quite fiercely, and I can imagine there must always have been a feeling of jealousy on her part towards my mother. And although my father is gone the jealousy is still there, at least I sometimes think so. In a way it must have made things more bitter for my poor little mother, but I never heard her complain and she was never impatient. Perhaps she realised and was comforted by Granny's passionate loyalty to my father's memory, so forgave everything else. I don't want you to think that mother's a saint or anything so inhuman, but she has stood up to life in a wonderful way and we're proud of her, Christopher and Watty and I, and grateful-as we've every reason to be."

"Yes," said Beatrice. "It's good of you to tell me about your mother. Now tell me about Watty. I've always wanted to be with boys, but I've never had a chance before."

"Watty's a funny fellow," said Cicely. "He was a delightful little chap, but he's getting to the self-conscious stage, terribly easy to affront, afraid to be laughed at or be made to look ridiculous. I adore him; we all do."

It was getting dark when they passed over a bridge that spanned a stream, ran up a short steep hill, and "Here we are," cried Cicely, bring up the car before a white garden gate, and sounding her horn fiercely. At the sound the house door opened, showing a lighted hall, and a boy came running down the flagged path, to be greeted with "Hullo, Watty! There's luggage here. Is Christopher in? *Christopher.* Come and help Watty; we're frozen."

Cicely took Beatrice by the arm and ran her up to the door, and she found her hand taken in a warm grasp, and heard a voice bidding her welcome.

"Come straight in here; you've had a long cold drive," Mrs. Sellars said, leading her guest into a lamp-lit room where tea was laid. Beatrice was almost too overcome with shyness to take in details, but she saw that her hostess was small and thin, with greying hair and a gentle plain face. In a large armchair by the fire sat a much older woman who, small and shrunken as she was, yet gave an impression of great vitality. She had a book on her lap on which lay a pair of tortoise-shell spectacles, and her dark peering eyes were fixed on the new-comers.

"My mother-in-law," said Mrs. Sellars. "Gran', this is Cicely's friend, Miss Dobie, who has come to spend Christmas with us. You remember I told you."

"You did not," said the old woman; then to Beatrice, "How d'you do? I don't know who are you; they tell me nothing in this house."

Cicely came forward and kissed her grandmother, remarking, "I can see you're in a surly mood, Gran'. What's upset you?"

"Wouldn't you be upset, if you were eighty-three, with no home of your own, and all sorts of young people coming in and out worrying you?"

"If I were eighty-three," said Cicely, "I'd be too jolly thankful to be able to hear and see-you can't deny that you can do both-and to have an angel like mother near me, and three such highly intelligent grandchildren arriving at intervals. . . . You're an ungrateful woman, that's what you are. Now, here's your tea, just as you like it. . . . What are you reading? Oh, *The Antiquary.*"

Old Mrs. Sellars looked at Beatrice as she said:

"When one is exiled from one's own land, to read about it is a comfort. You are from Scotland?"

"From Glasgow," Beatrice told her.

"I don't know it. We are Edinburgh and the Borders. It's not worth my while to try to get used to England and English ways, I just endure them. But these grandchildren of mine, poor creatures, they might as well be English. I don't know what their father would have thought of them."

"Mother," said Cicely, "let me pour out tea, and you will sit sociably by Beatrice and be at peace for a little. I'm pretty sure you've been on your feet since daybreak-Here are the boys. Well, is Ulysses resting in his lowly shed?" She turned to explain to the new-comer: "We've no proper garage, so we use what was once the hen-house. Oh, you haven't been introduced. My brother Christopher, Miss Beatrice Dobie. And Watty."

Beatrice found herself shaking hands with a tall young man in grey flannel trousers, a brown coat, and large boots, who smiled pleasantly but made no remark. Watty, the schoolboy, wore an alarming scowl. The two sat down to tea with their sister at a round table in the middle of the room, receiving with complete good humour their grandmother's caustic remarks and telling her little items of news; while Beatrice and her hostess made acquaintance with each other at a smaller table.

Mrs. Sellars, gentle, grave and deliberate, was very unlike her irrepressible daughter. Beatrice wondered if her spirit had not been broken by having to live with the formidable old woman with the hawk's eyes, who sat in the big chair.

"Have you been long in Oxlip?" she asked by way of making conversation.

"About twelve years," Mrs. Sellars told her. "Watty was a baby. . . . This cottage was left to me by an aunt, and after my husband's death, when we were giving up our Edinburgh house, it seemed a good idea to come here, more especially as it is near good schools. Oxford is not quite twelve miles away. And my mother-in-law came with me, not liking the thought of being separated from the children. I'm afraid she has never felt quite at home here, but really she is wonderfully happy. You'd be surprised at the interest she takes in everything that goes on; nothing escapes her. Granny likes to pretend that she is a thing of the past, a last leaf clinging to a November branch, but not a bit of it."

"Eighty-three is a great age," said Beatrice, glancing with awe at the little figure opposite.

"It seems so, but I don't believe one feels a bit older at eighty than one does at fifty, that is if one keeps one's faculties. It is not years but troubles that age one." She paused and then went on, "I think it is so nice of you to come with Cicely to spend your Christmas with us. It may make it easier for you to be in a strange place, with strangers, nothing to remind you of past Christmasses. We'll try to make you happy."

"You won't need to try," said Beatrice. "Merely being here gives me such a feeling of home. You don't know how grateful I am to your daughter for proposing it and to you for agreeing. Most people would resent a stranger being thrust upon them like this, but you-you look as if you liked it."

"Then I look what I feel. It pleases me very much when Cicely wants to bring a friend home. So many girls seem to have only one desire, to get away from home and all home ties. I'm afraid I'm rather puffed up with pride that my girl still thinks home is the best place. . . . You come from the city, Cicely says, so you won't know much about country life."

"Not of real country life. I've never lived like this in a village. We have a house down the Clyde, where we always spent the summer months, my mother and I, and gardened, and fished and climbed hills."

"There were only you and your mother?"

Beatrice nodded. "I never had any brothers or sisters, or even cousins, and as I didn't go to school I've never had a chance to know people of my own age. So long as I had mother nothing mattered, but now I'm beginning to see what I've missed. For one thing it makes me stupidly shy."

"A rare quality in these days."

"The rarer the better, I think. It makes one feel such a fool. How I envy girls like your Cicely. I don't mean that she is bold, but she's entirely unself-conscious, far too interested in the people she is meeting to care what sort of effect she produces."

They both looked at the girl, who was telling her grandmother something that was evidently very amusing; her brothers' eyes as well as the old lady's were fixed on her laughing face, all absorbed in her tale.

Presently Beatrice said: "How nice to have a boy in the house!"

"Yes," said Mrs. Sellars. "Watty is very much our baby still-though nothing would enrage him more than to hear me say it. A boy coming a bit behind is a great delight; he keeps us all young. Now, if you won't take any more tea, would you like to see your room? Cicely, take Beatrice-do you mind? the other is so formal-to her room? Our evening meal is at seven. I'm afraid you may think it early, but I don't like late washing-up. We have only one maid and it's only fair that she should get a little free time in the evening."

"Seven is a very good time to feed," said Cicely, putting her arm in Beatrice's. "Come and I'll help you to unpack. It's a work of art stowing things away in these small rooms; you keep bumping your head on the ceiling. Is there a lamp upstairs, Mother?"

They went up a short stair and Beatrice was interested to notice how every inch of space was put to use.

"Christopher's rather good with his hands," Cicely explained. "He made those bookshelves and fitted them in. We're always overflowing with books. They're about the only thing we have abundance of."

Beatrice's small room delighted her. True, the furniture was plain to shabbiness —a little old oak wardrobe and chest of drawers, a washstand of sorts, and the simplest of single beds, but there was a country freshness about its crisp curtains and valances, home-made rugs covered the worn carpet, the solid table by the bedside held a well rubbed-up brass candlestick and a stand of books, as well as a biscuit-box and a dish of rosy apples; a comfortable armchair stood by the bright fire and the whole effect was of peace and comfort.

"You like it?" said Cicely, "that's good. We'll get everything out, and Watty'll take the cases to the attic. This little wardrobe doesn't hold much, but there's a good cupboard here. Come and I'll show you the bathroom, the only one, alas! I'll give you a knock when it's empty in the morning. I'm afraid it's no good attempting a hot bath then, but sometimes at night it's pretty hot; you never can tell."

"It doesn't matter to me," said Beatrice hardily, "I always take a cold bath in the morning."

"Good girl! You're the kind to come to a country cottage. Now, I'll leave you. A bell will ring when the meal is ready, but don't wait for it if you're ready first. Gran's always in the living-room, very glad of a companion. Be sure and don't let the fire down; you will find lots of logs in that basket."

Very contentedly Beatrice put away her things, hung her frocks and coats in the big cupboard, making everything as tidy as possible. Then she studied the books by the bedside and sat down in the chintz-covered chair by the fire to consider them. It was odd to feel so completely at home in a strange place, among people she knew so little. Not even the young man and the schoolboy dismayed her, though she doubted if she would ever be able to address a remark to either. But probably they wouldn't trouble about her; she was used to being more or less ignored, and accepted it without question. One thing Beatrice knew, she was greatly drawn to Cicely's mother. Not that she in the least reminded her of her own mother, who had been so keen and alert and able to cope with life; Mrs. Sellars looked almost as if life had crushed her. Her bowed shoulders and lined face showed that she had borne a heavy burden of sorrow and care. . . What a pleasant room this was to sit in and dream. She went to the window and peered out. It was dark and very quiet, only here and there a lighted window; how unlike Portland Place, and how unlike Glasgow with its shrill clang of electric trams, and far away sounds from the ships in the Clyde. It was strange and delightful, Beatrice thought, to find herself in the heart of old England. Wouldn't Mrs. Lithgow be loud in her surprise when she heard!

When the bell rang she went downstairs and found Watty in the little hall waiting to escort her to the dining-room. His hair was tidily sleeked down with water, he wore a blue suit and clean collar, and his scowl was not so apparent.

"The dining-room used to be the kitchen," he told her, "but mother had another kitchen built to make more room. They built up the big fireplace too, and left a little one. Here it is."

Beatrice saw a long, low room, with a flagged floor, a gate-table with candles and holly berries, and a gleam of copper from the mantelshelf.

It was a warm, sustaining meal of steak and kidney pudding, apple tart and cream, and excellent coffee; every one ate as if they enjoyed it.

"How good home food is," said Cicely. "If you fed every day in a restaurant, as I do! I don't know what they do to food in restaurants, but they make everything taste the same."

"It's so nice," said Beatrice, "to get cream-and proper pudding plates."

"Isn't it?" Christopher grinned at her. "Nothing makes up for the lack of cream, to my mind. We never see it, of course."

"How are you fed on the whole, Christopher?" his sister asked him.

"Oh, pretty well-nothing to grouse about, though they do grouse, the little blighters." He turned to Beatrice. "I teach, you know. I'm a master in a prep. school in Suffolk."

"Oh," said Beatrice and could not utter another word.

"Yes," said Cicely, "I don't wonder you seem awed. You've probably read a lot of the stuff written about schools. But Christopher's is very disappointing. Quite dull; decent little boys and conscientious masters."

"I suppose," said Christopher, "it's just as it happens. There may be such places as novelists describe, but I haven't struck one. What I notice is that boys are changing a good deal." He looked at his young brother as he added, "For one thing, they're becoming gentler."

"Oh, shut up, Christopher," moaned Watty. "What a rotten thing to say!"

"Oh, I don't mean that they've lost their spirit, but the schoolboys of to-day can hardly recognise themselves in the schoolboys of yesterday, for instance, in the young barbarians of *Stalky & Co.* We seem to-day to produce a different breed, more like gazelles than bull-dogs."

Watty made incoherent noises of dissent, while his mother said, "At heart, I expect, the boy is eternally the same, but I've been surprised lately to notice a change in manners and habits. For instance, I've seen some of Watty's friends reading with every symptom of pleasure what we'd have called 'girls' books.'"

"Mother, *who?*" cried the outraged Watty.

Mrs. Sellars smiled at her young son as she said, "Didn't Tubby ask for another chapter of *Emma* the other night? . . . Now if every one's finished we'll go back to Granny. I'm afraid she will think us slow in coming. . . ."

Old Mrs. Sellars had her meals taken to her in the living-room as it hurt her bad leg to be moved, and she was waiting for them when they went in, sitting upright in her chair, one hand on her ebony stick, impatient to be amused.

Cicely presented her with a box of the peppermint creams that she specially liked, and said: "Well, Gran', what is it to be to-night? Cards or music or reading aloud? Shall I sing you some of the Songs of the North?"

"Yes, I've missed your singing. But we might have a chapter or two first. We're reading Miss Austen's *Emma* and it's most diverting. Where is it, Agnes?"

Her daughter-in-law produced the book and asked Cicely to read.

"*Emma,*" said Cicely, turning over the leaves. "I have read it but I don't seem to remember . . . what's it about?"

"It's about Emma," said Watty morosely. "She's an interfering creature; I can't bear her."

"Don't listen then, my son," his mother advised him, while Beatrice tried to refresh her friend's memory.

"Oh, you remember Emma, who liked to play at being Providence, and her little friend Harriet Smith, and 'poor Miss Taylor,' her governess, who became Mrs. Weston, and the hypochondriacal father who couldn't bear to let people eat things in case they'd be the worse of them, and Jane Fairfax, and Mr. Knightly — —"

"Yes. I do remember. Is this the mark?"

"Yes," said her mother. "The Coles are about to give a party; their love of society and their new dining-room having prepared everybody for their keeping dinner company-isn't it delicious?"

"It's only the 'best people,'" said Beatrice, "who are invited to dinner. You remember, 'the less worthy females' came in afterwards."

"The lambs!" said Cicely. "Mr. Woodhouse speaks: *I am not fond of dinner visiting, I never was. No more is Emma. Late hours do not agree with us. I am sorry Mr. and Mrs. Cole should have done it, I think it would be much better if they would come in one afternoon next summer and take their tea with us; take us in their afternoon walk which they might do, as our hours are so reasonable, and yet get home without being out in the damp of the evening.*"

Cicely sat close to her grandmother's chair and read in her clear, musical voice, making, with her sense of drama, the different characters live, so that even Watty listened entranced.

When she closed the book, Christopher turned to Beatrice and, laughing, remarked, "What a dangerous neighbour Miss Austen must have been! 'Round-cheeked, preternaturally capped, sedate!' . . . Isn't it Chesterton who says that Jane Austen may have lived in towns where women were protected from the truth, but there was precious little of the truth protected from Jane Austen!"

"But," said Beatrice, "she only laughed at people who deserve to be laughed at, like the vale-tudinarian Mr. Woodhouse, and the terrible Mrs. Elton; and Mr. Collins and Mrs. Bennet in *Pride and Prejudice*."

"Mrs. Bennet," said Christopher, "I can't believe in. She was too utterly foolish to be the wife of Mr. Bennet and the mother of Elizabeth. Have you read —— —"

But their conversation was at that moment interrupted by old Mrs. Sellars commanding that her granddaughter sing to her. So Cicely went to the piano and, after letting her hands wander up and down the keys for a minute, began to sing what she knew was an old favourite, *O gin I were a baron's heir*. From that she drifted to *Colin's Cattle*, and *I wish I were whaur Gaudie rins*.

Beatrice, forgetting in her pleasure to be shy, cried, "Oh, I didn't know you could sing like that."

Cicely, still idly playing laughed. "Did you ever read," she asked, "Sir James Melville's inter-view with Queen Elizabeth? She was very anxious to hear about Mary of Scots, if she were tall, if she could dance. '*She speired gin she played well. I said Raisonably, for a Queen.*' I sing raisonably, considering it isn't my job — D'you know this? . . ."

CHAPTER XIV

"Heigh-ho! sing, heigh-ho, unto the green holly!"

As You Like It.

At seven o'clock the next morning Beatrice was awakened from a dreamless sleep by the crowing of a cock. It was still dark, but she could hear movements in the house, and outside, somewhere, cows were lowing and milk-pans clattering. She was in Oxlip.

Snug in her bed she lay and thought over the events of the previous day, the run from London through the December mists, the arrival in the darkening, the kindly welcome given her-the family seemed at once to accept her as one of themselves-the evening with *Emma*, Cicely's songs.

Of course, she reminded herself, this was only a short episode, the result of a casual invitation given by a good-natured girl, but somehow it seemed to her that in coming to this place she had turned another page in her Book of Life. She remembered birthday mornings when she had come down rather palpitating to breakfast (for birthdays had never been unmixed bliss!), and her mother had said, "You've got a clean white page to-day, darling," and she had greatly disliked the idea. No matter how perfect that day she tried to keep her walk and conversation she was sure to stumble, and when she did she seemed to see a blot fall on the clean page. It was a relief to feel in a few days that it must now be comfortably smudged all over. But this morning she was not worrying herself about blots on the new page, only wondering what would be written on it.

A loud knock on the door and Cicely's voice shouting, "The bathroom's empty," made her jump quickly out of bed and, not waiting to light her candle, grope for her dressing-gown, towels, sponge, in a frenzy in case she took too much time and kept some one waiting.

When she got back to her room she found some one had put a lamp on her dressing-table, and before she finished dressing the light was beginning to come through the yellow blind.

Mrs. Sellars was already at the table when she got down to the dining-room, and Christopher was dealing with a dish of porridge by the fire.

He asked, "D'you like porridge, Miss Dobie? Good. Here's your bowl. Cream?"

"What luxury!" said Beatrice, "I'm accustomed to milk."

"We're very lucky about getting cream here," Mrs. Sellars said, "for in most villages you never see it. But we've a farm very near and the people who run it are most obliging."

Cicely came in with a covered dish of hot scones.

"These are in honour of you, Bee," she announced. "Our small retainer, Ruth, rose half an hour earlier to bake them, and very good they are!"

"Bacon and egg?" asked Christopher, "or cold ham and a boiled egg?"

Feeling rather overwhelmed by so much attention Beatrice made her choice, took a scone and told herself that breakfast in 'Twixt Bears was a truly delightful meal. The room itself was as gay as a crocus, for not only were its walls primrose yellow, but the table-cloth, napkins, crockery and window hangings were all of the same sunny shade. The chairs were plain Windsor chairs with blue cushions, and a thick, handmade blue and white carpet lay on the flagged floor. There was nothing "artistic" about the room, it was really country.

Beatrice was amused to see people pass the windows, and said:

"I feel rather as if I were in a play. You remember the bow-windowed room in *Quality Street*? We only need the snow-flakes."

"That's what we won't get, I'm afraid," said Christopher. "Watty has a constant feud with the weather-clerk on the subject. For years he made it a matter of prayer. . . . By the way, where is that warrior?"

"He's taken Voltaire for a walk," Cicely said. "They dashed out of the kitchen door as I was making the toast; they'll be here in a minute."

"Who is Voltaire?" Beatrice asked.

"Watty's dog, a funny little mongrel with a curious, sneering smile-at least Christopher insists that it's a smile, and christened him Voltaire. Watty has shortened it to Airy, but by any other name he'd smell as sweet. . . . Here he is! Yes, here you are, you precious thing! Did they say you sneered and called you ugly names and you such a darling," and Cicely embraced the animal, who bore it with patience.

"Intelligent conversation is impossible in this house," Christopher remarked pensively: "at any moment it may be broken into by sudden passionate endearments lavished on an entirely unresponsive hound!"

"Yes," agreed Cicely, and chuckled. "Like this. The difference between Edith Sitwell and — 'Oh, look at him, the precious woolly lamb! So coy, too. Have you been chasing the hens, wicked one?' "

"It's hard on a decent dog," said Watty, "to have to watch people making fools of themselves over him."

"Don't be morose, darling," his sister advised. "Voltaire is a very happy little dog in spite of our blandishments. Bee, doesn't he look as if he had come straight from a toy-shop? Such woolly legs. Such a round tubby body! . . . By the way, what are we supposed to be doing to-day?"

Beatrice, privately wondering what there could possibly be for anyone to do in a village in mid-winter, paused with a bit of toast on its way to her mouth to listen.

"My first job," said Christopher, "is to cut a lot of holly and ivy and cart it along to the church. I promised Mr. Snow."

"Oh," said Cicely, "I said I'd help to do the church; that'll take all afternoon." She turned to her guest. "I always help in the house for an hour or two in the morning, and then, I thought, we might run in to Oxford."

"Then," said Mrs. Sellars, "you might do some shopping for me; there are always things forgotten at the end."

"Oh, I would like to go to Oxford," said Beatrice. "It's a place I've always wanted to see."

"All right," said Cicely. "The place'll be packed, but we'll push our way through. I tell you what, we might lunch in Oxford and get back in time to help with the church. You'll be there to help, won't you, Chris? Your long arms are such a convenience and you don't seem to mind getting your hands pricked. Watty, would you care to go to Oxford?"

Watty was understood to say that he didn't mind if he did.

"Then," said Cicely, "you might give Ulysses a slight wash."

"Watty's going to saw some logs for me," said his mother. She turned to Beatrice explaining, "With one young maid we all have to help a little."

"I hope you'll let me help too," Beatrice said eagerly. "There's nothing I'd enjoy more; I love making beds."

"Good," said Cicely, "then you'll make them with me and that will let Ruth get on with other things. Mother, you aren't going to be very busy, are you?"

"Not in the least busy. Ruth and I have got things very far forward; it's wonderful how much you can prepare beforehand, and Ruth's sister is coming in to help."

"What a blessing Ruth is turning out so well," Cicely said. "You see, Bee, we've always had the same old cook-she came with us from Scotland. At least we thought her very old, though I don't suppose she's over fifty, and she surprised us very much last summer by marrying. The man's a widower, and suitably aged, but still it was a shock. The stars in their courses seemed to reel, didn't they, Mother? We couldn't imagine the house without *Colina*. Yes, that was her wonderful name. Jam-making time, spring-cleaning time, all the extra times loomed up before us like spectres. We hated Mr. Merry who was taking her away, poor decent man; we gazed reproachfully at Colina, but she was firm, said it wasn't that she cared so much for Mr. Merry, though she might get to like him better as time went on, but she felt she'd washed other people's dishes long enough and thought it was time she washed her own. So she became Colina Merry, and Ruth took her place here, and to our surprise was in many ways a change for the better. Colina had been apt to be sulky at times and needed to be considered and petted, whereas Ruth, brought up by a practical mother in a squatter of young brothers and sisters, expected nothing; we could never ask the dignified Colina to leave her work and 'run' here and there on errands, but Ruth goes like the wind anywhere, and what is more, enjoys it. Colina talked incessantly, Ruth seldom utters; Colina was slow, Ruth rushes at her work with almost maniacal fervour!"

"It's quite true," said Mrs. Sellars. "I like Ruth, but Colina was part of the old life and I miss her."

"But not so much as you thought you would," Cicely insisted. "Besides, we haven't lost her. She lives only half a mile away and watches our comings and goings with a jealous eye. If we ever really needed her I'm sure she'd leave Merry to fend for himself and return to 'Twixt Bears till the crisis was over."

"That's like our Fairlie," said Beatrice. "She was my nurse and stayed on with us as a sort of housekeeper and we all learned to lean on her. And she has suddenly arranged a marriage for herself with a widower, a lucky man he is too, for Fairlie is not only a splendid cook and manager, but she's a thoroughly comfortable person to have in a house. But, like you, I felt quite aggrieved and deserted, when she wrote and told me. . . . They're to be married on Hogmanay. I must remember to send a wire."

"You must," said Cicely. "Come along now and we'll start on the beds. Are you going to get Granny up, Mother? She seemed very bright when I took in her breakfast, and she said you had been in before me. It's not necessary to get up in the night and look at her, is it?"

"Oh, no. If I'm awake I go in, but she sleeps like a baby. Are you sure, Beatrice, that you want to make beds? It seems an odd way to treat one's guest."

"A very kind way," said Beatrice. "It makes one feel as if one belonged."

Beatrice was delighted with the bedrooms, their sloping ceilings and lattices windows, but Cicely hardly seemed to share her enthusiasm.

"They're pretty, of course," she said, "and roomier than they look, with those big cupboards; all the same I'd rather have modern rooms with high ceilings and big windows, and hot and cold water . . . What a mess Christopher's got here. All these books and golf-clubs."

"Is your brother good at games?" Beatrice asked.

"Yes. That helps him a lot. It's such a blessing he's keen on teaching, and that he really likes his boys. So many teachers loathe their job. If I had to teach-which God forbid —I'd prefer a prep, school. I like them better little and fubsy. I'm so sad to see Watty grow up. His voice is actually beginning to break. As I told you he's just at the stage when he thinks it rather clever to be morose, and regard the world as a bleak and mischievous place. . . . Mother says he's beginning to take his lessons more seriously; his report this time is quite good. I'm glad, for it's rather a strain on mother's small income keeping him at a good school, especially now when dividends are all going *phut*."

Cicely punched the pillows with vehemence as she said:

"Mother does *marvels*. It means, of course, that she gets nothing for herself, that her whole life is given to others; all the same, I believe she thinks it is worth it. And we three, Chris, and Watty and I, have jolly well got to make her feel that we're worth all she has done for us. . . . I'm not afraid of Christopher, there's something so decent about him. It's natural for youth to lean towards anarchy, but Christopher's all for law and order. But he's not a prig-though I called him one last night when he made some remarks about my lips. He said, 'Miss Dobie doesn't muck up her face,' and I gathered from his tone that the said face seemed to him pretty good as it was-Why, Bee, how beautifully you blush! I thought blushing was a lost art."

Beatrice, carefully smoothing a cover, said:

"If you had lived in 120 Portland Place you wouldn't ever want to see a made-up face again; you'd scrub your face with spring water, and wear your hair as nature made it even though it were straight as a bone; you'd adjure all scents and sachets and aids to beauty."

Cicely laughed. "Well, I grant you, such things are hopelessly out of the picture in 'Twixt Bears. Well now, have you any letters to write? It's a chance to post them in Oxford."

"I don't think so. I wrote them all at the Langham. I haven't a great number of people to write to."

"I'm not bothering this year," Cicely said. "It's too poor a Christmas to think of sending even cards to people who don't want them. I've had enough to do to get presents for the household; they're not up to much, but, happily, we're all easily pleased."

Beatrice enjoyed her run to Oxford. They parked the car in the Broad and set off for the shops, which were, as Cicely had predicted, packed to excess.

It was one o'clock before they had worked through the list of things needed, and they badly wanted lunch, but there seemed little chance of obtaining any.

"What about a hotel?" said Beatrice.

"Much too expensive," said Cicely.

"Oh, but at Christmas-time! And anyway, this is my show. You came to-day for me. Come along, Watty."

Beatrice had her way, and they ate their meal in peace, Watty being allowed to order all the things his boyish soul adored and seldom met with —hors d'œuvres, cider-cup, fruit-salad and ices.

Replete in body and light of heart they scrambled into the car, which seemed already full of packages.

"I like Oxford," said Beatrice.

"But you haven't seen Oxford," Cicely told her. "Another day I'll take you to the colleges. In the afternoon, when the dusk is falling, that's the time I want you to see it-oh, my goodness, we must hurry."

It was about three o'clock before they got to the church, where they found Christopher and about half a dozen other people, and were quickly given jobs. Beatrice was hurriedly introduced to every one present, but found some difficulty in sorting them out.

Coming home in the darkening she asked Cicely to help her. "When I'm being introduced I'm so occupied with the face of the person I'm meeting that I forget to listen to the name. Tell me, who is the pretty woman in black?"

"That's Mrs. Stopford," said Cicely. "She lives in a gem of a Charles II house on the road to Beel-on-the-Wold. The Stopfords have owned Broadmeadows for generations. She's a widow with a precious only son-Basil. He wasn't there to-day, but you'll meet him very soon. Mrs. Stopford is rich and very kind and most hospitable, a tremendous help, as you can understand to Oxlip and its inhabitants. The two pretty girls are twins, daughters of a retired soldier, Colonel Fairfax. They have that house covered with ivy on the village green. Yes, they're nice girls; mad, you know, but nice. Then there was the parson, Mr. Snow, and his wife. And the other couple are called Pugh. I like them most awfully. They've got a queer little house made out of a cottage and a garage, and they seem to find life such fun. Any money they have-it isn't much-is made from writing. They're both quite extra clever. That's the nice thing about Oxlip, we're all-at least nearly all-quite poor, so that there is no silly striving or pretending. I like London, but I often sigh for Oxlip."

That, it seemed to Beatrice, was not to be wondered at, as she went across the village green, and up the flagged path bordered by lavender bushes, through the hall, into the lamp-lit drawing-room of 'Twixt Bears. The blind was still up in the window at the garden end of the room, and the last of the daylight glimmered on the slow-moving Eden, while beyond lay, dark and shadowy, a great marsh-land where, it was easy to imagine, the Moor-wife did her brewing and nursed the Will o' the Wisps, as in Hans Andersen's story.

Mrs. Sellars was waiting for them with the kettle boiling. Granny Sellars was upright in her chair, reading *Guy Mannering* with dignity. A hurried washing of hands, with loud protests from Watty that some person unknown had stolen his nail-brush; laughter, talk, and tea-time so prolonged that Mrs. Sellars said it would be dinner-time before Ruth got the tea-cups washed.

And after dinner the time so galloped withal that they were lighting candles for bed when, to Beatrice, the evening seemed hardly begun. How different, she thought, from the way the hours had crawled when she sat alone in the Portland Place drawing-room beside an electric fire, reading, or meditating sadly, and longing for the time to pass that she might go to bed and finish another weary day.

As they were saying good-night, Mrs. Sellars said to Beatrice, "My dear, I'm so sorry you didn't get early tea to-day; you shall have it to-morrow without fail."

"Yes," said Cicely, "we're not accustomed to such luxuries here, but you have lived in King's houses, so to speak, and must miss them."

"But I don't," Beatrice protested. "I'd much rather not have it. I enjoy my breakfast so much better without it."

"It's not till nine to-morrow," Watty told her, "because it's Christmas. And we always have sausages at Christmas, the same as Sundays." And the two grinned at each other in a congratulatory way.

CHAPTER XV

"So thou through windows of thine age shall see,
Despite of wrinkles this thy golden time."

As You Like It.

For many years one Christmas Day had been very like another to Beatrice, but when she came down to breakfast the next morning she had a feeling that something very exciting was happening. It was all so different. In the Glasgow days, which seemed now so far away, she and her mother had always carried out the same programme; present-giving to the household in the morning, the Christmas service in the church they attended, a large luncheon-party of people who, if not invited, would have had to eat a solitary meal, and a dinner-party at some friend's house in the evening. It had all been decorous and happy, and Beatrice as she thought of it, felt her eyes fill with tears for the dear companion of those days. It seemed almost wrong that she should be feeling quite eager and excited on this first Christmas without her mother, and yet she knew that was foolish, for if her mother was aware of what was happening to her girl her generous soul would rejoice that life at the moment was bright for her.

When Beatrice opened her bedroom door she found Voltaire with a bright red bow on his collar guarding a white box tied with red ribbon, which bore the inscription, "Fudge for Beatrice, and a Merry Christmas." Picking it up she went downstairs, almost stepping upon Watty, who was flat on his face on the floor, working the present that Christopher had just bestowed on him. He had to explain all about it before they went into the dining-room, but once there, he was able to devote himself to the sausages which were a speciality of Oxlip, and excellent. The sideboard was heaped with parcels, and Beatrice found that she had by no means been forgotten; each one had given her a trifle, and she felt thankful that she had come well supplied with gifts for her kind entertainers.

"Not a bad morning," Christopher said, as he attended to her wants. "It looks as if it might brighten later on."

"It's not up to much just now," Watty complained. "Misty as anything. I don't believe the clerk of the weather *knows* it's Christmas!"

"Who's going to church?" Cicely asked. "Has Bee any conscientious objections to bowing in the House of Rimmon, Presbyterian and all as she is?"

"For the matter of that," said Mrs. Sellars, "we're all Presbyterians here, but there's nowhere else for us to go. And we are very well off, as it happens, for Mr. Snow, the rector, is a fine man, and well worth listening to. I think Beatrice will enjoy the service."

And Beatrice did. The church was well heated and smelt of warm evergreens and old stone and the dust of centuries. Above her on the wall was an oak panel with the names of all the rectors of the church, beginning in 1231 with one Hugh de Glastonbury, and finishing with the Rev. Norman Snow, M.A. Somehow, the feeling of age around her seemed to give a new meaning to the story of the shepherds and the angels, and the Baby in the manger. What a lovely story it was!

And the angel said unto them, Fear not: for, behold, I bring you tidings of great joy which shall be for all people. For unto you is born this day in the City of David a Saviour. . . .

It was pleasant to stand between Cicely and Watty and sing "*O come, all ye faithful,*" and when they all dropped on their knees at the end of the short service, she found herself praying, "O, please make my mother happy in Thy House," quite forgetting all she had been taught about the dead having no need for our poor human prayers. . . .

The midday meal that day at 'Twixt Bears was what Colina would have called a "pit ower," merely cold meat and potatoes in their jackets.

"We concentrate on the Christmas dinner," Cicely said. "And we're all invited to a tea-party at Mrs. Stopford's this afternoon."

"But," said Beatrice, "you mustn't think it necessary to take me. I'll stay happily at home and look after your grandmother."

"No need," said Cicely. "Mother isn't going. And Mrs. Stopford would be most disappointed if you weren't there. I think she took a fancy to you when she met you at the church yesterday, at least she described you to me as 'your charming friend.' "

Beatrice laughed sceptically and privately wished that they had all been going to have tea quietly at home, but, rather to her own surprise, she found the party most amusing.

Mrs. Stopford was a born hostess, watchful for her guests' comfort, quick to see any lack. She had an appealing manner and a way of making people feel that what they said was of supreme importance to her. Beatrice could not but feel flattered that her hostess should at once take her into her confidence, and pour into her ears all her hopes for her idolised son, also her fears. He was a handsome, well-mannered youth, though his good-natured mouth had something of weakness in it.

"The worst of dear Basil is he's so easily led," his mother lamented, "and you know what college life is, and how many temptations meet a young man. What I want for him is a thoroughly nice girl, a little older than himself, perhaps. Yes, I almost think it would be better. Only a year or two, of course. I hate any real disparity. . . . Money doesn't matter, although with everything so uncertain and the Government so odd about wanting to bring us all to penury, and values falling, it would be quite welcome; but what I mean is it isn't essential."

"I see," said Beatrice, at a loss what to reply.

"Yes, I knew you were sympathetic the moment I saw you yesterday, standing with your arms full of holly in the church. You looked as if you were feeling all the beauty and significance of it, your expression was so calm and sweet, almost up-lifted. . . ."

The girl, guiltily aware that she had felt nothing except that the holly was prickly and the church musty and cold, blushed, while her hostess continued in her confiding way —"I *always* know at once when I meet a kindred spirit. . . . And you are staying with the dear Sellars; I simply can't tell you what I feel about the Sellars. The mother! Isn't she wonderful, with her beautiful worn face? If I were a great artist I'd paint a picture of her, and call it, quite simply, 'The Mother.' And that amazing old grandmother! So very Scots in the sharpness of her tongue! And pretty Cicely! And dear Watty! Oh, and Christopher. . . . Ah, now there is a *man*. My Basil is as attached to him as if Christopher were his elder brother. . . . Yes, darling, dance of course. Basil, ring the bell and we'll get the rugs up. When would we frolic if not on Christmas Day?"

"That," said Cicely in Beatrice's ear, "is enough to blight anyone's spirits," but presently, all the guests were dancing, young and old, all except Watty, who, having steadfastly refused to learn the Terpsichorean art, sat on a sofa and glowered.

Beatrice danced with Basil and found him much more sensible than his anxious mother had led her to expect; she danced with Colonel Fairfax, she danced with Christopher, and, men giving out, she danced with Susan Fairfax and found her the most amusing partner of them all.

"You're stopping with the Sellars," she began. "Lucky for you. You must come to badminton to-morrow; we play in the village hall. Oh, and you'll come in very useful for our play. We actually need another girl."

"I'm afraid," said Beatrice, "I can't act."

"You mean," said Susan, "that you haven't tried. No one knows what they can do till they try. I'll coach you. I'm pretty good; and so is Sarsa, my sister-short for Sarsaparilla, you know."

"But-that isn't her name, surely."

"Well, it's been her name for a long time now, though I believe at her christening she was named Cynthia, but Sarsa goes better with Susan. We're twins, we two, aged eighteen; looks, but little money; ordinary as to brains; docile in harness. . . ." Beatrice giggled and Susan looked delighted. "I say, I'm glad I've made you laugh. I was afraid you felt rather sad-being in black and all that, but it's really no good being gloomy. It's awful, of course, when people die, but it isn't as if we're here for good either. We've got to follow, you to-day, me to-morrow, and life's such a funny thing and the world so full of comics that you simply must laugh. Hi, Sarsa" —she caught at the skirt of a girl passing —"meet Miss Dobie, as the saying is."

Susan's twin was Susan improved in every way. Her eyes were a clearer blue, her complexion purer, her nose straighter, her hair more golden, her figure slimmer and more graceful.

"Yes," said Susan, "Sarsa's the de luxe. I'm the cheap edition, but by moral worth and the cultivation of a manner pleasing alike to old and young, I hope to merit a share of public patronage." She surveyed Beatrice and added:

"Isn't it odd, every girl in Oxlip is a blonde, more or less (the poor gentlemen don't get a chance to prefer anything else), and here you are, blonder than any! . . . I hope you'll like us. We're a funny little land-locked community, though sometimes, of course, we mix with a wider world."

"Come off it, Susan," her sister advised, and confided to Beatrice, "She's showing off, you know, so don't encourage her. . . . It's lovely having Cicely back. I wish she didn't have to work in London. You're her friend, aren't you? I hope she'll bring you to see us. We live across the green from 'Twixt Bears, and we'd welcome you to any meal-including breakfast."

"Oh, thank you," said Beatrice, while Susan broke in, "It might be better to know when to expect you-better for you, I mean. We're not terribly efficient housekeepers, Sarsa and I, and sometimes there's not enough to go round, and our parent is put to shame before strangers. . . . What about lunch to-morrow? There's sure to be turkey left over. I'll speak to Cicely. . . . Sarsa, it's about time we were leaving, my girl. Have you forgotten we told Millie we'd lay the table ourselves, and it's going on for seven."

"Oh! my goodness!" shrieked the Twin. "I'll tell you what, I'll bolt. You say good night to Mrs. Stopford and explain. We'll never be ready in time. Good night. Miss Dobie —I promised Cook I'd make the brandy butter."

But the party was breaking up, every one hastening home to dress and dine, either in their own homes or with friends. A spirit of Christmas gaiety was in the air, and Beatrice, watching the laughing groups, did not feel in the least out of it.

At seven-thirty the Sellars family and their guest sat down to their Christmas dinner. The table was decorated in red and white and green. "Christmas colours," said Cicely, "red of holly-berries, green of mistletoe, white of snow. Nature seldom plays up, but we do our best by reminding her."

"How did you enjoy the party, Beatrice?" Mrs. Sellars asked. "All Oxlip was there, I hear."

"Not only Oxlip," said Christopher, "but for miles round."

"It was great fun," Beatrice said. "Mrs. Stopford is such a good hostess and looks after every one. Easy to know, too."

"I expect she confided in you," said Cicely. "It's a way she has."

"And," went on Beatrice, "I liked the Twins very much. Do they really keep house for their father? They look so young to have any responsibility."

"They've lots of sense, Susan and Sarsa," Mrs. Sellars said, "and aren't they a pretty pair? Were the Pughs there, Cicely?"

"Yes, but they had to hurry away, as they're dining in Oxford. Basil seemed in great form. I wish his mother didn't fuss him so. Her eyes seldom leave him. . . . I told you she'd taken a liking to you, Bee. She kept murmuring to me how sympathetic you were, and interjecting remarks like 'That Madonna brow!' 'Such serenity!' "

Beatrice, much abashed, murmured that it was very kind of Mrs. Stopford.

"Oh, she's *kind*," said Cicely. "There are moments when I feel I never wish to hear that word again."

"Dear me," said her mother, "what ails you at kindness?"

"Oh, you know quite well what I mean, Mother. It's not that I'm over-dosed with it myself. In my profession-you needn't scoff, Chris. —in my profession we're all striving so hard to keep our footing on the ladder that kindness is completely crowded out. But when I come back here and find some one like Mrs. Stopford, comfortably shut away from the stress of life, spending her time being kind, cooing soft things in the ears of other idlers, pursuing shadows . . ."

"You've lost the thread of your discourse," said Christopher. "Hadn't you better take your soup before it gets cold?"

Cicely laughed. "A prophet," she said, "you know the rest. Very good soup, Mother."

Christopher carved the turkey with the dexterity of one long accustomed to make a bird or a joint go round, and Watty helped Ruth to carry round the vegetables. It was a merry meal.

"I thought we'd have coffee beside Granny," Mrs. Sellars said, when they had finished their fruit, so they trooped into the living room where the old lady sat, looking most festive in her velvet jacket, which was one of her Christmas gifts, adorned with a spray of holly.

Cicely made the coffee, while Watty for once got his fill of chocolates, from an enormous box presented to him by Beatrice.

"And now, Gran'," said Cicely, "what shall we do? You choose. Shall it be bridge? Or, seeing it's Christmas night, shall we have something more communal?"

Mrs. Sellars, who was sitting back in an armchair, her hands for once idle, said in her gentle way, "Perhaps Granny would tell us about Christmas when she was a girl?"

"Yes," said Christopher. "Won't you, Gran'?"

If old Mrs. Sellars cared for anyone it was for her grandson Christopher, and her eyes always glistened less fiercely when they rested on him, but she received the suggestion with her usual lack of amiability. "Nonsense," she said, and added, darting a look at her daughter-in-law, "trying to humour an old woman."

She was sitting with the book Beatrice had given her as a present on her lap —*Albert the Good*, and Cicely with a "May I look?" took it up and immediately began to rave about the charming cover.

"Oh, but how sweet! Mother, did you ever see anything so nice? It's the picture of a pear, you see, and when you lift the flaps there is *the* pair-Victoria and her Albert. Such high-coloured, heart-shaped faces! The pets . . . Oh, Granny, were people really like that when you were young? You must remember Vicky very well, and even Albert."

Old Mrs. Sellars looked coldly at the girl as she said, "I'll thank you to give the Queen her proper title, Cicely. If there is one thing I dislike more than another about the young generation-and I dislike almost everything they say and do-it's their irreverence. Queen Victoria was a good woman and great queen, and it isn't for such as you to take liberties with her name now that she has gone to her reward."

Cicely received the rebuke meekly, merely remarking:

"I didn't mean to be irreverent, for I've the most profound respect for Victoria and her age. . . . You would be a child, Gran', when she was at her very happiest, furnishing Balmoral in tartan, playing with the children, exchanging mild jests with Albert. Did you ever see her?"

"I saw her at her Diamond Jubilee, a little old lady in a bonnet."

Cicely was turning over the leaves of the book. "Look at them," she said, "*how* I wish I'd lived then!"

Christopher turned to Beatrice, remarking, "Any one more completely out of place than Cicely in the Victorian age I can't imagine. She belongs to this age entirely."

Old Mrs. Sellars was speaking. ". . . There was certainly no softness in our upbringing. I rose at 6.30 on winter mornings to practise in a room without a fire!"

"But what was the use of that?" Cicely asked. "Your fingers would be too numb to feel the notes."

"It was good discipline." Watty here groaned, but his mother laid a restraining hand on him. "To-day everything is made much too easy. In my young days the country children thought nothing of walking five miles each way to school and were all the better for it; now they're conveyed in motors. I'm told that in some schools they actually ask the children what they'd like to do! No wonder they turn out the sort of young people they do. And are the children any happier? I doubt it."

"I don't think they are as happy," Mrs. Sellars said; "they taste everything too soon."

"Poor little wretches," said Cicely. "Let's leave them in peace, while we hear what Gran' did besides practising her music in a cold room. Didn't you ever get into any scrapes, Gran'? I believe you did. Tell us."

There was a short silence, while the old lady played with the holly in her coat, a little reminiscent smile on her lips. Then she said:

"You must know that there was a boys' school quite near our boarding school, and sometimes the boys had the impudence to write letters to the girls they most liked the look of. One to me had been intercepted, though I didn't know it. . . . We were all in the schoolroom that looked into the garden. It was the longest day, the 21st of June, very sunny. Suddenly, when we looked out we saw that two of the rascally boys had climbed on to the high garden wall. At that moment in came one of the governesses, saw us all at the window, and, horror-stricken at the sight of the boys, *drew down the blind.* Lottie Blake, who was always inclined to be pert-she married a soldier and died in India-said, 'Well, Miss Parsons, you've shortened the longest day. . . .' That was my last term —I went home after that-finished."

"Seventeen, were you? And pretty? I'm sure you were pretty?" Cicely leant forward looking into her grandmother's face.

"Mebbe I was. People said so, anyway, and I could have danced every dance twice over at my first ball. An Assembly they called it. It was held at the Tontine Hotel, in the big room with the musicians' gallery. I was in despair because my mother took ill and I was afraid I would have to stay at home, but old Miss Alison Hope offered to take me under her wing."

Mrs. Sellars paused and looked across at her daughter-in-law.

"You never saw Miss Alison, Agnes? She was a great character. Very tall and thin with a moustache. She always dressed in a distinctly odd way: her clothes were very voluminous, no matter what the fashion was, and she always wore in her bodice a very large cameo brooch. Her manners too were rather odd, for she had a habit of taking up a jam dish and calmly supping its contents. I remember one day, as a child, sitting round-eyed watching her performance, when a spoonful went astray on its way to her mouth. 'Where did it go, bairn?' she asked. 'Not on me, I hope, for there's nothing more unpleasant than a spoonful of jelly behind one's brooch.' "

"And was it there?" Watty asked, much interested.

"Oh, likely," said his grandmother, "but I forget. . . . Miss Alison had a nephew, a handsome young soldier. He was at my first assembly, and out of duty to his aunt, doubtless, showed me great attention. It was my first taste of the wine of life; one doesn't forget it even at eighty-three."

Christopher smiled at his grandmother, as he quoted:

"Girl, there were girls like you in Ilion."

"Yes," said Cicely, "they don't change, only the dress and manners are different."

It was quite late before they all went to bed, and Christopher, coming in from whistling on Voltaire, who was spending the evening with a friend, said:

"I believe it'll freeze to-night. That'll please you, Watty."

CHAPTER XVI

"But, my dear sir, if Emma comes away early it will break up the party."
"And no great matter if it does. The sooner any party breaks up the better."

Jane Austen.

As Christopher predicted frost came in the night, a really hard frost, and the whole world was changed the next morning. Gone was the mud, and the dreary mist that had hung close over woods and fields; now everything was a-sparkle. Hoar frost had turned the village into a German fairy tale.

"Just like it," said Watty as he came in, blowing his hands, to breakfast. "Why couldn't it have been like this on Christmas? Missed it by a day."

"Still," Christopher pointed out, "only by a day. It may pull it off next year."

"I doubt it," said Watty, made bitter by hope deferred.

Beatrice came in apologising for being late. She had been leaning out of her bedroom window, breathing in the air that was like wine, noticing how every sound came clear and sharp, entranced by the sight of the lavender bushes delicately rimmed with rime.

"Isn't it lovely?" she cried. "I've never really seen frost before, certainly not at such close quarters. In Glasgow one rather dreaded it, for so often it brought fog in its train, but this is so gay. I knew something had happened when I woke up. The very cocks crowed clearer!"

Mrs. Sellars smiled at the pleasure in the girl's face.

"Yes," she said, "people laugh at the British for talking so much about the weather, but they needn't. It's one of the most interesting subjects we've got. And don't you like books that bring in the weather? I do. It gives point to a scene, and there's no doubt weather has an influence on conduct."

Cicely, on her way to her place at table, with a plate of bacon and egg in one hand, and a cup of coffee in the other, stopped to remark that the weather as weather did not affect her at all. "Indeed," she said, complacently, "I'm just as happy on a wet November morning as in April when the daffodils dance."

"Then," said Christopher, "either you're posing or you're an unnatural creature . . . Is Glasgow a very ugly place, Miss Dobie?"

Beatrice, somewhat taken aback, paused. "Ugly?" she said; then in a burst of loyalty, "No, of course it isn't. Bits of it are dreadful as every city is dreadful, but it can be beautiful. It's built more or less on hills, and at night the lights hang festooned. And the river with the ships — —"

"I like a river," said Watty, "and shipyards, and ships going up and down. It must be fine to be an engineer."

"Not in these days," said Christopher. "Even school-mastering beats it. After all there's never any lack of boys, but ship-building's been pretty well at a standstill for some time."

"It's the saddest sight," said Beatrice, "to see a loch filled with swift ships laid up, idle and useless."

Mrs. Sellars sighed. "It's a strange new world and it's not a nice one. When one remembers the settled feeling of prosperity that once prevailed, the safety, the, the — —"

"The smugness," Cicely supplied. "Perhaps that had something to do with the muddle we're in now. 'Peace in our time,' they prayed, and played for safety, and on us the heavens have descended."

"Yes, but so far we haven't much reason to complain," her mother reminded her. "I'm almost ashamed when I think how much better off we are than most. . . . Well, what are the plans for to-day?"

"The Twins have invited Bee and me to lunch," Cicely said. "Where are you off to, Watty?"

"To see if the pond's bearing," said that youth, vanishing quickly.

Mrs. Sellars was about to rise in pursuit, but Christopher, who had risen to put out the flame under the heater on the sideboard, laid restraining hands on her.

"Don't worry, Mother," he said. "The ice won't be anything like bearing, and if he's fool enough to try, and goes in in the middle, it isn't deep enough to do him any harm. I say, Cicely, what about the show to-night? D'you think we could risk asking some people to make an audience? The chap's so keen about it."

Mrs. Sellars turned to explain to Beatrice that Mrs. Stopford, out of the kindness of her heart, had, in the previous summer, presented Watty with a small cinematograph camera. ("She has these impulses," Cicely put in.) Christopher had made a toy stage and fitted it up with tiny electric bulbs. "And," she concluded, "Watty wants to give an entertainment with the films he has taken."

"But how nice," said Beatrice.

"Not so very," said Cicely. "It's most trying for us all, I assure you. He's so anxious beforehand, poor Watty, and so downcast afterwards if his stunts don't come off. . . . I don't know, I'm sure. If the thing didn't work at all what would we do? I don't mean that the audience would mind, but what about the poor showman?"

"Does it often fail?" Beatrice asked.

"Almost invariably," said Christopher. "We haven't quite mastered it yet; but the other night it really worked wonderfully, and that's what put into Watty's head the idea of giving a show."

"Well, let's get an audience for him," Cicely cried recklessly. "What if the thing does fail? Watty must learn to laugh at failure, and at himself, or he'll never do any good in the world. . . . We'll only need sandwiches, Mother, and coffee, and we've loads of cake. . . . Would this room be best, Chris?"

"I think so. The two doors are such a convenience. My job's the lighting; also the musical numbers-in other words the gramophone records. Watty has his own ideas about what is suitable and has given me strict injunctions."

"What time shall I say, Mums?" Cicely asked. "8.30?"

"Won't it be rather a rush to get the room ready after dinner?"

"Not if we all help. I'm going to Granny now, and Bee and I'll go round the circle on our way to the Fairfaxes. That all right, Mother?"

"I think so. But you'll warn them, Cicely, won't you, not to expect too much?"

"Oh, we're easily amused in Oxlip," Cicely laughed.

The two girls dipped like swallows into three houses on their way to luncheon with the Twins and their father.

"How easy it is," said Beatrice, as they left the Stopford's house where their invitation had been enthusiastically accepted. "It's lovely to live in a village."

"It has its advantages," Cicely conceded. "Oxlip happens to be lucky in its inhabitants; we are all friendly with each other. But it can be very different. There's a village not far from this where practically no one is on speaking terms with anyone else. Awful? I should think it is. And yet taken separately they're quite pleasant people. It may be that they've simply got on each other's nerves."

"They should go and bury themselves in a city," said Beatrice, "that would 'learn' them."

"This is the Rectory," said Cicely. "You have met Mrs. Snow, I think. She has six sons, all clergymen, at least, practically all. Oh, Jane," to the maid who opened the door, "can I see Mrs. Snow for one minute? I know, it's mail day."

They found the Rector's wife seated at her bureau writing busily. "Now I know," said Cicely, "what that phrase 'immersed in correspondence' means. Are you too immersed to listen to my message? . . . This is my friend Beatrice Dobie, who is spending Christmas with us. You've met before."

Mrs. Snow took off her spectacles and blinked kindly at the girls. "I'm very glad to see you both. You'll stay and lunch with us? Norman is about somewhere."

"Thank you, but we're going to The Green. . . . Mother wonders if you and Mr. Snow would care to come in to-night for a little? Watty may or may not show us some films he has taken; anyway, we'll all have some coffee and conversation. Does it tempt you?"

"It does. Will you say to your mother that we'll be charmed. I know all about Watty's films. He's a friend of mine, Miss Dobie."

"Every boy is Mrs. Snow's friend," said Cicely.

"It comes, my dear, of having six sons of my own." She smiled at Beatrice and added, "They're all abroad, so no wonder my correspondence gets the better of me! It's my constant nightmare that I'll miss the different mails. I never have yet. Must you go? Well, we'll see you this evening. Thank you, my dear."

"Now, the Pughs," said Cicely. "Round here, 'ben a close and in a door-y,' as Colina's nursery rhyme said. Isn't the bright blue paint cheerful? They did it all themselves-Oh, here is Alice. No, thank you, we're not coming in, but could you bear to come to us this evening for a little? Yes, of course, Denis too. Not later than a quarter to nine. Watty's going to try to show us some films he's taken, and he'd be encouraged by your presence. That's good of you. We're lunching at The Green."

"And when," asked Mrs. Pugh, "will you bring Miss Dobie to lunch with us?" She turned to Beatrice saying, "I'd like to show you our funny little habitation. What about lunch to-morrow?"

"May we make it tea?" Cicely asked, "we've some people coming to us for lunch. That will be nice. Farewell for the nonce."

As they walked across the village green Beatrice remarked on the interesting face of the woman they had just left, and Cicely was only too glad of a chance to sing her friend's praises.

"Alice Pugh," she said, "is rather a wonder. As clever as they make them-her short stories are tremendously praised by people who know-yet thinking no better of herself for that, quite poor but quite contented, does most of her own work (Denis helps, of course) and cooks *the* most appetising food."

"Is 'Denis' clever too?"

"Very, in his own way. He couldn't write the wonderful spun-glass things Alice writes, but he's a good serious writer. Dull a bit: he's a scholar more than anything else. I'm not really surprised that he doesn't make much money. Happily for both, Alice admires him profoundly."

"It's very interesting," said Beatrice, "meeting people like the Pughs. You see, in Glasgow I only knew two classes-the well-to-do business people, and the very poor whom my mother tried to help. My relatives in Portland Place are business people with aspirations, and many of their friends are people who write and paint and make music and act, but it seemed to me they posed more than they worked. The Pughs are the real thing."

"Oh, they are," said Cicely, "and what's so nice about Alice is that she's not in the least narrow. Although I suppose you'd call her a real highbrow she's not precious; she can enjoy an ordinary story and wax enthusiastic about it, and she's easy to amuse and keeps her husband's spirits up when he declares that he sees starvation ahead, but when a windfall happens they let us all in to rejoice with them. It's far more amusing to be up and down than to know exactly where you are, and cut your coat neatly to your cloth."

"In a way, perhaps," said Beatrice, that child of a long line of careful business men, "but how difficult to housekeep!"

"Not a bit," said Cicely. "Bread and cheese when things are bad, and . . . Here we are; only five minutes late. Good morning, Millie" (to the fresh-faced maid who opened the door), "had you a nice Christmas? That's good."

Colonel Fairfax and his daughters were in the library, all three standing on the hearth-rug, all three absurdly alike. Many people wondered why Colonel Fairfax had not married again. His wife had been dead ten years, and a sensible woman at the head of affairs would have been good, they thought, both for the Twins and their father. But George Fairfax did not see it in that light. He had loved his wife very truly, and he could have said, like Austin Dobson's Georgian gentleman, that his ways were far too slow "to quite forget her." The Twins brought themselves up and ran the house to their own satisfaction and that of their father; it was a cheerful household.

Greetings over they sat down at a round table (round, Sarsa explained, so that there might be no jealousy about the head and the foot), and it was evident that pains had been taken with the planning of the meal.

Their father commented on it and the guests heartily agreed. Whereupon the Twins rose to their feet and solemnly bowed acknowledgment.

"Sarsa and I despise women who aren't good at their job," said Susan. "Whatever else a woman may do, she should first be able to cook a good meal and lay it prettily."

And Sarsa added, "Yes, but remember, we learned everything from Mrs. Cornfoot. If we'd had had a dragon of a cook where would we have been?"

"She wouldn't have been a dragon long with you, Sarsa," said Cicely. "You're warranted to melt the hardest heart."

"Yes," said Sarsa, dimpling, "I have rather a way with me."

"Conceited cat!" said Susan. "Cicely, I wonder you encourage her . . . Is Christopher coming to badminton this afternoon?"

"I'm not sure. He and Watty are busy fixing up the toy theatre for to-night. We hope you'll come and see Watty's films."

"Of course, we'll come," said Susan. "We helped him to take them. The best one is Voltaire playing with our Mungo. And the one of the boats isn't too bad. It'll be amusing to see them. Are you asking everybody?" She turned to Beatrice remarking, "That's the good thing about living in a village; there are so few of us that we can do everything together."

"It so happens," said Colonel Fairfax, "that in this case it is a good thing, for we are all agreeable together, but under other circumstances small village society can be rather terrible. I've seen it in Indian stations."

"The heat, perhaps!" said Susan, "making tempers short. My father," she explained to Beatrice, "was in India many years. Sarsa and I were born there just before the war began. We practically didn't know we had a father till we were quite big, for he hardly ever got home. Did you, Daddy?"

"No, I missed the nicest part of you."

"Oh, I wouldn't say *that*," said both the Twins together.

They went on, after lunch, to the village hall, where a number of people from the neighbourhood had collected to play badminton. Beatrice enjoyed watching the play, but nothing would induce her to take part, even after tea, when most of the others had departed, and Susan offered to teach her. She sat firm and shook her head.

"I'm not good at games," she repeated.

"That's feeble," said Susan. "Try anyway . . .," but persuasion was of no avail, and presently they all went home.

Cicely had sandwiches to make, and Beatrice helped her and earned compliments for her neat-handedness.

"There! That's heaps," Cicely declared, "for mother has made some savoury rolls and they're very popular, also little pastry tartlets. And there's that lovely iced cake you brought, and lots of little biscuits and chocolates."

The evening meal was hurried through that the room might be got ready for the entertainment, and they all helped to carry in chairs and arrange things. Then Granny Sellars was wheeled in and put right in front. Cicely said, "Only the first row will see anything, so Granny must be there, and Mums, and Mrs. Snow, and Mrs. Stopford, and Alice Pugh. The less worthy females-meaning you and me, Bee-will sit behind, and the Twins can squat on stools in front."

Beatrice had been told that they all decorated themselves as much as possible when it was Watty's evening, for he took these occasions very seriously, so she wore over her black dress a beautiful Spanish shawl that had belonged to her mother. Cicely was vivid in gleaming red. "It's a rag," she said, "but the colour's good. Isn't mother sweet in her old lace?"

"The dress itself is almost as old," said Mrs. Sellars, "but a good velvet is a wonderful thing for going on. Just look at Granny's."

"Yes," said the old lady complacently, "mine is pre-war. And my slippers too."

At that moment the Fairfax family came in, the Twins murmuring that they had put on for the occasion brand new frocks made by themselves.

"And," they added, "we painted our slippers to match!"

"The effect," said Christopher blandly, "leaves nothing to be desired."

"And here!" cried Cicely, "is Granny boasting that her dress was new before those children were born!"

The other guests arrived and were shown their places. Mrs. Stopford full of enthusiasm for things in general and the Sellars family in particular, Mrs. Pugh in a fichu, looking like a pretty edition of George Eliot; Mrs. Snow and her husband, both portly, in black.

Watty being out of the room, Mrs. Sellars seized the opportunity to apologise for the uncertain quality of the entertainment. "It may not come off," she said, "and it seems too bad to bring you here for such a performance, but Mrs. Stopford kindly gave him the camera and he is so keen about it, so we wanted to make a little celebration."

"Of course," said Mrs. Snow comfortably. "Dear Watty. We are glad of any excuse to have an evening with you, Mrs. Sellars."

"Indeed we are," said Mrs. Stopford, who, in a picture frock, with her white hair, was looking like some one out of a French memoir. "Basil and I jumped at the invitation. It's just the sort of evening I love and . . ." She faltered, meeting Granny Sellars' cold stare, and began to applaud vigorously as Watty emerged from the curtains that hung on either side of the table which held the toy stage with the screen. Christopher was invisible.

Watty, obviously very nervous, stammered out, "Ladies and gentlemen, I must tell you that these films aren't all taken by me. I bought the first. Ladies and gentlemen, it's very long and instructive about the Notre Dame in Paris, which is a church."

"Hear, hear," said Cicely, and the lights were put out. The gramophone began to bray, but was suddenly quenched, and Watty's voice was heard saying angrily, "I *told* you the Sonata was for the otter."

Cicely and Beatrice sank together in silent laughter, while the gramophone began again, this time with the *Marseillaise*, and Watty turned a handle with immense vigour. At first nothing happened, and the audience sat taut with dread in case nothing would happen and the show be a fiasco, but suddenly something appeared on the screen, and presently, a few inches at a time, the great cathedral was shown in its beauty.

"Wonderful!" said Granny Sellars. "I never thought to see Notre Dame again. I visited it with your grandfather when we were on our honeymoon; we studied it conscientiously with Baedeker. I almost recognise the gargoyles."

Watty, as showman, permitted himself to look pleased, and started winding up for his next film, which he announced had also been bought. It showed an otter diving for fish, to the strains of the Moonlight Sonata, in a weird green light supplied by Christopher. Then they had a film of some of the college boats in the races, but the popular feature of the evening was the film taken in the garden of 'Twixt Bears, featuring Mungo Fairfax and Voltaire Sellars doing tricks with Christopher. That had to be repeated twice. Then Watty said, "Ladies and gentlemen, that's all the show. Thank you for coming."

"Isn't he *sweet?*" Mrs. Stopford's voice was heard to exclaim, but happily Watty did not hear the remark.

The lights were put up, and there was a feeling of relief after a strain. Beatrice found herself beside Denis Pugh. She had been anxious to see Alice Pugh's husband, but found his appearance disappointing. He was slight and rather small, with a large head, and an anxious expression as if he distrusted life and what it might do to him and his. Also, he seemed disinclined for conversation.

"Shall we go into the other room now?" Mrs. Sellars asked, but Basil Stopford said: "Why not continue the entertainment? I suggest that the Misses Fairfax favour us with a song and dance?"

To the amazement and admiration of Beatrice the Twins rose without demur, and sang a song of their own composing, finishing with a neat step dance. In their flowered chiffon dresses they looked the prettiest pair, and loud applause greeted their efforts.

"Now charades," said Basil, and in a trice had chosen a team to go out and act a word.

To Beatrice it seemed little short of miraculous that people should be able to make up what seemed to her quite witty conversation on the spur of the moment, and she shuddered at the thought that anything of the kind might be expected from her.

To Christopher, who happened to be standing near, she said, "Aren't they very good? How do they *do* it?"

"Good? Oh, I don't know," said Christopher. "Denis is really good-he's our star-turn in theatricals-and Susan's a clever actress, but the rest of us are pretty sticky, I think. Don't you act yourself?" and laughed at the look of horror the suggestion brought to the girl's face.

It was Mrs. Snow who broke up the party, to the relief of the hostess, who feared the effect of late hours and excitement on her mother-in-law.

No one would have dared to suggest that Granny Sellars should go to bed. She had enjoyed the evening-she always liked a talk with Mrs. Snow, whom she respected as a good mother and a good housekeeper-and had been, for her, most amiable. Though she had to live in England, and pretty nearly everything was wrong with the world that could be wrong, still, it was pleasant at a time, she acknowledged to herself, to see friends and neighbours, to watch the antics of youth, and to feel in one's old heart something of the warmth and kindness of Christmas-time.

CHAPTER XVII

"Is my girl happy
That I thought hard to leave,
And has she tired of weeping,
As she lies down at eve?"

A. E. Housman.

Cicely had named a week when she had given her invitation to 'Twixt Bears, and Beatrice grudged every hour of that week passing. She felt as much at home as if she had known the Sellars all her life, and not only the Sellars but also their friends.

The Twins called her "Trixy" and wrote a song in her praise, which they sang to her with banjo accompaniment and great solemnity. Mrs. Stopford said she had never met anyone with whom she felt so much at one, which was gratifying, though Beatrice had a lurking suspicion that the lady must have made the same statement more than once before.

Mrs. Snow showed her photographs of all her sons, and read her bits from their various letters.

Alice Pugh talked to her of books and pictures and people, and at Beatrice's request, made out a list of books that she (Alice) thought should not be missed.

Beatrice told her "My mother and I loved books-old ones specially, though we bought all the best new ones, guided by the Book Society; in fact, I suppose we were the sort of people the Book Society exists to help-people who don't recognise the highest when they see it-but I've never lived among the writers of books-the *makers*. It makes it all so much more interesting, more exciting."

"Have you lots of time for reading?" Mrs. Pugh asked her.

"Lots. Practically all the time there is. At the moment I may be said to be at a loose end; I've got to try and decide what to make of my life."

"That sounds thrilling."

"Does it? It feels rather dismal."

"It's what I would have loved," Alice said, "to choose and see my path, as the hymn says, but somehow Denis was always there blocking up the horizon for me. I'm not sorry," she added, "we shall never make money, nor name, nor fame, but life is pretty good as it is."

Beatrice sighed as she said: "Oxlip is such a beloved place to live in."

"Well, don't be so doleful about it-you can make your choice of a place wherein to pitch your tent. If you've enough to live on you're a lucky woman."

"I know I am-in a way. But it must be great fun to work as Cicely works-as you do."

Alice laughed. "There's a great uncertainty in our way of living, if that is fine. . . . When does Cicely resume her editorial labours?"

"Tuesday. I go back with her."

"Tuesday," said Cicely, hearing the last sentence and joining the couple at the fire. "Tuesday, as ever was. Holidays go like a flash, but it was good of Jane Naesmyth to give me a whole week. I'm glad to go back in a way. I like London, it's the only place to live in, but I've been thinking, Bee, why don't you stay on for a bit at 'Twixt Bears? Mother would love to have you. You like the place, you say, and there's nothing immediate taking you back to London. Why not stay on for a week or two anyway, till Christopher and Watty go back to school? I own I'd like to think of you here with Mother, you can make things easier for her in so many ways."

"Do you really think" —Beatrice had flushed deeply —"that your mother would care to have me stay on after you go?"

"I'm sure she would," Cicely said heartily. "You've fitted in so comfortably it hasn't been like having a stranger at all. If you're sure you'd like to."

"Like?" said Beatrice. "Why, I'd love it. To be with some one like your mother means much to me, and in those few days I've grown so fond of Oxlip and its inhabitants that I hate to think of leaving."

"Then that's settled," said Cicely briskly, and Alice Pugh murmured, "So you see, the path lies straight before you."

Walking home together Beatrice was loud in gratitude to Cicely for her suggestion, so much so, indeed, that Cicely became restive.

"But it's not kind," she protested; "indeed it's rather selfish. It eases my mind to think of you here with Mother, helping her with Granny when she is in one of her moods, and able to do all sorts of little things to save her steps. You're almost too-too *deprecating*, Bee, my dear. I'd advise you to put a higher value on yourself. It doesn't do to go through the world oozing gratitude to people who are merely serving their own ends. If you don't take care you'll develop an inferiority complex. You're always so sure you can't do a thing when all you need is to try. The other day at badminton nothing would induce you to attempt to play. The same with charades. It's pretty feeble, you know, to behave like that. Everybody's got to begin some time, and how are you going to accomplish anything if you refuse to make a start?"

"Oh, I know," Beatrice said humbly. "But perhaps you don't realise what it means to suffer as I do from shyness."

"I don't know about shyness," said Cicely, drily, "to me it looks more like a form of self-conceit; you're afraid you won't shine and you prefer not to risk it. Bee, I'm being horribly rude I know, but faithful are the wounds of a friend. You tell me some home truths now."

But Beatrice was silent; Cicely's words had gone home, and to herself she admitted the truth of them. A scene came back to her mind, a scene she was never able quite to forget: a Christmas party at the Lithgows when Peggy and she had been girls of fifteen or so. They were playing a game. The figure of a tail-less donkey had been fastened to a screen and they had to try to pin on the tail. Each one in turn took the tail, was blindfolded and twirled round to lose the sense of direction and started off. Some never reached the donkey, confusedly walking in another direction till brought up against a wall or a window; others reached the donkey but pinned the tail to its head or legs, and each ludicrous effort called forth shouts of laughter. Beatrice remembered vividly how she had suffered in spirit with those who reached no objective at all. . . . At last the dreaded moment had come when she had to make the attempt. She had taken the tail and the pin in each trembling hand, and stood, with her breath coming short, as they tied the handkerchief round her eyes and twirled her round three times. Then, dizzy and faint, she realised that she was not properly blinded: the handkerchief had slipped and she could see just a little, enough to give her the direction. Very slowly and hesitatingly she advanced until she recognised a patch of donkey, then she pinned the tail almost where it should have been. It was not until she heard the sound of applause that she realised what she had done, then, tearing the handkerchief from her eyes, she gazed wildly at them all, the laughing children, the benignly interested grown-ups, longing to cry: "the handkerchief wasn't right: I could see! I cheated —I cheated," but her tongue was like a stick in her dry mouth and she could not make a sound.

"Well done, Be'trice!" Mrs. Lithgow had called out, and the company had cheered again. Only Peggy had remarked as she handed her the prize: "My word, Bee, you couldn't have done it more neatly if you had *keeked!*"

Beatrice had gone home a miserable child, to lie awake for hours crying over what she had done. She had cheated at a game, and no more terrible thing could be said of any Briton. And yet she had meant no harm, had desired no kudos-indeed she was hardly aware of what she was doing-to get the ordeal over, that was all she had cared about. But oh! how she wished that she had made herself a laughing-stock for the amusement of others rather than won by cheating. She had been far too deeply ashamed to mention the episode to anyone, but the thought of it had often come back to disturb, and now it seemed to rise up and accuse her.

Cicely was right; her words sounded cruel but they were true. Why had she been in such a state of fright over a silly game? Was it not because she had been afraid of being laughed at, had not liked to be made to look a fool? Peggy, she remembered, had never cared in the least what people thought of her actions, seemed, indeed, rather to enjoy being laughed at, but she, Beatrice, had clung to her dignity-or was it conceit?

Cicely, suddenly becoming aware of her companion's silence, turned to her, rather conscience-stricken.

"I say, Bee, was I rude just now? I didn't mean to be."

Then Beatrice, to her own great astonishment, started to blurt out all the story of the Lithgow party.

"So you see," she finished, miserably, "you were right about my conceit, it even made me cheat."

Cicely treated the confession lightly.

"I can quite understand how it happened," she said. "Parties are apt to be an ordeal to an only child. No wonder you were scared of them all hooting and laughing. Having no brothers or sisters you hadn't learned to laugh at yourself, so you were driven to cheat-and I daresay you've tormented yourself a hundred times with the thought of it?"

"Yes, but I don't believe I ever shall again-now that I've told you."

"That," said Cicely, "is what's called 'sharing.' I know a girl who belongs to a Group Movement and 'sharing' is one of their slogans."

"I rather like the idea," said Beatrice. "Do tell me."

"Oh, they confess in meetings and things-you wouldn't like that. Tell me, were you sincere when you said you'd like to stay on here for a bit?"

There was complete sincerity in the girl's tone when she replied: "There is nothing I'd like so much-if your mother will have me."

"Oh, Mother will have you very gladly, if you're sure you wouldn't be bored to death. I warn you it's very quiet without the boys. Mother doesn't care about leaving Granny much, though of course the neighbours look in very frequently and would take you out. If you stayed you would really be conferring a favour."

"Oh — —" said Beatrice unbelievingly. Then, "I can only stay if a proper arrangement is made about-board."

"Toots!" said Cicely, "you're no expense. I'm very sure Mother wouldn't hear of such a thing. We're not so poor that we can't afford to have a friend to stay with us. You save up your money till you need it. No, honestly, Bee, you will spoil it all if you insist on payment-Mother takes a real pride in being hospitable."

Beatrice said no more. Cicely's words had made it clear to her that the Sellars believed her to have a very modest income, and were glad that she should stay with them as their guest, and save her money for future needs. It was wonderfully generous, but could she let them continue in this belief? It was so difficult to say —"But you must let me pay! I've heaps of money." Then she would merely be a rich "parlour-boarder," or paying guest, and most of the freedom and intimacy of their relations with each other would be gone. And yet, in how many ways she could help if she only might! Mrs. Sellars spent practically nothing on herself; any money that would have gone on dress and small luxuries went to keep Watty at school. Cicely badly needed a hard-wearing fur coat, but would never dream of spending on herself the twenty pounds that would be wanted for it.

That night, after Granny Sellars had gone to bed, and Watty, too, had yawned himself off after a long day with Voltaire on the marsh, the four that were left gathered round the fire, which was too good to leave, and talked idly.

Cicely's thoughts were already with her work in London, and she was full of her plans and all she hoped to do. Her mother sighed to hear her and said, "I shall be left desolate on Tuesday when I lose both my girls."

"Well," said Cicely, "I must go, of course, but there's nothing very urgent calling for Bee. I was suggesting to her that she might stay on here with you, Mother, until she decides what she wants to do."

"Would you, my dear?" Mrs. Sellars asked.

"If you're sure I wouldn't be in the way I'd love it," said Beatrice. "I haven't made any plans yet. I'm afraid I'm not very good at plans. . . . I don't think I'll go back to Portland Place. My step-relations were very good about taking me in when our home in Glasgow was broken up, but it is such a busy house and I sometimes felt my room would be better than my company. I must get some voluntary work to do —I don't need to take a salary-and I'm hoping Cicely and Miss Naesmyth will help me about that, but, in the meantime, if you would let me stay on with you for a little time in this dear place, you'd be doing me a very great kindness."

Mrs. Sellars laid her hand on the girl's as she said:

"You're more than welcome, my dear. I was quite dreading your going;" while Christopher, rising to knock his pipe on the hearth said, "That's splendid!"

"Quite," thought Beatrice, "as if he meant it."

CHAPTER XVIII

"Sure this robe of mine
Doth change my disposition."

The Winter's Tale.

Cicely, before she departed in Ulysses, gave Beatrice many directions. "Remember," she said, "you're to be the daughter of the house. Don't let Mother work too hard, and don't let the boys get out of hand. When Watty goes Voltaire will be in your charge; give him a walk when you feel like it, but don't let him go down rabbit-holes or you'll have to wash him. Ruth will help you. Good-bye, everybody. A Happy New Year to you. Hope the play'll be a success. Be sure to write me every detail-Bless you, Mother. . . ."

Arriving in London without mishap, Cicely parked Ulysses and was soon in Miss Naesmyth's room.

"Well," said that lady, pausing in the act of opening letters, "you look well. Had a good holiday?"

"The best. Just wait till I get off my coat and hat."

Cicely was back in a minute, to answer Jane Naesmyth's enquiries about her mother and the others.

"Oh, Mother is very well. She liked your present most awfully-but I expect she wrote."

"Yes, she wrote. I was glad to see from her letter that Beatrice Dobie was a success as a visitor. Your mother seemed delighted with her."

"We all were," said Cicely. "She fitted in most beautifully and was so willing to be pleased, and appreciative of everything-in short, the ideal guest. Granny was quite civil to her. Watty took to her."

"And Christopher?"

"I think so, but Christopher doesn't say much. Oh, I see what you mean, but, of course, that is entirely out of the question. Poor old Chris, has no money and will probably never be able to afford to marry."

"And Beatrice came back with you?" Miss Naesmyth asked.

"No. I left her at 'Twixt Bears. She seemed to want to stay on and it's very nice for Mother to have her. She makes herself very useful, and you've simply no idea what a happy creature she is in an environment that suits her. Her eyes quite lost that anxious look that worried me when I met her first."

"She showed no partiality for the tops of wardrobes? . . . You remember you said she reminded you of a little cat you had that was so scared of people that it remained aloft."

"Did I say that to you?" said Cicely. "I said it to Christopher, and he was very short with me; seemed to think it rather an offensive simile-there's something very old-fashioned about Christopher's attitude to women. No, Bee wasn't a bit scared with us. She seemed to feel at home at once. And we never felt we had a visitor in the house. That's why I could leave her with Mother. As the late Lord Tennyson wrote, 'She'll be a better child to her than I have ever been.' Didn't you ever weep over the May Queen? *'Don't let Effie come to see me till my grave is growing green. . . .'* I say, what a pile of letters! But it's good to be back. Had you the quiet time you promised yourself?"

"Absolutely. Every one was away or engaged, and I had a perfect holiday. I read books I'd wanted for months to read; I wrote letters that had been lying on my conscience; I turned out drawers and burned rubbish; I had a grand parade of all my clothes and sent what I could use to be tidied, and gave the rest away to people who will be glad of them. Katie made me all the things I like best to eat. I feel perfectly rested and tidied up, and able for any amount of work."

"Fine," said Cicely, "we are two giants refreshed. Now, then, what about it?"

Later, as they went out together, Jane said:

"Of course, Beatrice Dobie is paying a board now that she is staying on indefinitely?"

"Well, no, she isn't," said Cicely. "She wanted to, insisted in fact, and pointed out that wherever she went she would be paying, but it was going to spoil things so. For one thing Mother would have hated the idea. And one more is very little extra expense; living's cheap in the country and we never keep household books anyway. Mother declares that it makes her so hard to note down every item, and as she never spends money except on necessaries she doesn't think it matters."

Jane laughed. "Your dear mother! that's so like her. I'd be miserable if I didn't keep careful books; it's the different way we're made."

* * * * *

Beatrice was rather surprised to find that things went on much the same without Cicely. True, they missed her greatly; her ready, merry speech was a loss, no less than her sunshine presence; but meals were still eaten to the accompaniment of small jokes and laughter, the fires burned as cheerfully, the lamps gave the same mellow light, nothing of the glamour left 'Twixt Bears with the departure of the daughter of the house.

Beatrice found many ways in which she could help her hostess. She took Cicely's place as lady-in-waiting to Granny Sellars, standing by while she dressed in the morning, and seeing her ensconced comfortably in the living-room for the day, with the daily paper, books, work, a magnifying glass, a bottle of smelling salts, not to mention two pairs of spectacles. The old lady found difficulty in deciphering the newspapers and liked to have the news read to her. Beatrice flattered herself that she could do that well. She had a sweet voice, and read distinctly and with intelligence, as she had been taught by her mother.

"It's a pleasure," she was told one morning, "to be able to hear what is happening, not to have the leaders yattered over as they are when my grandchildren read them. You might see if there is anything interesting in the correspondence."

Beatrice was in the middle of a letter complaining of something iniquitous that was happening somewhere, when Susan Fairfax suddenly put her head round the door.

"You're here!" she said, advancing; then, "Good-morning, Mrs. Sellars. I hope you are well."

"Fairly, thank you. You are an early visitor."

"Aren't I? I came with an S.O.S. to Trixy here. Lavinia Pierce has failed us. She was to have taken a part in our play to-morrow night and instead she's taken whooping-cough." Susan gave a small giggle which she suppressed instantly and proceeded: "It's dreadful for her of course, but it's dreadful for us too. Trix, will you take the part? There is literally no one else. It's only a sentence or two, Trix; you could do it on your head."

Granny Sellars leant back in her chair and drew her shawl round her, her face registering deep disapproval, while Beatrice, flushed and frightened, protested that she had never acted, and never could act, and would Susan kindly go at once and look for some one else.

"But I've told you," Susan said patiently, "that there is-literally-no one else. Oh, Christopher," as that young man entered the room, "help me to persuade Trix to act instead of Lavinia. She's got whooping-cough, poor thing. Tell her it's only a tiny part, and even if she's never acted before she simply couldn't fail in it. You remember it? The visitor, who comes in near the end with a message that puts the lid on? It's really important, although it's so small."

Meanwhile Beatrice, though still panic-stricken at the thought of speaking in public, had remembered Cicely's judgment-that the refusal to attempt anything in case of failure was merely a form of conceit, and had made up her mind that, even if she did make a mess of it, she must try.

Before Christopher could say anything, she turned to Susan and said: "If you're sure you can't get anyone else, I'll try, but I warn you that when the moment comes, as likely as not I won't be able to utter a word through sheer panic."

Susan immediately embraced her, then tardily remembering her manners, turned to apologise to Granny Sellars for her intrusion. She said: "Do please forgive me rushing in like this. I shan't keep you from the papers another minute, though what people find to read in them I simply don't know. . . . Rehearsal this afternoon at two, Trix. Here's the script. I hope you aren't cross with me, Mrs. Sellars?"

As the door closed behind the girl Mrs. Sellars spoke. "Ill-bred creatures those Twins are! What my mother would have said to a girl of eighteen (dressed so like a boy that one has to look twice to make sure what she is) bursting into a room without a by your leave, interrupting what is going on, and starting on some business of her own. Impertinent brat!"

Christopher tried to placate his elderly relative.

"Susan's all right, Granny," he said. "Only she gets so keen about whatever she has in hand she forgets everything else. She didn't mean to be rude when she interrupted your reading, but she had to obtain her objective, so to speak."

Granny Sellars replied only with a sniff, and Christopher turned to Beatrice saying: "It's jolly good of you to give us a hand. We've so few to draw on that when one drops out we're lost. Don't let yourself worry about it, for though we all forget our parts it won't greatly matter."

Beatrice shook her head, being unable to take such a light view of the matter, and as soon as she had finished her task escaped to her own room to study her part.

It was small, as Susan had said, only a matter of about three sentences, but it meant a good deal to the meaning of the play, and it was important that the audience should hear every word distinctly:

"I have a message from Lady Porter to her son."

Who was Lady Porter? Alice Pugh, she thought; and Basil Stopford was the son.

Beatrice had been at one rehearsal with Cicely, but every one had laughed and talked so much that it had been impossible to follow the action of the play. She remembered Christopher making rather wooden love to Susan, and Sarsa impudent as a stage housemaid, but had no recollection of Lavinia Pierce doing her part. She looked rather hopelessly at the directions. What was "up stage" and "down stage"? She would be told, doubtless, and also drilled in how she should say her lines, but the evening loomed before her as the Red Sea must have done before the children of Israel, and she could see nothing on the other side.

Christopher and she were both so busy repeating their parts that they never exchanged a remark on their way to the village hall that afternoon. When they reached it they found everything in a state of direst confusion. The village carpenter had promised to put up the stage the day before but had been prevented, he said, through excess of work, and had only now started and the noise he and his boy were making made rehearsing an impossibility.

"Terribly tiresome," wailed Mrs. Stopford. "It is so necessary that we rehearse on a stage in order to know our positions and so forth. Christopher, couldn't you get-what's-his-name?"

"Sammy?" said her son.

"Is it? No, of course it's Smith. Couldn't you get Smith to stop hammering for an hour? Urge him to go away and come back later. The stage is there, you see, though not finished, and we could use it. It's entirely his own fault not doing it yesterday; he was probably only putting up a hen-house."

"No," said Sarsa solemnly, "it was a funeral."

"Oh!" Mrs. Stopford was silenced for a moment, but she began again. "Well, anyway, he simply must leave us in peace till four o'clock."

Christopher asked the joiner if the stage could be used, and receiving a somewhat sulky answer in the affirmative, suggested that he and his helper might find another job for an hour or two.

Smith pointed out with some heat that jobs couldn't be picked up and laid down at a moment's notice, and continued to hammer. Then Mrs. Stopford thought of a plan: "What about having a rest at the Two Bears?" she suggested. "Have a cup of coffee or something and tell them I sent you."

In a moment Smith and his coadjutor had downed tools and made off, while Colonel Fairfax looking after them remarked pensively: "Now you've sent them straight into temptation. It wasn't the thought of coffee that lit that spark in Smith's eye."

The lady looked guilty. "You don't think —? I never heard that Smith drank. He's only glad of a chance of a seat by the fire and some one to argue with. He's a Socialist, you know."

"He'll probably be a Communist after to-day," Christopher prophesied. "Well, shall we begin?"

They began and stumbled through it somehow, and when her cue came Beatrice walked very stiffly on to the stage and in a voice which she did not recognise as her own, managed to repeat her few sentences.

"It wasn't very bad, was it?" Christopher asked her as they walked home together when it was all over, and Smith, maligned man, perfectly sober but suitably morose, had again begun to hammer. "I mean making your first appearance upon any stage? You came on with great dignity and didn't seem at all nervous."

Beatrice gave rather a shaky laugh. "I don't know how I managed to walk on or say anything intelligible, for I was absolutely demoralised with fright. It was all I could do to keep from giving a loud shriek and bursting into tears."

"As bad as that? It's cruel to ask you. But you've got the worst over now. I promise you, you won't care half as much to-morrow night when the audience is there."

"Oh, don't say that. I simply daren't think of the audience —a warm, big, breathing beast ready to spring at me! My only consolation is that I actually am attempting something at last. I've been a shirker all my life so far; if I was afraid of a thing I simply didn't attempt it. To you it must seem desperately silly."

"No," said Christopher, "it seems to me extraordinarily plucky. It's fatally easy to shirk, but I don't think one is so apt to give way to it after once having the feeling of satisfaction that fills one in attempting some difficult task and succeeding. . . . How did the performances strike you as a whole?"

"Oh, I can't tell you —I took nothing in. I was simply repeating over and over again, '*I have a message for Lady Porter, . . . Are you Lady Porter?*'"

Christopher laughed. "Never mind. After to-morrow we'll dismiss Lady Porter for good and all. All the same this may give you a taste for acting that you'll never lose."

"I doubt it," said Beatrice.

* * * * *

But that night when all was over and Beatrice stood, flushed and triumphant, with the rest of the company on the stage, bowing acknowledgment to the applause so unstintedly given, she felt the hitherto unknown delight of being one of a team. It was a very small success but it was her first.

CHAPTER XIX

"'Tis well: and I have met a gentleman."

The Taming of the Shrew.

While Beatrice was having her small triumph, and enjoying herself at 'Twixt Bears, her old friend Mrs. Lithgow was not entirely easy in her mind about the girl. The letters about the cottage and its occupants made her feel vaguely suspicious. Who were those people? How had Beatrice become acquainted with them? And why had she not gone with her own relations to Madeira?

It was the second day of January and Mrs. Lithgow and Peggy were sitting in the morning-room, working and talking. They had so much to talk about, the mother and daughter-the festivities just past, the doings of their various friends, Peggy's approaching marriage-they never, as Mrs. Lithgow put it, "ran out of crack."

They were discussing at the moment some of Peggy's relations to be, cousins from London who had come north for the New Year celebrations.

"They're nice," Mrs. Lithgow was saying, "nice, and willing to be pleased. I told Mr. Henderson that I was surprised he would go away to England to be a barrister when there is a Bar in Edinburgh, but he said there was more money to be made at the English Bar. That's quite a good reason. His wife's a gentle creature and very English. Do you know who she reminded me of? Be'trice Dobie. I felt all the time I was with her that I was talking to Be'trice. I asked Mrs. Henderson if she'd ever met Lady Dobie and she said she hadn't, but she often saw her name and her daughter's in the papers. Lady Dobie seems quite a leader of fashion. . . . isn't it a queer thing that Be'trice didn't go with them to Madeira? It would only have been natural it seems to me if she had spent the first Christmas after her dear mother's death with her own relatives. But mebbe they didn't press her to go; we can't tell. Be'trice said she didn't want to go and perhaps she didn't. Did you notice, Peggy, that though she never said a word against her step-sister, she was never what you would call warm about her? Well, if Lady Dobie wasn't kind to her it wasn't fair—a girl alone in the world."

Peggy looked up from the paper she was glancing at, and grinned. "No need to work yourself up, Mother, when you don't know the facts. Bee seemed to be having quite a good time in Portland Place. Probably she didn't want to go to Madeira—I'd have hated it myself, though a village in the depths of the country isn't my idea of perfect bliss either."

"Now, there's another thing," said her mother, "who are these Sellars? There's a son—I just hope he isn't a fortune-hunter. Be'trice is so unsuspicious, poor thing."

"They sound all right," Peggy said. "I never heard Bee come so near enthusiasm as in her description of the family and their habitation. If she's so fond of the country she should settle down in it. She could take a little place and run it herself-though that seems absurd when she has Greenbraes standing eating its head off. . . . Well, I'd better get on with these towels. Isn't it a blessing I'm sticking to L. Lithgow-Lendrum-for I've had so much practice in embroidering it?"

"Yes," said her mother, not listening, "I must write to Be'trice this very moment. It's disgraceful; I've never thanked her for the lovely present she sent."

"I thanked her at once for mine," Peggy said, self-righteously. "But you've had so many things to think of lately, and so much to manage, I'm sure Beatrice will forgive you."

"Well, I'll start now in case I forget, for my memory is something awful. The steps I give myself for nothing! Up to the top of the house-and then I can't remember what took me there."

"Just stand till it comes back to you," Peggy advised.

"I'd be standing all day at that rate," retorted her mother, and sitting down squarely at her writing-table, selected a pen, took one of her larger sheets of writing-paper and began.

"Fancy! This is the first letter I've written this year: I'll tell her that."

"Dearest Beatrice,

"My first letter this New Year is to you, and I'm sure I hope it will be a really good New Year to you in every way.

"You will have had some very sad thoughts during these past days, but what can we do? I must confess I always find this time of year very trying. Just to think of how many doors that were hospitably open to me are now closed by death! And there seems to be a lot of serious illness in our circle at present. I've three friends in nursing homes, two not expected to recover. You will be sorry to hear that Mrs. Murray is never much better. I saw her the day before yesterday-the last day of the Old Year-and she was wearing the lovely jacket you sent her.

"She is proud of it and so pleased that you remembered her. I would not be surprised if she went very suddenly. She is almost entirely confined to bed now. It is dull for Mr. Murray and the boys. I am perfectly ashamed to think that I haven't thanked you yet for your very kind present to me. It is just the sort of thing that appeals to me, and I use it every day. Mr. Lithgow, too, was delighted to be remembered, and he said I was to tell you that you are the first woman he ever knew who could choose good cigars. I heard him recommending them highly last night to all the gentlemen. For we had a party, you must know. Quite a big one. Mostly our own and Lendrum relations, among them a Mr. and Mrs. Henderson from London, cousins of Mr. Lendrum. He is at the English Bar, and seems to be doing well; quite a clever man. I asked Mrs. Henderson if she knew Lady Dobie, thinking perhaps she might have met you, but no. Everything went off well, lots of laughing and joking, as was natural at such an occasion, and I must say Peggy made the table look lovely. Peggy is as bright as ever. The wedding is fixed for 11th February. That seemed to be a date that suited everybody, and they are going to Ireland for their wedding trip. I'm sure I don't know why, a wet, unpleasant place in the winter, I should think, and so difficult to get at, and de Valera behaving like that and all, but they say they want to go to a place that is quite new to them both, and to cross the sea gives a suggestion of adventure. What it is to be young! But father and I can't help rejoicing to see the couple so devoted to each other. Harry is sometimes in before we have finished breakfast to tell Peggy something that has occurred to him about the house, or show her a letter, or tell her about a present.

"Peggy declares she came off poorly this Xmas, for people were holding off for her wedding. It's only natural if they were, but I can't say I noticed any falling off, but of course it was one of her jokes. Father says Brackenbrae-that's the name of their house, isn't it nice? and very likely it was once a bracken brae-will be a very cheery place with two people in it both so fond of a joke.

"I just hope that they will be able to keep their high spirits, for life is a struggle for every one just now. Not that we've much to complain of. I said to father last night that I was thankful we were in an essential trade; every luxury trade, except perhaps tobacco, is more or less on the rocks.

"I'm glad to see that you seem to have enjoyed your Xmas. I was just a wee bit surprised to hear that you hadn't gone to Madeira with your step-brother and his family; it would have been a fine change for you, but of course, it is no business of mine and I'm very glad that you had nice friends to go to.

"Did you say the Sellars were Edinburgh people? Father thinks he remembers a Sellars being Lord Provost or something in Edinburgh, but it may not be the same.

"I'm so thankful that we've got begun to a New Year. Hogmanay always did give me a creepy feeling, and it gets worse with the years. We turned on the wireless and heard Big Ben strike midnight and I just said to myself, 'What will have happened to us by next New Year?' It's a solemn thought. I hope I'm not faithless, but life is a frightening thing and the future dark to us all, and the most frightful things happen to quite decent people every day in the papers.

"But I did not mean to write like this and depress you, and you mebbe depressed enough already. Many a time I think of you, my dear, and I never forget you in my prayers. I hope some day soon you will marry a good man. I would not like to see you throw yourself away on a fortune-hunter, but I'm sure you won't; your mother's daughter has too much sense.

"Peggy sends you her blessing (so she says) and her love, and wishing you all good in the New Year,

"I remain,

"Your affectionate old friend,

"Nettie Lithgow.

"P.S. —What a queer name for a house —'Twixt Bears-has it anything to do with a Zoo?

"P.SS. —Be sure and let me know any particulars you hear about Fairlie's marriage, for I am greatly interested. I sent her a little present, and had such a nice grateful letter.

N. L."

This letter was lying on the oak chest in the hall when Beatrice came in with Christopher and Watty from an afternoon's toboganing, for snow had followed the frost, and Oxlip had thrown itself with enthusiasm into winter sports. The three came in laughing and talking and apologising for being so late for tea.

"It was such fun," said Beatrice, "we couldn't bear to stop. You didn't wait for us, I hope?"

"No," said Mrs. Sellars. "At least I gave Granny her tea at the usual time, but I waited-hurry now, Watty, and get off those wet boots and wash."

In a very short time they were all in the living-room devouring hot buttered toast.

Christopher sat beside his grandmother, regaling her with small items of news as he ate.

"Yes, every one was there, Gran': practically every able-bodied person in the place. It's a chance we don't often get."

"Were those Twins there?"

"They were; but why 'those'?"

"Ill-bred girls," said Granny Sellars. "I never saw worse manners. . . . Surely Mrs. Stopford wasn't tobogganing? A woman of her age."

"I don't know Mrs. Stopford's age, but she was certainly tobogganing, and enjoying it. Mr. Snow was her companion. Mrs. Snow looked on but refused to venture, said she'd heard that it was very dangerous for stout people to meet with an accident and have to lie in bed; it seems it's apt to give pneumonia."

Granny Sellars regarded her grandson suspiciously.

"I never heard of that," she said. "But Mrs. Snow was well advised not to make a fool of herself. I wonder at Mr. Snow's encouraging Mrs. Stopford in her folly, but of course she is rich and a good giver."

"You enjoyed it, Beatrice?" Mrs. Sellars said, holding out her hand for the girl's cup.

"Oh, I did," said Beatrice, her eyes shining. "I'd never tobogganed before. I've had the chance, often, but I never dared attempt it, somehow. But with Christopher and Watty there, not to speak of the moral support of the Twins, I felt bold enough to try, and once I began I couldn't stop. I'll be off to Switzerland next for winter sports, who knows?"

"That's what I'd like to do," said Watty wistfully.

"Watty never gets his fill of snow," said his mother, while his brother suggested that an antarctic expedition was the thing for Watty.

"Yes," said Watty, "that's what I'm going to be-an explorer," but Beatrice cried out in protest at the idea.

"You wouldn't want to do what that man did, remain buried under snow for months? That, to me, is the most wonderful, terrible feat ever accomplished. I can understand, in a way, the lure of flying over vast continents and strange seas, but to lie like that in darkness. . . . Most people would have gone stark staring mad. The thought of the weight of snow above one would have brought a feeling of unbearable suffocation. And the silence, the solitude. . . ."

"I know," Christopher agreed. "He must have had a marvellous grip of himself; absolutely no nerves."

"Perhaps," said Mrs. Sellars, "he was of a very meditative disposition, and welcomed the long hours of inactivity-to have time to think!"

"Or perhaps," said Watty, "he was like me, always wakened too soon in the morning, and was glad of a long lie for once."

"Tuts," said Granny Sellars, "I've no patience with those 'stunts' as they call them, speed records and so on, it's nothing but a tempting of Providence."

"It's such a strange idea that Providence can be tempted," Christopher began, but his mother broke in with "You're remembering that you're dining out to-night, Christopher."

Christopher groaned. "Am I not? The prospect has blackened my day. How I loathe dining out!"

His mother shook her head admonishingly at him as she said, "It is kind of Mrs. Eltham to ask you."

"Oh, no, it isn't. She needed another man and I was the handiest. I know those Eltham dinners. Mrs. Eltham, terribly vivacious, trying to goad her family into brightness and only succeeding in making them sulky. The house is cold, and the food is cold, and we play bridge after dinner and every one quarrels. To-night it may even be games. You don't know how well off you all are to be stopping at home."

Later Beatrice read her letter and smiled over it, for it brought her friend so vividly before her, her pessimism that was only on the surface, her interest in all and sundry, her complete satisfaction with her lot. Evidently Mrs. Lithgow was slightly suspicious of Beatrice's new friends. She wanted more information about the Sellars. Fortune-hunters were always at the back of her mind in connection with Beatrice, and Christopher was the suspect at present. Poor Christopher, thought Beatrice. Was there anyone less of a fortune-hunter? Why, he didn't even know that she had a penny. His kindness was entirely disinterested, nothing more than he would have bestowed on any guest of his mother. Besides, was it not fairly obvious that he was attracted to the Susan Twin? It seemed to Beatrice that he listened more attentively when Susan spoke, laughed more readily at her jests, was more tender to her faults, and surely that meant only one thing.

Well, she was a lucky girl, for though Christopher might not have worldly wealth, he had much else.

No, Mrs. Lithgow need not fear that Christopher had designs on her (Beatrice's) money. But, oddly enough, this fact seemed to bring the girl little satisfaction. Beatrice sighed as she folded up the letter.

CHAPTER XX

"His was the honest prose, the morning light, the cheerful naturalness of every day."

The Month of May.

One of Cicely's last injunctions, shouted to her brother from the car as she set off for London, was that he must show Beatrice Oxford, so one afternoon they set out accompanied by Watty, in Mrs. Stopford's car, which she had insisted on lending for the occasion.

"We could have gone by bus," said Watty ungratefully. "It's a nice jolty bus."

"I should like some shopping done," said his mother. "I'll give you the list, Watty; you won't want to see the Colleges."

Watty disclaimed all such desire, but wanted to know what exactly was expected of him. "I don't mind grocers," he said, "or butchers, but I won't enter a draper's shop."

"You won't be asked to," Mrs. Sellars promised. "Have you any objection to the fishmongers? No? That's a blessing. I'll make out my list."

Watty chose to sit beside the chauffeur, a valued friend of his, and Beatrice and Christopher talked intermittently as they rolled along. They knew each other well enough now to be at ease silent.

It was a pretty day, with sudden gleams of sunshine that revealed for a minute houses and floods and trees in a watery light, leaving them again in shadow, and Beatrice said suddenly:

"Before I ever saw Oxford I had a feeling it was a place I'd like to live in."

"I wonder!" said Christopher. "I expect you thought of it as a place of spires and bells, of grey walls and green lawns and a river, didn't you? But that's only one side of Oxford. There's precious little romance about the endless arid roads of villas, or about the people who live on vitamins and uplift on the hill tops."

"But," Beatrice protested, "those are the suburbs, and suburbs are much the same all the world over, —London, Glasgow, Edinburgh, Calcutta, and even, I shouldn't wonder, Moscow! It's Oxford itself I'd like to live in, if I could get one of those little old houses near the Colleges, that I saw when I was there with Cicely, with panelled walls and uneven floors. . . ."

"I'm afraid you'd find them rather stuffy, but we'll look out for one this afternoon, shall we? Is there any particular place you'd like to see? Or shall I take you the round?"

"I'd like to see Magdalen and Tom Quad-those names have always been familiar to me. And Balliol, because I had a second cousin there and . . . what was your college?"

"B.N.C.," Christopher told her. "It was my father's college. Well, if we tell Denison to have the car at Barnet House at 5.30 that will give us time to do all we want and have tea. Is that all right?"

They got out and Christopher asked his brother what he meant to do when he had finished shopping for his mother.

"Picture house," said Watty briefly.

"Well, meet us at that new tea-place —what is it called? the 'Bun Shop' —at about a quarter to five."

"All right. I know it," said Watty. "It's round the corner from the Plaza."

At that moment Beatrice sighted in a flower shop a rosy azalea, and thought of Mrs. Sellars' love for flowers.

"Just a moment," she said to Christopher and, rushing in, bought the azalea, as well as a cyclamen, pears, plums, grapes and a large box of candied fruit. It was impossible to get flowers in Oxlip, or any fruit except apples and bananas, and it was delightful, Beatrice felt, to get a chance of contributing even in such a very small way, to the upkeep of the household. That was her one crumpled rose-leaf that she should be a certain amount of expense to the Sellars. They had enough for all the necessities of life, but Beatrice knew that there was very little over for extras; indeed, had Mrs. Sellars not been a most capable manager there would have been nothing. It took practically all Cicely's salary to keep her in London; Christopher could only spare a little, and Watty at present was all expense.

"I can't send him to college," his mother had told Beatrice, "unless he gets a scholarship, but he has begun to work hard and his master says he has lots of ability. I would like him to go to B.N.C. But the difficulty is to know what profession to put him in afterwards. My people were all in India, the army and the I.C.S., but India isn't what it used to be. Christopher thinks the Colonial service. . . . Anyway, Watty's sure he won't teach, I'm afraid he has no call to the Church, and like the small boy in the *Golden Age* 'he holds the sacred art of healing in horror and contempt,' so we can't keep him in this country. Boys are really a greater perplexity than girls now; they are so often square pegs in round holes, and remain so determinedly square, whereas girls seem able to adapt themselves."

"Now, I'm ready," Beatrice announced, emerging from the fruiterers, and she and Christopher started upon their pilgrimage.

Christopher knew his Oxford thoroughly and loved it, and Beatrice learned much that afternoon. There was no boredom. When quadrangles palled and towers and garden-fronts became monotonous, they walked down the High and browsed in book-shops, explored exciting antique shops and stared at old prints.

And Beatrice felt that though she had learned much of Oxford that afternoon she had learned even more of Christopher Sellars. They had been good friends since the night of the arrival at 'Twixt Bears, but wandering together among age-old walls they had struck their first note of intimacy.

Christopher had talked of himself, recalling mad escapades of undergraduate days, as they looked at the rooms that had been his. He took Beatrice to the chapel to show her the brass tablet to the memory of his father, John Sellars, who had died from illness contracted in the Great War, and as he looked at it he said:

"I was away at school when he died, and before that there were the War years, but I have the childish years in Edinburgh to remember-Saturday afternoon excursions to the Pentlands, to Swanston. My father was a great lover of Sir Walter and of R. L. S., and he liked to tell me stories about them both when they were boys in Edinburgh. Sometimes he would take me to the Lawnmarket and tell me about Montrose, the great Marquis, or stand at the Market Cross and make me see the ghostly figure reading aloud the list of names that would not return from Flodden. I can't be sufficiently thankful that I have these memories of my father. Don't you like to collect a picture-gallery in your mind? Pictures that are one's own. No one else knows of them or has any right to them."

He stopped and said in a different tone. "That's one of the awful things about the lives of the children in the slums. They must have a sort of Chamber of Horrors as background: filthy streets, squalid rooms, drunken brawls. . . . But perhaps not. Time is the most wonderful alchemist."

"Perhaps," said Beatrice, "looking back they see what might have been rather than what was. Doesn't it depend entirely on one's temperament? Some can 'make believe' a garret into a fairy palace, while it takes others all their time to recognise a fairy palace when they see it."

Beatrice was finding it very pleasant to talk about serious things for once. She had been brought up in circles that believed in solid sense and avoided persiflage except perhaps at weddings and the New Year; she thought that constant light talk was apt to pall. So, by adroit questioning she encouraged her companion to talk of his work, his life at school.

"It's lucky for me," he said, "that I really enjoy teaching, and tremendous luck that I got into Heard's. Dr. Heard is such a good sort. That's a mild way to put it-he's magnificent. Did you ever read a school story called *Early Closing*? No? It gives you the best idea of life at a school of any book I know. There is a house master in it who is said to have 'feared God, mistrusted the Government, and moulded other men's sons to the best of his ability.' That's rather like Dr. Heard. He's a man you not only admire but like; the two don't always go together. The worst of it is I'm afraid he means to give up quite soon, he really isn't fit for all he takes on himself. Of course, he may get some one quite good in his place, but there's no use hoping we'll get a second Dr. Heard. It's his school, he made it; he gets the best out of all of us, masters and boys. . . . It's quite a small school, you know; he doesn't believe in having too many pupils, and it's a perfect place-lovely old house and garden, bracing air, space. . . . Most of the boys are sons of men on foreign service. It's specially important that they should get every chance, when very often they see almost nothing of their parents. To give them a good start, that's the main thing."

Beatrice was pondering. "But don't you grudge," she said, "letting the boys go on to other schools? Wouldn't you rather have them after their teens when they are more interesting?"

But Christopher would not own to such a preference, remarking that the early years were the most important.

"But," Beatrice insisted, "didn't some great Jesuit say that it was the first five years that really counted? In which case it would mean that it is the mother-or more likely the nurse-who is really the important factor?"

"There's something in that," Christopher acknowledged. "A stupid nurse and an over-indulgent mother can make things pretty bad for a small boy. It's a cruel thing to spoil a child and then send him off into the (comparatively) cold world of school."

"It is," said Beatrice soberly, watching the mist creep over the meadows.

"By morning," Christopher prophesied, "all these meadows will be under water. That's the worst thing about Oxford, the damp that soaks into the heart of everything. We get a touch of it at Oxlip, but then, of course, we are much higher. Come and see the rooms Shakespeare is supposed to have lodged in, passing through Oxford to and from Stratford. It's in a tailor's shop. They were making some alterations recently, taking down a wall, and found another painted wall behind, and a fireplace certified by experts to belong to the proper period. They have reconstructed the room, and behind the house is still the garden, with the mulberry tree in the middle under which he sat . . . so they say. What do you think of the new theatre at Stratford-on-Avon?"

"Haven't seen it," said Beatrice. "My mother, who brought me up on Shakespeare, always promised we'd go to the Festival at Stratford some April, but somehow there never was time, for we generally went abroad in spring. Stratford would still be there, Mother used to say, when she was older and not able for long journeys-but she died before she was old, and she was all that I had."

Even as she said the words Beatrice raged at herself. Seeming to ask for pity when she didn't want pity and making Christopher uncomfortable, for of course he didn't know what to say. At that moment they stopped, and Christopher said-in a relieved tone, Beatrice thought, "This is the place. Yes, it's quite all right; visitors are welcomed. As a matter of fact they charge a trifle to help with the outlay and the upkeep."

A young man led them up a narrow stair, explaining how it was the room had been discovered, and in her interest Beatrice forgot both herself and her companion, and eagerly studied every detail. Later, they picked up Watty who seemed rather dazed after the crook play he had been enjoying, and ate, abstractedly, an enormous tea.

All the way home through the misty evening Beatrice congratulated herself that they were not going anywhere that evening. The evenings at 'Twixt Bears were very precious to her. She looked forward to them all day. The curtains drawn, the dark night shut out, inside all was peace and quietness. Watty, who was clever with his fingers, working at some model; Christopher reading aloud beside his grandmother, who sat bolt upright, knitting, and listening intently; Mrs. Sellars and herself sewing.

But this evening disappointment waited for the girl, for after they had told of their afternoon's doings, Mrs. Sellars said: "I mustn't forget my message. The Twins came in just after you left asking you all to go to The Green to-night for a 'mystery' evening. I don't know what that means, they gave me no inkling, but they would like you to be there by eight-thirty."

"Some tomfoolery, doubtless," said Granny Sellars.

"There's a letter from Cicely," her daughter-in-law broke in. "I've just been reading it to Granny-here it is. She seems in excellent spirits."

"When was Cicely not in good spirits?" Granny Sellars asked, while Watty went out and fetched from the hall the flowers and fruit bought by Beatrice.

"I carried them in and forgot them," he explained. "Beatrice thought you'd like them. Ruth took the fish and the other things."

"Oh, my dear, this is sheer extravagance," Mrs. Sellars turned to her guest. "But it was very sweet of you to think of me and my love for flowers. I believe with care they will last till the snowdrops come. And fruit too! We mustn't let you into Oxford again; you're safer in Oxlip." She leant over her two pretty pots, and "I'll take them to a cool place," she said, "and bring them in here in the morning. Dear me, I can't help wishing you weren't going out to-night."

"And I!" said Beatrice. "I do so love home evenings."

But what really rankled with her was that Christopher seemed cheerful about going!

CHAPTER XXI

> "... I choose her for myself:
> If she and I be pleased, what's that to you?"

The Taming of the Shrew.

In spite of all her new interests Beatrice often found her thoughts wandering to the little bedroom behind the "antique" shop where Franky lay, and had been cheered to receive a letter from him, wishing her a happy New Year, and telling her what an endless pleasure her wireless was to him, so that it was a great shock to hear one morning from his father that the boy had died of meningitis.

Mercifully it had been short. He had complained of his head, had begun to wander, then had sunk into unconsciousness, from which he never wakened.

Beatrice was almost surprised to find how fond she had become of the yellow-haired boy who had always given her such a welcoming smile, and whose delicacy and deformity had tugged at her heart. As she thought of him tears came to her eyes, and yet, she told herself, there was nothing here for tears. She had known, and so had his parents, that the boy could never be strong. It was better that he should go now, happy and eager, than drag through years of suffering. Sixteen years had been the length of his span-long enough to light the path of his parents to the end-and now he had been taken home. He who so admired fine, big fellows, and who must often have felt acutely his own punyness, had he grown to "heavenly stature" now? Was it all made up to him already?

She was sitting at the bureau in the window that looked across the slow-moving Eden to the marshland behind, and as she sought for words with which to comfort Franky's parents, she looked out at the wide expanse of blue sky reflected in many pools, for the floods were still out, and thought that the world looked new-washed, and as young as the year.

Glancing behind her she saw that Granny Sellars had folded her hands on her book and dropped asleep. It was difficult to believe, seeing her look so pathetically helpless and frail, as if a rough wind would break her, that she would hardly be a minute awake before she said something in her high, definite voice to hurt some one. How old she was! And Franky dead at sixteen! *Whom the gods love* . . . was that why Franky's little candle had gone out so soon and poor Granny Sellars' was burning to the socket?

Beatrice's moralisings were interrupted by Ruth announcing in hushed tones, with an apprehensive glance at the sleeping figure in the armchair, "Please, ma'am, Mrs. Stopford," at which Beatrice arose quickly and with her finger on her lips, went to meet the visitor.

"I've the car here," Mrs. Stopford whispered. "Come out with me, will you? I want to talk to you."

"A minute," said Beatrice, "and I'll be ready. Mrs. Sellars has gone for a walk with Christopher, but they'll be back soon, and I'll ask Ruth to listen in case Granny Sellars wants anything."

She was downstairs again almost immediately, buttoning her coat as she came, and Mrs. Stopford applauded her quickness, remarking:

"What it is to be young! No mirror needed, a hat, a muffler, a coat, and you're ready. This is good of you, my dear. I felt I must confide in some one, and at once my thoughts flew to you."

The chauffeur tucked the fur rug round them and they were off. Then Mrs. Stopford told her news.

"I only heard it this morning," she said, "after breakfast. We had just finished, Basil and I —our guests are all gone-and I was saying how pleasant it was to be alone again, when he said abruptly, with no attempt at breaking it to me, 'By the way, Mother, I want to tell you that I've got engaged. No, you don't know her. Her name's Veronica Marston!' Beatrice, Basil —! The boy I've given up my life to since his dear father died; my first thought in the morning, my last at night, and he throws a bombshell like that at me!"

Mrs. Stopford leant back in her corner and looked in a frozen way at the wet fields through which they were passing.

Beatrice hardly knew what to say. She was not surprised that Mrs. Stopford was shocked-she was shocked herself. Imagine Basil! It was all very confusing. Mrs. Stopford's hand was lying on the cushions looking, somehow, rather pathetic. After a moment's hesitation Beatrice took it and then wished she hadn't for it lay in hers in a detached way that made her feel very awkward.

"Perhaps," she murmured, "you will find her a nice girl."

Mrs. Stopford made a sound suspiciously like a snort.

"She lives in Oxford," she said.

"But — —" Beatrice began and was interrupted.

"I know the type," said Basil's mother.

"But," Beatrice began again, "would Basil be likely to fall in love with that type?"

Mrs. Stopford sat upright and spoke rapidly in a hard, high voice, very unlike her usual cooing strains.

"Basil, my dear, is a man, and men can do the most unaccountable things. There's no telling what will attract a man. Basil says this girl has a beautiful soul which probably means that she has a plain face. That's what makes it so hopeless. I've always known Basil was weak, and I knew I might have to rescue him from the clutches of mature sirens or young ladies in the chorus, but when he talks of souls I can do nothing."

Beatrice became more puzzled. Mrs. Stopford herself had always seemed to her so soulful, almost embarrassingly so indeed, that she would have imagined the presence of a beautiful soul in her future daughter-in-law would have appealed to her above everything.

The lady went on:

"She is clever evidently, took Honours in History or something, while poor Basil simply *crawled* through his exams. That is so wrong to begin with; he will feel inferior. And I expect she will read nothing but Virginia Woolf and other highbrows, while my poor boy rarely tackles anything except crime. And he loathes poetry. It isn't my fault, I tried him with the best. The place was simply littered with anthologies and I read them to him myself till he begged me to stop. His father was the same. I tried to make him share my love for poetry, but it seemed to make him so uncomfortable I had to stop. He had his horses, he said, and I had my books, so we left it at that. If Basil had fallen in love with some girl given up to hunting or racing, I wouldn't have been surprised, but — —"

"But would you have liked it any better?"

"Anyway, she would have been one of ourselves. I'd have understood his point of view, and probably known all her connections. I know nothing of these Marstons; they may be butchers, or bakers, or candle-stick-makers. In theory I despise worldly position; I remind myself that our Lord was a carpenter, John Bunyan was a tinker, some of our poets little better than tramps, but all the same, Beatrice, it may be silly and snobbish to say so, but there is a difference between people who have been brought up in our way and the people who have not."

"Perhaps," Beatrice said cautiously, "but I don't think I quite know what you mean. I myself come of Glasgow stock, plain business people, with no pretensions to — —"

"Ah, but you're Scots, and that makes all the difference."

"Does it?" said Beatrice. "I don't see why. But to return to-Miss Marston is it? —when you meet you may find that you have been quite wrong about her. Anyway, you will have to try to like her, won't you? Because, otherwise, it might mean losing your son."

Mrs. Stopford's lips tightened and she said, "She shan't take Basil from me."

"If she has any sense," Beatrice went on, "she will realise that she must make friends with you and start at once about it, for her happiness and yours and Basil's all depend on it."

Mrs. Stopford gave a short laugh. "I don't suppose she spares a thought for me. If only it had been Cicely; that has always been my dream. I would so gladly have turned out of Broadmeadows for Cicely. It would have been such a happy arrangement; everyone pleased; no stiffness; no suspicion. It is too disappointing."

"Yes," Beatrice admitted. "I think it is. And what about Cicely?"

"I never knew if she cared. Probably not. Now, don't say this may turn out for the best, for I can't bear it."

"I wasn't going to say it. I was just thinking that it will be difficult for you to give this girl a chance, with Cicely always at the back of your mind."

"I am going to call on her to-morrow," Mrs. Stopford said gloomily. "I told Basil I'd rather he didn't go with me. It is better to meet alone the first time. I quite realise that the only sensible thing to do is to make the best of it and take the girl to my heart. We shall see how things work out. Anyway, it has done me good to pour it out to you. And now I think we've had enough of floods, let's go home by Stow-on-the-Green."

In her rôle of comforter Beatrice went back to Broadmeadows with her friend, and did not arrive at 'Twixt Bears till after six o'clock when she found Christopher on the point of setting out to look for her.

"Ruth said you had gone for a drive with Mrs. Stopford, but Mother got anxious and would have it something had happened. Here she is, Mother, safe and sound."

Mrs. Sellars rose to welcome back the wanderer, crying, "My dear, I got so nervous. There's nothing wrong, is there, at Broadmeadows?"

"No," said Beatrice rather uncertainly, "nothing really wrong. Basil has got engaged. Yes," in reply to Mrs. Sellars' gasp, "his mother was rather startled and came here to tell us about it, and I was the only one at home at the moment."

"Who is it?" Christopher asked.

"No one you know, I think." (Did Christopher look relieved? Beatrice was not sure.) "A Miss Veronica Marston, who lives in Oxford with her mother. Very clever, I understand."

"*What?*" said Granny Sellars. "I can't hear. *Who* is engaged? Not Cicely?"

Her daughter-in-law went over to her chair and said, "No, Granny, not Cicely. Basil Stopford. To a girl in Oxford. None of us know her."

"Oh! His mother should be thankful it's not one of those Twins." She glanced provocatively at Christopher as she said it, but Christopher was looking thoughtfully into the fire and did not respond.

"I'm afraid," said Beatrice, "that Mrs. Stopford isn't very thankful about it at all."

"Can you wonder," Mrs. Sellars said. "Basil is all she has, and if this has come as a complete surprise to her —! However, it may turn out quite well; better, perhaps, than if he had chosen a girl his mother knew."

"Was it a case of choosing?" Granny Sellars asked, acidly. "I always thought there was something weak about that young man's face. It's my belief any determined young woman could have captured him, and I suppose it was worth even a scholarly young woman's while when it meant not only Basil but Broadmeadows."

Christopher laughed, remarking, "What a cynical grandmother I've got! Basil is a very good fellow, and probably Miss What's-her-name thought too much of him to spare a thought for Broadmeadows. I can't say that I envy her having Mrs. Stopford for a mother-in-law; she is all that's delightful as a neighbour and a friend but — —"

"You would have been sorry for her to-day," Beatrice told him. "She was quite unlike herself; that rather lisping, gushing way she has of speaking had vanished, and her voice was hard and definite. She really is taking it very much to heart. To-morrow she is calling, in state and alone, on Miss Marston and her mother. I can't believe it will be either an easy or a pleasant visit."

"They say," said old Mrs. Sellars, "that a woman begins to be jealous of her daughter-in-law when her son is in his cradle."

"I don't see why she should," retorted her daughter-in-law. "She has him to herself through his childhood and his schooldays and his young manhood, and she must realise that as she took her husband away from his mother there is probably some girl destined to take her son away from her. It's only natural and fair. And it isn't as if-except in rare cases-there is any real cleavage. A man happily married can be as devoted as ever he was to his mother and make her a sharer in his new riches."

"That," said Granny Sellars, "depends on the man-and the wife-and the mother-in-law."

There was a pause, and Beatrice went upstairs to change; as she stood in her own little room so warm and inviting with a fire and a lamp, her thoughts left Oxford and flew to the bedroom behind the shop where Franky lay so still among his small possessions. She wished there was anything she could do for the poor parents, for she felt that they had probably few friends; they and their boy had been all in all to each other. Anyway, she would wire first thing in the morning to a flower shop she knew to send a wreath of spring flowers; it would at least show that she was thinking of the dead boy.

For a few days nothing was heard from Broadmeadows, then Mrs. Stopford came herself one morning with an invitation to Mrs. Sellars, Beatrice and Christopher to dine on a certain evening.

She explained, "I have asked Mrs. Marston and her daughter, and it would be a real kindness to me if you three would come. I know, dear Mrs. Sellars, that you don't care about going out at night, but I specially want you. Will you come? Beatrice would tell you about Basil's engagement? Yes. Well, eight o'clock on Wednesday. I am so grateful to you."

"We shall be very much interested to meet Miss Marston," Mrs. Sellars said. "We are all so fond of Basil."

"Yes. Poor Basil," said his mother, rising to go. "Well, Wednesday at eight."

"Dear me," said Mrs. Sellars, watching her visitor walking down the flagged path, "I never knew Blanche Stopford so uncommunicative. She generally sits for a good hour when she comes in the morning."

"And not a word," said Beatrice, "about the meeting with her daughter-in-law-elect!"

"That I was rather glad of. It showed her wisdom. We are to meet the girl, and Mrs. Stopford didn't prejudice us one way or another. My old velvet is very shabby, Beatrice, for a party."

"Not a bit," said Beatrice stoutly. "It looked so nice at Christmas-time with your lovely lace."

"Anyway," said Mrs. Sellars, "it matters nothing. All eyes will be on the bride. . . . Watty will have to look after Granny that evening. I'm quite excited already."

Beatrice never forgot that dinner-party at Broadmeadows. It seemed to her like a scene on the stage, and the men and women present merely players.

The 'Twixt Bears party had timed themselves to arrive on the stroke of the hour and found the company assembled in the small drawing-room which Mrs. Stopford called the boudoir. It was panelled in white, with one picture, a Hondecoeter, let into the wall opposite the fireplace, a polished floor and some good pieces of furniture.

As the Sellars party entered, Mrs. Stopford, dressed in black velvet, with her head held very high, was standing on the hearth-rug telling the company that the room was haunted.

"Oh, I assure you it is. Sit here on the hottest summer day reading a book in one of the window seats-it looks deliciously into the rose garden-and before long you will feel your feet and hands grow ice-cold, and find yourself listening intently for something, you don't know what."

Beatrice looked round the room. The Rector was there and Mrs. Snow, Colonel Fairfax without the Twins, a middle-aged man whom she did not know, and-seated on the sofa, dressed in white satin, the reason for the party-Veronica Marston.

She was beautiful, Beatrice at once decided. Her dark hair was parted in the middle and coiled in her neck, her slim arms were bare and she wore no ornament. She looked very stately, sitting there, not so much unaware she was the object of every one's attention as indifferent to the fact.

Mrs. Marston, who was engaged in conversation with the Rector, looked old to be the mother of such a young daughter. Her hair was grey; she had very black brows over dark eyes and a curious waxen complexion, while her mouth was drawn tightly over her teeth in what looked like a perpetual smirk. She was dressed unnoticeably in black and had none of her daughter's look of distinction.

They went in to dinner, and Beatrice, watching her hostess, thought of a deposed queen, so marked was her air of pensive dignity. Beatrice's partner was the strange man; he told her he was one of Basil's trustees, and had been asked to meet the fiancée.

"He's a bit young to marry," he said, "but I daresay it's all to the good. I always think this is a very charming place. I like the way it opens almost from the village street, with the lawns and garden behind looking across Otmarsh. It's lovely in the summer."

Beatrice agreed that it must be and added: "Mrs. Stopford is so good about sharing all the beauty; she never stops entertaining, and makes every one welcome."

"Oh, she does," said her partner. "It won't be easy for her to see another in her place; but it may work out all right. Basil was always his mother's first thought, and if he's happy, I don't believe she will mind about herself. It's a little difficult at first —I understand Miss Marston is a stranger."

Afterwards, in the drawing-room, when Mrs. Sellars was talking to Miss Marston, and Mrs. Stopford and Mrs. Snow exchanging confidences on the sofa, Beatrice sat down beside Mrs. Marston and tried to make conversation.

She found it difficult, for Mrs. Marston seemed to be keeping a guard on her words-or was it her accent? —and talked mincingly about the weather and the state of the roads.

Having waxed enthusiastic about the beauty of Oxford and met with no response Beatrice tried her with Scotland.

"I'm a Scot," she said "(as probably you've observed), and, of course, very proud of my native land. I wonder if you know Scotland well?"

"Not well," came the small mincing voice. "Once when I was very young I visited Edinburgh and the Forth Bridge. I believe it is very nice. Friends of ours go every year; they take a shooting-they are very wealthy-somewhere near Inverness, I think, or Aberdeen, and they always say it is very nice. But I can't say I am fond of grandeur in scenery. I like Bexhill."

Not knowing Bexhill Beatrice could not respond, so she made some remark about the Stopfords' charming house and asked her companion if she did not admire the drawing-room. Mrs. Marston's reply was guarded. She said it was "very nice," but for her own part she found polished floors, even when well covered with rugs, cold, and in her opinion there was nothing like a good thick carpet. Then she shut her thin lips very tight, and gave a glance at her daughter as if fearing she had said too much.

Altogether it was not particularly enlivening, and home again in 'Twixt Bears Christopher remarked that he'd seldom spent a more deadly evening. "It was as if a blight had fallen on the place," he said, "no one was properly at ease and Mrs. Stopford herself was so queenly that she had the effect of an iceberg. The only person who didn't seem to feel it was Miss Marston."

His mother agreed. "I've seldom spoken to a more composed young woman. Although she must be quite young there is nothing of the young girl about her, no pretty ways or any anxiety to please. Very pleasant, and no doubt very clever, though our conversation was far from intellectual. It consisted mostly of questions-rather like an interview in a registry office. But how beautiful she is! No wonder Basil fell under her enchantment."

"Yes," said Christopher, "he still looks a bit dazed. I saw you talking to Mrs. Marston, Beatrice. Isn't she devastatingly genteel?"

"Is that what she is? She seemed a gentle soul, and rather afraid, I thought, of her beautiful daughter. It must be disconcerting to think you are bringing up an ordinary duck and find you have a swan on your hands."

CHAPTER XXII

"Here is a letter: read it at your leisure."

The Merchant of Venice.

Marriage-bells seemed to be in the air, thought Beatrice, when, the morning after the Stopfords' dinner, she opened a letter from Fairlie describing in detail her own wedding:

"Everything," she wrote, "went off fine. Hogmanay was more like April than December and Greenbraes looked lovely. The Shields carried out all your instructions about the lunch. I set it myself just as we used to set the table for a dinner party at Park Place-flowers, and the napkins all standing up, and the glass shining. The ceremony was fixed for twelve o'clock, and the minister and Mrs. Bryce were there in good time and twenty guests all told. It was in the drawing-room, as you told us, with pot-plants to make it look nice, and I felt awful grand in my beige dress. Miss Caird made it *lovely*, and the lining of the coat to match and a hat trimmed with velvet. Mr. Gordon was quite composed, having gone through it before, but I felt like bursting into tears any minute. It was all I could do to make a sound when the minister asked me if I took this man. I had upset myself the night before thinking of your dear mother and the old days in Glasgow, and wondering if I was doing right taking him. It was silly, for of course I was very glad of the chance. I cheered up fine afterwards and enjoyed the kidney soup and the turkey and plum pudding, not to speak of merangs and fruit and coffee. Everybody present said they had never tasted a more luxurious dinner, and we drank your health, Miss Beatrice, in lemonade. Mr. Bryce came out wonderful. You wouldn't have thought that such a dry sort of man could have made himself so pleasant, and Mrs. Bryce the same. He made a beautiful speech about Mr. Gordon, said how much he depended on him in the church, and how much he was respected by every one and liked, and so on. He couldn't have said more if it had been his funeral. And then he started on me and gave me such a character that I was fair confused although in a way it was true enough. And he told stories and made us all laugh and some of the guests favoured with a song, so it was all very hilarious though quite well-behaved of course. A cup of tea and wedding cake was served and then we left by the four train for Edinburgh. I didn't take my good clothes away with me, they might have got spoilt, just wore my navy costume and my old coat with the fur collar, quite good enough for sight-seeing. I've often wondered how folk put in their time on their honeymoon and now I know it's a gey hard job! We stayed three days at a temperance hotel in Princes Street. Mr. Gordon thought it was a grand place, but me having travelled about with you and seen so many hotels I thought it very ordinary but quite comfortable. We went to see the pantomime and the Waverley Market and a service at St. Giles which I thought very old and sort of bleak. I like a cheery modern church better than yon. We went to the Castle, too, and saw the memorial. It's grand but awful sad. We saw David's auntie too. She is quite well off and has a nice house in Murrayfield, a widow with one daughter, who is in an office and gets a good salary. We had supper with them on the Sunday night and came home on Monday, and glad we were to be back. David is not at his best away from home. Sight-seeing and amusing yourself is very trying to a man's temper I find, indeed I began to wonder if I had been wise to take him. But you will be glad to hear that the minute we got home he was all right, whistling away as cheery as you like and helping me to get everything in order. Oh, Miss Beatrice, I would like you to see it. The room looks beautiful and so cosy with chenille curtains that draw across and all my photos and nick-nacks arranged on the mantelpiece and sideboard. But I believe you would like the kitchen best, it's so cheery with the new linoleum and the tins and grate shining. You would have thought that in all the years that I never dirtied my hands I'd have got out of the way of working, but not a bit of it. I love to work and it makes an awful difference when it's your *ain wee house*! David says it's easy seen I've been in genteel service (that was when I said I didn't like him to sit in his stocking soles) and I hope I'll always have nice ways.

"The minister and his wife are coming to tea with me to-morrow, so I'll have to put my best foot forward, d'oyleys on the plates and sandwiches and hot toast like a Park Place tea, just to show them that I know what's what.

"A line when you have time will be much appreciated by

"Your old nurse,

"Fairlie."

Beatrice put the letter into an envelope to send to Mrs. Lithgow who, she knew, would enjoy all the details, and then stood pondering over another letter she had received that morning. It was from Cicely in answer to the one she had written telling about Basil's engagement. Cicely only briefly remarked on the news, going on almost at once to talk of other things, but there was a postscript which said:

"*Does Basil look happy?*"

Beatrice wondered what she could reply to that. She would tell of the dinner, of Veronica-there was lots to say of her and of her mother-and as for Basil he still seemed dazed, as Christopher said-or was enchanted the better word? —as if he had heard the siren's songs and had hardly yet come back to common earth. . . . Fairlie, on the other hand, had never been off it, and saw with very clear eyes the faults of her mate. But she had got that for which she had probably always pined, a place of her own. She who had accepted meekly other people's taste, was free at last to indulge her own. Had she always pined, poor Fairlie, for chenille curtains and bright linoleums? What a blessing that she had got them, for so few people seemed to attain what they struggled towards.

As she went downstairs to read to Granny Sellars Beatrice reflected contentedly that so long as she was allowed to stay on at 'Twixt Bears she had nothing much to wish for. She would miss Christopher and Watty, of course, but they had to go, and with Mrs. Sellars left and the Oxlip friends, to repine would be impious.

They were playing badminton that afternoon in the village hall. Basil was not there, nor his mother, and there was naturally much talk of the engagement, the Twins especially being all excitement.

"Just think of Basil," said Sarsa. "We've known him almost from infancy and would never have suspected him of such conduct. Leaving all his friends and admirers in the lurch and getting engaged to an outsider. Daddy says she is beautiful-not pretty you understand, but beautiful, lofty, serene, calm-eyed goddess sort of person. What could Basil have been thinking of? He'll never live up to it, and so clever too-honours in everything."

"Sarsa, my dear," her sister advised, "we can't help perhaps feeling a little jealous, but need you make it so evident? It just shows how much there is in Basil that he ever thought of getting engaged to anyone like Miss Marston. Daddy was quite awed by her. How did you like her, Trix?"

"Oh, I hardly had a word with her, but of course I greatly admired her looks and the way she dresses and does her hair and sits and speaks and moves."

"Odd we've never heard of her before," said Susan. "We're often at things in Oxford."

"Oh, I've met her," said Alice Pugh. "Veronica Marston, isn't that her name? A tall dark girl with wonderful eyes, and very graceful. I saw her somewhere and asked who she was and was told she was at Somerville and was considered very good. She lives with her mother in one of those new roads. I understood that she was going to teach. . . . I'm not surprised at Basil, but I rather wonder she ever considered him. Not that Basil isn't delightful, only I doubt if they're suited."

Walking home with Beatrice, Alice Pugh spoke again of the engagement. "Basil is such a simple boy, it's a little like a union between a rabbit and a peregrine falcon. Besides, I always saw Cicely at Broadmeadows. Not that so far as I know she ever gave him a thought, but it would have been so perfect-as Mrs. Stopford would say. She seems to be taking this rather well, poor lady, though I'm told the other night she had perhaps too much the air of a queen about to abdicate-did that strike you?"

"Well, perhaps a little," Beatrice confessed. "She was rather wrapt away from common things. I mean she looked at us with a vague, pitying smile which made conversation difficult. But I thought she did very well in a trying situation. It must be dreadful to be asked suddenly to accept an utter stranger as your adored son's wife, and perhaps find that you don't much like the look of her."

Alice Pugh laughed. "Oh, I agree. A sense of humour is the only thing that can carry one through. And I doubt if either Mrs. Stopford or Miss Marston possesses such a thing. . . . By the way, I was given at Christmas a book I love, *The Stricken Deer*: Lord David Cecil's life of William Cowper. If you haven't read it you must. I'm sure you will enjoy it. I'll send it over to-night."

The days following were taken up preparing for the departure of Christopher and Watty. Beatrice was able to help in the way of putting in necessary stitches, washing hair-brushes and other small tasks. It gave her real pleasure to feel herself of use, and she was on the look-out always to save her hostess needless steps. She had found her way into the kitchen and made friends with Ruth, so that she felt at liberty to go there and help if there was anything extra, like people to luncheon or the evening meal, as often happened, for Mrs. Sellars had the true Scots sense of hospitality.

"How you must miss the boys," Beatrice said to her one day as they sat together sewing.

"Well," Mrs. Sellars said, "it won't be so bad this year with you here. I am consoling myself with that. But other times: the emptiness of the house and these three rooms so bleakly tidy, and Granny and I sitting here by the fire feeling so old and useless."

"By no means useless. Keeping the hearth warm for them."

"Yes, that is so. And once they are gone every day brings their home-coming nearer, and the letters are an interest, and if one knows the absent ones are well it's easy to be content doing the work that lies to one's hand. I'm thankful Granny needs a good deal, and when we are alone I give her practically all my time and attention, for though she wouldn't for the world admit it she misses the young life."

The last afternoon they went for a walk, Beatrice and Christopher and Watty, across the marsh, and finished up with tea at Colina's Cottage.

"We always have tea with Colina the day before we go back," Watty explained, "since she married Mr. Merry."

"There's not much 'always' about it," Christopher said. "Colina's been married a little over a year."

"Well, we've been twice," Watty insisted.

He was full of information that day, most of it strikingly incorrect, which he imparted to Beatrice.

"See that cottage?" he said. "There was a murder there. A man killed his wife."

"How horrible!" said Beatrice, much impressed.

"Well, it was really quite all right," Watty went on reassuringly, "and the man was dismissed with a pension."

"What are you talking about," Christopher asked his brother.

"Mr. Merry told me and he should know, for he says he's lived here man and boy for nearly sixty years."

"As a matter of fact," Christopher explained, "it was proved that it was after great provocation he struck the woman, and the blow hadn't really caused her death, so the man got off. But what the pension was for only Watty knows."

"Well, ask Mr. Merry," said Watty, as he went bounding over the tussocky grass after Voltaire, who loved nothing so much as a wild scamper over Otmarsh.

Beatrice remarked that Watty seemed in excellent spirits about going back to school.

Christopher agreed. "I expect," he said, "it's about fifty-fifty with most boys. They hate the moment of leave-taking, but once back and the routine of school lessons again begin they're as merry as grigs. Did you ever read Anstey's *Vice Versa?*"

"Oh," said Beatrice, "that book terrified me. It was too cruel. How I suffered with poor Mr. Bultitude! I was almost sick with anxiety when he finally does escape and goes home to find everything anyhow and the wretched Dick lording it at a party. It was hateful. Only this morning I was reading about Cowper as a boy being bullied almost to death by a wretch whom he only knew by his shoe-buckles for he never dared lift his eyes to his face. Do such things never happen now? Are you sure?"

"Oh, well, it's difficult to be quite sure. There will always be the born bully; and there will always be the delicate, too-sensitive boy, but a careful watch is kept. Of course, it does the ordinary little scallywag like Watty no sort of harm to fag for a strict prefect; it teaches him tidy ways and keeps him up to the scratch. Cuffs and lickings don't harm most boys any more than water does a duck's back. Your ordinary boy thrives on them. But the sensitive, timid, unapproachable boy is always a problem."

They walked on together for a little in silence, enjoying the fresh west wind, and watching the white clouds move across the sky.

"These wide distances," Beatrice said, "are so wonderful, they take your breath like a sudden sight of the sea. How far can we see? Ten, twenty miles?"

"Nearly forty. This place is at its best in spring, when the woods are full of anemones and primroses and the fields of cowslips, and every little village plot blazes with daffodils. The Oxlip church lifts its grey walls from a field of cloth of gold. I say, I hope you'll still be here when we come home at Easter."

Beatrice blushed and hesitated. "I'm afraid," she said, "that that would be too long a visit for even your mother's hospitality. But perhaps she would let me come back for Easter. I would love to see spring in Oxlip."

"I'll answer for my Mother that she will only be too glad to have you at any time. You help her such a lot. And not only that, it's a great pleasure for Mother to have you with her; she doesn't take to many people as she has taken to you. I like to think of you with her. Will you write to me now and again and tell me how things are in 'Twixt Bears?"

"Hi!" shouted Watty, coming bounding towards them, "you're going too far. You should have turned off at Bridges' Farm for Colina's."

"So we should," said his elder brother meekly, as they started to retrace their steps.

Colina was at the door of her cottage on the edge of the wood looking out for them, a trim little person with crinkly red hair turning grey. She wore a grey dress and a little black satin apron, which gave her, Beatrice thought, a delightfully douce appearance.

Watty and Voltaire sprang upon her with some violence, but she quickly reduced them to order.

"Give over, Watty, you're like a bear with your hugs; and keep your dirty paws off ma apron, dog." (She would have scorned to call him such a heathen name as Voltaire.) "Where's the beast been? He's fair clotted wi' mud."

"It was the puddles left by the floods on the marsh," Watty explained, "but I'm going to wash him to-night anyway. Let him lie on a paper on the rug, Colina. Here's one."

He picked up a newspaper which lay on the arm of a chair and would have spread it on the floor had not Colina grabbed his arm.

"Mercy! Not that. That's the *Fife Free Press* and I haven't got a word of it read yet. Here, take that. Now, dog, you lie there and don't wander about marking all ma clean floor."

It was a clean floor, Beatrice thought, and a very comfortable kitchen, large, with two windows, and a dresser with old lustre jugs and pewter pots.

"I've a room of course," Colina explained, "as well as a bedroom, but the laddies aye like their tea in the kitchen best, so I hope you don't mind, Miss. . . . We'd better just begin, Merry doesn't get in till half after five; he has a bit of a walk from his work. The kettle's boiling, I think. Open the oven door, Watty, and get out the toast."

Christopher, as he surveyed the table, said with conviction:

"Nobody can bake scones like Colina. Just look at them. You can see they're as light as air."

"Havers!" said Colina. "Sit ye down, then. You here, please, Miss Dobie and Mr. Christopher at the foot. And how may I give you your tea, please, Miss?"

Colina was anxious to hear all the news, and in the intervals of pressing viands on her guests asked many questions.

"And your Mamma's well? That's fine."

"And Granny's well, too," said Watty.

"The auld mistress is a warrior," said Colina. "And Miss Cicely's away again to that awful London! Yes, I was once there, Miss, with the Institute summer outing. We went in charrybangs and stopped first at Selfridge's and went down to the Bargain Basement, and didn't I lose the rest of them! What with the crowds and the noise I thought ma reason would go. I saw nothing for it but to walk round and round till I dropped. It was worse than the worst nightmare I ever had, and I was praying under my breath and half greetin', when suddenly I saw a face I knew-Mistress Trimble, the gamekeeper's wife from Watercaton. I've always looked on her as a plain woman but at that moment to me she was like a heavenly vision. I clutched her, I can tell ye, and a' the others were quite near. Eh, that was an awfu' day."

"But you liked the rest of it, Colina?" Watty reminded her.

"Oh, mebbe I did once I'd got over ma fright. Try that jelly, Miss, it's bramble, what they ca' blackberry in these parts. . . . And I was surprised to hear that Mr. Basil Stopford was engaged."

"Why surprised, Colina?" Christopher asked. "Wasn't it quite a likely thing to happen?"

"Oh, likely enough, I dare say, but . . . I hope he's getting a nice young lady."

"Very," said Beatrice. "At least, I've only seen her once, but she's certainly very nice to look at."

"I'm kinda vext for his mamma!" Colina said. " 'Ma son's ma son till he gets him a wife' —but she's no that old herself; she'll mebbe get another man."

"There's no saying," said Christopher gravely.

"Try the shortbread, Miss. It'll mind you of Scotland, though it's no' as good this time as it should be. However, it's a' guid that's in't, as ma granny used to say when the dumpling didn't turn out well. Merry likes shortbread, but he canna appreciate black bun. It comes of being English. . . . Oh ay, I'm quite settled down here, Miss, and I like it fine. Whiles I hae a longing to see my ain place, but a' ma folk are awa' so it's no the same. And Merry, poor soul, needs me, and him and me 'gree fine. He's very canny, mebbe that accounts for it. Eh, Mr. Christopher? But I aye think of Mrs. Sellars' as home yet, and Merry kens that if I'm needed I must go back. He's used to fendin' for himsel', bein' a bachelor so long. . . . Are ye sure ye canna eat any more, Watty?"

CHAPTER XXIII

"Madame, we'll tell tales."
"Of sorrow or of joy?"
"Or either, Madame."

King Richard II.

For a day or two after the male element had gone 'Twixt Bears seemed a strangely quiet little house, but very quickly the women in it settled down to their own occupations and company.

The weather was not such as to tempt people to go out and a daily run with Voltaire was often Beatrice's only outing, but she was quite happy in the house; with lots of small cares and duties the hours passed quickly.

Except for the newspapers in the morning, which she read aloud to Granny Sellars, she did not allow herself to read till evening when, all duties done, it was delightful to settle down to a long lamp-lit evening with a book-two books as a rule, for she liked to sandwich her reading, a novel to amuse, and something heavier, or, at least, more serious, to instruct. Her "serious" book for the moment was *The Stricken Deer*, which delighted her.

"Isn't it rather painful reading?" Mrs. Sellars asked.

"Not where I am now. He is at Olney with Mary Unwin, and his pet hares, happy for the time being."

"Why do you call it Cooper when it's spelt Cowper?" Granny Sellars wanted to know.

"Perhaps," said Beatrice, "it's the English way."

Granny Sellars sniffed. Then, "Read aloud a page or two," she commanded, "and I'll see what I think of it."

Beatrice obediently began to turn the pages to find something she considered suitable.

"This," she explained, "is after he recovered from the second attack of madness. He and Mrs. Unwin are at Olney, in a house called Orchard Side."

Old Mrs. Sellars peered with her hawk-like eyes at the girl as she said: "Did Mrs. Unwin live alone with Cowper? Most extraordinary."

"I don't think so," said Beatrice. "She was a widow with no home ties and devoted to Cowper. The poor man held on to her hand like a child in the dark. She could quiet him when he was at his worst."

"And didn't people talk?"

"Oh, yes, evidently, but I don't think Mrs. Unwin ever thought of what anyone would think, because she never thought about herself at all. The writer of the book says that her Evangelicalism was not the religion of respectability. If it taught her to shun the pleasures of the world as wicked, it also taught her to scorn its censures as trivial."

The old lady nodded. She liked that, and Evangelicalism was to her a blessed word.

Beatrice went on. "When Cowper began to recover he had to find something to occupy his time, so he started to write poetry. Here I begin: 'In winter, when the greater part of his work was done, his time was spent mostly in one room-the little wainscoted parlour, thirteen feet square with its spindle-legged chairs. . . . It was here, at the civilised hour of ten, in his dressing-gown and cap, that he had his breakfast, and Mary poured out his morning cup of steaming, scented bohea for him. Next he must see after the greenhouse and the hares and the birds and the cat. And now he must sit down to the two or three hours' writing which made up his very reasonable working day. . . . A walk followed, then dinner; and then possibly another walk, sharp, through the frozen or muddy lanes, with the sear leaves rustling round Cowper's feet, and Mungo leaping before him. . . . And now began that moment of the day that Cowper liked best-tea-time on a winter's evening. He liked tea better than any other drink-it gave him just the mild stimulus that his nerves required. And the little meal in the cosy, candle-lit room, alone with his best friend, and the winter's night shut out by curtains, was the very incarnation of that innocent security which all his life had been his idea of perfect happiness. The rain might drive on the window, the wind whistle along the deserted street; it only emphasised the warmth and comfort within, when the kettle hummed, and the cat lapped up its milk and Cowper and Mary laughed over the day's happenings. They were interrupted by the twang of a horse and the hollow sound of the galloping hoofs outside. It was the post arriving at the "Bull Inn." And a few minutes later a rush of cold air would blow into the house as the door opened to admit letters and newspapers that brought to Olney the news of Mr. Fox's last speech and the Duke of Devonshire's last rout, and Mr. Wilks' last enormity.' "

Beatrice stopped. "Isn't that delightful writing? 'Innocent security,' that's my idea of perfect happiness too."

Mrs. Sellars' eyes glowed with pleasure.

"Perfect writing," she said. "What a picture of peace. Port after storm! If only it had lasted!"

"Yes, but he was so wonderfully happy in between. And he was brave. So long as he had any control over his thoughts and actions he was gentle and polite and humorous even when he knew that another attack was coming on, and his nights were made a terror by nightmares and his bedroom candle every evening 'lighted him to hell'."

"It all seems very sad," said Granny Sellars, "and I'm too old for sad things. Are there any more pleasant, peaceful parts?"

"I think so," said Beatrice. "Oh, yes, there must be; all the times with Lady Austen, and his cousin Lady Hesketh!"

"Bless me! How many female friends had the man?"

Beatrice laughed. "Quite a lot, it seems. In his sedate way Cowper was something of a flirt."

"Well, I don't approve of it. A man who wrote hymns!"

"But it's too late to make a fuss, isn't it? They are all quiet in their graves for more than 150 years! But don't you think it is good to have a record of the gentle humour and the pretty and sweet manner of their days, as well as the tale of heroic courage and quiet patience under terrible affliction?"

Granny Sellars admitted it might be so, and added, "All the same, I'm surprised that there is a public for such a book in these days."

"A large public," said Beatrice. "I see Lord David Cecil-the author-says there is a great feeling just now for the eighteenth century: portraits, memoirs, furniture."

"Is there indeed," said the old lady loftily, "then let us hope they will learn something for their good," and she began to read her own book.

Presently Mrs. Sellars said: "Have you seen nothing of the Stopfords, Beatrice?"

"Yesterday, when I was out with Voltaire, I met Mrs. Stopford taking the dogs for a walk. Didn't I tell you? She didn't say anything much, asked for you and Granny and spoke about the weather. I mentioned the party, merely murmured something about enjoying it, but she didn't continue the subject. Perhaps she feels that now that the engagement is made public her mouth is shut, that it wouldn't be very fitting of her to discuss her future daughter-in-law? Don't you think very often when people make rather rash confidences to one about some family matter they are apt to regret it afterwards and blame-quite unjustly-the confidante? Anyway, I didn't persevere."

"Much better not. It struck me that evening at Broadmeadows that there was a feeling of strain, and that no one-neither Miss Marston nor Basil nor his mother-was particularly happy. But I may have been quite wrong-and anyway, it's no business of mine. Was that the bell?"

The door opened and Ruth announced "Mrs. Snow."

The Rector's wife was wrapped in an old fur coat with a shawl round her head, and she unswathed herself before coming into the circle by the fire.

"Norman's at a meeting in Oxford," she announced, "and won't be back till dinner-time, so I thought it was a chance to have a little talk. How are you, Mrs. Sellars?"

"Very well, thank you. I have really very little to complain of in spite of the Psalmist's remarks about four score years. I can still enjoy my food and a good fire and a good book."

Mrs. Snow whisked her knitting out of a bag that hung on her arm, and settled down in her chair.

"Now isn't that a blessing," she said. "And you're able to share in the family life and take an interest in everything. And the young people keep one young in spite of oneself. And you are looking well, Agnes. I think you're the better of having Miss Beatrice with you."

"Indeed I am. It is so melancholy when Cicely and the boys go as a rule, and this time I didn't feel it nearly as much. And what news have you of all your sons?"

Mrs. Snow nodded happily. "All well," she said, "and I've come over to tell you a bit of news which we only heard this morning. I'm longing to tell somebody-Robin's engaged." She turned to Beatrice and explained: "Robin is in the I.C.S., he's our 'worldly' son, all the others being clergymen or missionaries. Yes, Agnes, I think it sounds very suitable. She is the Commissioner's or Resident's (I always mix these things up) daughter in Barapore-Susie Challoner is her name, and she keeps house for her father: twenty-four, a very pleasant-looking girl. She wrote me such a nice letter, not gushing or silly, but so sensible and kind. She said that she has no mother of her own and she hopes I'll let her be a real daughter to me. And they both sound so happy. I shall be very glad to think of Robin with a house of his own, and from what he tells me of Susie and from her own letter I do think he is a lucky man. Oh, I've been doing nothing but build castles in the air since the postman came this morning! It makes the future so much more interesting and I can see that Norman feels the same. Perhaps the children (if there should be children) will come to us for all their holidays. Our boys have been so long in marrying-probably because of the problem of ways and means-that this is a great event."

"I should think so," said Mrs. Sellars. "How you will enjoy a daughter. And she must be a nice girl to write to you so understandingly. Robin was always a particularly likeable boy. He has done so well in India, and a good wife will be a great help to him. And as you say, it will make your already full life fuller still. Dear me, how delightful it is to hear good news."

"It's wise of him," said Granny Sellars, "to marry a girl who knows India and whose father is in the same service. Is it to be soon?"

"Quite soon," said Mrs. Sellars. "There's nothing to wait for, Robin says, except our blessing and they'll have that by this time, for Norman cabled almost at once. . . . I wonder what one could send them for a present, poor lambs! A cheque, says Norman in his lordly way. It won't be a very large one, things being what they are! But I have something else, something I've kept always for the first bride. A string of pearls. My mother left them to me, but I never cared to wear them, being better unadorned. I've kept them carefully and now I'll send them to good people to have them properly cleaned and re-strung and put in a nice new box and I'll post them away to Susie. How nice that sounds! 'My daughter Susie!' "

Mrs. Sellars smiled in sympathy and said, "Won't she be pleased. That is a gift worth having! I always admire *your* pearls, Beatrice."

"These were my mother's," Beatrice told her, putting her hand up to her throat and fingering her pearls. "I hate to be without them."

"Mine aren't nearly as fine as these," Mrs. Snow said, "but they're a good shape and a good colour and they've got a pretty clasp, an old one."

"You are generous to give them up," said Granny Sellars. "I don't suppose Mrs. Stopford will give her pearls to her daughter-in-law."

Mrs. Snow laughed as she said: "That's a very different thing. Mrs. Stopford's a comparatively young and a very pretty woman. . . . Her pearls are exceptionally fine. How well she looked the other night. Did you enjoy that evening, Agnes?"

"Well-not very much," Mrs. Sellars confessed.

"Nor did I," said Mrs. Snow, "though I'm sure I don't know why, for the dinner was, as it always is at Broadmeadows, excellent, and we were all old friends and full of good will, but there seemed to be something lacking. Norman said it was because our hostess looked like

Queen Mary of Scots on the eve of her execution. And certainly there was something rather withdrawn in her manner. And Basil wasn't his friendly boyish self at all, so preoccupied and quiet, and Miss Marston was so calm and self-assured —there is nothing of the timid young girl about her! Altogether, I came away feeling rather depressed about the engagement. Norman was impressed by the girl's looks and brains and says he doesn't know what she saw in Basil, but *I* think she is the one to be congratulated. I didn't like her."

"But we mustn't forget," Mrs. Sellars said, "that it was rather a trying evening for her, and though she seemed so entirely mistress of the situation, it may only have been seeming. And she is certainly very handsome as well as clever, and Mrs. Stopford may get to like her very much."

"I doubt it," said Mrs. Snow, knitting rapidly. "I thought the mother looked very cowed. Not that I see Mrs. Stopford allowing herself to be trodden on!" She gave an infectious chuckle, and Beatrice laughed too, and thought what a comfortable figure the Rector's wife looked, sitting there, in her plain, black dress, with spotless frilling round the high neck, her white hair brushed high in an old-fashioned way, and her frosty blue eyes sparkling. What a delightful grandmother she would make, the girl thought. Quick-tempered perhaps, but very human and understanding, with such a capacious lap for tired little bodies to rest in, and an almost inexhaustible stock of stories to amuse them with. She could sing too, all sorts of old crooning songs and nursery rhymes, and she would always have a good supply of sweets and sugar biscuits. Any small Anglo-Indians that came home would find themselves very well placed at Oxlip Rectory.

"What time is that?" Mrs. Snow asked suddenly. "Ten to seven! I must fly. Norman may be home any moment."

"Let me walk across with you," said Beatrice.

"Not for the world. It's only a step, and what could happen to me? As my old nurse used to tell me rather blightingly, nobody who saw me by daylight would run away with me in the dark! Good night, my dears. Forget any idle words I may have spoken!"

CHAPTER XXIV

"Naebody kens what the auld folk are thinkin'."

George Macdonald.

January passed with its floods and high winds, and February came with pale sunshine and softer air, and snowdrops pushing their way through the black earth. It was absurd, Beatrice thought, not to allow that February was the first month of spring. The lengthening days, the warmer sun-rays, the pushing up of strong green shoots, a certain liveliness among the rooks in the tall elm tops, swelling buds on the lilacs, the daphnes' flower, could only mean one thing, that, though cold weather might come and go for long, yet the elusive goddess had set at least one foot on the welcoming earth.

One good thing Beatrice found in being alone at 'Twixt Bears was that she was getting to know, every day a little better, her hostess. From the first she had admired her for her patience and her tact and her skilful management of the house, but she had hardly realised how much quiet humour she had, what a well-stored mind. It was a treat to have a talk with her! But the opportunities for a talk were not great, for Granny Sellars was exacting in her demands on her daughter-in-law's company. Although she was so often short with her, lying in the catch, and contradicting her, yet she could not bear to let her out of her sight for long.

One Sunday she had been more than usually trying, "miscalling" people she knew her daughter-in-law cared for, finding fault with the food, criticising the young people of Oxlip, with a wipe in passing at her own grandchildren. Her daughter-in-law bore it all with patience, agreeing when in honesty she could agree, and when she could not plainly saying so.

At last the old woman fell asleep, and looked so helpless and frail that all impatience was wiped out of the minds of the two women who watched her, and there was nothing but compassion in Agnes Sellars' face as she carefully tucked the plaid round her mother-in-law.

Beatrice went out for a short time with Voltaire, and had the pleasure of meeting Colina and being introduced to her husband.

"This is Mr. Merry," Colina said. "You've heard me speak of him," and turning to her perfectly silent husband she continued, "this is Miss Dobie, who came to tea with Mr. Christopher and Mr. Watty, but you weren't in. . . . All well to-day, Miss Dobie? There's a lot of influenza about. Merry, here, has had a touch of it. Ay, it is to be hoped the old lady won't take it, but it's not as if she was ever out and in the way of infection. Chilly to-day, isn't it?"

The couple walked on, and Beatrice next met the Twins, who were going out to tea. "Daddy will meet us at the Armours," Susan told her. "He wanted a long walk. . . . Come to tea to-morrow, Trix, dear. It's so dull with so many Sellars away, and Basil wrapt in contemplations of Miss Marston! Do come."

They went on, and Alice Pugh and her husband, coming in from a Sunday walk, waved a greeting. Beatrice thought for a moment of going in with them, but decided that she had better go home to tea. After tidying her hair and washing her hands, she was crossing the landing to go downstairs when, looking through the half-open door of Mrs. Sellars' room, she saw her hostess sitting there, and stopped involuntarily.

Mrs. Sellars wore a white shawl, for there was no fire, and her hands were folded on a book that lay open on her lap; above her head hung a portrait of her husband, a clever pencil sketch.

Beatrice could not understand why the scene seemed so familiar to her; then she remembered Whistler's portrait of his mother. That was it! Mrs. Sellars looked up and smiled at the girl, inviting her to come in. "This is my retreat," she said.

Beatrice glanced at the book, which was open at the fly-leaf and read, *"To my dear Agnes from John."*

"Tennyson's *In Memoriam*," said Agnes Sellars. "It is one of my favourite books, and I like to have an hour with it on Sunday afternoons. I sometimes don't even read it, but it helps me all the same." She turned her head and looked out of the window, away across the wide marshland to the hills in the far distance. "A wide view is a great comfort. . . . Now I can go down with my temper repaired. . . . Is it four o'clock?"

Beatrice looked at her wrist-watch. "A quarter past four," she said. "I'll go and see about tea, and you mustn't come down for another half-hour. Granny will have everything she wants."

The girl turned to go, but lingered for a second, loath to leave the room that seemed to hold peace within its four walls; the quiet face of its owner, the hands holding the record of a great loss; outside the tranquil grey day drawing to its close, with its Sabbath stillness broken only by a solitary bird-cry from the marsh, and the voice of a child helping to drive in the cows to be milked.

Several times through the evening that followed it struck Beatrice that old Mrs. Sellars was not in her usual good health. Not only was she cross-that was such a common occurrence as to be unworthy of notice-but she turned from her food which generally she enjoyed with gusto, and complained that it did not taste good. Beatrice noticed her daughter-in-law look anxiously at her from time to time, but it was not Mrs. Sellars' way to tease people with questions about their health, so she said nothing.

After supper they turned on the wireless to hear a service, but when Granny Sellars heard that it was from a cathedral she said fretfully that the intoning gave her a headache and she couldn't stand Church of England services anyway, so they turned it off.

Then Mrs. Sellars found a Scottish Church Hymnal and asked her mother-in-law to look out some hymns and they would sing them together. This pleased the old woman, and she chose hymns she had known and liked as a child, and Mrs. Sellars played, and Beatrice sang with unction, for she, too, had been brought up on —

> "There is a happy land
> Far, far away,"

and

> "When He cometh, when He cometh,
> To make up His jewels,"

and

> "Not all the blood of beasts
> On Jewish altars slain."

The familiar words and tunes seemed to calm Granny Sellars, and she talked amiably over her glass of hot milk about days that were gone, when she and her two brothers had learned those hymns together.

"Hymns were rather a treat to us," she told her companions, "after the long psalms; but they were considered poor stuff by our elders, only fit for childish minds. And I must say some of them are very silly, though nothing could be finer than

> 'When I survey the wondrous Cross
> On which the Prince of Glory died.'

And I always liked Horatio Bonar's hymns."

"In the new hymnary," said her daughter-in-law, "they have added some beautiful ones-Bunyan's Pilgrim Song, and some of Christina Rosetti's poems."

"Eh?" said Granny Sellars, suspiciously. "John Bunyan's all right, but I don't know what a Scots hymnary wants with Christina Rosetti's poems. A very morbid woman I always thought, with her talk of graves and directions how they were to mourn her; I never could be bothered with her. Not that I pretend to be a judge of poetry, though I've heard enough of it from a son who had a head full of it. And you, Agnes"—her tone was accusing—"you've seen to it that the children shared your love of poetry and fairy tales, though you know very well it won't help them through the world."

"Don't you think it will, Granny? It helped their father through the war. He sometimes said he couldn't have endured it had he not been able at times to get right away into a world of his own. I expect that was why so many of the young men wrote poetry in the trenches: it was a way of escape."

"Oh, well, maybe, maybe. It was a cruel war. I sometimes dream that it's still going on and waken with a pain at my heart. . . . Is it bed-time? Read the Bible, Agnes, and I'll get away to bed."

Beatrice woke in the night with a start and scratched a match to look at her watch. Three o'clock. Something had wakened her. Lying listening she heard a sound downstairs, so she lit her candle, put on her dressing-gown and slippers, going softly downstairs.

There was a light in the kitchen, and she went in and found Mrs. Sellars heating a kettle on a spirit-lamp.

"Is Granny ill?" Beatrice asked.

"I hope not, but I was rather uneasy about her last night so I've come down once or twice. She was sleeping the first time, but just now I found her awake and complaining of cold. The room is comfortably warm, but I poked up the fire and I'm going to fill this hot-water bag. . . . I wonder if she has got a touch of influenza. There's a good deal about. You might bring in this when the kettle boils, will you, and I'll go back."

When Beatrice took in the hot-water bottle the old lady refused it crossly, saying: "Take it away, I don't want it, I'm far too warm now. It's a drink I want-very cold well water. . . ."

Beatrice fetched a glass of water from the pipe in the scullery that came from the well and Granny Sellars drained it.

"Now, away to bed, both of you. I don't know what you mean coming disturbing me like this in the middle of the night. I'm sure I didn't call, or ring my bell. Don't come back till rising time. I can't bear to have people in soft slippers creeping about my bed."

"I daren't suggest taking her temperature," Mrs. Sellars said, as she and Beatrice went upstairs together; "but I'm pretty sure she's feverish. Well—I suppose we must just wait for the morning. I'll send Ruth to telephone for Dr. Brewster the moment the post-office opens."

"I'll run down every little while and listen at the door," Beatrice volunteered.

"No, go to sleep, child. It's nothing to me to lie awake."

In spite of protestations Beatrice fell asleep the moment she got back to bed, and did not waken till the little room was full of light.

Much ashamed she leapt up and had her bath and dressed in record time. She found Mrs. Sellars in the kitchen stirring something in a pan. She said: "Granny thinks she would like some gruel for breakfast. I don't know what to think of her. She declares that nothing ails her, and won't hear of the doctor, but she is flushed and talks fast and excitedly, and gives a nasty short cough that seems to hurt her. It is very worrying."

"But you will send for the doctor, won't you?"

"Oh, yes. Ruth has telephoned. Dr. Brewster knows Granny well and doesn't care how many insults she pours on him, and once he's really there standing by her bedside, she quite enjoys seeing him. He's a middle-aged man from Edinburgh, so Granny quite approved of him."

The doctor came about eleven o'clock and was very cheerful with his rather difficult patient, but when Mrs. Sellars and he came into the living-room where Beatrice was he said: "It's as you thought, influenza. You don't want a nurse, I suppose? No—I think I see Mrs. Sellars' face if I suggested such a thing. But there is nothing to do more than you are doing. Keep her warm and try to get her to take as much nourishment as possible. I'll look in again in the evening, though she told me just now that she had the deepest distrust of the whole medical profession, and had only lived to her present age through avoiding their ministrations."

The doctor left chuckling, but Mrs. Sellars, who knew him well, saw that he was anxious.

CHAPTER XXV

"I remember thee, the kindness of thy youth, the love of thine espousals."

The Bible.

For three days Granny Sellars was very ill, though never too taken up with her own feelings to fail to twit the doctor with being able to do so little for her; his helplessness seemed to give her a sort of grim satisfaction.

On the fourth day she rallied. Her heart was steadier, her breathing easier, she had some natural sleep, and Dr. Brewster said: "I believe we're going to pull her through after all, or rather let us say, she's going to pull herself through, for it's spirit that does it. Go and lie down, Mrs. Sellars, you're worn out. Miss Dobie'll take charge this morning. Don't let her talk, remember. I'll be in early in the afternoon."

Beatrice persuaded Mrs. Sellars to take the doctor's advice and go to bed till lunch time, and she installed herself in the sick-room, sitting behind a screen so that the patient might not be tempted to talk. But talk she did.

"Are you there, Agnes?" she began.

Beatrice emerged, and explained that Dr. Brewster had wanted Mrs. Sellars to go to bed for an hour or two. "You know," she finished, "Mrs. Sellars was up all night."

"And for all the good she did to me she might as well have been in bed," retorted the invalid. "A glass of water beside me and a night-light, and I'm contented. It was never my way to trouble anyone. But I must say Agnes is a good nurse, gentle and quiet and unfussy. I never was a good nurse: I hadn't patience, maybe, or sympathy. . . . Dr. Brewster was quite pleased with himself this morning; he says I'm better-that shows all he knows about it. Has the man never seen a candle flicker up before it goes out?"

"Oh, but you are better," Beatrice assured her, "you couldn't have talked yesterday. And now, I think, you'd better have a nap." She tried to draw the cover up, but Granny Sellars impatiently pushed her hand away.

"I want no nap," she said, "I'll be silent long enough."

She lay and looked at the girl who stood anxiously by the side of her bed, with a smile that seemed a mixture of envy, pity and ironic humour.

"Now don't fuss," she said. "I won't hold you responsible whatever happens! believe me, nothing can make any difference now. No, don't rush away and waken poor Agnes. She's very tired, I daresay, as she's been often through these thirteen years. It was a hard road for her, and I didn't help to make it easier."

For a minute Granny Sellars lay eyeing her young companion with a curious appraising look, then she said: "Be thankful, girl, if you haven't a jealous disposition to fight against: it embitters everything. I had too good a husband; his gentleness only made me more arrogant-and John was his father's son I had it all my own way, for they both hated dispeace and disputings. Then when I was left a widow, I expected John to be everything to me-and instead he fell in love with Agnes Graham."

The sick woman seemed to muse on this fact, and Beatrice tried to slip out of the room, feeling that the responsibility was too much for her and that Mrs. Sellars must come, but the moment she moved she found Granny Sellars' compelling eyes upon her.

"Can't I get you something," she faltered, but the offer was brushed aside, and the monologue began again.

"There was never anything wrong with Agnes," she said, as if talking to herself rather than to her companion. "I sulked and made the house miserable for him, but he was man enough not to heed me —I would have despised him if he had-and the plans for the wedding went on. I had my own house, my own money, enough to live on, and John made every arrangement he could for my comfort, but I was filled with nothing but resentment. I was a widow, dethroned, and Agnes was reigning queen. . . . They were both patient with me, too patient, it aggravated me that they wouldn't quarrel. . . . The children began to come. Christopher—I remember his father's face as he came to me and said, 'Mother, it's a boy'—and Cicely, and little Jimmy and Jill. I was always welcomed at their house, and I couldn't stay away, for I loved them, though Cicely, who was always impudent, called me 'Cross Granny.' Then came 1914. Agnes' mother died in the spring, and John joined up in August. I thought it was worse for me than for Agnes, and she let me say so. In 1916 little Jimmy and Jill died. When I saw Agnes after, I thought she had aged by ten years-her hair had lost its colour and her shoulders were bent. But I said to myself, 'She will get her husband back and be happy, but I will always be alone.' And they were happy, and Watty was born, and then John died. Agnes was all I had then, and when she made up her mind to go to Oxlip, I said I must go too. She couldn't have wanted me, but she made no objections, and I came and have been here ever since. I was seventy then, now I'm eighty-three —thirteen years I spent away from Scotland, in exile."

"But," said Beatrice, "you brought Scotland with you. Scotland wouldn't have meant much to you without your grandchildren and your daughter-in-law."

"And now I'm going back," said Granny Sellars, with a note of triumph in her voice, "to lie beside my two Johns. Christopher will take me and leave me there. I'd be thankful if I thought that finished it-just lying together in silence-but I know too well it doesn't. God is not mocked: we reap what we sow-unless-unless Christ — —"

Beatrice could bear it no longer-she flew upstairs to Mrs. Sellars, who was brushing her hair preparatory to coming down, and cried, "Oh, please, come down. Granny has spoken all the time, and she says she is going to die."

But when Mrs. Sellars came down she found the patient had dropped into a light sleep.

"Was she talking excitedly?" she asked Beatrice.

"No, oh, no; quite calmly, almost as if she were reviewing her life and passing judgment on herself. It was eerie to hear her. I wanted to go for you before, but she wouldn't let me. D'you think she's very ill?"

Mrs. Sellars stood looking down at the worn face on the pillow.

"Yes," she said, "very ill."

By the time Dr. Brewster came his patient did not know him. She had gone back to far-off days where they could not follow her: she seemed to be speaking to her mother. Just before the end she was quiet, and her daughter-in-law, kneeling beside her, said, "Don't you know me, Granny? It's Agnes."

The dying woman opened her eyes. "Agnes," she said, "Agnes and John. . . ."

* * * * *

Christopher and Cicely arrived the next day, and two days later Christopher took his grand-mother back to Edinburgh where, in the presence of a few old friends, she was laid beside her husband and her son.

Christopher described the scene to his mother as they sat in the living-room together the night he came back.

The table on which had lain her magnifying glass, her spectacles, smelling salts, had been taken away, but her chair still stood in its accustomed place, and the room seemed strangely empty without the little figure with the peering hawk's eyes.

Christopher glanced often at the empty chair as he spoke. "My goodness! Edinburgh is beautiful. I'd forgotten. Yesterday was a 'regatta' day, white clouds sailing, everything as clear as glass, the Forth, and Fife beyond. I thought how Granny would have crowed over the beauty! There were about a dozen men at the grave, none of them, I should think, less than eighty, and all looking as if they'd pretty well finished with the things of time. Three were distant relations, so the lawyer told me. I had never heard of them, and they were very friendly and offered me hospitality, and the others seemed to have known Granny when she was young. D'you know, I felt very sad!"

"I'm glad you did," said his mother, and Christopher went on, "I used to think, as a selfish little beast of a schoolboy, that it would be a very good thing if Granny were away; other people hadn't grandmothers always sitting there making nasty remarks. Granny would have been revenged if she had known with what an ache I saw her coffin lowered. But it was a comfort to leave her there, in her own beloved town, with the wind blowing as if in the rigging of a ship (you remember she always hated what she called the *lown* air in Oxlip?), and the Castle keeping guard, and her own people round her. Life can't be much fun when one has outlived most of one's contemporaries."

Cicely said, "I don't believe Granny cared a bit about that, and in her own way she enjoyed life. Like you, Christopher, I'm surprised at my own sense of loss. Honestly, I didn't think Granny meant anything to me at all, and now she's gone I find she meant a lot. She was part of the background."

"I think *I* shall miss her most," Agnes said after a pause, a break in her quiet voice. "Indeed I can't quite see life without her. She has been my care for thirteen years, and now I feel my hands are empty. I wake up in the night and am halfway out of bed before I remember there is no one needing me."

"My dear, you're tired out," said Cicely. "You've never been away from Granny practically all these thirteen years. No wonder you feel lost. You've got to re-make your life now, and I do hope you will get some fun."

"Oh, Cicely, fun! Why, I'm an old woman. I stood and looked at myself in the glass to-day, a thing I seldom do, and-well, I'll avoid a looking-glass in future."

Cicely chanted,

"The cruel looking-glass
That can always hurt a lass — —"

"But, Mother, that's where you're wrong. Face the glass, study your reflection, and see what can be done about it. No, I'm not being rude, Christopher. Mother's been letting herself go for years. I don't blame her, she had other things to do, but now when she'll have a certain amount of leisure the lamb must take more interest in herself. Mother, I know women years older than you are who look almost like girls — —"

"Yes," said Christopher, "*I* know the sort, with faces like hard-boiled eggs, and painted lips. Don't listen to her, Mother. Nobody wants you changed, but we'd like to see you look less tired. What you want is to get away from Oxlip into entirely different surroundings. Couldn't we arrange it before I go back to-morrow?"

But Mrs. Sellars refused to be rushed into anything.

"There's no hurry," she said, "and there's a good deal to think about and arrange. I am so thankful to have Beatrice with me. You don't know what a tower of strength she has been during this time." Mrs. Sellars put her hand on the girl's shoulder and Beatrice, sitting on a stool beside her, looked up gratefully.

"Indeed we do know," said Cicely. "You couldn't have carried on without Beatrice. It was a wonderful providence that she was here. . . Well, off we go again to-morrow."

"I wish," said her mother, "that you could stay on for a few days. I think you look tired. Have you been having late nights?"

"Well, yes, I have been going out a good deal; one must keep oneself amused, but I'm not in the least tired. Glad, really, to go back to work. There's nothing like it. I've had a lazy few days here. Make my apologies, Mother, to anyone who asks for me, especially to Mrs. Stopford. She made such a point of my dining quietly with her, and I couldn't face it. I'm sorry if she isn't pleased with Basil's choice, but it's no business of mine. Beatrice, I see your relations are back in Portland Place, the Lily-Maid conspicuous at all fashionable gatherings. Have you heard from them lately?"

"I had some cards from Elaine from Madeira," Beatrice said, "and my step-brother wrote me a long letter the other day, mostly about business. He said they were all well."

The brother and sister departed the next day on their different ways, leaving Beatrice dissatisfied. Why she should be she did not quite know, for she had no right to expect anything, but when Christopher had left at the end of the Christmas holidays he had seemed near and approachable, and this time he had seemed far away and preoccupied. That she took an interest in him Beatrice did not attempt to deny. How could she help it? He was practically the first man who had ever taken the trouble to talk to her, to be interested in her opinions. Socially, she had always been so sure that she was not a success that she had gone to parties and dances expecting to feel a failure-and generally did. She had been too self-conscious to make friends with men, and so afraid she was boring them that she was never quite natural, but in the easy, pleasant atmosphere of 'Twixt Bears she had forgotten herself and what impression she might be making and given herself up to being simply happy.

Christopher in his school in Suffolk had felt oddly near her, and it was both chilling and disappointing to find that when she met him in the flesh he seemed so far away. He had made no effort to see her alone. True, there had not been much time, but time enough for him to run over to The Green and see the Twins. That had rankled; she was ashamed that it should. Susan and Sarsa were so nice to visit, eager and welcoming and full of interest in everything, and it had been sad at 'Twixt Bears: a long day of life ringing at last to evensong made one think.

Anyway, Christopher must choose his own company, and Beatrice resolutely turned her thoughts to other things. What if she could persuade Mrs. Sellars to come away with her for a real holiday! She was not needed at home till the Easter holidays-they might go away together for six weeks. Perhaps they might go for a cruise. It would be splendid, Beatrice felt, to go away alone with Mrs. Sellars, to see her delight in new places, to give her every possible luxury, she who had worked all her life for others. What a companion she would make!

And she was Christopher's mother.

CHAPTER XXVI

"Oh, where, I asked, and whither?
He smiled and would not say.
And looked at me and beckoned
And laughed and led the way."

A. E. Housman.

It had seemed to Beatrice that Oxlip must be the most stable and settled of small communities, a place likely to remain unchanged, hospitable doors always open and friendly faces always at the windows, so that her surprise was great when it suddenly began to disintegrate.

The first shock came from her hostess.

Beatrice had found it very difficult to make her suggestion about a cruise, but one morning at breakfast, two or three days after Cicely and Christopher had left, she summoned up all her courage and, with a brightly coloured booklet in her hand depicting a deep blue sea, and brown skinned natives, and oranges in piles in the sunlight, said, "I've been thinking it would be rather nice to go for a cruise-doesn't that look rather alluring?"

Mrs. Sellars put on her tortoise-shell spectacles and looked at the bright picture. "*Very* alluring," she said. "I can't imagine anything more delightful, and I'm so glad to hear you are thinking of it. Of course you must go. It will be a splendid change."

Beatrice was about to propound her plan that Mrs. Sellars should also enjoy the change to new scenes and sunshine when that lady cut the ground from under her feet by lifting up a letter and saying in her gentle, deliberate way:

"It is odd that you should tell me of your plans just at this moment for, in a way, it's the answer to a letter I've had this morning. . . . Did you ever hear me talk of my oldest friend, Mary Livingstone? We went out in our prams together (our mothers were friends before us), we shared a governess, and went to school together in Paris. Mary Learmonth (as she was then) was the prettiest creature as I remember her with her gold hair, like a saint in a picture, and deep blue eyes, and was a great success when she came out. She married an advocate and settled down in Anslie Place where she still lives, but now her husband is dead, and she herself is crippled with arthritis and very much a prisoner. She has one girl, Betty, who seems to be very good to her, and this Betty has got an invitation to go with friends for a cruise to the West Indies, and Mary suggests that I spend the six weeks of her absence with her in Edinburgh. She puts it as a favour," and Mrs. Mrs. Sellars read:

"As you know I can't get about much and it would be a tremendous pleasure to have you with me. What talks we would have over old days! And I would gather any of the old lot who are still in Edinburgh. Elsie Dundas was at tea with me yesterday and she was so excited when I told her that I was asking you to take pity on me in Betty's absence. You will get a warm welcome, I assure you, Agnes, my dear. Thirteen years since you left us and never a glance back. It is outrageous. How can you stay away so long from your native Scotland! Besides, there must be things to settle about your mother-in-law's estate, and as you know your lawyer lives almost next door to me; you could collogue together most conveniently. With your family all away till Easter I really can't see anything to hinder your coming. Do, do, please come."

Beatrice felt as if all her castles in the air were crashing about her ears.

"But," she stammered, "but-will it really be a rest? You won't have to do any nursing?"

"Oh, dear no. Mary isn't as bad as that. Besides, she has a maid to look after her. It's a companion she wants. But I'm very reluctant to go. I'd much rather stay here with you. But if you are thinking of a cruise——"

"But I'm not!" cried Beatrice, "not if you won't come. That was my great plan, that we should go away together into the sunshine, and that you would do nothing for anybody for six whole weeks, but simply enjoy yourself."

"Oh, my dear, what a lovely plan! But of course I couldn't accept. Why, just think what it would cost!"

"Oh, that," said Beatrice, "that matters nothing. You see, I've hardly been spending anything at all for months-just think what you've saved me-and I'd love to spend it on you."

Mrs. Sellars shook her head, but smiled tenderly at the girl. "Dear Beatrice," she said, "I'm greatly touched. I'm more grateful than I can say for your generous thought for me, and not only for that but for all you have meant to me during these past weeks. If this letter hadn't come I would have been tempted to accept, but I could hardly go away simply to enjoy myself when I might be of use to an old friend. Not that I feel I'll be of much use, but it will let Betty go away with an easy mind and I'll always be some one for Mary to talk to-she was a great talker as I remember her. . . . Seriously, Beatrice, I do hope that you will arrange to go this cruise. If you fell in with a nice lot of people you might enjoy it greatly."

"I might," said Beatrice doubtfully. "Oh, well, we'll see. I don't feel like making any more plans for the moment. I'm not very lucky with plans it seems."

"Don't say that, my dear. I could find it in my heart to wish Mary hadn't written this letter. . . . But you are coming back to us at Easter. Remember that. I won't let you leave this till you promise."

"Of course I'd love to, thank you very much. But Easter seems a long way off. Will you shut up this house?"

"I hadn't thought about it. I suppose so. Ruth can go home to her mother on board wages, and do the spring cleaning through the day. Colina, too, will enjoy keeping an eye on things in general and on Ruth in particular. It will be odd to be in Edinburgh again-to walk over the hill from Ainslie Place and see the Castle! Just to think of it makes my heart miss a beat. I must have been more homesick than I realised."

After breakfast Beatrice got her hat and coat and whistled for Voltaire. It was a fine dry morning, though cold, and she felt that a long walk would be a good thing, so she set off across the marsh where she had walked with Christopher and Watty on the last day of the holidays.

She had had a bitter disappointment. What bad luck that this Mary person should have written now. Beatrice reflected that she had never thought of Mrs. Sellars except as a daughter-in-law and a mother; it was quite odd to think of her with a life of her own full of old friends and memories. There had been quite a new look in her eyes as she had spoken of coming over the brow of the hill and seeing Edinburgh Castle. How often she must have longed to lift her eyes and see that sight! Beatrice imagined her friend sitting in the drawing-room of the Ainslie Place house, with Mary Livingstone and Elsie Dundas-such Edinburgh names! —a different woman altogether, young again and free of anxiety, laughing over girlish nonsense out of the past. Beatrice felt almost jealous for Cicely and Christopher and Watty, and laughed to herself at her own absurdity.

Anyway, there was no doubt that Mrs. Sellars would be much happier back in her own land, among her old friends, feeling that she was being of use, than she would have been trying to enjoy herself on a ship, and Beatrice tried to feel philosophic about it. It had been a very happy interlude the six weeks at 'Twixt Bears; she had found herself taken into the heart of a family, had been allowed to make herself of use, and share not only the gladness but also in the anxiety and sorrow. She would never forget old Granny Sellars, the warped, unhappy old woman who had yet had something likeable about her and who was missed now that she was gone. She was a fortunate woman, Beatrice thought, to spend her old age among her own, and to die tended by hands familiar.

Well, now, what was to be done next? Beatrice dismissed the thought of a cruise. It would be too bleak to go alone; all her pleasure would have come from seeing her friend's pleasure; for herself it offered small attraction. She supposed she would go to London and try to fill her time somehow. Anyway, Cicely was there and Jane Naesmyth.

As she was returning from her walk she met the Twins, getting out of the Oxford bus.

"Hallo, Trix!" they greeted her. "Have you heard the news? We're going to London."

Beatrice stood still and stared. "Are you leaving Oxlip?" she gasped.

"Not for good," said Susan soothingly, "only for six weeks. You see we quite suddenly got a chance to let The Green, and it's been so deadly dull since Christmas we jumped at the chance. I want to study dramatic art and Sarsa wants to dance-take classes you know-and Daddy'll enjoy talking to people about the dreadful state of the world in his club."

"But," Beatrice said, "you can't start classes in the middle of the session, can you?"

"I suppose not," said Sarsa. "Never mind, we'll see what can be done, and anyway it'll be great fun being in London, though we'll have to be very economical for Daddy says he simply can't afford it. It will mean 'buses instead of taxis, and the pit at the play, if not the gallery, and a bun to lunch."

"That won't be economy," Susan said, "because lunch comes into the three guineas we pay for board."

"Yes," said her sister, "but a bun would cost less than a 'bus back to Kensington, supposing we were, say, in Piccadilly."

"Well, we'll simply have to see to it that we're within walking distance of the hotel at one o'clock," said Susan, "for it would be a thousand pities to miss a meal that's paid for."

"Of course it would," said Beatrice, feeling that London would be quite homelike now that there was a chance of meeting the Twins round any corner. "We must do some plays together if you have time. I'll probably be going quite soon, for Mrs. Sellars is going to pay a visit in Edinburgh."

"Edinburgh," said the Twins brightly, "that will be a nice change for Mrs. Sellars. Yes, indeed, we'd love to go to the play with you, Trix, dear, any time you like to ask us. We don't expect to be smothered in invitations, for we know very few people, and we've only one family of relatives, people called Wade who are older than Daddy, and lead a blameless existence in Cavendish Square. When do you leave 'Twixt Bears?"

"It depends on Mrs. Sellars. Next week probably."

"Then we'll all be packing up!" said Susan. "We're as busy as can be making clothes. We've been to Elliston's this morning-look at the parcels! Come on, Sarsa, and hurry up luncheon so that we can start at once. I'm filled with excitement at the thought of putting the shears into that gorgeous stuff."

Later in the day Beatrice took some books back to Alice Pugh. She dearly loved an errand to the odd, brightly coloured cottage, which was rich in nothing but books. She found Mrs. Pugh reading a weekly by the firelight.

"Come in," she cried, "and keep me from ruining my eyesight. I was too lazy to light the lamps, besides I like the spring twilight. . . . Please admire my bowls of daffodils-grown by me!"

"Lovely," said Beatrice, "all standing up like soldiers. They're particularly nice in this room. . . . We were thinking we hadn't seen you for an age."

"No. I seem to have been extra busy with one thing and another. But I meant to run across to-morrow to tell you our news."

"You're not going away?"

"Yes. How did you know?"

"Because," said Beatrice, "the whole of Oxlip is on the move: it's a regular landslide. Mrs. Sellars is going next week to Edinburgh, which means of course that I leave Oxlip. The Twins told me to-day that Colonel Fairfax has had a chance to let The Green and they are going to London, and now you — —"

"Amazing!" Alice Pugh held up her hands. "A wind suddenly arises that blows people through the world! Well, we hope we are going to see a little bit of it. Nothing is really settled yet. Denis has gone to London to-day to discuss things, but there is a good chance that he may be sent by a paper to write on the state of things in Germany, and, perhaps, Russia. Denis is an excellent linguist, as perhaps you know, and has studied very carefully the whole subject of world economics."

"And will you go with him?"

"Of course. D'you think I'd let him go alone? As a matter of fact, I'm hoping to be able to pay my own way by writing sketches on what I see. A woman always sees things from a different angle. D'you think there would be any chance of Cicely being able to persuade her chief to give me a commission? I think I could make my articles interesting. Oh, I know my books are dull, but this would be different."

She lay back in her chair and clasped her hands behind her head. "Oh, how gorgeous to get away! To make a pilgrimage in the spring! Even though I lift every penny I have in the bank it will be worth it. To cross the Channel again; to see new things; and meet people who are different, to eat exciting foreign food, to smell fascinating foreign smells. You know how different is the smell of a French town from an English one? And an Italian one is unlike either." She gave a long sigh of anticipation, then said soberly: "I do hope the interview to-day will go all right. This means so much to Denis: it's a job after his own heart, something he could do really well, but I can't help feeling a little anxious, for if he can put his foot in it he will. He's got what almost amounts to a positive genius for saying the wrong thing, and estranging the people he ought to placate. He promised me this morning to do his best to be practical and docile and everything a small man should be when he appears before the great, but —I'm doubtful."

"If the Editor has any sense he will see beneath the surface. . . . Well, I'll be glad if you have this adventure. You deserve it, for you've never shown yourself anything but contented in Oxlip."

"Because I was contented," said Alice Pugh. "We had everything we needed: a roof to cover us, fire, food, books, pleasant neighbours, and a wide outlook. I think Oxlip is an ideal place to return to after one has tried one's wings-as everybody ought from time to time. By the way, I hope we'll find you here when we return?"

"I hope so," Beatrice said doubtfully. "Let us know your plans. Mrs. Sellars will be so interested." She looked round the room, with its amusing decorations, and sighed.

"I do wish," she said, "that people would 'stay put.' It's horrible the way things keep changing."

"But think of the monotony of 'staying put.' "

"I like monotony," said Beatrice, as she went out into the twilight. As she walked across the Green watching the lamps being lit in the cottages and thinking of the Pughs and their affairs, she was suddenly accosted by Mrs. Stopford, who explained that she had been at 'Twixt Bears, heard where Beatrice was and had come to meet her.

"I've had a long talk with dear Agnes Sellars," she went on, "and I'm so glad she is going to have a change and a rest among her old friends. She definitely *belongs* to Edinburgh, dear Agnes, and it will do her a world of good to be back. I'm going away too."

"Oh," said Beatrice. "Where?"

"India," said Mrs. Stopford, "and what I want to ask is will you come with me?"

Beatrice began to laugh helplessly. "Forgive me!" she said, "but this day has been nothing but a succession of shocks. Isn't it rather late to go to India? I thought October was the proper time."

"Yes, yes," Mrs. Stopford said impatiently, "if you mean to spend six months seeing the country. I am only going out and coming back. I had a cable two days ago from a cousin of mine-she was brought up with us as children and is almost like a sister-telling me her husband had died suddenly and begging me to come to her. A good deal to ask you may think, and in ordinary circumstances I'm afraid I would never have thought of it, but with things as they are here, I've a feeling I'd be better out of the way for a little. And of course I'm very sorry for poor Molly Wheeler in her grief, and I'll be glad to be a help to her if I can-she is one of those helpless women who depend utterly on a man. Agnes Sellars said you had spoken of going on a cruise; it would be terribly kind of you to come with me. I sail from Tilbury to Calcutta on Saturday, and don't expect to be more than a week or so in India-then home. We'd be back about the middle of April."

"Must you know now, this minute, or may I take a night to think about it?"

"Why, of course, you must have time to think about it. Come to luncheon to-morrow and tell me, and if you say 'Yes' —as I devoutly hope you will —I'll ring up about a berth. There will be no difficulty about that at this time of year."

CHAPTER XXVII

> *"I have no relish for the country.*
> *It is a kind of healthy grave. . . ."*

Sydney Smith.

That night the two women in 'Twixt Bears discussed in all its bearings the question of a trip to India.

Mrs. Sellars said: "The point is do you want a glimpse of India-it would be the merest glimpse-and do you want it with Mrs. Stopford? I think myself Blanche would make rather a good travelling companion; she's even-tempered and enthusiastic and easily pleased. Her rather gushing manner is apt to make strangers think her too good to be true, but for thirteen years she has been a steady, reliable friend to us."

"It isn't of course a pleasure trip on Mrs. Stopford's part," Beatrice said. "She is really going to fetch home this widowed friend, but there's no doubt she is relieved to find a good reason for going away. Things are evidently not very comfortable and she feels they might be better if she were out of the way. Have you any idea when the marriage is to be?"

Mrs. Sellars hesitated for a moment before replying.

"I am wondering," she said at last, "if there ever will be a marriage. At least Mrs. Stopford said that 'Veronica' was behaving so oddly, never considering Basil's wishes, refusing to make plans or talk seriously about their marriage. It would be funny if it were not such a real trouble, for, though Blanche hates the thought of the girl marrying Basil she hates even more her treating him lightly."

"But what does the girl mean? Why did she ever become engaged to Basil if she only meant to play with him?"

"I don't know," said Mrs. Sellars, beginning to fold away her work. "Veronica seems always to have been a law to herself, accustomed to flattery because she is not only cleverer than most but out of the ordinary good-looking, all that joined to the natural perversity of a young girl. But I can well imagine how miserable it is making poor Blanche. She is right, I think, to go right away and leave them to settle things in their own way. And there is this about the trip, Beatrice, Blanche would be more than grateful for your company. You would be doing a really kind thing."

"As well as seeing something of the world," said Beatrice. "I only wish Cicely had the chance. She longs to travel. As for me, I don't think I'd ever ask for change if I were once settled in a place I liked."

"I can sympathise with that feeling-all the same, I doubt if it should be encouraged. I think if your mother were here she would advise you to see as much as you can, and attempt to do as much as you can while you are young: even in old age there is no need to let go."

"Oh, I know. I can see that you're right; it only requires a screwing up of courage. And I'm not such a mollusc as I was when I came here in December. I've learned a lot. You are all so nice to me you give me confidence in myself. . . . By the way, did Cicely's letter come to-night?"

"Yes, and one from Christopher. They're over there on the bureau."

"Let me get them-may I really read them? Cicely writes such amusing letters. I always think she could write a novel."

Mrs. Sellars shook her head. "I'm afraid it doesn't follow. Some of the most vivid talkers and letter-writers I know are hopelessly dull when it comes to telling a story in print. . . . Isn't it a good thing Cicely is so happy in her work with Jane Naesmyth. And I never feel the least anxiety about her living alone in London, for in spite of all her nonsense she has sense. I know she has all sorts of odd friends, and goes to some very queer places, but she is always the same Cicely, steady and clear-eyed, who sees the good behind the bad, and can love the sinner while hating the sin. Even in her childhood there was something strong and protective about her, she was the friend of every destitute creature and ill-used animal, and had such faith in the largeness of our charity that she never hesitated to bring them home; it was sad, sometimes, to have to disillusion her."

It was always a treat to Beatrice to hear Mrs. Sellars talk of her children, and the eager interest she showed encouraged the older woman to further confidences.

She went on: "Christopher was more imaginative. He is very like his father, both in appearance-that long Scots face-and in disposition. His wish, I am sure, would have been to go across the world. He never said anything, for he felt that his father being gone his place was in this country. And I think he likes teaching, and there are long holidays when he can get away for a bit to climb: mountaineering gives him something of the thrill and excitement of life. You see he says in that letter that Dr. Heard is seriously thinking of retiring. I wonder if that will make a great change in the school? I do hope not, but, anyway, it will make a very sad change for Christopher; he is devoted to 'the Head.' "

Later on, as they were preparing to go upstairs to bed, Beatrice said, "Then, you think it should be India for me?"

"Sleep on it," Mrs. Sellars advised, "and see what you feel about it in the morning. I have no right to advise, but I think it might be an enjoyable trip. . . . Is the front door locked?"

* * * * *

In the morning light the trip seemed less alarming and more attractive, so that when Beatrice walked into the library at Broadmeadows and her visitor sprang up from the fender-stool crying eagerly, "Well—?" she said, "If you really think you can stand me as a travelling companion I'd love to go with you."

Mrs. Stopford kissed the girl saying, with gratitude in her voice, "You are indeed a good friend. I was wondering how I could face the voyage alone, now I shall look forward to it. And it won't really be so boring as a so-called pleasure cruise for they won't always worry us to play games and dance and get up concerts and so forth. There won't be many on board-only those who have to go, poor things-and I think we can arrange each to have a cabin. Come to lunch now and we'll discuss everything. As I told you, we sail on Saturday week from Tilbury. I thought that would really be easier than tearing away to Marseilles."

"Much easier," Beatrice agreed. "We'll miss that long train journey; I don't believe I'll mind the Bay as much as the Channel; you can be ill in the Bay at leisure."

"That's the proper travelling spirit," said Mrs. Stopford, "making the best of everything."

"I'll do anything," Beatrice assured her, "but fly. It's the thought of the noise, and the fear of being sick into a paper bag that unnerves me; also the prospect of being killed any moment. A ship is a more or less natural thing, but an aeroplane. . . . About clothes-what shall we need?"

"Only a supply of washing frocks, and probably you have tennis things that will do admirably. Some tidy clothes for evenings-not too smart, an evening coat to sit about in on deck, a wrap-coat and tweeds for the beginning and end of our pilgrimage."

As they sat over their coffee, Mrs. Stopford asked Beatrice if she were busy that afternoon.

"I was wondering," she said, "if you'd mind going to Oxford with me? Basil has gone to London for a few days —I persuaded him to go-and I think I ought to go and see Veronica in his absence. It would make it easier to have some one with me. Yes. These are the terms I am on with my future daughter-in-law. It may be my fault. I don't know. I did try to seem pleased about the engagement, but I never could act and probably my efforts weren't very convincing. And she makes no pretence at all about caring anything about *me*. She doesn't consider her own mother, why should she bother about Basil's? Indeed, to be frank, she doesn't much bother about Basil either. She really is an extraordinary creature; rolls over everything to get her own way-more like a tank than a girl."

Sorry as Beatrice was for Mrs. Stopford she had to laugh at the thought of Veronica as a tank.

"Yes, but she is," Mrs. Stopford insisted. "Quite calmly and complacently she ignores other people's plans and wishes and tastes and arrives at her own goal perfectly satisfied. However, don't let's talk about it. I've always loathed people who insisted on telling me about their family affairs. Isn't it enterprising of the Twins to get their father uprooted and conveyed to London? He will be terribly bored, poor man, without his garden and his dogs and the birds on Otmarsh, but he will appreciate them all the more when he returns."

"Yes," said Beatrice. "The Twins seem to have some idea of studying something-dancing and dramatic art, I think they said, but they were rather vague about it."

"They would be wise to go in seriously for something of the kind, for they are really clever, and such attractive creatures to look at. I've written to a friend who knows a lot about the theatre, a good-natured woman who doesn't mind taking trouble, asking her to call on them and advise them. They are rather pathetically on their own, poor babes."

"Yes, but not in the least afraid. I think they will always stand up to life like valiant pilgrims."

"I hope so. Their mother was a delightful creature; her death was a cruel blow to poor Colonel Fairfax, and an irreparable loss to the twins. Mrs. Sellars has been a second mother to them. I am so glad she is to get a holiday from us all."

"Yes, but she's going to a friend crippled with arthritis," said Beatrice, ruefully.

"Oh, but that's all to the good. I don't believe she would go only to enjoy herself, the crippled friend makes a reason. It will be a change, and then she will love being back in Edinburgh; it's my belief she has ever been anything but homesick in Oxlip, though she never hinted at it. Agnes Sellars reminds me of Christina Rosetti's queen who gave no sign though 'her white brows often ached beneath her crown.'"

"No," Beatrice objected, "that makes her much too bright and good for human nature's daily food, and she isn't. Those years with Granny Sellars have taught her to keep her temper under complete control, and I've hardly ever seen her even irritable, but she isn't in the least dull; she can sum up people very shrewdly, and she has both humour and enthusiasm."

"Oh, I know, I know," Mrs. Stopford cried. "There is no one I've more respect and affection for than Agnes Sellars. And I'm particularly pleased with her at the moment for going to Edinburgh and leaving you free. You are sure you don't mind going with me to Oxford? Well, I'll go and get ready. I ordered the car at a quarter to three. I thought that would get us there at a good time-luncheon well over and tea still beneath the horizon."

After they were seated in the car the butler placed carefully on the floor a great bunch of carnations and a bowl of flowering bulbs.

Mrs. Stopford looked at them discontentedly as she said:

"I don't believe myself Veronica wants them, but Basil likes me to take flowers."

"Anyone," said Beatrice, "would be glad of such an offering," and little more was said until they reached their destination.

The Marstons lived in a small new villa in one of the many new roads that lie round Oxford. A maid, still in her morning print, with a cap set rakishly on a mop of red hair, opened the door and, saying that both Mrs. and Miss Marston were at home, showed the visitors into the drawing-room.

Beatrice looked round in an interested way. The furniture was very ordinary, a "suite" and an upright piano and rather an ugly carpet, but the prints on the walls were few and good, and there were one or two good pieces of old china. The fire was low and the room, chilly from a recent cleaning, smelt strongly of furniture polish.

Mrs. Stopford laid her offering of carnations on a chair and Beatrice put the pot of bulbs she was carrying on a table, and they sat down to wait. Some one was evidently hurrying in the room above; footsteps ran backwards and forwards; drawers were opened and shut; doors banged. Presently Veronica appeared, charming in a light tweed coat and skirt and a small hat to match. She had been working, she announced, in rather aggrieved tones, and had dressed before coming down to see them as she was going out quite shortly.

"You shouldn't have let us interrupt you," said Mrs. Stopford, while Beatrice remarked that it must be annoying to break off from study to see visitors.

Veronica looked out of the window and made no reply, so Mrs. Stopford began a sort of monologue about the spring weather and the celandines and the great winds that blew away the winter's ills, which was interrupted by the entrance of Mrs. Marston.

Evidently it had been she whom they had heard dressing in a hurry, for she was fastening her belt as she came in, and her hands were still sticky with "vanishing" cream. They were rather hard-worked looking little hands, and Beatrice, noting them, as well as the signs of haste, felt remorseful that they should have come early and disturbed what was probably a much-needed afternoon rest. Mrs. Marston, who was much more forthcoming in her own house than she had been at Broadmeadows, begged Beatrice to take off her coat, and hoped that the visitors meant to stay tea.

When she said this Veronica turned cold eyes on her mother which had the effect of making the poor lady nervous, and she dropped first her handkerchief, and, when that was retrieved, her spectacles.

"Must you, Mother?" said Veronica, sighing with ostentatious patience as she picked up the articles.

Mrs. Stopford at that moment claimed the daughter's attention, and Beatrice entered into conversation with Mrs. Marston who confided in her that they had begun spring cleaning.

"I know it's early," she said, "but you never know what may happen. When February comes I can't rest. We try not to disturb Veronica, her study is always kept to the last. This room is done." She looked over the rather bleak apartment with satisfaction, and Beatrice said: "I've been admiring your pictures."

"*Have* you?" said her companion with obvious surprise. "They're Veronica's taste. All my drawing-room pictures are banished to bedrooms, and my framed photographs, and all my silver things—I used to have such a pretty room, but the taste of the present day is different." She sighed and went on: "The men are coming to-morrow to the dining-room carpet. All morning I was busy getting the room ready, so I was glad to lie down, not expecting visitors, and to think that Mrs. Stopford of all people should come!"

Beatrice sympathised about the broken rest, and said that as Mrs. Stopford was so soon leaving for India she was getting all her visits paid.

"Going to India?" said Mrs. Marston. "I didn't even know she was thinking of such a thing."

"No? I expect she came to-day to tell you. It was very hastily arranged, I believe. I only heard about it yesterday when she suggested I should go with her. And I'm going."

"Oh," said Mrs. Marston, and after a minute added, "Mr. Stopford-Basil I should say-will miss his mother in that big house."

"Oh, I don't think he means to stay at Broadmeadows; there's some painting to be done, and the servants are going to spring-clean, so I think he will be mostly in London-or Oxford."

"Oh," said Mrs. Marston again.

After a pause Beatrice said, "You will miss your daughter badly when she marries."

"Yes," said Mrs. Marston with her lips, but for a moment her eyes met Beatrice's eyes and they seemed to tell a different tale. There was a gleam in them-was it hope, satisfaction or what? Was she seeing a home where she was free to do as she liked, with no daughter to lord it over her, where she could entertain her own friends without let or hindrance and say and do what she liked without fear of criticism? It was only for a moment, then her eyes dropped and she said in her most genteel accents: "I see Mrs. Stopford has brought beautiful flowers. How kind! I always think it must be so pleasant to have a lot of glass."

Ten minutes later, having refused Mrs. Marston's invitation to stay to tea, the visitors departed. As they were getting into Mrs. Stopford's Daimler, another car drew up beside theirs, driven by a good-looking young man with a pipe in his mouth, who leapt out and entered the gate they had just left, and as they drove away —

"Ready, Veronica?" they heard him shout.

"So," said Mrs. Stopford, "that was why Veronica was so smart! Poor Basil!"

Beatrice found nothing to say, but presently she remarked in detached tones: "I like Mrs. Marston. Whoever Veronica marries I hope she will marry soon and let her mother get some enjoyment out of life."

CHAPTER XXVIII

"There's muckle adae when cadgers ride."

Old Scots Saying.

When Mrs. Sellars began to look over her clothes, preparatory for departing to Edinburgh, she found that much was needed, and Beatrice and she had to make several excursions to Oxford for hurried fittings. "You see," Mrs. Sellars said, "I've needed practically no new clothes for years, but I mustn't disgrace Mary Livingstone, so I'll get a new dinner dress-my old velvet will do for home evenings, helped out by the lace one Cicely got me. And with one good coat and skirt for spring days, and your lovely coat for cold ones, I'll feel almost too smart. I do think it was good of you to give me such a beautiful coat, Beatrice. I've always coveted a seal-musquash coat-they are so soft and comfortable looking-but I never hoped to own one. All the same I feel I shouldn't have allowed you to do it; it was too much."

"Too much!" said Beatrice, "as if I could ever hope to repay what you have done for me. You simply can't realise what you did by having me here and making me feel one of yourselves. . . . I think that coat and skirt is going to look very well. I do like a pin-stripe. We mustn't forget about hats. I didn't much care for any we saw the other day, but in a side street I came on rather a nice little hat-shop: it might be worth seeing what it can produce."

"But what about your own things, my dear? One would think that a visit to Edinburgh was more sartorially important than a trip to India!"

"Oh, I shan't need much. I've ordered some washing things; they will do for summer, and two useful sort of evening dresses that won't soil readily, or get out of order, for board ship. Everything else I have."

One morning, two days before they left 'Twixt Bears, Beatrice looked up from a letter and said, "To-night, when we sit at peace by the fire, I'm going to read you what my friend Mrs. Lithgow thinks of India."

"Oh, do, I'll look forward to that. Alice Pugh is coming to tea, isn't she?"

"Yes, and the Twins. Don't let me forget meringue biscuits at Fullers; they adore them. Did you hear they've invited us to a mannequin show to-morrow afternoon? All the things they've been making. Aren't they amazing?"

When Mrs. Sellars had left the room Beatrice sat on, smiling to herself over Mrs. Lithgow.

Peggy had been married with more hilarity than pomp and circumstance on the 11th February, and Beatrice had received the *Herald* and the *Bulletin* —the latter with a good photograph of the wedding group-and when Mrs. Lithgow found time to write, a detailed description. It had evidently been the happiest and heartiest of weddings, the bride and groom radiant, the sun shining on pretty bridesmaids carrying spring flowers, and the air thick with good wishes.

"I must say," wrote Mrs. Lithgow, "it was a pretty sight. Peggy looked her best, for her dress was most successful-the head dressmaker at Masons took a real interest, and that makes such a difference-and she came sailing down the aisle on her father's arm, her face beaming when she saw Harry waiting for her, and it was easily seen that she *had not a qualm*. I can tell you I felt a thankful woman, for there is nothing better that you can wish for any girl than a perfect companionship in marriage.

"I think everybody enjoyed themselves, indeed, I thought they were never going away! And the refreshments were excellent-everything good, and *so* varied. It was a great disappointment to me that Mrs. Murray was not able to be there, poor body, but Mr. Murray came, and they sent a very handsome present, a beautiful screen, Chinese, I think. Peggy is afraid that it will look a little out of place at Brackenbrae where everything is Glasgow made-they were both determined to patronise local industry, but of course it will stand in the drawing-room whether it suits or no.

You can't look a gift-screen in the mouth as the saying is, and we are not going to affront old friends by putting it into a bedroom.

"We have only had two p.pcs. from the happy couple, but they seem all right so far and are enjoying Ireland. We miss Peggy sadly in the house, but we've little to complain of so long as we have each other; and soon she will be in her own house and running in here every day. . . ."

The letter that Beatrice proposed to read to Mrs. Sellars was full of warnings:

"It is nice," Mrs. Lithgow wrote, "that you should see something of the world before you settle down, and I hope you will enjoy the voyage and everything else and that all will go well. But *be very careful*. Don't have much to say to the men on board even if they want to make up to you. How can you tell that they are not married or worse? And be careful of the food. There are so many cases of ptomaine poisoning, with cockroaches in the soup and cold storage going wrong. I had a friend who went to India-your mother knew her, Isa Duncan was her name-and she got sand in her lung (or something of that kind) and was never the same again. Indeed, poor thing, she died, after a long time of ill-health. But I don't want to discourage you, only to warn you. I suppose you know all about the lady you're going with? For on a sea-voyage you are likely to see the worst side of her, especially if she happens to be a poor sailor. . . . You would be very thankful to be able to help Mrs. Sellars when the old lady died. I happened to take up the *Scotsman* one day when I was lunching at the club to glance at the deaths and the first thing I saw was 'Oxlip-Sellars.' It gave me quite a start until I saw it was the old lady. She had reached a long age and I am glad they brought her back to Edinburgh. Not that I would care to lie in that east windy place myself, but it was home to her. We have been having an uncomfortable sort of time for the past ten days, chased from room to room by the servants spring cleaning. I was very busy myself doing out wardrobes and presses, but now it's done and we were all ready to welcome the couple when they came home yesterday. They arrived about eight in the morning, sailing up the Clyde to the Broomielaw, so breakfast was their first meal in their new home, and Peggy said never did a meal taste more delicious. That's the mood she has come back in. They dined here last night. Peggy wore one of her trousseau frocks, and Harry had on a dinner jacket! They say they mean to dress every night. Peggy says it isn't swank, it's more self-respecting. I think, perhaps, she is right, but Father says they needn't expect him to follow their example; his old velveteen coat is good enough for him (what Peggy calls his 's'plush jacket!').

"It seems the weather in Ireland was good, and they liked it so well they mean to go back in summer, and want us to join them. Father is quite keen about it, but I don't like islands; even Arran always gave me a queer cut-off feeling.

"When we stood at the door last night and watched the couple get into their car, laughing and carrying on like a couple of school-boys, Father gave a long sigh and said it seemed a very queer thing to bring up a daughter and give her everything in the world to make her happy and then to see her going off with a stranger, and more than contented to go! I had to remind him that it had been the way since the world began, and it would be that way till it finished, and some people seem to think that it is going to finish quite soon now, and, indeed, it is difficult to see how we are to get out of this tangle unless there is a second Flood and we're all washed off the face of the earth. Did I tell you Mrs. Murray is much worse? I went to see her to-day to tell her about Peggy and Harry, but she wasn't able to take much interest. It did vex me to see her. I doubt it won't be long now. She asked for you and when I told her you were going to India she said: 'A long journey.' I tried to cheer her by telling her you would send her p.pcs. from all the different places you stopped. Write to her Beatrice, before you sail; sick folk are like bairns, a little thing pleases them. . . ."

Mrs. Sellars and Beatrice left on the Thursday morning.

Colina was at 'Twixt Bears before breakfast to see that they got off properly, and to help Ruth to leave the house in perfect order. It was obvious Colina was slightly envious of Mrs. Sellar's trip to Edinburgh. "I hevna much patience," she said, "with people who talk about being homesick, but I must say it gives me a queer lonely feeling to see the mistress go and me left with none but English round me. But of course I'm not the wearying kind and I've plenty to occupy me, and six weeks'll soon pass, and they'll a' be back. It's you that's takin' the long road, Miss. Are ye no feared?"

"I expect," said Beatrice, "that I'm as safe on a ship as I'd be in a London street-or an Oxford one either."

"Eh, that's true. Every time ye cross the road ye take your life in your hand. We live in dangerous times. But they're interestin' times. I fair enjoy the papers. Merry reads them out loud to me in the fore-suppers. I've plenty to keep me busy through the days, what with hens and one thing and another, and I wasna brought up to sit down and read till the day's work was done, but I look forward to the evenings when I can sit with my work by the fire and hear Merry read. He's a quiet soul, is Merry, quite content to bide in the house, once he gets in, and read, and he kens a lot about politics and foreign affairs. Whiles he has me fair *avert* when he talks about Communists and Nazis and such like. All the same I'm glad he's intelligent, for I could not abide to live with a fool. When you marry, Miss, see you get a man who can sit doun and enjoy a book, not one of the kind that aye needs amusing."

Beatrice laughed, and agreed that a man who could be "buried in a book" was less trouble than his more restless brethren, and Colina hurried off to strap a bag for her one-time mistress.

At Rugby, Beatrice saw Mrs. Sellars into the Edinburgh express and went on herself to London.

She had booked a room at the Langham and reflected as she sat down to lunch that it was just two months since she had been there before. Only two months, and she felt quite a different person. For one thing she was richer by a host of friends. She counted them over proudly. Alice Pugh, Mrs. Stopford, the Snows, the Twins, and-above all-the Sellars. What a difference the Sellars had made on her outlook on life! She still felt that she sometimes came woefully short, but she was trying not to shirk, to make the most of what came in her way, to get enjoyment out of all her various experiences.

There were a good many small things to buy at the last moment, but she found time that afternoon to visit Franky's parents.

Cicely came to dinner, looking, Beatrice thought, rather thin and fine drawn, but she seemed in the highest spirits, full of all that she had been doing of both work and play.

"So Mother is really off," she said. "I believe she will love being back in Edinburgh. It may hurt a bit at first-so many memories will meet her-but the pleasure will outweigh the pain. I don't remember ever seeing Mrs. Livingstone, but I was brought up on stories of 'Mary Learmonth' and 'Elsie Dundas' and all the others who were at school with mother. Can't you imagine them reminding each other of this and that? And you've a bold spirit, Bee, setting off for India at a moment's notice. I only wish I were in your shoes. I do so long to see the world and you don't much, do you?"

"Not much," said Beatrice. "It does seem unfair. Never mind, the world won't run away, and there's lots of time before you, I hope."

"I hope so indeed. Mrs. Stopford is so pleased that you're going with her, Basil says."

"Do you see Basil in London?" Beatrice asked.

"Oh, yes. I dined with him last night."

"Oh," said Beatrice, wondering what it all meant.

"It's odd to think," Cicely said, as she helped herself to salmon, "how short a time it is-only two months-since I came here for you that day in December. You were a stranger then, and now you seem one of ourselves-part and parcel of Oxlip."

Beatrice looked down at her plate as she said, "I couldn't ask for anything better." Then raising her eyes she said, "Cicely, you will never know what you did for me taking me home with you that day. Think how rich you have made me in friends-yourselves first, of course, then all the others."

Cicely waved away her friend's earnest gratitude. "All you needed was to acquire 'a guid conceit of yourself.' You were too humble, too easily crushed. By the way, can you give me the Twins' address? I hear they're to be in London till Easter, and I must do something about it. Not that I expect they will need my patronage; they are bound to be a success wherever they go. So long as they meet lots of the right sort of people."

"I wish you had seen their 'mannequin show,' " said Beatrice. "All the things they had made themselves; it was funny and rather pathetic. Mrs. Stopford is giving each of them a coat and skirt from Bradley's. Isn't that a nice present? They can run up house-frocks very cleverly, but street clothes are the puzzle for small allowances. I was wondering, Cicely, if I might make them a present without offence? I thought, if you approved, of posting as I left a note to each of them, £10 I think. Would they be hurt?"

"I'm sure they wouldn't; overjoyed more likely. But, good gracious, girl, how can you go flinging about £10 notes? You will need every penny you have for your trip to India."

"Not every penny I have."

"Had a windfall?"

"Not exactly, but anyway I've more money than I need."

Cicely looked at her friend with eyes of awe. "Say that again," she demanded. "It's the most remarkable utterance of modern times."

Beatrice laughed and blushed and begged Cicely not to be so absurd. "It's owing to you, really, and to your mother's kindness in keeping me so long. I've hardly spent anything at all since I went to Oxlip. . . . Cicely, aren't the accidental happenings of life terrifying? Just think if I'd never met you that Sunday at Miss Naesmyth's, then I'd never have seen 'Twixt Bears, never known your mother or your brothers or dear Granny Sellars!"

"It's a solemnising thought," Cicely agreed, "and it would have been our loss as much as yours." She watched the other diners for a minute or two, then said, "By the way, Christopher seems rather disgruntled about this trip of yours. Did he write and remonstrate with you?"

"No," said Beatrice, enraged to feel her face grow hot, and looking down at the bit of toast she was crumbling to avoid Cicely's clear gaze. "Of course not. He doesn't write to me. Anyway, I don't see why he should object."

"Nor do I," said Cicely. "But men are the *oddest* creatures. . . . Poor old Christopher has got a lot to worry him just now. When Dr. Heard gives up it may make a great difference to him. And his whole heart is in the school. . . . However, as Solomon says, it's no use worrying. . . . Aren't you going to see your relations before you leave?"

"Yes, I'm going to call to-morrow some time."

"I see. Just blow in breezily and announce 'I'm off to India, folks.' You've come on, Bee, in the last two months; there's no doubt about that."

Beatrice remained calm under Cicely's chaff.

"Well," she said, "if I had written and said I was to be two nights in London they would have felt they had to ask me and I'm much better here. Samuel, my step-brother, knows I'm going and quite approves, but I didn't say when."

"Oh, it's all right, only you used to be such a punctilious creature, such a lesson to the free and easy manners of the youth of to-day. I say, shall we go to a show after dinner? There's a good picture, I'm told, at the Regent Street place."

"Well, let's. We'll have coffee in the lounge. There's no hurry for a picture."

* * * * *

Beatrice called at Portland Place about five o'clock the next afternoon, but as she had expected found no one in. Payne took her into the library where she scribbled a note to her step-sister saying that she was at the Langham rushing about London before sailing for India the next day, was sorry to miss every one, but hoped to see them all on her return. The result was a telephone call from Sir Samuel asking somewhat resentfully why she had not come to them, and begging Beatrice (rather in the manner of Mrs. Lithgow) to be very careful on board ship because of the sharks that abound there.

Beatrice, thinking that she must look even sillier than she really was, promised to be everything that was most discreet and went back to the Fairfaxes who were dining with her that last evening. They were going to the play, and Beatrice had taken the precaution of engaging a Daimler car for the whole evening, to do away with the awkwardness of letting Colonel Fairfax pay for taxis which he could not afford.

The Twins were in the highest spirits, one in white, the other in geranium red. "I rather think," Beatrice told them, "that you are what is known as the 'cynosure of all eyes.' "

"Oh, are we really?" said Susan delighted. "I do love to dine in public. It's so interesting to have a lot of people to look at. I don't know how I am ever to get used to being at home again with nothing to look at but the four walls of the dining-room? Sarsa, d'you see that girl in pink velvet? Isn't she lovely? And *she's married*! I saw her ring."

"She could easily be married," said Sarsa; "she must be twenty if she's a day. I wonder which of those men is her husband? I hope for her own sake it's the fair-haired one-he has a look of Christopher. But it may be the fat black one."

"Don't stare so, children," said their father.

"But, Daddy, country cousins always stare," Sarsa reminded him. "You won't let us be late, Trix. We *must* be in our seats quite five minutes before the curtain goes up, and it takes quite a while to get down to Shaftesbury Avenue."

"We came here by the tube," said Susan, "and managed nicely. Daddy won't enter one when he's alone, says he has a horror of being set adrift down a tube! He walks or takes a bus, usually walks."

Beatrice begged them not to worry about being in time. She said, "We can eat our dinner in comfort, for I've got a car for the evening. Coming home it will drop me and take you on to Cromwell Road."

"Oh, Trix, you're very extravagant," said Susan.

"But very sweet," said Sarsa. "How I'm looking forward to 'The Yeoman of the Guard,' the first Gilbert and Sullivan I've ever seen."

"I remember," said her father, "seeing it in London in 1908. There are some lovely things in it, '*Is life a boon?*' and the quartette, '*Strange adventure, maiden married.*' . . . I used to know it all by heart. We did it at Balapore the next year. Rawson took the tenor part-Fairfax. He died of cholera, poor chap, shortly after."

He sighed, and Susan said:

"Nearly all Daddy's stories end in gloom."

CHAPTER XXIX

"Now if we set sail to-morrow,
You and I,
If the waves were liquid silver, fair the breeze. . . ."

Margaret Veley.

Of all miserable things surely the getting on to a ship is the most miserable, at least Beatrice thought so, as she and Mrs. Stopford set sail from Tilbury on a typical February day.

It had been quite gay at Liverpool Street, with Cicely there and Basil, not to speak of several of Mrs. Stopford's friends who had bestowed flowers and chocolates and good wishes in abundance, but at Tilbury the rain was pouring, and they were chilled by a cold, blustering wind. The *Mandoa* lay out in the river, and there seemed to be such a crowd of passengers that it was surprising how they all got on to the tender.

Mrs. Stopford was an old traveller and once on board immediately found a steward to show her the cabins, and remained in her own until luncheon, putting everything as she wanted it. Beatrice, however, was restless, and leaving her luggage as it was, she found her way to the top deck. It was interesting to watch the bustle and confusion and to gaze furtively at the passengers, wondering what they would be like when she got to know them.

They had hardly finished luncheon when a bell rang. It had such a tocsin-like sound that Beatrice looked at Mrs. Stopford, who said: "It's to warn all who are seeing-off friends to leave the ship."

Beatrice's face paled. "Oh, why did they come?" she cried. "Surely it would have been easier for them to say good-bye at home. I wondered why that girl looked so miserable; probably that's her husband."

"East-going ships are always sad," Blanche said. "They always mean separation. A woman leaving all her children at school and going back with her husband must carry a load of care. But they are marvellously plucky. After a day or two you see them playing deck-games, and dancing, as if they hadn't a worry in the world. I do admire them. . . . Shall we go up and see the last of England?"

As they leant over the side, watching the tender grow smaller till faces were indistinguishable and the waving handkerchiefs made a white blur, Mrs. Stopford said:

"Most of the passengers will come on at Marseilles; it gives them a few days longer at home. It is only the people with lots of time like ourselves, or who haven't the money for the long train journey, who go from Tilbury. Well, we're leaving a dull and rainy England; it will be a pleasure to see the sun."

Beatrice agreed, but her spirits were very low at the moment. England might be dull and rainy, but somewhere in it, among the green Suffolk downs, was Christopher, and now every minute was taking her farther from him. In a way she was glad to be going away, and it had given her a momentary satisfaction to hear from Cicely that Christopher had not liked the idea of her taking the trip-it was something to know that he was sufficiently interested in her to be annoyed by anything she did-but she could not help feeling depressed. She had hoped there might be a line from him or a wire-it would surely only have been friendly, but there had been nothing.

Mrs. Stopford was speaking. "Basil isn't going back to Broadmeadows till the end of next week and then only for a day or two. He didn't mention Veronica, nor did I, but I can't help thinking he is getting tired of being treated as a thing of no importance, and is asserting himself. High time too. It has done him good being in London. I thought him looking well, didn't you?"

"Very well," said Beatrice. She had been struck by the air of complete satisfaction with which Basil and Cicely had walked off together, and wondered much what was going to happen.

Later, they went to their cabin to tidy for tea, and when Beatrice joined her friend she was a different creature.

"I've had a wire from Mrs. Sellars," she said, rather breathlessly, "a long one. She is well and happy and sends all sorts of messages to us both. My step-sister wired too."

But neither of these messages accounted for the fact that the girl's face which had been pale was now softly flushed, her eyes bright, and her mouth turning up at the corners. With the telegram the steward had brought her a little box which, he explained, should have been in her cabin when she came aboard. The box contained a few early primroses lying on moss and on the top a scrap of paper with the words, "Love from Christopher."

That was all, but it was enough. Not even a rough Sunday in the Bay could depress Beatrice with that message to hearten her.

Buttoned into a warm coat she marched up and down the deck, every now and again running down to see how Mrs. Stopford was getting on in her cabin. That lady, feeling that discretion was the better part of valour, remained in her bunk, passing the time snoozing when she was not reading a light novel. It was a pleasant change when Beatrice came in, smelling of fresh air, her cheeks aglow, her bright hair escaping from under a jaunty cap, and seating herself on the sofa gave an account of herself.

"I've made friends," she announced, "with a Government official, a high-up one; such a precise, little, dried-up man, absurdly named Samson. He seems to like a listener, and he's been telling me about all the different voyages he has made. He has been all his life in India-at least since he was twenty-three —and this year retires for good. I asked him if he were glad. 'Glad?' he said, 'Why should I be? I've hated it most of the time, but I'll miss it. It's dull in England without work. My wife died two years ago; I've two boys, one at the Cape and one in Nairobi; there's nothing for me but rooms in London and hanging about the Club in the hope of meeting men I used to know, who'll talk about India.' Wasn't that rather sad?"

"I advised him," Beatrice went on, "to take a cottage in the country, with a garden. He doesn't know how much interest and excitement there is in a garden, poor man. Besides, as I told him, you can't make friends in London, not real friends such as you make in the country."

Blanche Stopford smiled to herself when Beatrice left her, and thought how pleasant it was to have such a contented, unfussing travelling companion. In a short time the girl was back again.

"I swoop on you like a gull," she said. "How are you feeling? Yes, keep on sniffing the smelling-bottle. There are no women on deck except Angel-Face —you know the pretty woman at our table with the blue eyes and golden hair? She is being given brandy by a red-faced colonel. The wind is awful but it's rather jolly. No, I don't feel a bit ill, only I shan't risk eating anything. There's a poor shivery ayah in a tweed coat trying to control a wicked little boy who wants to climb on to the rail. His mother can't leave her cabin, and I told him I'd give him a beating if he didn't desist. *He swore at me!* Oh, yes, a thoroughly bad boy, but rather a dear. I'm going to take him up some of my chocolates."

The next time she came the afternoon was waning.

"There's a woman in a cabin along there with *the* most wonderful pyjamas. . . . Couldn't you take a cup of naked tea? I'll get the steward to fetch it freshly made and weak. Then you might feel like sitting up for a little, perhaps. The wind's going down; they say we'll have a quiet night."

The next day was better and Mrs. Stopford was able to go on deck, and by the time they reached Marseilles she was fit for anything. They explored the town and visited the sights, and Beatrice sent picture post-cards to every one she thought might like the attention.

A number of fresh passengers came on and the ship woke to life. As it happened, there were few girls on board and Beatrice had no lack of cavaliers; though, as she told her friend, she did not find them very exciting companions.

"They all want to talk about themselves," she said, "but I don't mind as I'd really rather listen than talk. It's rather depressing, though, for life has disappointed most of them. They don't want to look forward, all their pleasure is in looking back to the days when they first went out, with everything before them and no limit to their hopes and ambitions. Nearly all the people they tell you of are dead, and most of the things they worked so hard for have been scrapped. India seems such a hopeless proposition. I'm afraid I always skip reading about it in the papers. It isn't as if we had grudged India our best brains and some of our finest young men, and they work themselves to death without seeing any fruit of their labours. Everything is done with the best intentions, and yet everything seems to work out wrong. I'm terribly sorry for those poor 'sun-dried bureaucrats' who will go home to live in Sidmouth or somewhere and have nothing to do but play golf and rage over *The Times* or the *Morning Post* where Indian rule, or mis-rule, is discussed."

"Oh, I don't know," said Blanche Stopford, who at that moment was feeling very comfortable herself. "You must remember that they have a good pension-and that is something to be thankful for in these days. And they can live among their own kind and have cosy times grousing about everything in the present, and recalling the brave days when they were, if not Kings in Babylon, at least of vast importance in their own provinces."

Beatrice laughed as she said, "I daresay you're right. A legitimate grumble is something to be thankful for. . . . See what a lovely time Angel-Face is having! What amuses me is the way she fits them all in. She gives the story-book-looking Colonel his time after breakfast; three turns round the deck; arch ejaculations from the lady, and a deep 'I assure you, dear lady,' from him. Then the Commissioner of Boggley Wallah has the honour of settling her into her chair —a pretty performance: rugs, books, smelling salts, a box of *marrons-glacés*. He sits beside her and talks while she gazes wistfully out to sea. They are interrupted by that nice young soldier with the very red head, who brings her her beef-tea and seats himself on the deck at her feet. She looks down at him with a sort of girlish maternal air, and her hand hovers over his red head but never quite descends, while he tells her jokes he has heard from the barber. Presently she sends him away and opens a book-but seldom turns a leaf. At 12.30 the good-looking doctor appears and suggests a walk before luncheon. And that is the morning. In the afternoon she sleeps in her cabin till tea, and emerges very sweet and fresh, ready to play deck-games or promenade, then to dress again, dine, play bridge or dance, always before an admiring audience. A great life! She certainly is deliciously pretty in a film-star way, and I don't think she's a cat: she's always very civil to me any time we meet. Perhaps she's married to some decent dull man in some out-of-the-way place and stores up admiration, as a bee stores honey, against empty hours."

"Is that why bees store honey?" Blanche asked lazily, idly amused at her companion's chatter. "D'you know, my dear, you're developing a sense of humour."

"Am I?" said Beatrice, much amused, for it had always seemed to her that Mrs. Stopford's great lack was the saving salt of humour. "I quite thought I had one! Isn't it odd how a thing may seem simply wildly funny to one person and not in the least amusing to another. You remember Hugh Wakefield in *77 Park Lane*? I laughed till I ached and the man in the next stall never even smiled. That seemed to make it funnier, and every time I looked at his impassive face I went off into fresh paroxysms. But there are awful moments when by everything you hold sacred you ought to be grave, and some one trips over a chair and in a moment you are a ruin of helpless laughter. You remember Martin Ross in *Irish Memories*?"

"Are you an Irish M.R. enthusiast?"

"I should think I am," said Beatrice. "My mother and I read them aloud, and sometimes we laughed so much we couldn't go on. The McRories! And the night when Major Yeats fled with the hound and the cook put the cuckoo clock into the flour-bin!"

"Yes," said Blanche, "my husband adored them and kept reading them aloud to me. It may be some lack in myself but I never found the Irish very funny. I once stayed in Ireland with some people and I hated the sort of slip-shod, untidy way the house was run. When the butcher didn't send the meat they seemed to regard it as a good joke! And everything was damp. I was glad to get away."

"Then," said Beatrice, holding up the book that had been lying on her lap, "I shan't urge you to read this. It's very Irish and full of the charm of all the things you dislike. You know, we needn't have burdened ourselves with so many books; there's an excellent library on board."

"This," said Blanche, looking down at her omnibus volume, "will almost last me the voyage. I find it very interesting-the life of a woman from childhood to old age: we pursue her through three long novels; it's a *rich* book."

"Then," said Beatrice, "if you read it all the way out, may I read it all the way home? I can't think why some people object to long novels. The longer the better for me-if they can keep it up to the finish. Think of *Royal Flush* and *Broom Stages* and *Judith Paris*. I was desolated to part with the people in each of them. . . . Well, shall we go down to dress? Isn't it amusing how important meals are on board ship?"

It was a pleasant voyage; the heat was not too burdensome, and the days ashore at Port Said and Colombo were quite entertaining. The older and the younger woman fitted into a most comfortable companionship, and when they boarded the pilot on the Hooghly and realised that soon they would reach their destination, Blanche Stopford said with real regret, "I'm sorry the voyage is over. It has been so peaceful. I left home feeling jangled and out of tune, seeing everything in wrong perspective, and now, thanks to the air and the sea-and thanks to you, Beatrice, for you've been a dear all the time —I feel a new woman."

"I'm glad," said Beatrice. But that night in her cabin she told herself that she was thankful the voyage was nearing an end. All the time she had been talking and laughing and playing, her thoughts had been in England. She was in a fever to get back before the Easter holidays finished; she could not bear the thought of missing spring in Oxlip with Christopher, when the daffodils would be out, as he had said, making a cloth of gold round the grey church.

Not that she flattered herself that Christopher would miss her. That would be too much to hope. True, he had sent her primroses with his love; but she was stern with herself about that, refusing to allow herself to make too much of it. He had done it out of a friendly feeling for a girl rather pathetically alone in the world. That was all.

And as Beatrice sat on the edge of her bunk and heard the Hooghly water softly flapping against the side of the ship, she sighed as maids have sighed in uncertainty from the beginning of time.

CHAPTER XXX

"O mistress mine, where are you roaming?"

Twelfth Night.

Mrs. Stopford had engaged rooms at a hotel in Calcutta for Beatrice and herself, but Mrs. Wheeler wired that she expected them to stay with her in a house she had been lent in Harington Street, and when they landed they were met by a dignified servant in spotless white who conducted them to a waiting car, and said their luggage would be brought on at once.

It must be confessed that Beatrice got something of a shock when she beheld the lady they had come to comfort and assist. Accustomed to widows who would have fulfilled St. Paul's idea of "widows indeed," Mrs. Wheeler in her most becoming mourning came as a surprise. She seemed able to take a most vivid interest in everything that concerned herself and her own well-being, and determined to miss nothing that she could help.

She greeted Mrs. Stopford with enthusiasm, her companion with indifference. Again Beatrice had the feeling of being in the way that had so afflicted her at Portland Place, for Mrs. Wheeler led her cousin away to her own room, remarking, "Darling, I *must* have you to myself for a little. How it brings everything back to see you," and her handkerchief went up pathetically to her eyes.

An ayah took Beatrice to her room, which she found delightfully large and airy. After being cabined and confined for weeks it seemed almost absurd to see such a sea of floor space, with a white-curtained bed like a small ice-floe on its surface.

The ayah padded about with bare feet, clucking with her tongue over creased dresses and hanging them up to the air, putting others away in the *almirahs* and filling drawers with under-clothes.

Presently Blanche came in and sunk down on a large cane chair. "Are you all right?" she asked. "We're in luck to be in this cool, airy house. I daresay we would have found the hotel pretty stuffy! That reminds me, we must send our address to the hotel in case letters come. There may be some now."

"Oh," said Beatrice, her heart giving a jump as she thought that perhaps Christopher might have written, "I could only hear from the Sellars, for no one else has my address. I told them not to forward letters. I didn't expect there would be anything of importance; I haven't very many friends."

"I envy you, my dear. I've far too many. No, that's wrong, one can't have too many friends, but I've too many acquaintances; idle creatures who sit down and scrawl off notes, never thinking what a nuisance they are to answer. And, really, I've been a very busy woman, what with the Institute and the Village Industries as well as Broadmeadows to look after. Of course Basil will take over that responsibility when he settles down, and everything else will come to an end for me automatically. It will seem strange at first, in London, away from all my village interests, but I daresay I'll find others."

"You will be badly missed in Oxlip," said Beatrice, and then, to change the subject, remarked, "Mrs. Wheeler seems wonderfully-composed."

"Yes," said Blanche. After a minute she went on, "There are all sorts of ways of taking sorrow-some drown in it and never rise; others are made reckless by the pain of it and are glad of any alleviation, careless of what the world may think of their conduct; others, again, are quite incapable of feeling anything acutely, and can't even convincingly pretend grief. Poor little Molly! She was a great deal with us when we were children. She is some years younger than I am and I've never got over a feeling of responsibility for her. I didn't expect to find her inconsolable-though her letters sounded as if she were. The pathetic thing is, she doesn't in the least realise what she has lost. Bill Wheeler would have stuck to her through anything and never ceased to care for her, being made that way. Perhaps there is a certain-But I mustn't discuss poor Molly. Bill would have hated to hear me criticise her; he always covered up her faults and invented excuses for her. . . . Well, my dear, you and I must see something of Calcutta now that we are here. I wonder if it would be rash to attempt the journey to Darjeeling, I've always had a great desire to behold the Himalayas."

But it was evident almost directly that Mrs. Wheeler had no intention of allowing her cousin and Beatrice to enjoy themselves together. Always she had something to suggest, some pathetic little plea to put forward, that effectually spoiled any plan they had made for the day. Often Blanche had to give in, but now and again she remained firm.

"You must remember," she told her cousin, "that Beatrice came this trip out of kindness to me; it would have been a dreary voyage to me without her and I've got to see that she enjoys her short time in India."

"Well, who is hindering her?" Mrs. Wheeler asked. "I'm sure my friends have been very good asking her to do things. She can play tennis every day and dance every night if she likes. And they only ask her for my sake, for she is really very dull as young girls go now. Don't you think so?"

"No, I don't," Blanche said shortly. "And as for asking her out of kindness that's nonsense. For one thing the mere sight of her must be a refreshment. She's like a rose in a desert place."

Mrs. Wheeler gave a little laugh. "Oh, I grant you a perfect wild-rose complexion. But that sort of thing has gone out so completely. A complexion out of a box is so much more amusing, and can be changed for every mood. With the real thing a girl can only be dull and primly proper-like your Beatrice."

Blanche restrained herself and said, "Well, we won't argue about it, Molly. We're going out to Tollygunge this afternoon. The Beatsons are calling for us."

Molly Wheeler put her handkerchief to her eyes, as she said, "I suppose I must try to become used to loneliness."

"You won't be lonely this afternoon, anyway. Haven't you people coming for tea and bridge?"

Mrs. Wheeler was hurt but dignified. "It is rather hard," she said, "when one is making a great effort for every one's sake to bear up under a crushing blow, to find oneself misunderstood by one's oldest friend. Do you suppose I have any heart to see people or to try and dress becomingly or play bridge? I do it because it seems more unselfish than to shut oneself up and give way to grief. I ask myself what my dear Bill would have wished me to do." She threw herself down among the cushions on the sofa crying, "Oh, Bill, Bill, come back to your little girl!"

"Poor Molly!" said her cousin, realising that this grief, if transient, was real. Bill had always been the final refuge. When friends and admirers had failed her-as they always did sooner or later, for she tried them too high-it was on her faithful Bill's shoulder that she wept out her disillusionment before proceeding to pastures new. And he, decent, long-suffering man, with no illusions left, had always been able to feel for his silly little wife, and comfort her.

In a short time Mrs. Wheeler sat up and carefully re-arranged her face, and all day was very dignified in her manner towards her cousin.

Beatrice, on the whole, enjoyed her time in Calcutta. Mrs. Wheeler's peevishness did not trouble her; she was very willing to make allowances for a woman left widowed and childless; and other people were kind. She developed a sudden friendship with the young cheerful wife of a civilian, fresh from Devonshire, who was glad to find a companion. Together they explored shops and markets, and in the cool of the evening watched tennis and drove in the Maidan.

"Are Anglo-Indian women difficult to get on with?" Beatrice asked her new friend.

"Not really," said Betty Fawcett, with all the assurance of four months spent in the country. "Some of them are a bit shrewish-climate and years telling, you know-but I haven't met anything yet that is positively malignant. Partly, I expect, because I'm no beauty. And Barty, bless him, is no lady's man, so there is not much competition for either of us. 'Tis better so. We enjoy a quiet life and I'll be glad when Barty finishes his secretarial job here and we get away to the Mofussil. Being country-bred I want a house of my own and a garden, and animals galore.

And it won't be half so wearing for Barty. Here in Calcutta these *chaprassis* with their piles of documents give him no peace. I get so sick of them. Not, mind you, that I haven't enjoyed my cold weather in Calcutta. It's been jolly, and I've had a chance to wear out my trousseau frocks. It was very gay round about Christmas-time —but give me the country every time."

"And you like the thought of spending your life in India?" asked Beatrice-Beatrice who was counting the days before she got back to England.

"Oh, I didn't say that. But I've got to like it. It's Barty's job and I'd rather be with Barty in Hades than with anyone else in Paradise-if you know what I mean."

"Yes," said Beatrice, slowly, "I know what you mean," and tried not to feel envious of this round-faced girl with the Devonshire complexion, who was so satisfied with her little sandy-haired husband.

It was the evening that they went on a launch, Beatrice and the Fawcetts, to the Botanic Gardens, that the wonderful thing happened. Beatrice came back to the house in Harington Street feeling rather tired and out of spirits. The heat was beginning to try her, and she longed to be on a ship heading for clean, cool Western lands.

Somehow it had made her very homesick to see Betty and her husband together, to watch their glances at each other, the surreptitious way they clasped each other's hands.

When she reached her bedroom there was a flimsy envelope lying on her dressing-table. Who could be wiring to her in India where she knew no one? It might be from England —a cable; in which case there must be something seriously wrong. Beatrice stood a yard away and surveyed the envelope as if it were an evil thing, then she tore it open and read —

"Will you marry me. Christopher."

For a few seconds the words conveyed nothing to her, then suddenly her heart seemed to leap into her throat. She leant forward and stared at the reflection of her own face in the glass as if she had never seen it before. . . . Thoughts rushed through her mind. Betty and Barty Fawcett, she need not envy them any more: Christopher was hers, they would belong to each other utterly through life and death.

She sank on her knees, her head bowed on her arms among the brushes and bottles on the toilet-table. She did not consciously pray, but her heart sang a pæan of love and gratitude.

Presently she came back to earth and realised that it was high time she was getting ready for dinner. Still feeling rather dazed she took her bath and got into the dress the ayah had laid out for her, and, as she heard the rumble of the gong, folded carefully the precious cable and put it into the safest recess of the evening bag she was carrying, and went downstairs.

It was odd, she thought, that no one seemed to notice any difference in her, she, who in a moment, by the reading of five words had been lifted out of this common earth.

Blanche Stopford asked about the expedition, and Molly Wheeler wondered how anyone could possibly want to look at things like Botanic Gardens. "That little Mrs. Fawcett," she said, "makes a great pretence of freshness and interest and high spirits. It's a pose, of course. She feels it goes with her complexion. She will soon give up the one and lose the other. They say her husband is clever, but I've always found him deadly dull: the sort of man who looks at his dinner with more interest than his partner. Were you alone with the couple? You must have felt rather in the way."

"Yes," Beatrice said, "I did a little. It's rather nice to see two people so happy about each other."

"It won't last," said Mrs. Wheeler, "there's nothing in that round-faced girl to hold a man. Blanche," turning to her cousin, "you must come with me to-morrow to Hall and Richards. I'm not satisfied with one of the evening frocks they're making me and you will help me to talk to them."

"Wouldn't you have been better to wait till you were back in London to see about clothes?" Blanche suggested mildly.

"And what would I have done on board ship? I've practically nothing but what I'm wearing, and I can't look a fright, not with the Austens on board and Lady Solomon who dresses so exquisitely."

"Very well," said Blanche. "I'll go with you to-morrow, though, I warn you, I'm not much good at scolding people. But I'll listen to you and murmur assent. What do you want to do to-morrow, Beatrice?"

"Oh-nothing," said Beatrice, "I'm very happy just sitting about thinking."

Molly Wheeler stared at the girl.

"You're lucky," she said, "to have pleasant thoughts. Some of us dare not think."

Later that night Beatrice, safe once more in her room, printed carefully two words —"*Yes. Beatrice.*"

CHAPTER XXXI

"Albeit my body be absent
My faithful heart is vigilant."

Alexander Montgomerie.

Perhaps it was not surprising that, the moment Beatrice despatched her reply to Christopher, she fell a victim to a thousand doubts and fears. It was so unbelievable. Might there not be some mistake? Had she been too quick? Had she jumped at the offer, to use Colina's expression, "like a cock at a grosset"?

For a day she alternated between hours of misery and minutes of wild happiness, then another cable came —

All my love. Christopher.

That settled everything. After that she gave herself up to dreams. Often she said to herself in these days, as she sat through the hot hours in darkened rooms sewing, writing letters, talking to Blanche Stopford, or in the cool of the evening, driving, or watching tennis, "Surely this must be the happiest time in my life." She could have cried with Charles Lamb, "Here let me stay and build a sanctuary; I am content." To know that she was loved, to rest in that assurance, it was enough; almost she shrank from going home to the realisation of her dreams.

Presently she found that this new happiness woke her to life in an amazing way. Her appreciation of everything was deepened; meals were more enjoyable, a play more interesting, music more full of meaning, beauty more entrancing, because Christopher loved her. She felt more affection for her friends, more tolerance with irrelevant people, and a new pity and understanding for the lonely and disappointed. Even Mrs. Wheeler received a share, but happily she did not acquaint the lady with her feelings, for nothing would have angered that rather wanton widow more than to know that Beatrice out of pity was trying to like her.

Mrs. Wheeler, as the time for leaving drew near, needed more and more help and advice from her cousin, so Beatrice was much alone, and would have been more, had not Betty Fawcett, who greatly regretted losing so soon a congenial companion, constantly suggested things they might do together. She found the Scots girl a perfect listener, and poured into her ears details of her home life in Devonshire which she so delighted to recall. On her part Beatrice was only too pleased to hear of the kind, busy mother, and the father who lived for his pedigree cattle, and the sisters, one older and one younger than Betty, and the two schoolboy brothers. Through Betty's eyes she saw the serene Georgian house standing among its green lawns, very shabby as to carpets and cushions, but full of sunshine and happiness. She heard of Barty's first appearance, one summer day, at a neighbouring house.

"It was a tennis party," Betty told her; "we played together, then he took me to have tea. Next day he came over with the Bridports to tennis at our place. He says he knew from the first-and I think I did too. And now I know that everybody else saw it too. Neither of us noticed that we were always being given opportunities of meeting-picnics, tennis, dinners with a dance afterwards. People were really frightfully decent. And then we got engaged-that was in August-and we were married in October, just before Barty's leave was up. It was such a pretty wedding, in our village church, with Nancy and Joan, and two girls we had grown up with, as bridesmaids (Barty has no sisters), and all the neighbours there to wish us well. And Daddy kept saying, 'Bless the girl, what does she want to leave us for!' and practical Mums said, 'Well, it's a blessing to have one provided for in these hard times,' and then cried a little because I was going so far away. But all the girls envied me going to India, and Daddy promised that Nancy would come out to us for a cold weather. That's one reason why I'm so keen for Barty to get an Assistant Commissionership or something, in some fairly nice place, for Nancy would simply love the life-as much riding and tennis as she liked-and dancing at intervals. She wouldn't care for Calcutta."

"That," said Beatrice, "will be something to look forward to-your sister's visit."

"Oh, yes, if I needed anything. It may be different in a year, but after nearly five months I'd grudge a little giving up our solitude-even for Nancy. Barty's splendid. He never grouses and he's never irritated at my mistakes (and they are many). He is always thinking of things that'll give me pleasure. My goodness, it makes me shiver to think what I'd have missed, if anything — a cold, maybe, or a headache-had kept me away that day from the Bridport's party. I say, if ever you're anywhere near Seaton you might go and see my people. They'd love it. You could tell them all about me. Parsons is my father's name, and Knole Corner the name of our place. Do go. You might easily be taking a motor tour in Devon and Cornwall, mightn't you?"

"I might," said Beatrice, but said nothing more. Not even to Blanche Stopford had she mentioned Christopher's cable. There was time enough to tell; meantime it was her precious secret.

Mrs. Wheeler became increasingly occupied, and seemed always at the telephone, or talking to the people who streamed in a procession through the house. One day Beatrice said to Mrs. Stopford, "Surely Mrs. Wheeler is very popular," and Blanche laughed, remarking, "Your surprise is hardly flattering! There's a lot to see about when you leave a country for good, and though Molly has only been in Calcutta since October she seems to have no end of friends."

Beatrice thought of a sentence she had read somewhere, "*Her new friends liked her, she had no old friends*," and felt a cat.

"Sorry to go, Beatrice?" Blanche asked her.

"In a way. It will be much shorter going home from Bombay, won't it?"

"Much. I can't help wishing we were sailing all the way, but Molly wouldn't hear of it. It means that we see a little more of India, that's something."

At last they were on board ship.

Beatrice was sharing a cabin with Blanche, and Mrs. Wheeler had managed to wangle one for herself.

Mrs. Stopford could not help feeling some surprise at her cousin's behaviour. Remembering that she had taken the voyage in order to be a strength and support to a bereaved friend, it was somewhat chagrining to find the friend so exceedingly self-supporting. Anyone more thoroughly capable of looking after herself than Mrs. Wheeler could hardly be imagined, and she evidently enjoyed the part she was playing-that of a youngish, pretty woman left to face a hard world alone. The pathos of her most becoming mourning, the appealing gaze of her large eyes, her wistful response to kindness, made most of the men pity her and long to protect her. A small minority fled from her presence.

Fortunately it was a good voyage, and she could wear all the clothes she had ordered with such care in Calcutta-and look her best. She sat surrounded by friends-the ornate wife of a wealthy merchant, Mrs. Bobby Austen, Lady Solomon, a tall woman with a perfect figure, who looked about as amiable as a ferret, and half a dozen men. Together they talked, played games, drank cocktails, and gambled. Mrs. Stopford and Beatrice had tried at first sitting in the group, but had almost at once dropped out without being missed. They did not know the people the others referred to by nicknames, and found the conversation deadly dull.

The two women made their own group: a girl, Patricia Baird, going home alone after a cold weather with a brother; Mrs. Curtis, the charming wife of a soldier in Peshawar, who was rushing home to see her children at school, while her husband was away on a special mission; two young men, Donaldson of the Political Service, Conway, a soldier-and a very cheerful group it was.

Six months earlier, Beatrice would have felt awkward and shy among them all, but now, wrapped in her own bright dreams, she had entirely lost her self-consciousness, and treated both young men with gay friendliness, listening to them much as she listened to Watty at 'Twixt Bears, and enchanting both. As she had told her friend on the voyage out it was a good thing she liked to listen, for every one had a tale to tell her. Mrs. Curtis had three children at school, and before they reached Marseilles Beatrice knew everything there was to know about Brian and Margot and little Peter. She had pored over snapshots of the three and exclaimed at their size and good looks; she had read blotted, ill-spelt letters, and understood what they meant to the mother who treasured them.

Patricia Baird was a great amusement, the most out-spoken young woman Beatrice had ever met. Her brother, she said, had been relieved to get rid of her, and it seemed probable that she was speaking the truth. She was very tall, rather like a du Maurier drawing in an old *Punch*, with a most kindly and cheerful countenance. But her hair, which she wore in a coil at the back of her neck, was always coming down, and she had generally forgotten some rather important part of her attire. She blurted out things just as they came into her head, and the effect was often startling in the extreme, as she was rather a clear-sighted young woman. It was impossible not to like her.

Beatrice had to listen to her confidences. "My mother'll be frightfully disappointed to get me back un-engaged. People at home have an idea that India simply teems with eligible young men. Such a mistake! I met no one but the most pop-eyed, dull things, and even they-such as they were-were engaged. Not that I regretted the fact! —You see I'm the eldest; and there are three others coming on, and Mums swoons at the thought of taking us out in a procession. And I'm so big and untidy. You'd laugh if you saw my mother. She's tiny, with the most exquisite hands and feet and of a discretion — —! She keeps saying she can't imagine how she came to have such a daughter and blames Dad, who has a sister rather like me-Aunt Patsy! *I* think much the nicest of our relations, but that's not saying much, goodness knows. I've been a disappointment to Mummy all my life. When she came to Speech Day at school, I shamed her by falling over my feet when I went up to the platform; and I got all tied up in my veil and train when I was presented. And the mothers of neat, tidy girls said sympathetically, 'You have such a *large* girl!' Fortunately all the others are pretty and neat. Of course it would have been perfectly all right had I been the boy I ought to have been: size doesn't matter in a boy, it's rather admirable."

"It's all right in you," said Beatrice stoutly; "the first glimpse I had of you I thought you looked so handsome, and jolly and cheerful. It's a great thing, I think, to be a little unlike everyone else. So many of one pattern are turned out, it's very monotonous."

"You're very neat yourself," grumbled Patricia, "stock size I should think. I've got to get everything made for me, and it's very expensive, and Dad does nothing but complain about losing money, till one hardly feels one ought to be alive. Have you parents and sisters and so forth?"

"No," said Beatrice, "I'm entirely alone."

"Cripes!" said the large girl in a vulgar manner. "What fun! You mean you can do entirely as you like. Answerable to no one? What luck some people have!"

"Think what I miss," said Beatrice.

"As to missing-Oh, well, I admit I'm looking forward to being at home again with my young sisters, telling them all about it, and giving them their presents. And Mummy is rather a dear when she stops for a moment being ambitious, and Dad is always a lamb even when he grouses. I suppose I'm fortunate really. . . . Then Mrs. Stopford is no relation? I thought at first she was your aunt."

The two young men competed with each other to secure Beatrice as a companion, and, for the first time in her life, she told herself with amusement, she knew what it meant to be sought after by the male sex. Had she known it, it was Christopher she had to thank for the experience. The consciousness of being loved had deepened the beauty of her face, and had warmed and softened her manner, so that like Mercy in *The Pilgrim's Progress* she was the more alluring. Her thoughts were so entirely with Christopher that she was blind to what was going on before her eyes, and it was a great shock to her to find one night as she sat with young Donaldson while the others danced that she was receiving her second proposal in a fortnight.

Startled, she cried, "Oh, stop, please stop! I never imagined such a thing."

"You don't like me then?"

"Oh, yes, I do, indeed I do, but-there is some one else."

"I might have known it," said the poor young man, "I was a fool to think you could be free to care for me. But you were so kind and gentle you raised my hopes."

Beatrice, feeling miserably guilty, sat silent, fervently wishing herself elsewhere, and presently her companion said:

"Well, that's that. Don't let it worry you. I'm not sorry to have had the experience. And I daresay it's all for the best. As a matter of fact, one is as well not to marry in India-it saves complications. Till I met you I'd made up my mind to celibacy."

Beatrice laughed, much relieved. He was a decent youth this, and something of a philosopher. She thought of Mrs. Lithgow's warning about the men, "married and worse," she might meet on board ship, and wished that good lady could know that her fears were groundless.

The next day they arrived at Marseilles.

CHAPTER XXXII

"Journey's end in lovers meeting."

Twelfth Night.

There was the usual turmoil on leaving the ship, tipping, saying good-bye, thrusting into cases the last few things, but at last they were on the train and the last lap had begun.

Mrs. Wheeler was one of those travellers who by sheer force of will get the best of everything. Mrs. Stopford and Beatrice stood near, listening shamefacedly, while she bullied porters and harangued attendants, and flattered officials, until she got what she wanted.

Beatrice, who would have crept into any hole rather than make a fuss, looked helplessly at Blanche, who said with a shrug, "Molly was always like that. I suppose she must think it worth while. While she is settling in let's go and have some coffee or something and read our letters in peace."

Beatrice eagerly agreed, for she was in a fever to look at her letters; Mrs. Sellars had written, and Cicely, and Christopher.

Christopher's was opened first, glanced over, and put away to be read at leisure. The opening words told her all she wanted to know. A sip of such happiness was enough at the moment, the full draught was for later.

Mrs. Sellars' letter was written just before she left Edinburgh, and seemed to bring with it a breath of that old grey city. The holiday had been everything that was delightful, and now she was looking forward to being at home again and having the house full for Easter. Cicely's long epistle brought some rather startling news. Veronica Marston had broken her engagement to Basil on the one day and the next had married another man.

"Basil," Cicely wrote, "is perhaps more humiliated than hurt. As a matter of fact, I think relief is his chief feeling. V. M. has given him a very poor time lately, and he realises that he is well quit of her, but of course it is beastly for him, and I would dearly like to tell the woman what I think of her. What was the sense of her ever getting her claws into Basil if she only meant to drop him? I expect she may have been tempted by the thought of the flesh-pots and then found that in conjunction with Basil (poor lamb!) they were too deadly dull. I believe the man she has married is brilliantly clever and expected to do great things, so that is all right.

"... I am longing to see you back. We shall be dull at 'Twixt Bears without you. I go there to-morrow. It will be nice to hear all Mother's news and to see the boys again. Somehow it seems a very long time since my last holiday and I'm tired. ... I shall be at Victoria to meet the boat train."

Beatrice sat with her letters on her lap thinking over what they contained. She was not really surprised to hear of Basil's broken engagement: it had never looked like lasting. ... She wondered if Veronica's husband was the man who had come to the gate with the car the day she had called with Mrs. Stopford. She remembered thinking that he looked a determined person, one not likely to stand much nonsense; probably Veronica had met her match. Well, it was a blessing she had married some one, for now the little mother who loved spring cleaning would have peace to do as she liked.

Mrs. Stopford at that moment lifted her eyes from the letter she was reading, and "I suppose you've heard the news?" she said.

"Yes," said Beatrice, "Cicely has written."

"Well, I hope Basil realises that he has come out of it better than he deserves. He was a silly boy to let himself be gobbled up. ... From the first it was a farce. I could see that he bored

Veronica horribly; and when she was rude to him, his puzzled dog-like look drove me almost crazy, but I managed to keep quiet and let things take their course. Now that we are free of her I can see that there is much that is admirable about Veronica. She is honest, I believe. And her tank-like methods are rather amusing so long as one doesn't stand in her way. And she is beautiful. Though I didn't like her I enjoyed looking at her."

"I liked her mother," said Beatrice. "She will be glad to have the house to herself; she looked as if she had rather a crushed existence. But I think she will regret Basil; he would have made a kind and thoughtful son-in-law."

Blanche Stopford nodded. "Basil won't be any the worse of this experience, and, to be candid, neither shall I. It is desperately difficult not to be a fool over an only child, but I shall walk warily now. By the way, d'you see in the *Daily Mail* a great story about Miss Elaine Dobie's engagement to that stunt airman, Dick Darcy?"

"*No*," said Beatrice. "How very interesting. Oh, I hope he is nice as well as brave. I always liked his face in the papers. Elaine will make a lovely bride. I must give her something very special—I wonder what?"

They drank the coffee they had ordered, and as Beatrice laid down her cup she said, with an obvious effort:

"Mrs. Stopford, there's something I want to tell you. It's about Christopher and me."

"You and Christopher! You-you're not engaged?"

Beatrice nodded.

"But when? I don't understand."

"He cabled," said Beatrice, "when we were in Calcutta. Somehow I didn't want to tell anyone out there, it had nothing to do with India, so I waited. You don't mind, do you?"

"My dear, I'm too delighted to mind anything. It's the best bit of news I've heard for ages. Dear Christopher. If I'd had a daughter I'd simply have thrust her on him. He's so *decent*. Perhaps that doesn't sound extravagant praise, but it means a lot. Decency goes right through and lasts to the end. And Agnes for a mother-in-law! You're a lucky, lucky girl. . . . Well, we've finished a wearing day with exciting news, and I'll have the night to think it over. I never can sleep in the train anyway. . . . But now I must go to Molly in case she's feeling neglected. Go to bed, my dear. I'll try not to disturb you if you're asleep when I come."

Asleep! Beatrice smiled at the thought. She had better things to do than sleep. Had she not Christopher's letter to read, her first love letter, and to-morrow—to-morrow she would see him.

* * * * *

During the journey from Paris and the Channel crossing Beatrice had time to work herself into a state of nervous fright about the meeting, and when she got out of the train at Victoria and stood on the platform, clutching her dressing-case, jostled and pushed by eager passengers, she looked bewildered and miserable.

Then a hand came over hers and took away the weight of the case, and looking up she met Christopher's kind eyes, and in a second all her silly doubts and misgivings were gone, and she gave a long, contented sigh. They were together and all was well.

Cicely was also on the platform, and Basil had come to meet his mother, and having seen Mrs. Wheeler and her luggage drive safely away, they all repaired to the Grosvenor Hotel, where the travellers had arranged to spend the night.

Basil, it turned out, had taken seats for a play that was having a great vogue, and his mother invited the party to dine first at the Grosvenor: that being arranged she and Beatrice were left for a brief rest.

"I can't say I particularly want to go out to-night," Mrs. Stopford said, as they went up to their rooms in the lift; "indeed I was looking forward to going to bed early and making up some arrears of sleep—I never sleep well on board ship-but I didn't like to damp Basil when he felt he had done so well getting seats. It's about the most run on play at the moment, I believe, and very good."

"I've wanted to see it," said Beatrice, "since ever it came on. The critics have been positively fulsome about it, and I like historical plays."

Beatrice would have liked almost anything at the moment. It seemed pure bliss to her the prospect of sitting beside Christopher watching perfect acting in a good play.

Cicely knew. She had given Beatrice a bear's hug, and whispered, "The nicest thing that ever happened. You can't imagine how pleased mother is: she will tell you to-morrow."

Beatrice was surprised to find how little of an ordeal this home-coming was; she had dreaded set speeches and sly looks and a certain amount of archness, such as she would certainly have met with, say, in the Lithgow household, but here, except for an added warmth in their greetings, no one made any fuss.

While they walked in the foyer of the theatre during an interval, Christopher explained why he had been so precipitate.

"You know, I told you that I had dallied with the thought of some day running the school, but it was never anything but a far away bright dream. Then, when Dr. Heard decided to retire I gave up hope. Suddenly, he sent for me and told me, what I knew, of course, that his heart was in the school and he couldn't bear to think of it falling into the wrong hands. Then he said that he thought I'd be the most likely person to run it on the lines it had always been run on. ME! In the most generous way he offered to help me with money-he knew I hadn't a penny-and so made it possible for me to accept. You can imagine my feelings! Not only was I half off my head at the thought of getting the school-but now I had something to offer you. I daresay I might have waited till you came home, but I was filled with fears of the men you might meet out there, and on board ship, who would all want to marry you, so I sent off the cable the very day the Head spoke to me. Was I right? Might you have been tempted to stay out there?"

Beatrice, thinking of young Donaldson's proposal, blushed deeply, and Christopher nodded. "I thought so," he said.

"No, no," Beatrice cried, "there was never anyone but you. *Nothing* would have tempted me. . . . Oh, is that the bell?"

"Yes, I'm afraid we must go back to our seats. What wretchedly short intervals they have in this play," and they went back to Mrs. Stopford, who had been yawning wearily into her programme at the length of the wait. The play, it is to be feared, did not get the attention it deserved. Basil and Cicely seemed to have so much to say to each other that the play was more of an interruption than anything else; Mrs. Stopford was struggling with sleep, and though Christopher and Beatrice listened it was through a sort of haze of happiness: their own love story was so much more real than any enacted on the stage.

Mrs. Stopford was staying in London for a few days, but it was arranged that Christopher and Beatrice would go to Oxlip by the late afternoon train.

"There's one thing we must do," Beatrice told Christopher. "We must go to Portland Place and see my relatives. I'll ring up my step-brother before he goes out and see if he can arrange anything."

"Of course," Christopher agreed, "your step-brother will want to talk to me. I'm afraid he'll think you're making a poor marriage. The only thing I can do about a marriage settlement is to insure my life well."

"But why should you," said Beatrice, "when I've got lots of money?"

"Lots? I thought you had just enough to live on. Cicely said so."

"I know, she thought so. But that was my fault, though I didn't really mean to leave a false impression. My father was a rich business man and I was his only daughter. My money is very well invested so I really am rather disgustingly well off for these bad times. It sounds an affected sort of thing to say, but I've never been very keen on money-perhaps because I've always had more than enough! But now I'm very glad about it, for it will be of use to you in the school. You won't need any from Dr. Heard. . . . You don't mind, Christopher?"

Christopher's face was rather white.

"In a way," he said, "it's a big let up. If you care to invest some money in the school, I don't mind telling you it'll be a great help, and I don't think you'll be let down-not if I can help it, certainly. On the other hand, I'd have liked to feel — —" he hesitated.

"That I was dependent on you," cried Beatrice. "But I am, Christopher. I am dependent on you for everything that matters-for all my life." It was the public lounge, people were streaming out and in through the revolving glass doors, a few feet away stood Mrs. Stopford-Christopher could do nothing, but as he looked into the eyes of the girl he hoped to marry, and saw there such shining love and trust, his own, vastly to his surprise, became dim.

CHAPTER XXXIII

"You and you no cross shall part:
You and you are heart in heart."

As You Like It.

It was arranged on the telephone next morning that Beatrice should take Christopher to lunch at Portland Place that day. Sir Samuel himself had spoken, so Beatrice was able to break to him the news of her engagement. He had been quite friendly, but Beatrice felt that he was reserving his congratulations until he had made the acquaintance of the young man and heard what he had to say. It may have been imagination, but Beatrice thought there was also some restraint when she spoke of Elaine's engagement.

It was a lovely spring morning, and Christopher was in high spirits. "Is there anything so fresh as Bond Street on a spring morning?" he cried. "Talk about the country! See how the shop windows blink, look at the flowers, smell that indescribable smell. . . . The first thing I do is to buy a ring."

"Not in Bond Street," Beatrice protested.

"Not quite, but almost. In Conduit Street. A jeweller I know about. I got Mother a present there when I was twenty-one —it is much better to give a present on one's birthday than get one-and they were so kind and helpful I vowed that I would go back to them. Here it is. I want a ring," Christopher announced with some bravado on entering. "Diamonds, not large, but good. Will you show us one?"

They were given chairs, a velvet cover was laid on the top of the glass cases, and a middle-aged man with a kind face and depressed moustache produced rings in bewildering variety.

"Oh, not like that," Christopher protested, "not in the least like that. If you'd show us one likely ring we'd ponder over it for a little. Cover them up, my eyes dazzle."

The shopman obediently put away all the rings except one, which he held out to Christopher saying, "These are good stones, sir, and a pretty setting, I might almost say an original setting."

Beatrice put it on. It fitted perfectly. She held up her hand and the diamonds emitted fire. "I like this one," she said.

"Sure? Remember, I'm not likely to be able to give you another till our silver wedding day. Do you feel it's your ring?"

"I feel it's my ring," said Beatrice.

"Then, that's the job done." He turned to the shopmen. "How much? Don't listen, Beatrice-may I sign a cheque?" As they left the shop Christopher said, "Well, that hasn't taken long. If only I'd got this interview with Sir Samuel over, I'd be the happiest man on earth."

"Don't worry about Samuel," said Beatrice. "He'll pretend to be very sharp and business-like, but really, he'll be most relieved to think I'm going to be somebody else's responsibility. It's odd to think how I used to creep up Portland Place feeling the smallest thing that crawled, of no account to anyone, a nuisance to my relatives. To-day my feet are positively spurning the ground. It must be the ring. D'you think it's a magic ring?"

"Yes," said Christopher, "it gives you the power to lay a spell on all who come near you making them your bond-slaves."

Beatrice was laughing as she rang the bell of 120 Portland Place.

The door was opened by Payne, who permitted himself a reserved smile at the sight of Beatrice, and showed them into the library where Sir Samuel was waiting.

After a brief interchange of courtesies Samuel suggested that Beatrice might go upstairs and see his wife and daughter, while he and Christopher had a talk, so with a reassuring smile at her lover Beatrice unwillingly withdrew.

For a wonder, both Lady Dobie and Elaine were in and greeted her with warmth. Betha, indeed, was arch.

"Here is our run-away, at last," she cried. "Naughty, naughty girl to desert us as you did! But you look blooming, doesn't she, Elaine? and we are simply longing to meet your young man. Is Samuel cross-examining him in the library? Too bad. But it will soon be over. . . . And you've just arrived back from India? Surely a very rapid trip."

When the first flood of Betha's conversation had been stemmed Beatrice explained to Elaine that she had seen only a notice of her engagement when they landed at Marseilles, and rather shyly wished her happiness.

"Thank you, darling," Elaine said lightly. "It seems quite an old affair; we've been engaged for a fortnight. We'd have liked if Dick could have been here to meet you and your fiancé to-day, but it wasn't possible, and you are going straight away back to the country, aren't you? But you'll come to our wedding, won't you? It's to be in June. I'm afraid it's going to be rather a crowd: there are so many whom we *must* invite."

Betha broke in, "I don't think I shall survive it. You've no idea what it means, Beatrice, to marry a popular hero. Dick is terribly popular, and everything he does is 'news,' so of course the Press keeps demanding fresh details and photographers dog them both. Did you see the *Daily Whoop* yesterday? Both of them in the Park; rather charming, I thought. And there are studio portraits in the *Sketch* and *Tatler*, and two paragraphs in that witty *Sketch* article about well-known Society people. Talk about publicity! And entirely unsought, for, of course, we'd never think of trying to call attention to ourselves, as so many people do, I'm sorry to say. How pleasant for you, dear Beatrice, to become engaged to the man of your choice without fuss, and be able to marry quietly. Elaine would love that, I'm sure, but we feel we owe it to our position to do things properly. There is the question of wise spending. What are the poor shop-keepers to do if those who can afford it don't spend money on weddings? Elaine is going to have ten bridesmaids (chosen for their looks) and two pages-it ought to be a lovely show. And you really like the idea of marrying a schoolmaster and spending your life among little boys?"

"Adore it," said Beatrice.

Sir Samuel was most urbane when he brought Christopher to the drawing-room and luncheon passed very pleasantly. Beatrice could see that Christopher was making a good impression on his step-relations to be, but she was surprised to find how little her relations' opinions about anything mattered to her now. She wondered how she could ever have been so silly as to wilt under their neglect, or take it to heart when they called her provincial. She was thankful that her road and theirs lay far apart.

The moment luncheon was over Beatrice got up to go, for she knew Betha would be panting to be out and away on her everlasting round.

Walking back down Portland Place in the sunshine Beatrice suddenly stopped. "Oh," she said, "I forgot to ask for Higgins and the kitten. What ingratitude!" and she told Christopher of the lonely hours she had spent in her bedroom, when the kindly maid and the kitten had been her great comfort.

"You poor child!" said Christopher.

"Silly creature, you should say," said Beatrice. "Oh, d'you mind coming with me to an old furniture shop near here? The people who keep it are friends of mine. I was fond of their boy, a delicate little chap who died at Christmas-time. I've bought things from them time and again-they are very reliable-and it might be a good place to get some things for our house."

"*Our* house," repeated Christopher blissfully.

"Tell me exactly what it's like," said Beatrice, and Christopher told her of the dower house in the grounds that Dr. Heard had used for himself. "Eighteenth century, it is; smallish: drawing-room, dining-room and library-all panelled, on the ground floor, and about half a dozen bedrooms upstairs and garrets above them. The Heards put in bathrooms-there were none! Also central heating and electric light."

"Lovely," said Beatrice, "I'm rather glad we are to have a house of our own, and very glad that it's an old house. Won't it be amusing making it just as we like it? Tell me, is the drawing-room on the right as you go in?"

Franky's father seemed thinner and shabbier than ever in the revealing spring light, but he showed a faint pleasure on beholding Beatrice, and on being introduced to her fiancé, asked if his wife might also have the honour.

She came and offered her congratulations, and when Christopher turned away to look at something, said to Beatrice: "I'm sure I'm very glad, Miss. I used to think you were lonely like and he looks a pleasant gentleman."

"Thank you," Beatrice said. "I hope you're feeling better."

"Oh, I'm quite well, only-when the weather is fine it seems to make it harder. Franky did like good weather."

"I know," Beatrice said, holding the worn hand of Franky's mother, and seeing again the bright smile and the yellow hair that had once lightened the dark shop and the drab lives of his parents. "I know. But now he doesn't need our uncertain sunshine. Where he is the day is always fair."

"So they say," said the woman and sighed.

The couple spent an interesting hour looking for furniture and ended by buying eight dining-room chairs, a table and a sideboard, also a corner cupboard for the drawing-room, a bureau and a fine Aubusson carpet.

Beatrice asked her friend to let her know if he got in anything specially good, and told him where to send what they had bought that day, as well as what he had stored for her.

"Come and have tea and ices at Gunter's," Christopher said, when they got out into the street. "I was so busy being polite that I couldn't enjoy your step-relations' excellent lunch. They were very civil, weren't they? But perhaps it's as well we shan't have to see too much of them. I don't suppose poor schoolmasters swim very often into their ken."

"And all the better is it for the schoolmaster," said Beatrice. "They did try to be pleasant to-day, and Samuel is really a kind soul. Didn't you think Elaine lovely?"

"Very, in an exotic sort of way. I hope she'll be happy with her airman."

"I do hope so," Beatrice said fervently. "I've a weakness for Elaine, she fascinates me against my better judgment, so to speak. But I can't somehow feel that this marriage is anything but what she'd call 'a thrill' —not very permanent. Oh, I don't know. Perhaps I'm only being catty. We'll have to hurry, my dear, if we're to get back to the Grosvenor and catch the 5.30 train at Paddington."

It would have amused Beatrice had she heard the conversation in the Portland Place dining-room after she and Christopher had left.

"Well," said Betha, "that's satisfactorily settled, and I must say I'm thankful. It would have been a nuisance to have Beatrice back, especially at this time. We are all so rushed and need every corner we have."

"I don't think it would have been a nuisance," said her husband, "I liked having Beatrice in the house, and I miss her still at breakfast-always a lonely meal for me. But I'm glad she's marrying such a decent fellow. I confess I liked the look of him, and if he hasn't much money at least he belongs to a good Edinburgh family, which is something. You didn't think of asking Beatrice to be one of your bridesmaids, Elaine?"

"No, Papa," said his daughter sweetly.

"Well, I think you might. I like the old way of having relatives to follow the bride, instead of a retinue of alien young women chosen because they matched in height or for some equally absurd reason."

"Papa!" Elaine protested.

"Yes," Sir Samuel went on, "I must say I intensely dislike these show weddings. Thousands of silly, idle women crowding round to get a free show, and the bride, and bridesmaids simpering along like paid puppets. There's an indecency about it that I deplore."

"Must you make a speech, Papa?" Elaine sighed; while Betha broke in indignantly, "I must say, Samuel, you aren't very flattering to your own daughter. The fact is you've never got over your upbringing: you still have middle-class values. I believe you prefer that commonplace schoolmaster of Beatrice's to dear Dick with his dash and daring."

"Mother," moaned Elaine, while her father said, "Well, Beatrice's young man has better manners for one thing; and he's a fellow I can understand. He has to work his way and he does it cheerfully. Probably he'd like to go stunt flying as much as anyone, but he knows it's not for him. He and Beatrice will have a useful and happy life, I believe."

"Till death does them part," said Elaine. "Oh, I am sure they will be an example to every one. Beatrice, timid, constant soul that she is, will never glance away from her Christopher. And that's as it should be, of course, Papa. I thought her looking very pretty. That anxious, lost-dog look has gone and she has gained assurance. I felt to-day that she didn't care a hoot for any of us, and was only longing for the meal to be over that she might get away with her schoolmaster. Can't you picture her mothering all the homesick boys and nursing any who are ill? And won't she take a delight in running her house and making a 'peaceful fireside clime' for Christopher when the day's work is done. She is sure, too, to have hordes of children; quite one of the nation's assets, in fact."

Sir Samuel got on his feet, his expression more of sorrow than of anger.

"Ah, well, my girl, it's easy to sneer, but you may live to realise that it's the simple things that really matter. I hope I haven't lived an entirely useless life." Unconsciously he squared his shoulders as if addressing an audience, "And now that my face is towards the West (although I have many years of work before me yet, I hope), I have moments when I doubt if anything really matters except following the precepts we learned at our mothers' knee."

He left the room hurriedly, being deeply moved at his own words, and his wife and daughter looked at each other with raised eyebrows.

"What we brought on ourselves!" said Elaine. "My father's passion for speech-making grows on him. And, bless his heart, why shouldn't he lecture his own women-folk? —I rather agree with him, you know, Mother."

"Nonsense, Elaine. But I can tell you this, these Puritan ideas of your father's that I thought I had rooted out are getting stronger. I can see the day approaching after you and Stewart are gone, when I shall be hauled back into the pit we began in. Awful! I only hope your father will be in better temper this evening, or how am I to tell him about Stewart? And he says he must have the money immediately. I'm afraid he's in a bad mess. I'm sure life is difficult enough for everybody without people making it worse by sermonising."

CHAPTER XXXIV

"Between the Windrush and the Colne
There stands a little house of stone,
A little wicked house of stone."

J. B.

As Christopher had told Beatrice, Oxlip was at its best in springtime. She had thought it perfect in drear-nighted December, but now, with the greening trees, the woods starring with primroses and anemones, celandines brightening with their yellow gloss shadowy corners, and above all, the daffodils, standing valiantly in great clumps, armies of them, now it was of an enchanting loveliness.

And 'Twixt Bears, newly cleaned, smelling of beeswax and turpentine, with all its buttercup-yellow curtains hanging crisply, full of flowers and sunshine and birds' song, was a joyful place to return to.

So thought Beatrice, and so thought Mrs. Sellars, who was unfeignedly thankful to be at home. "Not," she said, as they sat by the fire that evening after Watty had gone to bed, "that I didn't enjoy my holiday. It was delightful, though I was inclined to be 'perplexed with leisure.' Breakfast in bed every morning—I who so long to get up-and driven everywhere, hardly allowed to put my feet to the ground, all done in kindness, for Mary is kindness itself. She was inclined to be selfish as a girl, but she has learned the lesson of suffering so well that she seems never to spare a thought to herself. How humble I felt before her! I had lost touch with most of my friends, but Mary managed to gather many of them, and to hear all that happened to them was like reading a chapter from the Book of Life! Sad stories, happy stories: one getting every possible good thing, another losing the little she had. It was a wonderful holiday, although they told me, like Granny Sellars, that I was a poor degenerate Scot, when I prepared to depart with alacrity! But one's heart is where one's treasure is, and how could I help being glad I was going home? And I didn't know I was coming home to such joyful news. My dear, I am glad. I had a suspicion that Christopher cared for you, but I saw no hope of his being able to marry for years. Dr. Heard's generosity changed everything."

"But, Mother," said Christopher, "there's yet another surprise for you. It seems I'm marrying an heiress. It never occurred to Beatrice that we didn't know she had money — —"

"Oh, yes, it did," Beatrice interrupted. "But Cicely seemed to take it for granted that I had only just enough to live on, and somehow I could never bring myself to tell you that I was-in a small way-an heiress. I think I was rather ashamed of the fact, though now I'm glad. D'you think it was secretive of me? Are you hurt?"

"My dear, I'm very thankful. I was afraid you and Christopher might find it rather difficult starting under an obligation. Not that I'm in the least sorry for young people having a struggle-when are you going to bear the yoke if not in your youth? —but I don't like debt."

"Nor I," said Christopher. "But getting the school meant so much to me that I simply couldn't resist the temptation. For behind it was the hope of Beatrice." He turned and looked at the girl as she sat beside his mother. "It will be sad, my dear, if it turns out a bad investment for you, but I don't think it will somehow. Nothing is very firm these days, but the small boy should be as stable as anything."

Beatrice smiled at her schoolmaster as she said, "It hardly seems right to be so happy in these anxious times, when so many people are miserably anxious.

"Be happy," said Mrs. Sellars, "and be humble and grateful. Happiness helps every one who comes in contact with it, it keeps alive faith and hope: that is why a happy book is such a gift to the world. Oxlip seems to have its share of happiness just now. I met the Twins looking so gay they might have been dancing with the daffodils. Did you hear? An uncle is sending them both to study at the School of Dramatic Art-is that what you call it? So there's no saying what we may hear of those children some day. And the Snows are happy at the prospect of welcoming their son and his wife in the early autumn. And Blanche Stopford is her old self again . . ."

"And the Pughs?" Beatrice asked eagerly. "Have you heard anything of them? I've only had one postcard."

"Cicely said something in one of her letters, just what I can't remember. We'll hear when she comes. You know she is bringing Jane Naesmyth for the week-end by way of celebrating the engagement. I do hope the good weather will hold on."

It did, and on the Saturday they were all able to go for an expedition. Ulysses, that famous old roadster, led the way, driven by Christopher with Beatrice beside him, and his mother and Watty and Voltaire behind, and Basil followed with the others in his Bentley.

Their destination was a half-ruined house, Casey Lovell, which stood in a remote valley among the Cotswolds. The drive in the sunshine was lovely, through wide pasture-lands, past grey churches and sleepy villages and winding streams, until they ran steeply downhill into a hamlet sunk in peace and buried in blossoms, which boasted a very old and comfortable inn.

The cars were left there and tea ordered, and the company started to walk across the fields to Casey Lovell. For Cicely the place had a special fascination, and she begged Jane Naesmyth and Beatrice who were seeing it for the first time not to look until she had guided them to the best view-point, so they went with downcast eyes through rank grass and under crumbling gateways until she said, "Now".

Among age-old yews there stood a house of the time of William and Mary, a honey-coloured house. One wing was inhabited, and casement windows with small leaded panes stood open to the sunshine. The enclosed space made by the angle of the house was roughly tidy, wallflowers and polyanthus and forget-me-nots flowered in a narrow bed under the windows. A stream of pale green water slipped over its paved bed, steps led down to it, and the stone sides were hung with creeping plants. A bridge, so frail that it seemed as if a touch must set it crumbling, spanned the stream, and the remains of what must have been a water-garden lay on the farther side.

"Can't we see inside?" Jane Naesmyth asked, instinctively lowering her voice.

"No," said Cicely in the same hushed accents. "Somebody lives in it, I don't know who —a bailiff, perhaps: somebody not too troubled with imagination, certainly. If ever there was an eerie place! Walter de la Mare might have written *Mrs. Gill* here."

"What is the story of it?" Jane asked.

"We've tried to find out but nobody knows. All we can make out is that it is supposed to be haunted. It's in the market now; they want £10,000 for it, for there's a good deal of land. If I were suddenly told I was a millionaire the first thing I'd do would be to write a cheque for that amount and Casey Lovell would be mine!"

"You'd be afraid to live in it," said Watty, who was consumed with a desire to walk over the frail bridge.

"I'd never think of living in it," said Cicely. "It would be enough to know that it was mine and that I'd saved it. I'd have it preserved very cautiously but I wouldn't tidy it up. I like the rough grass and the cows. I'm terrified somebody buys it and makes it horribly perfect, with every bit of furniture a museum piece, and stone statues and lead squirrels in the garden! I'd almost rather see it going to wreck and ruin as it is now." The spell of the place was upon them and they stood watching the old house drowse in the sunshine, while Cicely quoted —

"Between the Windrush and the Colne
There stands a little house of stone
A little wicked house of stone."

The spell was broken by Watty suddenly addressing Christopher with "Hand that dog a colossal wallop, will you? he's scratching himself again," and after that they went back to the inn for tea.

Jane Naesmyth and Beatrice found themselves together at a table that was spread most hospitably with brown and white bread and butter and a large glass of gooseberry jam, not to speak of cress sandwiches and an excellent plum cake.

"Well," said the older woman, "this is rather different from our first tea together, Beatrice, on a dreary October day in the train, when life was looking very black to you. You were alone and frightened, do you remember?"

"Do I not?" said Beatrice. "Even now, with the sun shining, and Christopher near and everything bright, I don't like to think of that time. You don't know how gratefully I often think of *you*. If you hadn't out of the goodness of your heart invited me to your house nothing at all would have happened."

"Something different would have happened. . . . It is seldom that things work out so pat, but very pleasant when they do. I hope the years will bring you more and more happiness, my dear."

* * * * *

That evening, after dinner, Mrs. Snow and her husband, and the Twins and their father, came to 'Twixt Bears to spend a friendly hour.

The Twins were radiant and had so much to tell that they showed no inclination to listen. They gave Beatrice and Christopher their blessing and said the engagement was no more than they had expected, and went on to talk of their own life-work.

"We don't mean to marry," Sarsa said loftily, "we mean to have a career."

"We could do both," Susan pointed out; "we might have a career and marry later if anyone asks us-nobody has yet. But, though disappointing as to proposals we had quite a successful time in London; heaps of invitations and flowers and sweets. Mostly, though, from elderly gentlemen; the young are so apt to be penniless. But it will be interesting to have some really hard work to do. You *have* to work, I'm told. All kinds of lectures as well as dancing and fencing and acting. Who would have imagined that Uncle Robert would think of such a thing? And he has arranged that we board with an exemplary household, so Daddy will be allowed to live happily at The Green and work in the garden. We, of course, will be home for the holidays and see that all is well with him."

"You are great managers," said Jane Naesmyth, much amused.

"Yes, aren't we?" said Sarsa.

Mrs. Snow pleased Beatrice by telling her stories of Christopher as a schoolboy. "He ages with our Robin," she said, "and in the holidays they were seldom apart. I'm almost as fond of Christopher as if he were my own. He has his faults, of course: terribly obstinate you'll find. Dear me, what changes in these last few weeks! Basil's engagement-that always seemed to me unlikely, your sudden trip to India, Robin married, and then this news! You must come in and see the Indian papers. I've kept them all, and the photos are good-at least they're recognisable."

"I'd like to see them. Tell me, have you heard from Alice Pugh?"

"One postcard. She is the worst of correspondents. Odd, because one would think that a woman who writes books wouldn't mind a letter or two, but there it is. I wish she were back. There is something so stimulating about her. I never went to see her without coming away more interested in everything. She is so generous with all that she has, her witty thoughts, her books, her recipes-what a cook! —even her clothes-she'd lend you anything. I wonder what that dull, little Denis Pugh did to deserve such a wife!"

"You'll admit," said Beatrice, "that he realises his luck."

"Oh, I daresay. How well Mrs. Stopford looks —a different woman. That engagement weighed on her more than she would have cared to admit. You liked being with her in India? She wasn't too-over-whelming as a companion?"

Beatrice laughed as she said, "I know what you mean, but no, not in the least. Travel is an acid test, and Mrs. Stopford came through it more than creditably, and I hope I didn't utterly fail. Anyway, we never had a jar, and returned closer friends than when we left."

"You went out to bring back Mrs. Stopford's widowed cousin. Poor thing, it must have been a sad voyage for her."

"Ye-es," said Beatrice, and added, "there are widows and widows, you know."

"I see. Then your support was not required."

"It was not. Mrs. Stopford and I supported each other while Mrs. Wheeler (the widow) was the centre and soul of a large gay group!"

"Dear me!" said Mrs. Snow, much intrigued. "In that case her poor husband is as well away. . . . How pretty Cicely looks! I never saw her in pale blue before. There is something very sweet about pale blue, it reminds me of a dress I had as a young girl. . . . I won't have coffee, Watty, thank you, it keeps me awake at this time of night, but I'd like some lemonade: I've talked myself thirsty. Well, had you a good report this term, Watty?"

Watty muttered something, feeling that Mrs. Snow might have had the sense to let that subject alone. Not that the report was bad, but reports belonged to the grimmer side of life, and need not be mentioned except by one's parents or guardians. Mrs. Snow looked after him with an understanding smile. "Funny things, boys," she said. "So easily offended. I remember our Jim. Nobody dared speak to him at one time for he would have fought you for a word. They grow out of it," she added, comfortably.

"I wish I knew more about boys," said Beatrice. "Watty is actually the only boy I've ever seen 'close to'. And I'm going to live my life in a world of boys."

"So you are. And very entertaining you'll find it. When is the marriage to be?"

"Well, I thought in the summer holidays, but Christopher says why not get married right away? The summer term is, he says, in many ways the pleasantest and easiest, and would make a good beginning for me, and when school starts again in September I'd feel quite experienced. As it happens Dr. Heard and his wife have managed to get the place they had had an eye on and are gone, and our house is being done up. It seems it needs very little, so we could go into it almost at once, with what furniture we have. There seems no very good reason for delay; we want the quietest of weddings, so very little preparation is needed; Mrs. Sellars raises no objection."

"Then it may be any old day," said Mrs. Snow, who sometimes surprised her friends by using expressions culled from the conversation of her sons. "Dear me! Youth is so sudden. But why not? Norman is at your service any moment. It must be in the church. I hate register office weddings-unblessed, dusty affairs."

"Of course it must be in the church," Beatrice said. "You know, Mrs. Snow, I can hardly believe this is me. I was so alone when my mother died —I had practically no one of my own, not even a great friend, for mother filled my life and I wanted no one else. And friends were raised up in the most marvellous way. Jane Naesmyth, and Cicely, Mrs. Sellars —I can never be grateful enough to them."

"And what," said Mrs. Snow, "about your gratitude to God? Don't you believe in answer to prayer? And don't you suppose your mother prayed for the safety and happiness of the child she was leaving?"

Beatrice nodded. "I like to think my happiness is due to my mother's prayers. I'd hate to feel she was out of it. It keeps her part, as I hope she always will be, of my life. . . ."

* * * * *

Before Cicely left with Jane Naesmyth on Monday morning, it had been arranged that the wedding should take place in Oxlip Church on the last Friday of April.

Cicely had a few words with Beatrice before she left. "I think you'll be happy, my dear; Christopher is a stayer. And certainly we are happy about you. I never imagined Mother could see Christopher married and be pleased, but she is-because it's you. Bless you, my dear. I'll be back on Thursday night. Send me as many commissions as you like . . ." She hesitated for a moment, turning over some of the things on the dressing-table, and then said: "I want you to know that I'm going to marry Basil; not yet, some time in the autumn probably. We've always liked each other-the Veronica episode was only a brief madness, I don't mind about it a bit-and the fact is I found it quite impossible to entertain the thought of anyone else. So there it is-we're both faulty creatures, but it's to be hoped we'll manage to make a fairly decent thing of our life together-Yes, Jane, coming," and Cicely ran downstairs, followed by Beatrice.

After the car had departed they lingered, Mrs. Sellars, Christopher and Beatrice, among the flowers in the front garden.

"Christopher's mother," said Beatrice suddenly, "what am I to call you? I can't say 'Mrs. Sellars,' for that is formal and horrid. I can't say 'Mother,' for mother means only one person to me. 'Mums' doesn't come easily to my Scots tongue. May I call you 'Mamma'?"

"Yes, do. I like 'Mamma.' "

"Most appropriate," said Christopher, "for there's a distinctly Victorian flavour about you both. Well, now that is settled what shall we do to-day? I'll have to be in London to-morrow and Wednesday settling up things, Thursday will be occupied, so this is really our last day together at this time."

Mrs. Sellars had gone indoors at the call of Watty, and Beatrice said:

"I'm going to Cheltenham with Mrs. Stopford to get a wedding garment-she knows of a good place. What about taking your mother away for the day? It's going to be fine, and it would be nice for you both to be by yourselves for once."

Christopher looked suspiciously at his bride to be.

"Are you by any chance trying to be unselfish?" he asked.

"Not in the least. I'm looking forward to shopping in Cheltenham, and I want you and your mother to have a nice day."

"I see. Well, it's quite a good plan. Mother! Mother!"

Mrs. Sellars came to the open window of the living room and asked what was wrong.

"Can you come out with me for the whole day?" Christopher asked. "We'd have lunch some-where-perhaps at Burford, and go and see the church and the place where they make rugs and things, you always enjoy that, and come round by Wychton and beg tea from the Ashleys, and so home. How does that strike you?"

"It sounds delightful," said Mrs. Sellars, "but Beatrice — —"

"I told you, didn't I," said the girl, "that Mrs. Stopford was taking me to Cheltenham to-day to see her dressmaker. If I don't see anything I like it will have to be made for me at lightning speed. How lovely for Christopher to have you to himself for a whole day. You must go. Just leave everything."

"Yes, I'll go," Mrs. Sellars said, nodding her head in a determined manner. "I'm learning in my old age the wisdom of gathering rosebuds while we may."

CHAPTER XXXV

"It is not the fashion to see the lady the epilogue."

As You Like It.

"At Oxlip Church, Oxfordshire, on April 28th, by the Rev. Norman Snow, M.A. (Oxon), Christopher John, elder son of the late John Sellars, Writer to the Signet, Edinburgh, and Mrs. Sellars, Oxlip, to Beatrice Ann, only daughter of the late Joseph and Jane Dobie, Glasgow."

Mrs. Lithgow read aloud the announcement to her daughter Peggy, then laid down the *Glasgow Herald*, and took off her spectacles.

"That," she said, "isn't put in with much show. You wouldn't think from that that Joseph Dobie was one of Glasgow's merchant princes. Well, well, so that's the finish of Be'trice. I can't help feeling that old Joseph Dobie would be vexed to know that his girl was married in an English church; but, anyway, I'm thankful she has married a Scotsman. A Writer to the Signet sounds quite respectable for a father, but I can't help thinking that with all her money Be'trice might have done better."

"Oh, I don't know," said Peggy, who was sitting on the arm of a chair lazily teasing a kitten, "he's very good-looking from the snapshot she sent us, and evidently very nice. And the school is his own, remember. It seems a fine old place."

"I daresay it is," said her mother, "but I can't say I care much for fine old places myself. It's very sad that she's settled out of Scotland."

"So we think—I'd hate it myself-but Beatrice will be happier in England than ever she was in Glasgow. She was never really at home with us-not as she seems at home with those people in Oxlip. Our jokes didn't appeal to her and she seemed often to creep into herself. . . . When we were little together I thought she was sly——"

"That's an ugly word, Peggy. What made you think of such a thing?"

"Oh-nothing," said Peggy. "I see now that she was just scared of us, poor child, and that made her seem aloof and queer."

"Peggy," Mrs. Lithgow protested. "I never thought Be'trice either the one or the other. I'm sure no one could have been more prettily grateful for any kindness shown to her: her letter telling about her engagement almost made me cry. I took it up to read to Mrs. Murray and found Be'trice had written to her too. 'My mother's friends,' she called us. And I think it was very mindful of her to get Mrs. Sellars to write to us about the wedding, describing it all. And very well she does it. She must be a nice woman."

Mrs. Lithgow took up the letter in question and brooded over it for a minute and Peggy said:

"Primrose-yellow would be very becoming to Beatrice, and I like the description of her walking across the green with her mother- and sister-in-law to be, and the village children scattering flowers; and the daffodils and the tombstones and the old grey church."

"Oh, it's all very nice," said her mother, "but it's not my idea of a wedding. What a contrast to Sir Samuel Dobie's daughter. I'm fair tired reading about that girl's wedding, and looking at pictures of her and her airman, here, there and everywhere, and her Pekinese and her this and that. Is it twelve bridesmaids she's to have? Tuts. There are the two extremes, and Be'trice has gone to the one and the Dobie girl has gone to the other. Yours, Peggy, was the happy medium."

Peggy chuckled. "You're right, Mother," she said. "Harry and I are distinctly middling."

"And the happiest thing to be," said Mrs. Lithgow. "Yes, Mrs. Sellars writes very sweetly about Be'trice. That Mrs. Stopford had lent her house for the lunch, and their intimate friends were all there. I seem to know them quite well from Be'trice's letters-the Twins and Mrs. Snow, and Miss Naesmyth too. Nice wee touches she puts in about Watty, and his dog with the bridal bow of white satin ribbon, and Be'trice and Christopher going hand in hand out of the door to start their life together. I think that's awfully nice somehow. I like to think that Be'trice will always have a kind hand to hold on to, for she was never meant to battle alone through life. By the way, Peggy, did I tell you she said in her last letter that she and Christopher had decided to keep Greenbraes as it is, for they mean to spend most of their holidays there? I call that very sensible. The children (if they have them) will get a chance of knowing something of their own land. And how pleased Fairlie will be to have her dear Miss Be'trice near! Did I tell you I met Fairlie? Ucha. She was coming out of the Sauchiehall Street Woolworths, looking very prosperous. I said I hoped she was happy in her marriage, and she said Oh, yes, quite as happy as she had expected to be for she had always known a man would be a trial. Very cynical, I thought, but I expect she was rather late in starting. Well, you and Be'trice haven't been too long in starting and I earnestly hope you will both make a success of marriage. . . . I was just thinking, Peggy, if father and I ever take that motor-tour in the south we've been planning so long, it would be nice to go to Suffolk. I'm not very keen on scenery as you know, and new places aren't very interesting if you know no one in them, but to see Be'trice in her own house-that would be worth going for. You know, I don't believe the poor girl knows a thing about housekeeping. How could she? Janie Dobie didn't bring her girl up as I brought up mine, to know how everything ought to be done. As I often said to you, 'Can do is easy carried about.'"

"You did indeed," Peggy agreed, "and Harry is reaping the benefit of your wisdom to-day. Probably Beatrice will have a housekeeper."

"Oh, very likely, but she'll be none the worse of a few practical hints from me. And I'd like to see for myself what sort of man this Christopher is: you can't make much of what a girl in love says about a man."

Peggy looked at her mother with amused eyes. "You're a comic, Mother," she said.

"I'm sure I'm not that," said Mrs. Lithgow. "But I notice you young people are all inclined to be amused at your parents-poor out-of-date things that we are! I suppose it was always so, and, bless you, the parents don't mind. It isn't as if we hadn't all come the same road. . . . We'd often like to warn you about when to be careful, but we know it's useless-you must make your own mistakes and find your own way through. All that really matters is that the way should lead upwards."

"Mother," said Peggy uneasily, "you talk as if you were eighty and finished with things."

"Not a bit of it." Mrs. Lithgow's tone was brisk. "I'm hoping and expecting that Father and I will have many years yet together, and now that you've made me get one of those bashed-down looking hats I feel quite modern."

"And look it," said Peggy. "You've no idea what a difference it makes. It'll be lip-stick next," she added wickedly. But this was going too far, and as Mrs. Lithgow rose to tidy away her letters before going to do her morning shopping, she said in a tone of rebuke:

"Peggy, I wonder to hear you!"

Made in the USA
Columbia, SC
01 February 2023